SHE FELT AS IF SHE'D BEEN VISUALLY FRISKING HIM

The late-afternoon sun backlit his hunky, decidedly masculine frame, casting his face and those thickly lashed eyes in shadow. Her gaze drifted to his hands again as she remembered how they'd felt, keeping her steady in those first moments after the crash. He looked like the perfect guy. All gorgeous, courteous, manly-man rescuer of damsels in distress.

She felt a hot rush of attraction zip right through her recently traumatized system. And by trauma, she didn't mean the car crash. She blamed it on that, though, all the same. All that adrenaline and pain, making her a little lightheaded. Had to be it. Otherwise, she was quite certain she'd have looked at him and felt nothing. Because not only had she sworn off men in general, she'd sworn off men who made her girl parts tingle very specifically.

One thing was certain. Looks were deceiving. Because there were no perfect men. "Just perfect idiots," she muttered, lifting her hand from the wheel, as if taking an oath. "Yes, your honor, guilty as charged. No need for a trial. The evidence is overwhelming." She looked at him again . . . and, yep, definite tingles. *Book me, lock me up, and throw away the key, judge. Because that's apparently the only way I'm going to save me from myself.*

Sea Glass Sunrise

DONNA KAUFFMAN

ZEBRA BOOKS
KENSINGTON PUBLISHING CORP.
http://www.kensingtonbooks.com

ZEBRA BOOKS are published by

Kensington Publishing Corp.
119 West 40th Street
New York, NY 10018

All Kensington titles, imprints and distributed lines are available at special quantity discounts for bulk purchases for sales promotion, premiums, fund-raising, educational or institutional use.

Special book excerpts or customized printings can also be created to fit specific needs. For details, write or phone the office of the Kensington Sales Manager. Attn.: Sales Department. Kensington Publishing Corp., 119 West 40th Street, New York, NY 10018. Phone: 1-800-221-2647.

Zebra and the Z logo Reg. U.S. Pat. & TM Off.

First Printing: June 2015
ISBN-13: 978-1-4201-3745-3
ISBN-10: 1-4201-3745-X

eISBN-13: 978-1-4201-3746-0
eISBN-10: 1-4201-3746-8

10 9 8 7 6 5 4 3 2 1

Printed in the United States of America

For Joyce Lamb
Some sisters are born, some are chosen,
and some come to be because the universe
is being really generous.
I'm so glad that lovely bit of generosity
has touched us both
. . . and we were smart enough to recognize it!
For the lunches, the late nights,
and most of all, the laughter.
This one is for you.

Chapter One

So, there was going to be a June wedding after all. Only it wouldn't be Hannah McCrae in a gorgeous white dress, walking down the aisle.

No, she'd be swathed in wildflower blue. Or spring leaf green. Or dandelion yellow. Or some other color found only in nature and bridesmaid's dresses.

Hannah didn't slow down as she passed the cheery, hand-painted sign welcoming her to Blueberry Cove, Maine. Chartered in 1715. Population 303. "Make that three hundred and four," she murmured, still undecided on when she was going to share that little tidbit with the rest of her family.

She should be happy for her big brother and his impending nuptials. And she was happy. Truly. Logan deserved all the love and fulfillment in the world and she was thrilled he'd finally found them. Alex MacFarland had gotten herself a good guy. Probably the last remaining good guy on the planet.

Not that Hannah was biased or anything. Or cynical, for that matter. Okay, so maybe she was a little cynical. All right, more than a little. Who could blame her after the year she'd had?

Hannah wove through the narrow streets of her hometown on autopilot, too distracted by her thoughts to soak up the sense of belonging, the unconditional love she always felt simply entering the Cove. Unable to sleep, she'd left her Old Town Alexandria row house at four that morning, then driven north for thirteen straight hours, fueled solely by the promise of that much-needed hometown group hug. Well, that and the king-sized bag of chocolate-covered pretzels presently tucked in her lap.

She dug in for another fix. They'd been an impulse buy when she'd filled her tank after passing through New York City. She couldn't even say why. She hated salty and sweet together. Of course, she'd also hated finding out the guy she'd been giddily anticipating a marriage proposal from at any second had already proposed to someone else. In fact, he'd not only proposed to someone else, he'd married her. Four years ago. Which meant Hannah had spent eighteen months dating a married man. *Eighteen monumentally stupid, blind-as-a-bat, how-could-I-be-such-an-idiot months!*

She was a trial attorney, for God's sake. A damn good one. She earned her living by knowing when people were lying to her. How could she not have known? How could she not have had at least some inkling of a suspicion long before Tim's very petite, very blond, and exceedingly pregnant, sweet-faced wife stalked into Hannah's office, in front of God and everyone—and by God, she meant Findley Holcombe, the senior partner of Holcombe and Daggett, and by everyone, she meant, well, everyone—and announced, quite loudly, using language that could only be described as salty, just what Hannah could do to herself, and stop doing to her husband?

Yeah, Hannah thought, and shoved the pretzel back in the bag. She hated salty and sweet.

As the Rusty Puffin pub came into view, she felt a tug

in her chest, and a knot form in her throat. She wanted nothing more than to pull over, run inside, and be immediately folded into one of her uncle Fergus's big bear hugs, but she couldn't trust herself not to fall apart all over him. No way would she get out of there without telling him why she was a wreck, which would be as good as telling the entire town. Instead, she whispered a silent *I love you*, knowing she'd see him soon enough at the wedding rehearsal the following afternoon, and continued toward the coast road that would take her out to Pelican Point . . . and home.

She didn't see the pickup truck until it was too late.

One second, she was glancing over at the tall shoots of summer lupines, in all their purple, pink, and white stalks of glory, and—dammit—digging out another chocolate-covered pretzel. The next, she was slamming her brakes and swerving to miss the tail end of the big dark green dually that was suddenly somehow passing right in front of her.

She missed the truck's rear bumper by a hairbreadth, but the hand-painted sign on the far side of the intersection advertising BEANIE'S FAT QUARTERS, THE BEST LITTLE QUILT SHOP IN BLUEBERRY COVE! wasn't so lucky.

It all happened so fast, and yet each second seemed to be somehow elastic, as if she could live a lifetime inside of every single heartbeat of the accident as she was swerving through it. So many thoughts went through her mind as she careened toward the sign she knew Beanie's husband Carl had so proudly painted for his wife when she'd opened up her little shop, what, fifteen years ago now? Sixteen? Hannah had just graduated high school. Carl had done the town sign, too, right in his adorable little potting shed-turned-art studio, touching the signs up like new every spring after the winter season did its number on them. And yes, okay, that made two good men, but Carl had gone to his great reward just last year, so that left Logan as the only one still breathing.

So many thoughts raced around inside Hannah's brain in those weirdly elastic, terrifying, life-threatening seconds. The things she should have said to Tim during their final confrontation—on Christmas Eve, no less; that she should have told Logan and her sisters what had happened; that she should have come home for Christmas or the New Year, or both, and leaned on them instead of shouldering the holidays and the six months that had elapsed since then alone. That maybe she should have tried harder to make her newfound notoriety in the Capitol Hill legal community work for her, that she still felt terribly guilty for being involved with someone who was married to someone else, even if she hadn't known, and hating—*hating*—that she'd ultimately caved, quit, and come running back home to the Cove with her humiliation tucked between her legs like the tail of failure and shame that it was.

Then Carl's once-beautiful sign raced right up to the hood of her car and no amount of further wheel yanking and swerving was going to save her from smashing right into it. There was a small explosion as her air bag deployed, punching her in the face and chest, just as her shoulder harness jerked her tightly against her seat back. Her thoughts were yanked instantly back to the present as she plowed straight into the stack of brightly colored plaid quilting squares painted on the bottom corner of the sign. *Sorry, Beanie,* she thought inanely, along with *Shit, shit, shit!* as she finally slid to a stop a mere speck of an inch before hitting the cluster of tall ash trees that stood just behind the sign.

She instinctively batted at the white, puffy bag, trying to keep it from smothering her, as she struggled to regain clarity of thought. Her head was buzzing from the adrenaline rush, her pulse was pounding in her ears, and her face hurt. A lot. So did her shoulder. Then the driver's-side door was being pulled open and there was a man crouching next to her. At least, given the deep voice, she assumed it was a man; she was still wrestling with the air bag.

"You okay?" he asked, his voice all deep and dark and smoky in that bass vibrato kind of way that sent shivers down a woman's spine. Though, in all fairness, her ears were ringing from the impact and she was pretty sure shock was setting in, so it could have just been an aftereffect of the collision.

He effortlessly collapsed the air bag with one broad palm. "Whoa, whoa," he added quickly, putting those broad, warm palms gently but firmly on her wrist and shoulder when she tried to wrestle off her seat belt. "Let's make sure you're okay before you move too much, all right?"

She wanted to be the cool, competent, in-control—always in-control—attorney she was. Not the exhausted, injured, bordering-on-hysterical idiot who stupidly and blindly dated married men yet still got the shivers over a smoky, hot, sexy voice. Sadly, the latter was the best she had to offer at the moment. "What . . . happened?" she managed, her voice sounding oddly tight, bordering on shrill. "Where did you come from?"

"I came from your left, through the intersection. You ran the stop sign. Not sure how you didn't see me."

She leaned her head gingerly back against the headrest, eyes still closed, willing her brain to get straight and her face to stop throbbing. "What stop sign? There's no stop sign going that way."

She felt his broad hands grow even gentler on her arm. "Well, then I took those big, red octagonal things with the word STOP on them the wrong way, but let's not worry about that. You didn't hit me."

"Yeah," she said, her breath coming out in small pants, her heart still feeling a little out of control as the shakes started to set in. "Good. I'm sorry. For scaring you. I—I'll be okay. You don't need to stay. I just need a few minutes, that's all." And a few painkillers. Possibly a few stitches. And a very long nap. "It's not . . . your problem," she gritted out, bolstering herself for another attempt to undo her seat belt. Though she might want to shoot for opening her eyes first. Yeah. Maybe a few more minutes. "Thank you, though. For stopping."

"Well, the sign is DOA," he continued calmly, in that spine-tingling voice of his, as if she hadn't just summarily dismissed him. "And given the steam rising from under the hood, your car might need more than a little CPR, too." She heard him pushing at the air bag and she felt him angle in for a closer look. "Looks like you took a bit of a hit from the air bag canister when it popped. And, uh . . ."

At the odd edge in his voice, she cracked open one eye and caught sight of a head of tawny, sun-streaked brown hair. She couldn't see his face, because he was staring at her . . . boobs? *Really?* She'd have snorted in disgust if she hadn't been pretty sure doing so would make her face fall off. "Someone from town will tow me," she said, barely restraining the urge to pull his head back. By the hair. *Now get your stupid man face out of my boobs.* She sighed. Six years of college, summers spent clerking for a federal court judge, a law degree, and a fast-tracked position in one of Capitol Hill's premiere litigation firms . . . and the best she could do was *stupid man face*? Maybe she needed more than a long nap.

"Good." He glanced up then and met her slitted gaze

with an easy expression and eyes the color of warm honey. "You might want to call the paramedics while you're at it."

Oh God. She closed her eyes again, not wanting to know what her face must look like. Given how badly it hurt, she was guessing not great. *Oh shit! The wedding!* She shut that train of thought down immediately, knowing it wouldn't help her at the moment. "How . . . bad . . . ?" she managed, too afraid to open her eyes again and look in the rearview mirror. Maybe she had far worse injuries than whatever had happened to her face, only she couldn't feel them because she was in shock. Maybe—

"Well, I'm not sure," he said in a serious tone, "but I think you've been gut shot by Willy Wonka."

She frowned, winced, then gingerly lifted her head from the headrest and peered downward. The air bag had smashed the chocolate pretzels into a crumbly, chocolate blob and plastered them across the front of her once-beautiful Helona Georgette white silk blouse. She let out a long, shaky sigh of relief and closed her eyes again. "Bastard," she breathed, then was surprised to feel her lips curving upward when he chuckled, even though the hint of a smile only intensified the throbbing. It was a nice sound, his laugh—rich, deep, and inviting, just like his voice, and his eyes, she thought.

"Wiggle your toes," he said, and she cracked her eyes open again. "Make sure your legs are okay, and your back."

"They're fine," she said, but wiggled her toes inside her leather flats, just in case. "Are you a doctor?"

"Contractor," he replied. "I'm going to call someone to come get your car, come take a look at you." He straightened. "Sit tight for a few minutes."

She wanted to insist once again that he go on his way, but what came out was, "I think I can manage that."

She also managed to open her eyes enough to watch him

step to the front of her car and survey the damage. The deflated air bag was in her lap now, so her view through the front windshield was unobstructed. She should be looking at the damage to her car, too. Or reaching for the rearview mirror to take a gander at the damage to her face. What she did instead, however, was take a gander at her Good Samaritan.

He wasn't a local. At least not one who'd lived in the Cove for any length of time. She hadn't been home in a couple of years, but she'd have remembered him. A contractor, he'd said. Probably in town temporarily then, on a job of some kind. Or maybe not working in the Cove at all, but just passing through on his way down to Machias, or up to Lubec. It was all too much to ponder and her face hurt too much to think it through. So she let her head loll back on the headrest, focused on releasing the post-crash tension from her neck and shoulders, and used the moment to mindlessly enjoy the view.

He was tall. And big. Not like a gym-obsessed muscle-head or anything. More like a lumberjack or, well, a contractor. The kind of man who'd gotten those broad, thickly muscled shoulders, and biceps that strained the armbands of his short-sleeved polo shirt through honest, hard labor. His chest filled out the soft, dark green cotton pretty nicely, too. Her gaze drifted downward, approving the flat stomach where his shirt was tucked into the waistband of his jeans. His approval rating climbed further when he bent down to look under her car, giving her a nice view of the back pockets of those jeans. Not a baggy, saggy inch of denim to be found there. No, sir. Not when he straightened again, either. *Damn.* Her gaze had moved back to his face, cataloging the honey-colored eyes, tanned skin, the smooth angle to his jaw, and that mouth wasn't bad either . . . when he lifted his gaze directly to hers, as if he'd felt her watching him.

Maybe he had, she thought, a little dazedly. She felt like she'd been visually frisking him.

The late-afternoon sun backlit his hunky, decidedly masculine frame, casting his face and those thickly lashed eyes in shadow. Her gaze drifted to his hands again as she remembered how they'd felt, keeping her steady in those first moments after the crash. He looked like the perfect guy. All gorgeous, courteous, manly-man rescuer of damsels in distress.

She felt a hot rush of attraction zip right through her recently traumatized system. And by trauma, she didn't mean the car crash. She blamed it on that, though, all the same. All that adrenaline and pain, making her a little lightheaded. Had to be it. Otherwise she was quite certain she'd have looked at him and felt nothing. Because not only had she sworn off men in general, she'd sworn off men who made her girl parts tingle very specifically.

One thing was certain. Looks were deceiving. Because there were no perfect men. "Just perfect idiots," she muttered, lifting her hand from the wheel, as if taking an oath. "Yes, your honor, guilty as charged. No need for a trial. The evidence is overwhelming." She looked at him again . . . and, yep, definite tingles. *Book me, lock me up, and throw away the key, judge. Because that's apparently the only way I'm going to save me from myself.*

Calder Blue wasn't sure if the woman still strapped in the driver's seat of the banged-up Audi was waving at him or blocking the sun from her eyes, but he didn't wave back. He also didn't take his eyes off her, though he couldn't have said exactly why.

She wasn't his type. On first glance, she was all money and status and high maintenance wrapped up in the veneer of fierce independence. She hadn't wasted any time making sure he knew she was perfectly capable of taking care of herself, despite glaring evidence to the contrary. In his experience, women like that always ended up being the clingiest, the neediest, though they'd deny it to their dying breath. They shoved that fierce independence front and center like a thick, impenetrable wall, then all but begged a man to batter his way through it. In reality, that wall would always turn out to be a thin, barely held together smokescreen designed to hide things like deep-seated insecurity, massive self-doubt, and low self-esteem. When that wobbly facade came tumbling down—and it always did—the real-world light would then shine into all those hidden neurotic nooks and crannies.

Give him a down-to-earth, capable woman who didn't waste time labeling things or shoving anything in anyone's face, but simply took care of business because that was how the world turned, offering a hand when she could, taking a hand when she needed one. A smile, a wave of thanks, or you're welcome was all that was needed. No endless analysis of every little thing. Not giving a damn what anyone else thought of her. That, to him, was true independence.

And yet, he didn't look away. From the once-shiny car, or the tailored clothes and tasteful, understated jewelry she wore. Her sleek, dark hair was pulled neatly back in an expensive-looking gold clasp. Hair that hadn't dared get even a little mussed up despite an exploding air bag. Her face . . . well, for the moment, that was a different story. It was going to be a little tender for a while. He didn't think her nose was broken, just lacerated, but he wouldn't be surprised if she was sporting a pair of shiners by this time tomorrow. Even with the cut to the bridge of her nose, the partly swollen lip, and the slightly wild look in those dark blue eyes of hers, she was an elegant, cool beauty. A stunner, actually, in every sense of the word. *Lord only knows the issues you've got, sweetheart, but I bet most men wouldn't think twice before trying to breach your walls.*

Given the way she'd coolly instructed him to be on his way, despite very clearly not being anywhere close to fine, he'd bet her walls were a little more solidly constructed than most, probably from years of practice. Well, he wasn't most men, and those thick walls didn't represent a challenge so much as a screaming red flag. One he was more than happy to accept at face value.

So no, he didn't wave back. He did curse under his breath, however, when he realized he was checking her raised hand for a wedding ring. "Jesus, Blue, don't you ever learn?" he muttered to himself, then turned his back to her as he slid his phone out of his pocket.

Before he could dial for help, the sound of tires spitting gravel had him turning around again. *What is it with the folks in this town?* He caught sight of a little green Prius swerving from the middle of the intersection to the side of the road where he'd parked his truck, barely missing clipping the front bumper before it came to a stop, half on the road and half off. *Can't anyone here read a damn stop sign?*

A woman of shorter-than-average height with a compact, curvy frame popped out of the car. She had a wild mass of dark curls sprouting every which direction and was wearing a—what the hell *was* she wearing? It was a full-length formal dress, rose colored and shiny, really shiny, as if it was made out of satin. On crack. There was some sort of off-the-shoulder thing going on and a hideous, mutant flower made of the same unnatural material, only a few shades darker, attached to the other shoulder. The whole of it looked like a prom dress gone horribly wrong. Except she was a good half dozen years or more past prom age. *Carrie: The Reunion,* he thought, somewhat morbidly fascinated.

She gathered up the skirt, which was voluminous, revealing what looked a lot like brightly flowered . . . were those rubber garden boots? *Oh, why the hell not?* Then left her car door hanging open into the roadway as she rushed toward the banged-up sports car.

"Hannah!" she cried as she ran toward the driver's-side door. "Hannah? Oh my God, are you okay?"

Hannah. The name sounded a lot more down-to-earth than suited the woman still strapped into the Audi. She looked more like a Danielle or Blair, or some private club name like Sloan or—*or Tenley.* He immediately shut out thoughts of his ex and stepped around the front of the car. "She's okay," he said, "but she needs a tow, and it probably wouldn't hurt to have a paramedic take a look at her."

Prom Queen of the Walking Dead jerked back in surprise at the sound of his voice, then instantly spun on him. "Did you do this?" she demanded. "Did you run her off the road?" She stalked toward him, which, despite her small frame, was scarier than it should be, mostly due to the getup she had on. Mostly.

She stuck her hand out. "Insurance information? License?" She lowered her hand before he could give her anything, not that he'd planned to, and patted her hips and middle, then swore. "Stupid dress. No pockets. Wait right here while I get something to write with," she told him, finger in his face, which was when he noticed the god-awful green lace gloves she was wearing. "And on," she added.

"No need," he told her as she spun on her rubber-booted heel, making her spin right back again, then reach up to grab the tiara—how on earth had he missed that?—that swung precariously from the wilds of her dark hair to dip over one side of her forehead.

"You already gave that to her? Well . . . good. That's good. What happened? Have you been drinking?" She tried to remove the tiara, but it was hopelessly stuck in her hair. More swearing.

He started to reach out to help her, then thought better of it. He worked with his hands for a living, so probably better not to give her a chance to bite them off. "Your friend ran the stop sign," he said calmly. "She swerved to keep from hitting me—and she didn't hit me, by the way—only the sign there wasn't so lucky."

"She's not my friend, she's my sister. Well, we're friends, too. I mean, we're close, not geographically, but—wait, she ran the stop sign? What stop sign? That intersection doesn't have—" Prom Queen whirled around, almost sending the drunken tiara flying.

Calder sighed and pointed. "Unless I'm hallucinating, and at the moment I'm not entirely confident in saying I'm not," he added, "it does. Four of them, in fact."

"I was born here and I can absolutely guarantee you that—" Her shoulders slumped as she looked at the inter-section. "Hunh. What do you know? When the hell did they do that? And why? This town barely has enough traffic to warrant the single traffic light we do have, and that's in the heart of it, much less a four-way stop on the outskirts."

"I couldn't say. I was just going to call nine-one-one and ask a recommendation on a tow truck from whoever answered."

"Sal's," she said, without glancing at him. "I'll call him. I'll call my brother, too. He'll send Bonnie over."

"Bonnie?"

She looked back at him now. "The paramedic." She said

it as if he were dense, or a little slow. "My brother is the police chief."

Of course he is. Calder began to realize that any hope he had of making the meeting with his great-uncle anywhere close to on time was already lost. And that was a problem. A big one. But life happened. Hell, wasn't that how he'd ended up in Blueberry Cove in the first place?

"Don't call Logan."

Calder and Prom Queen both turned to find Hannah standing behind them, one hand braced on the roof of the sports car. She didn't look too steady on her feet and he was already moving toward her before he realized it.

"His wedding is this weekend," Hannah said, looking oddly regal despite the banged-up face and messed-up shirt. Maybe it was the still-perfect hair, or the too-straight set to her shoulders. "He doesn't need—"

"Oh God, Hannah," her sister cried, rushing past him to Hannah's side. "You're bleeding!"

A wedding, Calder thought, pausing a step. *Well, that explains the dress. I guess.* He shuddered to think what the rest of the wedding party looked like.

"I'm fine," Hannah assured her sister. "I just need to clean up a little, maybe get some ice and a few ibuprofen in me, possibly with one of Fergus's whisky chasers, and I'll be good to go."

"You're in shock. You should be sitting down." The shorter woman looked her sister over and gasped. "Oh no! Your blouse—"

"Willy Wonka," Hannah said, still sounding shaky, but her gaze lifted from her sister then, and found his. A hint of a smile curved her puffy lip. "Bastard," he and Hannah both said at the same time.

He shouldn't be smiling. He definitely shouldn't be thinking how beautiful she was, even all banged up. And he absolutely, positively shouldn't be saying, "I can give you a ride into town, get you somewhere you can clean up. Get some ice." His smile grew slightly even as he mentally kicked himself for being the idiot he clearly was. He blamed it on the town. Obviously they were one cuckoo short of a full nest and he'd been elected to fill the void. "Either in a baggie, or in a glass. Or both."

Hannah's sister blinked at them both, then sprang back into action. Calder had the feeling she sprang a lot. It was dizzying. Although, in fairness, it might be the dress, the crazy hair, and drunken tiara making it seem that way.

"I can take care of my sister," Prom Queen said. She turned to Hannah. "I was just heading out to the Point. You can come the rest of the way with me." She tossed Calder a look as if he were somehow still the bad guy in all this, then looked back at her sister. "We'll call Sal and get him to tow your car—which, you were right, I do love it!" She gently took Hannah's arm and tucked it in hers. "So cute! Or, it was. And it will be again," she rushed on to say, as if her sister were in a far more fragile state than Calder was coming to believe she actually was.

Hannah was definitely shaken from the wreck, and a little banged up, but she wasn't waiting to be rescued. In fact, now that she'd been given a few minutes to pull herself together, it seemed to him she was handling things much as she'd claimed she would. She wasn't turning down her sister's offer of help, either. She was calm, rational, doing what needed to be done. Maybe not the girl-next-door exactly, but . . . somehow he found himself thinking he'd been a bit hasty with his initial snap assessment.

"I don't think she's going to fit in your car," Calder told Prom Queen. "I can give her a ride." What the hell, he'd already screwed up the big Blue family reunion. He'd just have to call Jonah and let him know he'd be there a bit later than planned. It was already destined to be one giant cluster anyway.

"It has a passenger seat," Prom Queen informed him. "Just because I drive an environmentally friendly car while you drive that monster gas hog, is no reason to—"

"I was referring to the balloons," Calder said, nodding toward her little Prius, which was presently stuffed to the gills with an array of silver-, white-, and rose-colored helium-filled balloons, some of which were trying to escape out of her open driver's-side door. "And if you can figure out how to haul five hundred pounds of feed and a four-horse trailer behind that thing, I'll gladly give up the gas hog."

"Oh! The balloons! Crap!" And with that, Prom Queen was hotfooting—or booting, as the case may be—back toward her car, leaving her abruptly released sister to steady herself against the hood of her damaged vehicle.

Calder stepped in to help, but stopped short when she straightened and lifted a hand to stall him. So, still a little Ms. Independent. He caught sight of her stiffening shoulders. Maybe more than a little.

"You'll have to forgive her," Hannah said. "She's—that's Fiona—she's an interior designer by profession and in charge of planning our brother's wedding, so she's got a million details on her mind at the moment. And then I go and get in an accident. She's usually not that rude or scatterbrained."

Calder wisely kept his opinion to himself. "Just being protective of her family. Nothing wrong in that. Why don't we get you over to the paramedic or the ER if you'd rather go there, and we'll let your sister handle calling in for the tow."

Hannah surprised him by merely nodding. "Thank you. I appreciate that. I'll need to call Beanie, too."

"Who's Beanie?" It surprised him that he actually wanted to know.

"The owner of the sign I just took out. Her husband built it and hand-painted it." She looked over at the pile of shattered planks. "I feel awful about ruining it."

"Sounds like the kind of guy who wouldn't mind making another one. I'm sure it will be fine." He motioned toward his truck. "Is there anything you need from your car?" He lifted a hand. "I'll get it, just tell me."

"He can't make another one," she said instead. "He passed away last year. That's why I feel awful."

Calder stopped and looked at her, and saw she was on the verge of tears. And likely not the sweet trickle of a single tear sliding down a pale cheek, either. He didn't know her, but despite his earlier rush to judge—okay, maybe his ongoing rush to judge—something told him she wasn't a crier. Something also told him that it probably wasn't the sign that had her feeling suddenly undone. Maybe it was all of it, the accident, her brother getting married, and now adding to her sister's list of worries. Maybe the sign was simply the final straw. He didn't know. And he shouldn't care.

"Come on," he said, gently taking her elbow, but keeping his hand there when she would have pulled away. "We'll get it all figured out."

She was taller than he'd initially thought when she'd been in the car. Somewhere around five-nine, maybe five-ten. He didn't know what kind of heels she had on, but, regardless, she wasn't much shorter than he was, and he came in at six-one. Lithe and lean, not much in the curves department, either. That much he'd accurately ascertained from his blouse assessment earlier.

She paused as she noted the sign on the side of his truck. "Blue Harbor Farm." She looked back at him. "I thought you said you were a contractor."

"I am. Family business. Fourth generation."

"And the farm?"

"First generation," he said with a smile.

"You?"

He nodded.

"Sounds like a lot to juggle."

"If you ask my father, it's a waste of time and money. If you ask my brothers, a hobby that got a little out of control."

"And if I asked you?"

He kept his smile in place, but his answer was serious and heartfelt. "The thing that kept me sane through a hellacious divorce." His smile grew slightly. "Continues to keep me sane working with family."

"I'm sorry," she said. "About the . . . hellacious part." She waved a hand briefly, but said no more. She held his gaze, then looked at the sign again, more, he thought, for somewhere else to look. Other than at him. He wasn't sure what she'd seen in his expression, but banged up or not, she seemed a pretty sharp sort. So probably . . . too much.

He saw her eyebrows lift. "Calais?" she said. "You're a long way from home."

"Not that far. Hour and fifteen to the company office, hour-forty-five to the farm."

"Unique town, Calais. Sort of umbilically attached to Saint Stephen across the border in New Brunswick, right? Interesting blend of cultures."

"*Mais oui, bien sur.*"

She smiled a little at that. "I guess you grew up speaking French and English, living so close."

"It's predominantly English on both sides of the border. I speak French because my mother is French Canadian. I grew up with both languages." He opened the passenger door to his truck.

"You didn't have to do this," she said, as he helped her up to the passenger seat.

She levered herself into the truck with a natural, graceful ease, making him wonder if she was a dancer, or some other thing that elegant women did with elegant bodies like the one she had. She required only a little assistance from him, which was just as well, he thought. Putting his hands on any more of that elegant body wouldn't be wise. She was the kind of distraction he never needed in general, and definitely didn't need right now.

She pulled on her own seat belt, wincing a little as she did, then immediately leaned her head back and closed her eyes. "But I'm very grateful you did."

"Not a problem," he said, palming the door, intending to close it.

"Hannah," she said, quietly now, so he knew she was in more pain than she'd been showing, making him pause. "I'm Hannah. McCrae."

"Calder Blue," he responded.

"Ah. Blue Harbor Farm," she added, as if recalling the sign on his door. "Any relation to Jonah Blue?" she asked through barely moving bruised lips, eyes still closed.

"Great-nephew."

"I thought I'd met all the Blues."

"Different branch of the family."

She opened her eyes then, and turned all that dark blue on him. Despite whatever pain she was in, and whatever worries she might have, her eyes were still surprisingly sharp, and quickly assessing. "You mean—as in Jedediah Blue's branch?"

"The very same."

"Your branches don't talk to each other. For like . . . a hundred years."

"A little longer, but that is true, yes."

"How long have you been in Blueberry?"

"Just heading in, actually."

She leaned her head back and closed her eyes again, but her lips curved upward just a hair and stayed that way, even when she winced at the pain.

"Something amusing about that?"

"Not at all. It's . . . I just realized that your bombshell is going to be a lot bigger than mine."

Chapter Two

"Dear Lord, what have you done to yourself and just days before the wedding. Sit down and let me have a look at you." Barbara Benson pulled around the chair next to her beat-up metal desk and gestured to it.

Hannah knew better than to offer even token resistance, and frankly, she found standing upright highly overrated at the moment, so she sank gratefully onto the thinly padded seat. Sergeant Benson was the closest thing Hannah had ever had to a mom. One she remembered anyway. Though she supposed where Barbara was concerned, "mom" was a relative term. Barbara was in her late sixties and had raised her own brood of children while simultaneously performing her duties as sergeant, receptionist, secretary, dispatcher, Mother Superior, and general savior of everyone's asses in Blueberry Cove. She'd performed those duties for Hannah's brother, Logan, as well as the previous three police chiefs. Hannah was pretty sure Sergeant Benson applied the same handbook to child-rearing duties as she did her police duties. And Hannah wouldn't have changed a single thing about it.

"I missed you, too," Hannah said wryly, trying not to wince as she smiled.

"Got word from Sal that you took out Carl's sign with your fancy little hot rod."

"It's not a hot rod," Hannah said, dutifully tipping her face up for examination.

"It's not a pickup truck or a sport utility vehicle. Something useful."

"No. It's actually fun to drive." *Or was.* "In fact, it was a pickup truck that ran me into Beanie's sign."

"Way I heard it, you ran the stop sign."

Hannah sighed. Small towns. And Blueberry was the smallest of the small when it came to everyone knowing everyone else's business. She'd have to get used to that again. Though, admittedly, she'd learned that the Capitol Hill legal community was a close second when it came to high-functioning grapevines. It was a miracle no one here knew what had been transpiring in her life back in D.C. for the past six months. Just because she hadn't told a single member of her family didn't mean that somehow word wouldn't make its way back to the Cove anyway. Hannah was certain it hadn't though, because Barbara would have been the first one to call her if it had. And then, only if Uncle Gus hadn't beaten her to the punch.

Hannah had already planned to make up an excuse for why Tim wasn't with her at the wedding. She'd come clean after the ceremony was over and Logan and Alex were off happily honeymooning, but not now. Not yet.

"When did that happen, anyway?" Hannah asked. "The four-way stop, I mean. And all the way out there? Why? Fiona ran the damn thing, too. Darn thing," she automatically corrected when Barbara gave her The Look. Hannah reached for her purse so she could dig out two quarters for the swear jar that had sat on Barbara's desk for longer than Hannah had been alive.

Barbara reached over and filched a dollar when Hannah opened her wallet, then dropped it in the jar. At Hannah's raised brow, she said, "Price of swearing has gone up, just like everything else."

"You know," Hannah said, mildly, "Fiona's convinced that having a swear jar in a police station, even one as small as ours, probably put every one of your kids through college. What does the loot go to now that they're all grown and married? The grandkids' college funds?"

Barbara leaned closer and examined the laceration on the bridge of Hannah's nose, making clucking noises. Hannah knew from experience that was her version of swearing. "Always had a hankering to see Alaska," Barbara said, as she finished her perusal and moved back behind her desk. She was still frowning at the state of Hannah's face, but there was a decided twinkle in her eyes when she added, "Preferably from the deck of a cruise ship."

Hannah laughed, then flinched and gently put her hand over her nose and busted lip. "I can't believe I have to play maid of honor with this. I don't think even Fiona's amazing cosmetic skills are going to save me. Logan's going to kill me when he finds out. If Alex doesn't first."

"What did Bonnie have to say about it?"

"She said my head must have been jerking forward when the air bag exploded, because the impact was harder than it usually is. I bought an older-model car because I liked the look of it better, which made the air bag technology dated." She raised a hand to stall the lecture. "I know, I know. Happens sometimes, apparently. So . . . lucky me. It's not broken, thank goodness, just a deep laceration from the canister hitting me, three stitches. Lip isn't pretty, but no stitches there, so there's that. Bruised shoulder, but nothing worse." Although . . . tell that to her shoulder, which felt as if it were on fire. "And I'm probably going to have two black eyes from the impact."

Barbara clucked again, but mercifully spared her the full-on safety lecture. "Trust your sister," she said instead. "She can make anything look good." At Hannah's twist of a half smile, Barbara waved her hand. "You know what I meant. And Alex isn't exactly one to worry about things like that and neither is your brother. Although he might not be too thrilled with you drag racing through town and wiping out the signage."

"I wasn't drag racing," Hannah said, letting the exasperation come through. "I wasn't even speeding. I just . . . I didn't see the stop sign, that's all. I was distracted by the lupines." *And the wreckage that is my personal life.* "So . . . why *do* we have a four-way stop there?"

"It's all the changes coming to Half Moon Harbor. Town council thought we needed to be a step ahead of the increase in traffic. There's one at the other end of town, too, at Point Road. And talk of putting in a second light by the courthouse park."

Point Road. If it hadn't been for the accident, she'd have already driven that long, scenic route around Pelican Bay out to Pelican Point, to home. She missed the rocky shoreline, the constant sea mist, the aging family home that had once been the lightkeeper's station, the even older and more crumbling original keeper's cottage. And oh, she missed her lighthouse. Hannah knew the Pelican Point lighthouse was well into its much-needed restoration, close to being done actually, last she'd heard, because Alex was the one heading up that project. She couldn't wait to see it. For the first time in her life, it would be fully functional. She couldn't even imagine it.

The town was celebrating the tercentennial of its charter date later that summer, and the lighthouse was closing in on its bicentennial, so the idea had been to link the two together and celebrate their history and heritage at the same time. But the Cove as a whole was well north of the standard tourist trade, and neither a restored lighthouse nor their little town celebrations, no matter how important or historic, were going to bring a crush of outsiders, certainly not long enough to warrant permanent traffic signs. She said as much to Barbara.

"You're right, it won't," Barbara said, scooting her chair in, lips pursed as she started methodically going through folders on her desk, filing things, shoving other stacks aside, clearly annoyed, but trying not to be. "It's the schooner tours that will be operating out of the harbor and the new yacht club that will raise those kinds of issues."

"Right! The schooner! How did I forget about that? I guess it's been bringing in sightseers already. It's not every day you can witness a life-size version of a seventeenth-century tall ship being built. I can't even imagine it, not really. I'm anxious to see it, and to meet the Monaghan who came to resurrect their shipbuilding heritage." Along with the McCraes, the Monaghans were the other founding family of Blueberry Cove.

"He's a handful, that one. What they once would have called a scalawag," Barbara said, but her expression made it clear that while she might like to hold his reputation against him, she simply couldn't. Made Hannah all the more curious to meet him. "But he does fine work," Barbara went on. "Very impressive. His forebears would be proud indeed."

"I look forward to seeing it. But tours on one boat out of Half Moon Harbor, even one that big, can't mean a huge increase in—wait. Did you say . . . yacht club? What yacht club? Who here even has a yacht?"

Barbara met Hannah's gaze with a level one of her own. "It's Brooks Winstock's schooner, you know. Brodie is building it, just like his ancestors once did, but Winstock is the owner, and he's the one who'll be operating the tours. Or who will own the business that operates the tours. Winstock also happens to have a yacht. And lots of friends with yachts. So, he decided to build himself and his pals a club."

Now Hannah understood the annoyed look. "Brooks Winstock decided *what?* When did that happen?"

Barbara's expression became a bit more pointed, in a way that would have made Hannah squirm in her seat even if she weren't hiding a big, fat secret.

"Well, if you'd bother to come back home more often than once every few years, or keep in touch more regularly, you'd know when it happened."

There's the lecture. Hannah knew better than to think she'd escape without one. Oddly, instead of irritating her, it made her feel . . . well, not comforted, but like she was home. Like she mattered. To someone.

Barbara leaned back, but stopped short of folding her arms over her buttoned-up, uniformed bosom. Not that it mattered. Her steely gaze did much the same. "Speaking of which, what is Tim the Titan of Finance's excuse this time? And don't bother telling me he's coming because it's all over your face that he's leaving you to pull wedding duty alone. At least he didn't keep you from coming home this time."

"No," Hannah said quietly, no longer annoyed by Barbara's nickname for him. He had plenty of far worse ones now. "Tim isn't here. He's not coming to the wedding. It's just me." The urge to simply unload and tell Barbara exactly how truthful a statement that was, to tell her every last thing that had happened, was so strong Hannah wasn't sure she could hold it in another second. Then she noticed, or made herself notice, the door to Logan's office in her peripheral vision. *No, you can't. Not until after his wedding.*

Hannah knew that the mere mention of Tim by her family and loved ones would cause her to relive the heartache all over again. But she'd promised herself she wouldn't shed so much as a single additional tear over him, and willed her eyes to stay dry now. Surprisingly, despite her thumping, battered heart, they did. Maybe it was the accident trauma. Maybe her body could only focus on handling one type of pain at a time.

"I know you all were looking forward to finally meeting him, but he's not why I haven't been home." Hannah could blame Tim for a lot, and did so, freely, but she'd never been one to push off blame that was rightfully hers on someone else, no matter how tempting. "I would have come without him, it's just been really—"

"Busy. Yes, so you've said for the past three Christmases."

"It hasn't been three, it's only been . . ." She trailed off, did the math, and felt . . . sad. And annoyed with herself. *Had it really been that long?* It felt, in some ways, like a lifetime longer. Hannah lifted a shoulder, then flinched, as she was reminded, quite painfully, that that was the shoulder the seat-belt harness had done a number on during the crash. "It's not because I didn't want to be here. And I'm sorry. I truly am." That much was true. "It's just, in my business, holidays are a big time for networking and I was—we were both—trying to make a name for ourselves in our respective firms. This is the time in our lives we had to strike if we wanted to climb. If you don't make your mark early, you generally don't make one ever. I just—" *Used to think that was important.* Her shoulders slumped a little under the weight of . . . all of it, not the least of which was the subterfuge she'd decided to continue upon her return. "Logan understood, and Fi. Kerry hasn't been back for even longer, and—"

"And she's been on another continent at the opposite end of the earth," Barbara commented pointedly.

Hannah glanced down. "I've missed all of you, terribly." She knew the statement sounded heartfelt and sincere, because it was. Never more than after the past six months. She looked back up. "I'm really glad to be home." She felt tears threatening now, and it made her face hurt that much worse, so she frowned slightly to try to quell them, and said, "So, what's the deal with Winstock and the yacht club? Where on earth could he even build such a thing? Between the Monaghan shipyard and Blue's fishing docks, there isn't much real estate right on the harbor—"

"He took Delia's place. Right out from under her. Tried to snatch himself part of Monaghan's, too, but got his fingers smacked away from that particular cookie jar by a friend of Grace's with deep pockets."

"Grace? Grace who?" Hannah's temples began to throb in earnest. Maybe she should have had more to eat in the past fourteen hours than chocolate pretzels and Diet Coke.

Barbara must have seen something of the pain because her expression softened and she leaned forward and placed a firm hand over Hannah's. "Honey, you've got a lot to catch up on. And plenty of time to do it. Later. For now, you should head on out to the Point, see your brother, let Fiona fuss over you a little. Get some sleep. You've had too long a day already and some big ones coming up."

"I—Logan's not still here in town?" She glanced at his office door again, which stood half open. She'd known he wasn't in there or she would have already had the best big-brother bear hug ever, but she'd assumed he was in town somewhere. "That's why I came here after seeing Bonnie. I figured he could give me a lift."

"No, he headed out early today, something about the restoration had him heading back. It's almost seven now anyway, so he'd already be gone." Barbara smiled, and her love and affection for Logan shone clearly in every line of her face. "He's been a lot better about not spending all his hours working these days. Does a soul good to see it. I tried to radio him when I heard about your accident, but he must be outside somewhere on the property, because I couldn't get a signal."

"That's okay. Fi will fill him in. I spoke to her and she knows I'm okay."

"Ask me, I think he lit out of here to go make sure everything was ready at the Point. He's so excited having the three of you back home all at once, but a little nervous, too."

"Nervous? What on earth for? The Point is our home. We grew up there together. And last I heard, Kerry won't be here until the day before the wedding." *If she comes at all,* Hannah thought, but kept that to herself.

"His life has been turned upside down since you've last seen him. In a good way," Barbara assured her. "The lighthouse, all the other restorations and renovations. Alex being out there with him now. It's different—it's a home to him in a new way."

"I—I guess you're right." Hannah let the realization sink in. "I hadn't thought about it like that." And she couldn't. It was too much to think about it that way, like she was losing her childhood home. The truth of it was, the idea of her big brother, after all he'd been through, making a home there with Alex, the two of them taking the Point into a new generation, would—did—make her truly and sincerely happy. It was just . . . a lot, at the moment. Her eyes might have misted again, and she was afraid even happy tears would turn into the big, ugly kind, so she pushed them back once more.

"I'm really glad they are happy. I'm dying to meet Alex," Hannah said sincerely. Better to focus on the good things instead. "We've spoken several times about wedding stuff and I like what I know of her so far." She smiled, ignoring the pain, inside and out. "She's definitely got Logan's number, and I'm a fan of anyone who can jerk a knot in him from time to time. He's been the big kahuna long enough."

"You'll like her even more when you meet her, I can promise you that. What about you?" Barbara asked after a beat. "Are you happy?"

Barbara had caught Hannah off guard with that one, and though Hannah saw the love she'd missed even more than she'd realized, along with no small dose of concern in the older woman's eyes, she wondered if maybe she'd been too hasty in assuming Barbara didn't know anything. She knew Barb would be hurt when she found out Hannah hadn't confided in her, and more than a little upset to learn Hannah hadn't confided in anyone else, either. Feeling that burden a little too keenly, she ducked her chin.

You're getting pretty damn good at ducking things, she thought, then stuffed another dollar in the swear jar. Just because. "I'm happy to be home," she said. At least that much was the truth. Then, after a short sigh and a little breath to help square her shoulders up again, she quietly asked, "Why didn't you tell me all this was going on? With the club, and the diner? We talk at least once a month."

"More like every three or four this past year," Barbara corrected, "and not at all since Christmas. But who's counting?" She ignored Hannah's abashed expression and instead reached across her desk and placed her hand over Hannah's wrist. "Honey, I didn't tell you because I knew you had a pretty good amount of something going on in your life as it was. It's not like you to go that long without a call, even as busy as you are. I figured you didn't need to get worked up over stuff going on here. It wasn't like you could have done anything about it, anyway."

So, Barbara didn't know what had happened, but she knew things weren't good. Hannah wished that made her feel better, instead of worse.

"Still, I should have known. Should have called more."

"Phone works both ways, so don't go taking it all on yourself. And you're home now," Barbara said in her matter-of-fact way that made it clear the subject was closed. "You'll know more than you ever wanted to know about things no one ever wanted to know about, most of them by sundown. Which it will be shortly. We should see about getting you a ride home. You need to be resting, not sitting here gabbing with me."

Hannah nodded absently, but her mind was skimming back over all the news Barbara had shared with her already. "I can't believe that, about Delia's. We all used to go to her grandmother's restaurant, until it burned down. I always admired Delia for starting up her own place after that. God, I can't even count how many times I holed up in a booth there during high school. How long has it been since she opened?"

"Twenty years."

Hannah's eyes widened. "Wow. I'm officially old as dirt. I should go see her. I need to anyway. We're co-maids-of-honor. Maybe Alex will let her carry that ball—or bouquet, as it were—given—" She gestured to her face. "Where is she? Did she get a new place? When did this—?"

"Delia's fine, still has her grandmother's little cottage. Happier than I've ever seen her, in fact. You'll hear all about that soon enough." Barbara stood, and tugged Hannah to her feet, hugging her before Hannah straightened fully. Barbara was a fierce force to be reckoned with, and it always surprised Hannah because she barely hit five-foot-five, and that was in her uniform-issue heavy-soled shoes.

"I'm going to get Deputy Dan to give you a lift," Barbara said. "Sal said your car—well, that's for later. I'm sure he'll be in touch, and between Logan, Alex, and Fi, there will be a car available when you need it." She picked up her radio and flipped the call button.

Hannah put her hand out. "Don't take Dan off duty to drive me all the way out to the Point. It looks like I'm going to need a rental, so I'll just go take care of that now."

"You're not driving," Barbara said, and when Hannah opened her mouth to argue, she merely pointed to the chair, then radioed Officer Brentwood.

Barbara had tagged him as Deputy Dan on his first day, because he was young, with blond hair, blue eyes, and the kind of peach-fuzzed cheeks that would probably follow him well into maturity.

Her handset squawked just as the door opened to the station house and in walked . . . Calder Blue. Sergeant Benson clicked off the radio, all business. "What can I do for you?"

"Actually, I was looking for Ms. McCrae," Calder said, his gaze moving easily to Hannah's.

"Is something wrong?" Hannah asked him.

"I went by the fire station house and the medical clinic, but Bonnie said you were at the police station. Is Beanie filing charges or something? Signage homicide?"

"What? No. I came to see Logan—my brother—after Bonnie was finished with me."

"Right. The police chief."

"Why did you go to the clinic? I'm a little banged up, but I told you, I'm fine. Unless—are you . . . is something else wrong?"

He walked toward her and held out his hand. "I stopped to put gas in my environmentally challenged truck and found this on the floorboard." He was holding her stuffed-to-the-gills leather day planner. "Must have fallen out of your purse. I figured you'd need it sooner than later. ID for the insurance paperwork and such."

She was a slave to technology just like everyone else in her field, but she'd never been able to quite part with her handwritten file book. Once upon a time she couldn't have breathed without her day planner, and that time hadn't been so long ago yet. So, it was shocking to find out she'd gone this long without even realizing she'd left it behind.

He stopped in front of her and gave her a closer look, taking in the cleaned-up face and bandaged gash on the bridge of her nose. "But I guess having a police chief brother jumps a few hurdles."

"Being born and raised in a town the size of Blueberry pretty much removes the hurdles all together." She took the leather-bound book from him, running her finger over the elastic strap that held the bulging contents between the hand-tooled covers. "But thank you. I didn't even realize I'd lost it. Saved me the additional panic attack I'd have had when I finally figured it out." Would she have panicked? She wasn't so sure now. What did she really need it for anymore? Shouldn't that make her sad? Instead she just felt . . . numb. She belatedly noticed Barbara eyeing the two of them with open interest. "I'm sorry. Barb—er—Sergeant Benson, this is—"

"Calder Blue," Barbara finished for her, her voice all business once again as she turned a shrewd, speculative gaze on him. "I'd heard you were coming to town to work for Winstock but didn't think you'd have the nerve to actually do it."

"Winstock?" Hannah said, then looked back to Calder as she put it together. "That's why you came here? As a contractor? Not to end a hundred-year-old blood feud, but to make sure it lasts another hundred years? You could have stayed home and accomplished that."

His expression remained smooth, giving away nothing, his gaze clear and still very much on her. "Contractors build things. It's my job."

"It's a yacht club," she countered. "Which we need like we need a . . . well, a yacht club. Which is to say, not at all. Not only is Winstock shoehorning it in between a founding father's shipyard and your own family's generations-old fishing business—which employs a fair percentage of the working folks in this town, I might add—but he apparently took down a town icon to do it. The O'Reillys have been feeding residents of the Cove since long before I was born. O'Reilly's restaurant was like a second home to me as a kid, and Delia's Diner was the social center for me and my friends throughout high school. It's the same for a lot of other folks who lived here—" She could hear her voice getting shrill and wasn't even sure where all the anger was coming from. Well, okay, if she wanted to play armchair psychiatrist for a half second, she knew exactly where it was coming from. But, questionable job choices notwithstanding, Calder Blue was not Tim. And she was better than someone who would make all men pay for the crimes of one.

She held up one hand, took a moment to gather herself. "I'm sorry. What jobs you choose to take are none of my business." She held his gaze coolly now, calm and once again collected. It would have been easier to pull off if she didn't know what she must look like at the moment. "I appreciate your dropping this off. Thank you again for your help today. My apologies for whatever trouble I've caused you."

"Not a problem," he said, and though she swore there was a thread of amusement in his tone, it was not at all visible on his face. He looked to Barbara and tipped his chin. "Ma'am." He turned and walked back to the station house door.

Hannah watched him go, then swallowed a string of swear words when she realized her gaze had lowered and snagged on those nicely fitting back pockets of his. She opened her wallet and handed Barbara a five-dollar bill just on principle as he reached for the door handle. He was this close to being gone, out of her life. Yet, that didn't stop her from blurting out, "What did Blue say? Our Blue, I mean. Jonah. Does he know what you're planning to do?"

Calder paused and looked back at her. "I don't know what he thinks, or what he knows. I'm headed that way now, so I guess I'm about to find out. Now, if you'll excuse me, I'm running a little late. I got a bit . . . sidetracked on my way in." Then he flashed her a smile that was only about a hundred times more lethal than that velvety smooth baritone of his, and pushed out into the hushed, pink light of dusk.

Hannah swallowed against a suddenly dry throat. She

might have leaned a slightly unsteady hand on the back of
the metal chair.

"So. That was interesting."

Hannah turned to find Barbara staring at her with open
speculation. Hannah instinctively gave the older woman
her own version of The Look, the same look that made
first-year associates quail in their crisply starched suits
and sensible shoes, even as she knew it wouldn't so much
as ping Barbara's sturdy armor. Which it didn't. "Whatever
it is you think you're insinuating, don't."

"I'm just saying there was enough . . . ah, *energy* spark-
ing between you two that I'm surprised something didn't
spontaneously combust."

"I can't imagine what you're talking about. I barely have
enough energy to stay upright. I feel like a wrung-out
dishrag at the moment. And he's on his way to his own fu-
neral." She felt Barbara's gaze like a sniper laser and was
surprised there wasn't a little red dot glowing somewhere
on her person. "I almost sideswiped his truck, then more or
less ordered him to get lost when he tried to help me. I've
been on the road since before dawn this morning, and, yes,
I was more than a little freaked out by the accident, so I was
tired, shrewish, and Fiona added rude and impatient to the
list of the fine McCrae traits on display. For his part, he was
kind, considerate, and played Good Samaritan to the end."
She lifted the day planner as if showing evidence to the
jury. "I have no idea why, but I can guarantee you it wasn't
because of anything I did or said." She lowered the day
planner, looked at it, then back at the closed station door.

"Seems a little at odds, then," Barbara said, all calm and
infuriatingly knowing, "with the kind of man who'd come
all the way back to the birthplace of a centuries-old family

feud, with the intent to piss his relatives off further by messing with their current status quo."

"Yeah," Hannah said, absently playing with the elastic strap again, gaze still on the door. "It does."

Barbara let a slow smile cross her face when Hannah looked back her way. "So . . . why was it you said that Tim the Titan of Finance wasn't escorting you to the wedding?"

Chapter Three

Calder swallowed a sigh and perhaps a swear word or two as he pulled into the gravel lot and spied Jonah Blue standing at the ready, on the dry-land end of Blue's Fishing Company's main pier. The sun was setting over the pine tree–dotted ridge that fringed the hill rising up behind High Street at Calder's back, casting Jonah's tightly pinched features in a stark, mauve-shadowed relief that didn't warm his expression in the least. Calder told himself he should feel lucky the old man wasn't toting a shotgun. Although he supposed that didn't rule out something equally lethal. Like a nice, sharp gutting knife.

Feeling a little too close a kinship to a lobster swimming into a trap, he slid out the cab of his truck . . . and tried not to grimace when the sharp briny scent hit him. Calder had discovered that the air had a salty tang anywhere you went in Half Moon Harbor—in most of the Cove proper, for that matter. He liked it well enough, thinking it added a more immediate, visceral element to the historic, seafaring ambience of the little town. But down here, right on the fishing docks, it took on a layer of catch-of-the-day that was fairly aggressive.

His thoughts slipped to Hannah McCrae and her rather heated argument for keeping change from coming to Blueberry Cove. *We need a yacht club like we need . . . a yacht club.* He found himself quelling the urge to smile at that. Folks never liked change, even when it would benefit them directly.

He took in the look and feel of the decidedly blue-collar harbor, from the half dozen main fishing piers, the network of other docks that zigzagged between them, and the throngs of pot buoys, dwarfed only by the stacks upon stacks of lobster traps piled everywhere, to the shipyard just around the curve with its centuries-old boathouses and . . . Calder's eyes widened and his gaze hung up for a moment, and then another one, on the four soaring masts of the behemoth, full-size replica of what seemed to be a seventeenth- or eighteenth-century tall ship sitting proudly on the shipyard grounds. "Holy . . . schooner," he breathed.

He swung his gaze back over to the fishing piers that comprised Blue's, and finished his thought, which was that he had to kind of agree with Hannah McCrae. What the hell was Winstock thinking, shoving a yacht club in the middle of all this?

Unless, of course, Winstock didn't plan to stop his harbor remodel with razing a local diner.

Which still didn't explain why he'd specifically dragged a St. Croix River Blue into the mix, Calder thought as he looked at his great-uncle, who hadn't moved so much as a hair, what little he had left anyway, much less lifted a hand—or a gun—in welcome. He simply stood there, holding his ground, much as Calder assumed all the Blueberry Cove

Blues had before him, and waited. Of course, the old man didn't need a gun, or a gutting knife. Jonah Blue cut quite an imposing figure all by his lonesome. *So much for imagining him as a weathered, hunched-over old man.*

The Cove branch family patriarch was somewhere in his mid- to late seventies, and the sparse bit of hair that sprouted in a ring around his otherwise baldpate was snowy white. But that was where the ode to aging began and ended. Jonah was an easy six-four, maybe an inch taller. But where Calder had a fair share of hard-earned muscle lining his frame, Jonah was simply a hulk of a man, born and bred. Broad at the shoulder, thick through the chest, solid shank arms, and big, meaty fists. The lower half was just as imposing, legs thick and long as sturdy oaks, set on feet that likely required special-ordered boots. It would take more than a stiff wind and a heavy surf to topple that old man.

Good thing I only want to talk to him, and not wrestle him, Calder thought, ranking his odds as only slightly better than they would be grappling with a grizzly. He resisted the urge to hitch his belt or do any other type of male-pattern ground pawing, and opted to simply walk up to the man, stopping a respectful five or six feet away.

"I'm Calder," he said easily. When Jonah didn't so much as blink, he went on. "You must be Jonah. Please accept my apologies for being so late. I was involved in an accident outside of town and needed to see to the other driver's welfare. I tried to call." *And you couldn't be bothered to answer. As usual.* "I left a message."

Nothing. Not even a blink. Hard blue eyes silently stared him down.

Calder didn't offer his hand. No point giving the man a second chance to insult him. "I appreciate your agreeing to see me." It hadn't been so much *agree* as *didn't flat-out refuse,* but Calder wasn't going to quibble. "As I said in my note to you, I was hoping to get your input. Not about family business, but about my business here in the Cove." He had every intention of talking family business at some point, but from what little interaction he'd had with the man, Calder had a pretty good idea that wasn't the way to get Jonah to start a conversation. Work was something Jonah understood and respected. They both did. Seemed a good place to start. He held the man's gaze, stare for stare, though he was careful to keep his expression open, congenial.

"You already accepted the job," Jonah said at length, his Down East accent as thick as his voice was rough and rumbly. "Nothing to talk about."

I accepted the damn job to have an excuse to come here and talk to you, you old buzzard. Though Calder was beginning to question the wisdom of that decision. "Nothing's been signed. Ground isn't broken yet," Calder replied. "I was hoping to get your thoughts on the project. Monaghan's, too." *And take a closer look at that tall ship now, while I'm at it.*

"Bit late for opinions now," Jonah said flatly. "What's done is done."

Calder continued to hold the older man's gaze directly, wondering if Jonah's remark was aimed at the contracting business . . . or the family feud business. "Nothing's done until it's done. Never too late to change course, if you discover there's a more worthy destination."

He saw what looked like a flicker of disgust pass over the man's face, but with that locked jaw of his, it was hard to tell. "Shows what you know then. Which, no surprise to me, is very little." He moved for the first time, but only to shift his head a few inches to the left, so he could spit some tobacco juice.

Surprised, Calder wondered where the man could stuff a wad of chew, his jaw was so damn tight.

"Might as well head on back up your river," Jonah said, at length. "Your like isn't wanted here at Blue's."

He said it as if Calder's being a Blue was somehow . . . less Blue.

"Once the town folk find out why you're here, you won't be wanted by them, either. Seems you River Blues still haven't figured out how to tell the difference between where you're wanted and where you're not."

It was quite a speech, Calder thought. But rather than put him off, or piss him off, it did quite the opposite. *The old man wants me gone, and it's not because I'm a St. Croix Blue,* he thought, surprised yet again. Calder didn't know Jonah Blue from Adam, but he did know people, how to read them, how to work with them, for them, or get work out of them as the case may be. The success of the family business depended on it. Same could be said for Blue Harbor Farm. Jonah might well hate Calder with the kind of deep-seated mistrust that only a life spent being taught to mindlessly hate could engender, but that wasn't why he was giving Calder the bum rush. Or not entirely the reason. Jonah Blue was afraid.

Which begged the question . . . afraid of what?

"I don't run from a challenge," Calder said.

"Must not be a Croix River Blue then," the old man snorted.

Calder had walked right into that one, but ignored the barb. "What our ancestors did to, with, for, or against each other has no bearing on me, or why I'm here. Life is short, Jonah, too short for petty grievances and borrowing other people's troubles." Okay, so maybe he was a little annoyed.

"Memories are long," Jonah shot back. "And some

grievances should never be forgotten." His emphasis on the latter, and the disgust with which he'd spat it, implied he thought the gash that had separated the two branches of Blues ran much deeper than Calder apparently understood.

"What about forgiven?" Calder asked, figuring this might be his only shot at the man, so might as well go for broke. "What good does holding on to animosity do? That kind of hate only eats at the one who harbors it, while doing nothing to the one it's aimed at. Seems like a waste to me. And a shame."

"Thought you didn't come here to discuss family business."

Calder surprised himself—and, judging by Jonah's momentary blank expression, the old man, too—by grinning. "Who said I was talking about family?"

"What the hell are you talking about then? Because if you've got something else to say, then get on with it. You may not have a clock to punch, but my days end early and start even earlier. I don't have time to—"

"The folks of this town, the ones who work here, and have for their whole lives, just as their parents did before them, don't strike me as the kind who are applauding someone like Brooks Winstock for building them a yacht club none of them will be able to join," Calder interrupted.

He paused. He could see Jonah's chin jutting as he moved his tobacco, and chewed on Calder's words, though clearly he'd rather be doing pretty much anything else. Calder took full advantage of the moment. "When Winstock sent a bid request to my company, I knew it wasn't because Blueberry Cove suddenly needed a contractor located close to two hours away. I knew something else had to be up, but I couldn't figure out what. So, I overbid the project."

That opened those steely eyes a fraction wider, but the curiosity was quickly snuffed by a look of disgust. "Greedy bastard, just like—"

"Careful now," Calder warned quietly. Jonah might be able to snap him like a twig, but that didn't allow the old man free rein to trample on Calder's immediate or distant kin, and the sooner Jonah knew that, the better off they'd both be. "I don't give a damn about the money. I overbid it because I suspected Winstock didn't care how much I asked. He wanted me here for other reasons. If I was wrong, it was a job I didn't want anyway, so no harm."

There was a long beat, but Jonah finally said, "So, he took the bid. What does that prove? You're still takin' the man's money, more than you're due. Makes calling Winstock a schemer a bit of pot calling the kettle black."

Actually, Calder hadn't taken a dime yet. He was here to discuss the project and sign the contract, and, in fact, he fully expected Winstock to find some way around paying him his full asking price. But Jonah was so hell-bent on making him into some kind of bad guy, Calder didn't bother setting him straight. "Like I said, it's not about the job or the money."

"Then you're a bigger fool than I thought. Why bid a'tall?"

Calder had to hide a grin. So the man did care, even if he wouldn't admit it to Calder or himself. "Because I knew it had something to do with the fact that I was a Blue—it was the only connection, and a pretty damn direct one— and I wanted to know why. If my hunch was right, he was going to accept any bid I offered, just to get a St. Croix Blue to step foot in Blueberry Cove."

"What business is it of yours what's going on here or why? Can't see where you sticking your nose in is going to mean anything good, no matter what. Should've just turned him down."

"Winstock made it my business. He wanted someone from the wrong side of the family tree, at least as residents of the Cove consider us to be. Don't you want to know why? Aren't you the least bit concerned that he knocked down an iconic diner, owned by someone from a family that has been feeding the fine folks of this town for generations, without so much as batting an eye? You're right next door."

Jonah's gaze went from wary and speculative to glass hard in a blink. "He's got no claim to this property. And no price tag high enough to change that fact," he said, clearly insulted.

"Seems to me he's not much concerned about following proper channels, or he'd have thrown some money at the diner owner." Calder noticed the way Jonah's expression shuttered. "He didn't even try, did he?" Calder had suspected as much from what Hannah had said, but he hadn't been sure until that moment. No wonder she'd been so worked up about it. "I understand he tried some end run around the shipyard owner, too. So, he's not even interested in giving his fellow townsfolk a leg up to get what he wants. He just wants you out of his way."

"This has nothing to do with you and yours," Jonah said tersely. "Done quite well without interfering in each other's business now for well on a hundred years. I expect we can manage a few more without you riding to the rescue." He all but spat the last words.

"With all due respect, it's not up to you what I do or don't do, or why I choose to do it. You don't know me. Never met me. Nor I, you. I was raised to think about

Jeremiah's branch of the family much the same as I imagine you were raised to think about Jedediah's. And you know, I thought it was a pile of horseshit then, and nothing I've heard or learned since has ever changed my mind. Holding the sins of the fathers against their offspring, who haven't so much as laid eyes on each other in generations? What possible good does that do?"

"Stops them from doing any more harm to each other," Jonah said, his eyes flat, his tone even flatter. "All that matters."

"Seems to me it's more a bunch of stubborn old men who'd rather sacrifice what this family could be—"

Jonah spat again, only this time it landed right at Calder's feet, just a speck from his booted toe.

Nice aim.

"Head on back up the St. Croix," Jonah said, his expression closed tight. He eyed Calder up and down. "Unlike the River Blues, we know how to stay and fight for what's ours."

"That's just it," Calder said, keeping his tone smooth though his own jaw was starting to ache a little from being clenched tight. "You're not supposed to fight the ones who are already on your side. Blood is thicker than the water in this harbor, Jonah. At least that's what I was raised to believe. I just choose to believe that means all of my family. Including you."

"Don't you understand? It's the blood of this family that taints that harbor, boy. Some sins don't simply go out with the tide. Now I've got nothing else to say to you. Do what you will in this town. Folks'll stand up for themselves well enough. But steer yourself clear of this property." With that, he turned and walked back down the docks toward the big boathouse at the end of the pier. He didn't look back.

"That went well there, didn't it then?" came a voice from behind Calder.

He turned to find a man about his own age, close to the same height, His thick, sun-bleached hair, tossed about in the harbor breeze, made him look like a surfer dude on the wrong stretch of coast. And judging by the Irish brogue, a really distant wrong coast. The guy had a broad grin on the kind of face that probably made women swoon. If not, the accent would surely do the trick.

"Indeed," Calder finally said in response. "Making friends and influencing relatives everywhere I go." He took a step forward and stuck out his hand. "Calder Blue. You must be Brodie Monaghan. I was on my way over to see if I could somehow piss you off next."

Brodie chuckled and took Calder's hand in one equally broad and improbably more calloused and gave it a firm, welcoming shake. "A Blue, are you now?" His gaze tracked the old man's progress toward the big boathouse at the end of the pier. "I take it you must be from the other branch." His grin widened. "Here I thought I had a hard time winning the folks of this fine town over. And they liked my forebears."

"They're that hard-assed then?"

"The hardest of arses, mate. Once you win them, though, you've got a crew who'll rally a cry for you at the wave of a pot buoy flag, and stand beside you until the last one has fallen." His eyes crinkled more deeply at the corners. "So, there's that."

"Aye, indeed," Calder said, chuckling. The Irishman could probably sell a swatter to a fly and make him happier for it. Calder nodded toward the shipyard. "You build that monstrosity?"

With the sun now dipping below the tree line, Brodie

glanced at the shadowy hulk of the massive schooner. Honest pride and profound joy filled his handsome features so fully, Calder thought the man might burst with it. Like a kid who'd been told he could work in Santa's workshop the rest of his days.

Passion like that earned Calder's respect. Lucky was the man who never worked a day in his life because his profession was also his joy. Calder knew something about that, though not necessarily in the way his family approved.

"Always had a thing for building model boats," Brodie said.

"I'd hate to see the glass jar you plan to stick that one in."

"Oh, aye, but I do. I put a call into Stephen, you see. Asked if he could whip something up. Good with domed things, he is."

"Stephen?"

"King. Him being a Mainer and all."

Calder chuckled again, pleased to know there was at least one Cove resident who wasn't going to immediately try to run him out of town. Or toss him in the harbor. Of course, while Monaghan was also something of an outsider himself, he had found a way in. Perhaps he'd be a valuable resource in more ways than one.

"What brings you to the Cove?" Brodie asked. "You drew the short straw and were elected to come down with the olive branch?" He tucked his hands in the front pockets of his close-to-worn-out work jeans, pulling the faded T-shirt tight across shoulders that Calder knew had earned their well-honed shape from hard, honest labor. "You might get farther with a six-pack and pouch of chew," he added. "Better yet, a case of each."

Calder grinned. "I'll keep that in mind." He noticed the Irishman's work shoes were of the boat shoe variety and, like the rest of his clothes, had seen better years. They also didn't match, but given the gleaming beauty presently dominating the open shipyard field, Calder doubted Monaghan's eye for detail was lax anywhere beyond his sartorial choices.

"Not the elected bearer of the olive branch," Calder said at length. "It was my choice. Business."

"What's your work then?"

"Contractor."

And . . . poof, out went the twinkling light from the green eyes now steadily assessing Calder with a shrewdness that would seem out of character for the charming rogue he presented himself to be. Yeah, Calder had known that sharp intellect had to be there under the layer of charm somewhere. A man didn't learn to build something like that ship without some serious smarts.

"So . . . Winstock hired you," Brodie said, his gaze assessing. "Interesting. Not a coincidence, then, you being a Blue."

"I doubled my bid estimate and he didn't even try to negotiate me down. So I sincerely doubt it was a coincidence." It was a calculated risk, revealing that. Calder hadn't had much time to read the Irishman, but he went with his gut. "Heard he made a grab at your property."

"We worked around it," he said by way of response, then nodded toward the tall ship. "I built that for him instead. Not much competition for my bid, either, as it happens. Though admittedly I didn't have quite the stones you did. Double, ye say?"

Calder was still looking at the schooner. "Any man who can build that poses enough threat in any whose-is-bigger contest to earn my respect."

Brodie barked out a laugh and the grin was firmly back

in place. "Might have underestimated you, Black Sheep Blue." He gestured to his shipyard. "Care to walk?"

"Can I see your toy boat?"

"Are ye askin' me to show you mine, then? Because you should know, I'm not at all interested in seeing yours."

Calder chuckled. "Not to worry. Besides," he added as they ambled back down the harbor road toward the shipyard, "no point in shaming the locals straight off."

Brodie shook his head, made a tsking sound. "So, that's how it's to be then, is it?"

"Begin as you mean to go on."

"Good to know," Brodie said, laughter still in his voice. He slapped Calder on the back with just enough force behind it to make a point, and motioned him toward the shipyard. "Welcome to the Cove, mate."

Chapter Four

"Oh . . . wow." Hannah let the car roll to a stop along the Cove road as she stared down the short stretch of Pelican Bay shoreline, then out to the Point, where the McCraes' lighthouse stood, a proud old sentry, historic and beloved. The sun was just rising above the horizon line behind it, casting it in a pinkish-golden halo of light.

Just shy of two hundred years old, and long since decommissioned, Pelican Point had been in the care of the McCrae family from its inception, both an honor and a burden. Hannah had always felt a little guilty that Logan had been left to somehow find a way to maintain the lighthouse, the keeper's cottage, and the rambling main house. "But look at you now," she breathed, astonished by the end result of the renovation that had begun a little more than a year and a half earlier.

Even from this distance, she could see that the uniquely shaped exterior, a sort of boxed-out square with angled corners, had gotten a complete face-lift. The salted-over and weather-damaged windows set into the tower walls had been replaced and the morning sun glinted off their clean, glossy surface. The whole of the tower appeared to have been resurfaced, as well as repainted a resplendent, beacon white. "And the station house . . ." *My house. Home.*

She felt tears gather at the corners of her eyes and ignored the sting as the bruised skin around her eyes— which had indeed grown a ghastly dark purple overnight— tightened. She'd been more than a bit unsteady after Calder had left the police station the evening before, and Barbara had gone into full drill-sergeant mom mode. She'd made the decision that Hannah was done for the day. Barbara had bundled her off to the pharmacy to pick up the pain meds she'd been prescribed before taking her back to the Benson household and putting a bowl of homemade chowder and a grilled cheese sandwich into her, then tucking her summarily into one of her guest room beds.

Hannah hadn't put up more than a token resistance, mostly because her body had pretty much been one hundred percent in favor of being horizontal on a soft mattress, and because she wanted this specific view when she was awake, alert, and feeling a lot more steady on her feet.

Home.

So many feelings, thoughts, and emotions swamped her: that she was back to stay, how badly she'd missed this view, missed her tower. That it would be Logan and Alex's home now . . . and she'd have to find herself a new home. Where would she land? In town? On the coast road? Some little bungalow, tucked away in one of the many inlets?

Her gaze hung on the lighthouse as her heart thumped inside her chest. She didn't feel much steadier this morning, as it turned out, and the enormity of the decision she'd made, to come back home to stay, to live full-time in the Cove, made her feel shaky. Not because it had been the wrong decision. She didn't regret leaving her life in D.C. behind. But . . . where to begin? She hadn't lived here since she'd been in college, and then only as a pit stop between semesters, clerking, internships, and the like. Her world had been full of dreams then, of life in the big city, of being engaged in a more vital, immediate, impactful world.

"Well, you got what you wished for," she murmured. Her life on Capitol Hill had certainly been . . . impactful. Ten years later, here she was, back home again. Only, as the old adage so wisely proclaimed, she couldn't go home again. Not really. She was back in the Cove . . . but had no idea what home would actually mean to her now. "Home, and yet . . . not entirely home."

Dabbing carefully at her eyes, she avoided so much as a glance at herself in her rearview mirror, and pulled resolutely back onto the road . . . toward home. *Yes. Home.* Pelican Point had always been that, so deep a part of her she couldn't separate who she'd been as a child growing up here from the place itself, as if they were forever entwined. Beloved, and steeped in memories that swept the scope from tragic and challenging to wondrous and perfect, the Point represented where she'd come from, why she'd become the person she had. It was her foundation, her home base. And in that regard, it would never change.

Hannah took a deep, slightly less shaky breath, feeling better, steadier.

The list of all the things she'd yet even to begin to figure out—not only where in the Cove she would live, but how she was going to use her legal skills to earn a living there— began to clamor again as she turned down the long driveway that led out to the main house. She shut them off. There would be plenty of time for all that later. Right now, there was a wedding to prepare for, and a homecoming to enjoy.

As it turned out, it was Alex who came out to meet Hannah. Fiona had texted both of her sisters with photos of Logan and Alex on her past few trips home, so Hannah recognized the shorter woman with the trim, athletic body and wavy, dark hair. She was smiling broadly as she approached the car Hannah had ended up borrowing from Sal that morning; her little Audi would take some time to repair. Hannah was thrilled to finally meet Alex in person, so she was surprised by just how many butterflies were fluttering in her stomach.

"Hi," Alex said brightly as Hannah opened the car door and slid out. "I want to hug you, but Fiona said—"

"A hug would be really nice," Hannah said, and they more or less fell into each other's arms.

"I'm so happy to finally meet you," Alex said, her tone more fierce than her hug, which Hannah knew she was keeping purposely gentle.

"Me too." The hug went on another moment longer, and Hannah whispered, "Thank you."

Alex leaned back, surprise on her pretty face. "For what, loving your brother?" Her smile shifted to a grin that begged one in return. "Oh, my pleasure, trust me."

Hannah smiled, winced as it pulled bruised skin, but didn't stop smiling. "Yeah, that might fall into the category of TMI, at least as it pertains to older brothers." She shifted her gaze from Alex to the house, stunned all over again by just how much had been accomplished in such a relatively short time. "I meant thank you for this." She took in the new shakes, the renovated and freshly painted frames around all the dormers inset into the roof, the siding, the porch . . . all of it. She looked to Alex. "You fixed my heart, my soul," she said. "The house, but even more, the tower. It's . . . majestic now. Like it should have always been. I can't believe you did that." She laughed a little self-consciously. "How *did* you do it?"

Alex beamed with pride, clearly pleased by Hannah's reaction, and maybe a little relieved as well. "It's what

MacFarlands do," she said simply. "We let the lights shine again."

Hannah could only shake her head. "You have no idea how much that—" She paused, let out a watery laugh. "I'm not usually so emotional."

Alex stepped in and gave her a gentle, one-armed hug. "It's okay. I'm loving every moment of this reaction, trust me. Makes all the hard work ten times more worthwhile." Her smile shifted from one of beaming pride to one of simple happiness. "I know what the tower means to Logan. I mean, he's told me . . . the whole story. About his fiancée and—"

"He did?" Hannah shook her head. "What am I saying? He's marrying you. Of course he told you all about his past, especially about the tower, since you're the one in charge of restoring it."

"I know that the tower is a big part of all of your lives." She grinned. "Fair warning, Logan has shared many—*many*—a childhood tale with me about life with his three sisters."

"Ah, well . . . now that we're all going to be home again, please allow us to help balance the scales."

Alex's eyes danced. "I was so hoping you'd say that."

Hannah laughed and felt a little silly for being so nervous. It was going to be okay. Just being there felt so good. It was an enormous relief to finally be on ground she could trust to remain solid and steady. "I hope, for Logan's sake, our stories don't change your mind about your future husband-to-be."

Alex laughed, but Hannah was more charmed by the blush that accompanied it. Alex didn't seem the blushing type. "Nothing is going to change my mind about marrying your brother," she said, clearly over the moon about her fiancé. "He's the best person I know."

Hannah's smile was watery—again, dammit—as she nodded. "The very, very. And if you tell him I said that before I at least have a chance to give him a hard time, I will flat-out deny it." She swore under her breath, hoping the tear fest would stop for good, and soon. "You have to know that I am not a crier. They called me the Iron Maiden in court." *And a whole host of new things outside of court.* "But now I've come home . . . I can't seem to stop." In truth, the tears had started with Tim's betrayal, but she couldn't—wouldn't—go there. "I could blame your impending nuptials for making me all mushy, but I've decided I'm going to place the blame squarely on Calder Blue's shoulders." *His nice, wide, manly-man shoulders*, a little voice helpfully supplied. *Stop that.*

"Calder Blue?" Alex asked.

"The man who gave me these," she said, and pointed to her black eyes, which Alex had been exceedingly kind not to stare at.

"I thought you were in a car accident. But—someone struck you?"

Hannah sighed, wishing now she'd never mentioned him. Why had she? "No, I did all the striking. I guess if I want to find an unwitting scapegoat, I should be blaming Beanie's road sign." She smiled briefly. "It was just more satisfying to blame Calder."

Alex's gaze became more speculative. "Would he be the arrogant, pickup truck guy?"

"Who called him that?"

"I did."

Hannah turned to find Fiona coming down off the front porch and closing ground fast. "Why? He was the quintessential Good Samaritan."

Alex's eyebrows rose a fraction at Hannah's turnabout, but she wisely stayed out of it.

"Did you or did you not just lay the blame at his work-booted feet?" Fiona didn't wait for an answer. "Let me see your face." She took Hannah's chin gently in her hand and tipped it this way, then that. "Barbara warned me it wouldn't be pretty."

"Gosh, don't fawn and stroke my shattered ego or anything." Hannah shifted her chin from Fi's grasp and stood straighter. Funny how they fell back into the rhythms of their childhood, no matter how long they'd been apart. Hannah the stalwart leader, Fiona the determined caretaker. All they were missing was Kerry, the eternal troublemaker.

Fiona didn't falter. "What did Bonnie say?"

"That I'll live. Do you think you can do something to cover this, or at least reduce the Frankenstein factor for the rehearsal later?"

"Hannah," Alex interjected, "please don't worry about that. I'm just thankful you're here and that you're okay. That's all that matters."

Hannah gave her a grateful look. "That is pretty much the nicest thing anyone has said to me since I got back." *Or, for that matter, since Tim's pregnant wife showed up in my office.* "You're like the anti-bridezilla."

Alex gave her a crooked smile. "Then my work here is done."

Hannah turned back to her still-clucking younger sister. "Although I'm thinking maybe we need a second medical opinion. Psychiatric this time." She gestured to Fiona's outfit. Currently, her sister was swathed in a skirt made of yards—and yards and yards—of the most awful shade of mauve tulle, with big green-sequined flowers sewn quite unfortunately in far too many places all over it. The skirt of many horrors was topped with a strapless, bandeau-style sequined tube top that matched the flowers. All of this was made magnificently worse by the matching headband that sported trailing strands of . . . something that looked shredded and badly in need of recycling, topped with little green sequin flowers marching, upright, across the flat band. "Weren't you wearing something equally psychotic at the scene of the stop-sign crime yesterday? What *is* that?" She wanted to look away, but it was like rubbernecking at a bad train wreck of fashion. "Are you being punished? Is this some kind of humiliation-through-community-service thing?"

Fiona rolled her eyes. She was the sister who did that the most, too. "It's for this afternoon's rehearsal. Remember, I sent you a note telling you to bring the worst bridesmaid dress you owned, or could beg, borrow or steal."

"You had to wear that dress in an actual wedding?" Alex asked, horrified. "Complete with the head gear? Really?"

Fiona nodded, then reached up to center the headband. "And the one yesterday. In fact, there are more." At Hannah's and Alex's gaping expressions, Fi looked at Alex and added, "It's because you get the horror of it all, and therefore would never inflict similar bridesmaid crimes on us, that you are fast becoming the best sister-in-law-to-be ever." She turned to Hannah. "Our dresses are beautiful. Stunning. Although we might have to work on yours. Have you lost weight? And why? You're already the tall, skinny one. Cut the relentlessly curvy sister here a break, will ya?"

Hannah just smiled. Even Fiona's fretting and clucking felt good. Familiar. It came from love, so she let the warmth of family seep in and soothe the aches and pains. "Hey, at least you can fill out the front of that thing without requiring David Copperfield illusion engineering."

Fiona stared down at her full, perfect breasts. "Yes, the booby fairy was kind to me. So very, very kind." She smiled sweetly up at her sister.

"So, I get why you're dressed like that today, at least from your crazed perspective, but you still haven't explained why you were wearing that other getup yesterday."

"Oh, I went to see Delia, so we could go through her closet. I brought that one with me, thinking seeing one of mine would make her feel more inclined to join in the fun." She grinned. "Oh my God, wait until you see the dress she decided to wear! It puts the fabulousness of this to shame."

"She had options? Like . . . she had to decide which one was worse? Than that?" Hannah immediately raised a hand. "Never mind. I don't think I want to know. Am I the only one who has never been subjected to such horror? I mean, there has been the occasional too-lemony shade of yellow or unfortunate butt bustle, but . . . what kind of friends do you have, anyway?"

Fiona was laughing now. "Hey, you should have seen that dress yesterday before she helped me fix it. Oh my God, we were laughing so hard, so I just kept it on."

"You . . . fixed it?" Hannah said, dubiously, trying not to recall the unnaturally shiny monstrosity her sister had had on the day before and failing. Spectacularly. Where was post-accident amnesia when she needed it? "Really? What part?"

Fiona's topaz eyes gleamed. "Yours is even more delicious."

Alex was watching the interplay between the sisters with open interest. "I can't decide if I am hating that I was an only child, or if I owe my dad yet another debt of gratitude for stopping at just the one."

"Sisters rock," Fiona said at the same time Hannah put in, "Wouldn't trade this little shrimp boat for all the lobster rolls in Maine. Perky tits notwithstanding."

Fiona's expression went all soft and mushy, and she nudged Hannah ever so gently. "You could stand to eat a few of those rolls. Just sayin'."

Hannah looked at Alex. "I hope you'll come around to the idea of not being an only anymore, because you're about to add three siblings to your family tree, whether you want to or not."

Alex's smile wobbled a little. "I don't cry either, so you need to cut that out right now." Then Fiona opened her arms and they all found themselves in a sloppy, teary group hug.

Which was how Logan found them. "Did somebody die?"

Fiona looked up first, and snuffled loudly. "What? No. We're welcoming Alex to the family fold."

"Please don't leave me," Logan said to Alex with utmost sincerity. Then he turned to Hannah and his face split wide with a grin. "Welcome home, you."

Hannah flew into his arms, then snuffled inelegantly all over his plaid work shirt. He was rock solid, as always. "I've missed you so much."

"Let me see this face," he said, leaning back. He tipped up her chin and gently brushed the tears from her bruised cheeks, his own suspiciously bright.

"Welcome home, indeed, right?" For the first time, she was grateful to Calder and what had happened in that intersection. It gave her a convenient excuse for the waterworks she couldn't seem to switch back to the off position. And if everyone was busy worrying about her injuries, they wouldn't notice her natural spark had been dimmed for entirely different reasons.

Fiona took her sister's arm. "Come on, let's go see what magic we can create, then I'm going to show you the dress you're wearing to rehearsal."

"You didn't need to do that."

Fiona eyed her without even a shred of curiosity. "You actually brought a bridesmaid dress? Let me guess. It's tasteful, elegant, and not remotely mortifying. We're shooting for humiliation in satin and tulle."

Hannah thought about trying to brazen her way through it, but then broke and said, "Yeah, I got nuthin'."

"That's what I thought." Fiona steered Hannah inside the big, rambling house, through the living room to the landing of the main stairs.

"I can't wear anything of yours," Hannah protested, "unless part of the humiliation factor is a floor-length dress that hits me just below the knees."

"You're not that much taller than me, Gargantua, and give me some credit. I trolled the secondhand stores. And Delia's grandmother's attic trunks." She grinned and the light that twinkled to life in her dark gold eyes was nothing short of evil. "I think we found a winner."

Hannah groaned and followed her sister up the stairs, across the open balcony hallway to the two smaller bedrooms that had once been hers and Logan's. He'd long since claimed the master at the top of the stairs, and Fiona, whose childhood room had been off the kitchen on the main floor below, had taken her old room as soon as she'd left for college. Logan's old room was now the guest room Hannah stayed in when she was home. Kerry had always had a room out in one of the additions that stretched out the back of the house toward the water, which had suited her more bohemian personality . . . and kept the riotous music and higher-decibel lifestyle she enjoyed at enough of a distance as to make her sibs feel less homicidal toward her. Most of the time.

"This wasn't my idea," Alex called up the stairs after them. "I'm fine with everyone just coming in jeans, T-shirt, and flip-flops."

Hannah glanced down over the balustrade at her. "You

did ask Fiona to help with the wedding preparations, right?"

Alex nodded. "She's a brilliant New York interior designer and my future sister-in-law. What's not to love about that combination?"

"See? Thank you," Fiona called down over the railing, beaming triumphantly.

Hannah gave her sister a quelling look. "Public shaming in horrifying bridesmaid apparel, that's what is not to love." She glanced back at Alex. "So, yes, I blame you, too."

"Now, now, play nice," Logan said, chuckling.

"Oh, we are," Fiona assured him, her smile turning to treacle. "Wait until you see the happening tuxedo jacket I found for you to wear."

Despite being a towering lumberjack of a man, Logan visibly blanched.

Hannah hooted, suddenly feeling miles better. "Are you certain you know what you're getting yourself into?" she called down to Alex as Fiona all but dragged Hannah into her bedroom.

Alex grinned up at them. "Oh, I have a pretty fair idea. You should see what she's making *me* wear tonight."

Hannah realized the tears had stopped. And she was smiling. Laughing. The pain of the accident forgotten, the pain of . . . everything else, shoved aside for now. Home. And family. *The cure for everything.* Then she had another thought and turned back to Fiona. "Did you get something for Kerry to wear? Because . . . you didn't tell her to bring something, did you? God only knows what kind of tribal getup she'll have found. She's probably haggling with customs right this second over some kind of fang-covered bikini top. Or worse, they've already done the full-body cavity search and she's in some small holding room somewhere.

You know how she is. Has anyone heard from her? Is she still due in on Saturday?"

Hannah closed the door behind herself and turned around to find Fiona standing in front of her, eyes swimming in tears. "Oh no! Oh my God. What happened to her, Fiona? Tell me right now. I'm an attorney. I know people, highly placed people. We'll help her no matter what she's done. We'll—ooph!"

Whatever else she might have said was squeezed out of her lungs by her sister, who had wrapped her up in a tight hug and was holding on for dear life. And, accident trauma or not, Hannah didn't even take a whole second before wrapping her arms around Fiona's soft shoulders and hugging her right back.

"I've missed you so much," Fiona said, sniffling again, her face pressed against the annual police picnic T-shirt Barbara had given Hannah yesterday so she could get out of her Willy Wonka death-by-chocolate shirt.

With the memory of her now-ruined silk blouse, Hannah's thoughts went immediately to Calder Blue's twinkling, whiskey-colored eyes as they'd shared that private joke grin. *Bastard*, she thought, but realized she was grinning again now, even as tears pricked at the ends of her eyelashes.

"I have, too."

"It's so good to have you home. To be home." Finally, Fiona loosened up her death grip and noticed Hannah's T-shirt. "Barbara?"

Hannah nodded. "My blouse—well, you saw it. Everything happened so fast, and I guess I was more out of it than I realized. I didn't even think about my luggage until I got to Barb's last night. It was still in the back of my car. I picked it up this morning from Sal and he loaned me his nephew's car to use."

"So, I saw," Fiona said, waggling her eyebrows. "Sweet."

Hannah didn't want to think about cars. Driving in general still made her feel vaguely queasy. "I haven't had a chance to change yet."

"I'll get Logan to bring your stuff in." Fiona smiled, her eyes filled with love. "God, I feel like it's been forever since we've talked. Really talked. So much has been going on and I feel awful for not keeping up with you and, well . . . I've missed leaning on you. I try not to be the needy little sister, I really do. You always have your act so together, and I keep thinking that will be me someday." Fi's smile turned sardonic. "And we both know that is *so* never going to happen. I mean, let's face it. The big three-oh is officially in my rearview mirror. I'm single, no prospects, no kids, my life is upside down, my business—" She waved a hand. "See? There I go. But I do want to talk to you while you're here . . . maybe bend your ear a little. Get some sisterly life advice."

Yeah. I don't think I'm the one to talk to for life advice, Hannah thought. If Fiona only knew. Thankfully she didn't, and she wouldn't. Apparently she had her own life stuff going on, because, well, frankly, when did Fi not have life stuff going on? But Hannah would happily listen. Especially if it meant stuffing her own problems on a shelf for a little while longer.

Logan was the oldest McCrae sibling, but while they'd all three turned to him for things like killing spiders, changing tires, and intimidating ex-boyfriends, he was not the one they turned to for life advice. And though Barbara had always been a sounding board of sorts for all three McCrae girls, and loved them unconditionally, her brand of advice was more along the lines of the no-nonsense wisdom passed down by grandparents and well-intentioned clan elders.

So Hannah had, at a pretty early age, become the default

mother figure for her two younger sisters. She remembered their parents, gauzy though her memories had become over time. She'd been five when they'd been killed in a car accident, the victims of a late-season, freak ice storm, but at barely three and just shy of two years old, respectively, Fiona and Kerry had only the many stories they'd been told to form their memories.

Just as she'd always done, Hannah put aside her own fears and insecurities to do her best to keep her siblings on even ground. The hard part wasn't keeping her own life mess to herself; it was trying not to feel guilty that she'd been a little relieved to have Fiona and Kerry not needing her ear or shoulder lately.

Kerry had flown the family nest quite young, and for some time now had generally only needed her oldest sister for things involving international legal matters and the occasional help securing a bail bond. Fiona was the more traditional younger sibling, who turned to her big sister for help and advice on what Hannah had come to call the Big Three: job, living situation, men. Most of life's problems fell under one of those categories, along with their occasional overseer: finances. Though, in all honesty, her sisters had generally taken care of themselves in that department. Where Kerry was concerned, Hannah tried not to think too much about how she was making that happen.

And I've hit the Big Three trifecta, Hannah thought dourly, having recently divested herself of all three.

"We'll have time, Fi," she told her sister, dragging her thoughts firmly back to the here and now. "Whatever it is, we'll figure it out."

Fiona hugged her again. "Thanks. I knew I could count on you." She looked up; then just as quickly as she'd fallen apart, her expression cleared and turned shrewd and observational.

"Now, let's see what we can do about your face. Then we'll work on the dress."

Hannah might be the pro when it came to tackling the Life Big Three, but Fiona was the queen of the Girl Big Three: clothes, food, and makeup.

"I think I might have maxed out even your admirable skill set," Hannah said. Without even looking, she could feel the color settling in more deeply around her eyes as the ache settled in with it. And not the kind of color one applied with a magic makeup wand.

"Never underestimate the power of a great foundation," Fiona said, gently pushing her sister to sit on the delicate antique bench seat positioned at the foot of the old sleigh bed.

Oh, the stories that sleigh bed could tell, Hannah thought. So many nights of laughter, of tears, of plotting and planning, discussing the important subjects of their lives. At least they'd seemed life-or-death at the time.

Hannah sighed and thought how nice it would be if she could just crawl under the old quilt, curl up in a ball, and sink back into that time when figuring out how to sneak Billy John Buckley her phone number without Logan finding out, so Billy could invite her and Fiona to the Cove's winter festival skate night with him and his younger, equally cute brother, had been the biggest crisis in their lives.

"Let me get my bag of magic tricks," Fiona was saying, already bustling about again.

"If only the bridesmaids could wear veils, too, we'd be all set." Hannah watched her sister move about and gather her things. Always most comfortable when she was doing something or creating something with her hands, that was Fi. Hannah wondered what was going on with her, what she hadn't confided to her big sister, noticing for the first time, as she looked past the outrageous getup her sister was wearing, the tiny stress lines pinching the corners of Fi's eyes and mouth. Here Hannah had been selfishly glad not to have to fake her way through phone conversations with her closest sib, happy and relieved knowing that at least Fi was doing well. Only clearly that wasn't the case. Guilt made another stab.

"Want to talk now?"

Fi just got even busier sorting through what appeared to be a toolbox containing enough paraphernalia to make up the entire cast of Cirque du Soleil. Hannah might need all of that help and then some.

"Let's just focus on the rehearsal this afternoon and the celebration tonight. Fergus is so excited to be hosting the dinner afterward at the pub, it's almost comical. God, I love him."

"Is that really what Alex wanted? Dinner at the pub? I mean, we all love Gus to pieces, but—"

"Oh, they have a special bond, those two. You'll see. It's ridiculously sweet. He was one of the first people she met here. In fact, he was the one who initially hired her for the lighthouse project. Without telling brother dearest."

"Really? How did I not know that part?"

Fi just gave her a look that said, *Uh, because you have no time for a life?* "Anyway, he offered and it was exactly the right thing for her. You should see him. He's all but dancing a jig, absolutely loving being part of the big event."

Hannah smiled, her heart bumping a little harder inside her chest. "Then you're right, it's the perfect thing. I'm glad she's connected so well to Gus—to the whole town, to hear Barb tell it. She's made her own place here, and not just via Logan. That's a really good thing."

"They're great together. She doesn't take any of his stuff and he's like this complete idiot around her. So it's enormous amounts of fun." Fiona's eyes sparkled with the shine of happy tears. "I love seeing him like this."

Hannah tipped her head back and willed her eyes to dry. "Okay, no more sappy wedding talk. We'll need to strap Kleenex boxes around our waists at this rate. And it's making my face hurt."

"Well, it's killing me, so only seems fair."

Hannah tipped her head forward again and narrowed her gaze at her now innocently smiling sister. "If it wasn't for your crazy makeup skills—"

Fiona snickered. "Remember when Kerry was what, like twelve, and pissed off that Logan wouldn't let her wear makeup to school, so she decided to practice her burgeoning eyeliner skills on our dead-to-the-world brother?"

No one slept as hard and heavy as Logan had when he was younger. The giggle burst forth from Hannah at the long-ago memory, and she didn't care about the pain, even as she put a hand over her bruised and banged-up lip.

"Oh my God, and Logan got a call to go help Jessica's dad on his fishing boat, at like, what, four the next morning? And never looked in the mirror?" They both fell into gales of laughter.

"I'm surprised she lived to see high school," Fiona gasped.

"I'm still surprised she lives to see her next birthday. Ow," Hannah said, holding her face as giggles snorted out.

"Serves you right," came a voice from the doorway. "Sitting here dissing my good name when we have a perfectly good brother to roast over the coals."

"*Kerry!*" Both Fiona and Hannah shouted at the same time and scrambled up to gather her into a tight group hug.

Kerry McCrae was average height and build, but with the finely sculpted body of an athlete. And that's where any resemblance to being a civilized human being ended. Fiona and Logan had wild, amber-colored eyes, and Hannah had stormy blue ones, but all three of them had thick, dark, almost black hair, of varying lengths and textures. Logan's was relentlessly rumpled, Hannah's sleek and shiny, Fiona's a wild mass of corkscrew curls that drove her insane. So no one knew, exactly, how it was that Kerry had somehow popped out with wild red curls and green eyes so bright and sparkling, they put emeralds to shame.

Fergus had often teased her that she was but an unruly forest sprite the wee folk had left as a babe under the magic oak tree that had grown up through the middle of Eula March's antique store in town. Kerry had been a very impressionable ten-year-old when Fergus had come over from Ireland and into their lives. She'd loved his stories and had taken that one particularly to heart. An unruly forest sprite, indeed.

Having just recently turned thirty, she still looked every bit of the role. Her hair was wildly out of control, with random braids flying out here and there and odd bits of who knew what tied to this strand or that. Her latest grand life adventure had been living in Australia and New Zealand, so her skin was brown as an island native's, which made her brilliant emerald eyes shine somehow mystically from her angular and beautiful face. She hugged them back with a fierceness that made Hannah feel as if her heart could explode with the joy she was feeling.

"Look out, Blueberry, the McCrae sisters are back!" Fiona sang, as they all bounced up and down.

"And we're having a wedding!" Kerry crowed, then led them in some kind of aboriginal-style dance that, when the typically more staid and proper Hannah gave herself completely over to it—including the bit Kerry called "tribal twerking"—had them all collapsing on the big, sleigh bed in peals of laughter.

God, it was so good to be home.

Chapter Five

Calder paused on the sidewalk and looked up at the towering oak tree. There was nothing particularly special about the tree itself, except for the fact that it was growing straight up through the interior of a small antique store, and right out through the roof. MOSSYCUP ANTIQUES, the oval sign read. The background was navy blue, the store name in raised white script, and the oak tree—a mossycup oak, he presumed—was in beautifully rendered gold relief in the background. "*Founded: At the Beginning*," he murmured, reading aloud the small line of script under the store name. Hmm. *The beginning of what?*

He'd noticed the eccentric little place on his way into town the day before—it was hard to miss—and decided he'd stop in on his way in that morning to talk to Owen Hartley, owner of Hartley's Hardware and the new mayor of Blueberry Cove. More importantly to Calder, he was apparently the town historian as well.

Calder's meeting with Winstock had been pushed back from dinner the previous evening to a late lunch today, midafternoon, so he'd headed back home to the farm the evening before, right after leaving the police station. His thoughts drifted, as they'd done with a little too much regularity, to Hannah McCrae. He found himself wondering what her story was, even knowing it didn't matter. Couldn't matter. She was in Blueberry for a wedding, then would go back to Virginia. At least that's what he assumed, given her little Audi had Virginia plates. Driving in that morning, he'd wondered how her injuries had fared, what her face looked like now, how she was holding up under what was likely a crush of last-minute wedding details.

Recalling her sister Fiona's getup the day before, he smiled. Yeah, he didn't even want to know what all was going on with that. Just as well he was out of her particular orbit. Now if he could just stop thinking about her.

Switching mental gears, curious to see how the roof construction was configured around the oak tree, he reached for the door and noticed the long brass handles were actually flamingoes shaped as . . . He bent down for a closer look. "Croquet mallets?" The whole town was certifiable. He was thinking maybe his branch of the family had escaped the Cove to save their sanity when the door swung open and he had to jerk back to keep from being smacked directly in the face with a flamingo mallet.

"It's okay, Eula," the woman was saying as she backed out of the shop, a moderately sized leather-strapped oak steamer trunk cradled in her arms. "I've got it. I just— ooph!"

Calder hadn't been able to both straighten and move out of her path at the same time, so had opted for not getting his face clobbered. His arms came around her as he fully righted himself, his hands covering hers as he kept the steamer trunk from pitching to the sidewalk. He just managed to catch the door on the toe of his boot before it hit her in the elbow. "I've got you," Calder said, bracing her in the shelter of his body until they were steady.

She turned her head to see who had her, causing him to

duck back in order to keep the lace-covered brim of the little hat she was wearing from clipping him across the cheek.

"You." She said it like an accusation.

He would have known those stormy, dark blue eyes anywhere. He was grinning before he thought better of it. "Every day."

She started to turn, but he tightened his hold for a moment.

"Mr. Blue—"

"Calder. And, just—wait," he instructed. "Don't pull. Something on your dress is caught in my, uh . . . belt buckle." It was only because he was a whisper away from her face that he saw her cheeks flush a little. It would otherwise have been almost impossible to tell, since she had enough makeup troweled on to rival a wax museum mannequin. He guessed it was to cover the damage from going one-on-one with the air bag and losing. "I'd ask what on earth it is you're wearing, but it's probably best you don't explain. Hold on." He shifted, trying to free himself from the white lace edging the voluminous layers of purple satin that made up the wide skirt of the antebellum ensemble she had on.

"I've got the trunk," she said tightly, sucking in her breath when he inadvertently brushed against the curve of her backside, though how he'd managed that kind of contact through all the fabric between them was beyond him. "Just, get unstuck," she said, sounding more than a little breathless.

His body wasn't remotely concerned with figuring out how it had made contact with the softly rounded curve of her backside; it was too busy enjoying the aftereffects of such contact. *What are you, fifteen? Copping a feel?* "Trying," he managed, knowing if he didn't free himself quickly it was only going to get more embarrassing for both of them.

"Please," she said, sounding strained now. "Rip it if you have to, it's not like it could possibly hurt the dress."

"True." He made sure she had hold of the trunk and shifted them both back a step so he could release the door. It swung closed in front of her as he straightened his stance and reached down between them to untangle the intricate scrap of lace from where it had somehow completely woven its every tiny strand in and around the prong of his belt buckle, as if they'd done some kind of slow bump and grind. He tried not to brush his fingertips over her surprisingly curvy backside any more than he had to. *Stop thinking about bumping. And grinding.* He tugged a bit harder than he'd meant to and jerked her right up against his—*Jesus, Blue, just rip the fucking thing, will you?*

"Hold still," he ground out, when she shifted against him. She might have groaned a little, or maybe that was just his own private fantasy. "There," he said a second later. "Got it."

She turned around so fast they almost bumped chins and he had to grab the trunk to keep it from effectively cornering him right in the balls.

"Sorry!" she said. Realizing what she'd almost done, she reached for the trunk, but he kept his hold on it. "I can take it now. You don't have to—"

"Just . . . I got it. Okay?" He closed his eyes for a brief moment, willing his body to calm right the hell down. Then, when that didn't work, he just thought, *Fuck it all*, and lowered the trunk so it blocked her view of him from belt to mid-thigh. *Seriously, go get laid or something. Because this is just sad, man.*

She must have seen something on his face, in his expression, because her face went from pink to red, and she stammered when she spoke. "Oh—right. Okay. Fine. Just . . . right. No problem."

Oh, she was a problem, all right. He still liked that he flustered her, liked it way too much. He was finally able to take in her full regalia and could only shake his head. Rather than comment, he looked back at her face. Her hair had been pulled back into some intricately woven, sleek bun all tucked in at the nape of her neck, but her features were still partly hidden by the dipping brim of the plum satin froufrou hat she had perched on the side of her head and the dark netting attached to the brim, which swept over her forehead and down across half of her left cheek. As a way to minimize anyone's view of her bandaged nose and banged-up face, it worked pretty well, but that bit of genius was mitigated by the fact that the getup itself would draw twice as much attention to her in the first place.

"Interesting disguise," he said. "How's the nose?"

With her hands now free, she lifted one to briefly shadow the exposed part of her face, then let it drop back to her side, appearing a bit annoyed with herself for caring what she looked like to him. Which, he discovered, he liked as well. A lot.

"The doctor says I'll keep it," she said. "But the lip is touch and go."

He grinned, surprised by the dry humor, and found his gaze drawn to that bruised and banged-up lower lip. He had the strongest urge to lean in . . . and soothe it with his tongue.

"Well, you do have two of those, so there's that."

"True, but having only one fully functional makes that whole whistling thing a bit of a challenge."

His grin widened. She gave every appearance of being a tall, elegant, cool sip of very expensive gin, yet her wit was sharp, very down to earth, and . . . well, earthy.

Interesting. Very . . . very interesting. "Yes," he said. "How would Bogey have ever landed Bacall if he couldn't put his lips together"—his gaze dropped to her mouth— "and blow?"

He watched her throat work and her pupils expand, and knew he shouldn't feel that little punch of triumph in his gut. And, okay, maybe a bit lower as well. Yeah, maybe he shouldn't go there at all.

"Old film buff?" she asked, pulling herself together and managing to look down her bandaged nose at him all at the same time.

"Classics never go out of style." And she was that, he thought. A classic. He took in her getup once again. "So, where are you off to in your, uh, Sunday finest? On this sunny Thursday morning."

She looked down, but rather than appear embarrassed, she smoothed her hand down the exceedingly shiny and very purple skirt, which spread outward over an untold number of what appeared to be white lace petticoats, at least from what he could see in the opening that split down the front of the skirt. Then she lifted a hand to carefully straighten her bonnet, and looked him straight in the eye with a small smile that could only be described as saccharine sweet. "Actually," she said, her voice a syrupy drawl, "why, I was just running a few errands in town before dashing off to save Tara."

He barked out a laugh. Now who was charming whom? "Why, Miss Scarlett, flash one of those smiles, and I do believe you could save Tara and the entire Confederacy, even this deep into Yankee territory."

He watched her mouth soften into a more natural smile, and was pleased with himself more than was wise. Even banged up and bruised, she was a very beautiful woman, but the unexpected wry humor was the far more dangerous weapon.

"I'm afraid to ask," he said, "but assuming this dress is to go along with the getup your sister was wearing yesterday, and that this has something to do with that wedding you mentioned, just who is your brother marrying, and why does she hate you all so much?"

"Actually, the dresses were Fiona's idea. They're for the wedding rehearsal later today, which I'm going to be late for if I don't get going. With everything that happened yesterday, I forgot to stop here and pick up my present for Alex—the bride," she elaborated. "We're having the rehearsal dinner party in town at the pub, which is where Fi is now, decorating. I want it to be a surprise, so this was the only way to hide it from her."

Calder looked down at the trunk he was still holding. He knew a little bit about antiques, partly from his work, which included a fair amount of restoration, as well as from his aunt Jo, who ran a little antiques shop in Calais. It was a beautifully made piece that someone had painstakingly taken a good bit of time to restore right down to the intricate scrollwork on the brass corner pieces and front locking mechanism, not to mention the design and letters that had been hand-carved and branded directly into the wood planking. "It's quite a piece. I don't know her, but I'm sure she'll like it."

"She's in charge of all the restoration work on Pelican Point," Hannah said. "Our historic lighthouse," she added, when he didn't show any sign of recognizing the name. "My ancestors were the lightkeepers of the tower, dating all the way back to its inception, almost two hundred years ago now."

"She'll appreciate the craftsmanship that went into restoring this piece, I'm sure."

"Oh, I know she will. That's her work." At his surprised look, she added, "Alex helps Eula occasionally—Eula is the shop owner here—with some of her restoration work. I found out she was particularly fond of this one, so . . ." She trailed off with a light shrug.

He looked back at the piece. "I'm sure she'll be touched by your thoughtfulness. Your brother appears to be a fortunate man. She is a very talented woman."

"You know something about antiques?"

"Some. I know more about restoration."

"A shame you aren't here to bring one of our many weathered buildings back to life, then. We could use that a lot more than—"

"A yacht club. Yes, I imagine you could. But that's not the job I was hired to do."

"More's the pity," she said, adopting a bit of her Scarlett accent again, even as her smile shifted back to one of cool politeness. "Well, I should be on my way." She reached for the steamer trunk.

"I've got it," he said, not because he needed the shield any longer, but . . . *because you're an idiot who needs to get his mind back on business and off her . . . bustle.* "Where did you park the horse and buggy?"

"I opted for just the horse." She motioned to the midnight-blue Mustang convertible parked curbside, just a half dozen yards down the street from his pickup truck.

He cast a glance from the sports car back to her, but wisely said nothing.

"I promise I'm looking both ways before entering intersections," she said, following his gaze.

"Did I say anything?"

"Your condescending grin speaks volumes for you."

"My grin never condescends," he said . . . grinning. "But I'm glad to hear you're observing proper road safety protocols. Still, I wouldn't let Wonka ride shotgun again if I were you. Not in that dress."

Her lips twitched at that. "Yes, well, we certainly wouldn't want to do anything to damage this . . . fine piece of couture. Now, if you don't mind, I have a plantation to save."

He followed her to the car and set the case inside the trunk after she popped the lid with her keyless remote. *Walk away, Blue. Just, nod, smile . . . and walk away.* "How long are you in town?" he heard himself ask. *Christ.* Then it was his turn to be surprised when a look of, what— uncertainty? Worry? Worse?—flashed across her face. What the hell was that about? Wasn't she just in town for a family wedding?

"I really should get going," she said.

"That's not an answer." And why on God's green earth was he pushing it? *Why the hell are you still standing here?*

She smiled politely, then stopped when it pulled at her busted lip, making him want to soothe it. Again. "I'm afraid it's the best one I have at the moment." She stepped up and closed the trunk with a snap, then moved around and opened the driver's-side door. Before he could help her, she proceeded to tuck her voluminous skirts into the car with a smooth elegance and ease that shouldn't have surprised him in the least.

Lauren Bacall, eat your heart out.

He did step up then and helped close the door as she pulled the last bit of her skirt in and out of the way, then smoothed it down under the leather-wrapped steering wheel. *Mustang Scarlett.* An incongruous sight, to be sure, but something told him that incongruity was a common theme where Hannah McCrae was concerned.

She started the engine.

"Might want to put that top up," he said, continuing with the drawl. "Wouldn't want you to lose that fine bonnet now."

In response, she merely reached up and tightened the starched bow under her chin, which was when he noticed how the ribbon and artful sweep of hair across her forehead, under the hat brim, served to hide the rest of the accident damage. Still, she had on an awful lot of makeup, and he wondered just how bad things really were underneath it all. The nose and lip alone had to be throbbing, no matter what pain relievers the nice paramedic had given her. Then she flinched a little as she pulled on the seat-belt harness across her shoulder, so yeah . . . she was hurting. A lot more than she was letting on. Pretty brave trooper to go through all the trouble of getting herself laced and buttoned and strapped into that crazy getup just for a wedding rehearsal. The things folks did for love of family. *Yeah,* he thought. *Tell me about it.*

"Thank you for the help," she said, clicking her seat belt in. "Again."

He let a hand rest on the open window frame of the door. "If you need to escape the insanity, I could always hijack you away somewhere for a bit." He quelled his internal voice, knowing he should just let her go. He wasn't sure why he hadn't already done so. She just as clearly neither wanted nor needed his help. *Exactly. So who's the needy one here?* But it wasn't that he needed her. He didn't. It was just that for some reason he felt compelled to . . . care for her.

"Thank you, but that won't be necessary." She made a big show of adjusting the rearview mirror, tightening her bonnet again.

So, she was, what? Stalling?

"You sure?"

She looked back up at him then, the brim of her hat and his body both serving to block the late-afternoon sun from her face. "To be perfectly honest, I'm not sure of many things at the moment, so it seems unwise to add anything else into the mix."

So . . . not so much an "I don't want to" as "I really shouldn't." He lifted his hand from the car door, but held her gaze as he let the grin slide across his face. "You know what they say, Miz Scarlett. Tomorrow is another day."

"Indeed it might be." She turned on the engine and gunned it a little. "But frankly, Mr. Blue, I'm not in a position right now to give a damn."

Then she peeled off down the street, horses thundering, leaving him as he'd known she would . . . eating her dust.

Well, you got one thing right about her, anyway.

"Frankly, Mr. Blue," Hannah mocked herself with an eye roll as she slowed down to a crawl and carefully navigated the shiny blue Mustang through town. It belonged to Sal's nephew, Micah, who was stationed overseas with the army at the moment and had left his prized possession with his uncle for safekeeping. Sal thought it would be a good way to give it some road time after being garaged for so long. Normally Hannah would have been more than happy to put some miles on the blue beast. All she had to do was even think about getting her foot close to the gas pedal and the thing leaped forward like the uncivilized stallion it had been named for. She would have enjoyed letting it loose to have a good galloping run. But nothing was normal for her right now. And being behind the wheel of any car, especially one so powerful, so soon after the accident, was making her feel queasy and borderline paranoid that something else awful was going to happen.

Just get back on the horse and ride it already! She gave a rueful smile, thinking that sentiment applied to so many things in her life at the moment. Not a single one of which she felt remotely ready to climb back up on, much less let loose for a long ride. And that visual made her thoughts swing right back to Calder Blue. *Oh, for the love of . . .* She groaned, tempted to pull over, lean forward, and just rap her forehead repeatedly on the steering wheel. However, she'd already been punched in the face with one steering wheel this week, so clearly that wasn't going to knock any sense into her.

She turned into the parking lot of the Rusty Puffin. She'd promised Fi she'd help decorate for the rehearsal party after stashing Alex's present in Gus's office, but at the moment her thoughts weren't on hanging copious quantities of tissue-paper wedding bells and crepe-paper streamers. Her thoughts were still all tangled up with Calder Blue. And climbing up on . . . things. And riding them. Hard.

"Seriously, the man gives you one little alpha grin and you're all Scarlett O'Hara to his Rhett Butler, Bacall to his Bogey. You're in no shape for that," she lectured herself. "So why do you respond to him?" *Because there is nothing little about that man,* her inner voice so helpfully offered. *Or his Bogey. Probably.* She swore under her breath and pulled into the space next to Fiona's little Prius and shut off the engine. No more horses. No more climbing.

She didn't even like big, muscular men. Tim had the type of body she'd always found herself attracted to. His was the lean, long-limbed physique of a distance runner. *Probably got it from all the beds he was hopping in and out of while making all those empty promises. And one very real baby.*

She shuddered at the memories, but wasn't quick enough in clamping down on it to shut out the memory of that charming, lying bastard face of his, how he'd smiled down at her as they lay tangled up together in her soft linen sheets. She'd loved the way their bodies matched each other in their long litheness, how elegant his fingers had looked as he'd traced them over her pale skin, his beautiful blue eyes so laserlike in their focus, making her feel so utterly cherished, as he softly stroked her cheek, down along her shoulder, over her rib cage, her hip bone, seeming so completely absorbed in her as he earnestly told her she was his exquisite, porcelain goddess.

Her stomach knotted up in equal parts disgust and fury. The fury was aimed at Tim for so calmly and easily abusing everything she'd felt for him, but the disgust she felt she reserved completely for herself, for being stupid enough, besotted enough, and—God—vain enough to buy into that awful, ridiculous, over-the-top praise of her supposed virtues in the first place.

She forced those images out of her mind, only to have them replaced by warm honey eyes, a fast grin, a hard jaw, and chiseled lips. The way Calder had drawled out that *Miz Scarlett*, if he'd truly been a Southern gentleman, there wouldn't be an untwirled parasol or dry petticoat on the plantation.

Calder's knowledge of classic films was yet another good reason for her to avoid him, she decided. She loved classic films. The last thing her beat-up and betrayed heart needed right now was some guy quoting iconic film dialogue to her clearly susceptible-to-flattery ego. *Especially a charming, sexy-as-hell guy who gives really good Rhett Butler.*

And who'd offered to hijack her away from all the wedding craziness. She wondered what a stolen afternoon with someone like Calder Blue would be like. *Climactic, for one.* Oh for God's sake. What was his deal, anyway? What was his angle? He had to have one. Because . . . why else the interest in her? Clearly it wasn't her charm, good looks, or lovely personality.

Maybe, from now on, she should approach the interest men showed her the way she did her case files, like a litigator. He was a guy from the wrong side of a centuries-old family feud who . . . what, decided to stroll into town like some kind of bad-ass cowboy at high noon and not only take on the Cove Blues, but also build something that was the source of a lot of anger and unrest in the Cove? Why would he do that? Was it possible he didn't know the majority of the townsfolk were against the club being built? Could he truly think he was doing a good thing? That growth was always a positive?

Her phone rang, making her jump, as her thoughts were jerked back to the present. She saw on the screen it was Fi, picked up. "Yes, dear?" she said in a put-upon, nasal drone.

"Funny. Listen, could you do me a giant favor? I need more white crushed gravel."

"Of course you do. And please don't explain why."

"I can't. No time. But also no time to make it back out to the nursery for more, so I called Owen and he's got something he thinks will work. Can you be an awesome sister and get it for me when you leave Eula's?"

"I actually just pulled in here at the Puffin. I'm outside in the parking lot. Can Kerry do it?"

"No, she and Gus had their big reunion moment and are already thick as thieves in the kitchen cooking up God knows what."

"Is she already dressed for rehearsal? And remind me to kill you dead again for making me come into town dressed like this when I could have stayed out of sight back out at the Point. Where the rehearsal actually is."

"It took me all morning to do your face, missy. You owe me. And there would be no time to get us all laced up and done after decorating the pub for tonight. So just roll with it. And yes, Kerry is all geared up, too. All we have to do is get this done, drive out there, and we're ready, set, go. I just need the gravel."

"I already went into Eula's looking like a sad extra from *Gone With the Wind*." *And ran into Calder. Literally*. She tried to keep her thoughts from going to how it had felt to be pressed up against his big, hard body, how his hands had felt covering hers, then later . . . covering her ass. Well, okay, so they hadn't really *covered* it so much as brushed over it, but she'd sort of thought about what it would feel like. At the time. But not now. And never again. She cleared her throat. If only it was so easy to clear her mind. "You know, not every event has to have a theme."

"But they're so much better when they do. It's funny, and it's fun. I thought it would keep us from getting stressed or . . . I don't know. I wanted us to be playful, spontaneous, silly, goofy. The world could use more of that. We need to embrace the fun."

"Well, you've got the silly and goofy nailed. I definitely feel both of those things," Hannah said dryly, but she heard in Fi's tone that same thread of anxiety or weariness, or . . . whatever it was that she'd seen in her sister's face earlier that morning. Hannah hadn't asked how long Fi was going to be staying in town, but happy wedding event and her own issues notwithstanding, Hannah decided she was going to make a point of getting her sister aside and sitting down for a good long talk to find out what was going on.

"Well, I can't argue with that," Hannah continued. "Fun has been a foreign concept in my world of late." The last time she'd been anything close to playful had been when— *shut it down. Now.*

But when she forcibly blanked out images of Tim, they

were replaced by Calder. He had made her smile. And she had been a little silly with him. With the whole Scarlett, Tara thing. It had felt good. Maybe too good. She had a lot of serious stuff to work through before she could afford to play and be silly. At least with members of the opposite sex, anyway. And she wasn't going to be either of those things with him, at any point in time. The moment the townies found out he was building the yacht club, and learned he was involved in a long-standing family feud, he'd be the town pariah. And she'd had enough notoriety in her life, thank you very much. She'd left D.C. to get away from that. The last thing she was going to do was come home . . . and get herself all caught up with the new black sheep in town.

"Earth to Hannah," came Fi's voice over the phone. "Owen has the gravel all packaged up and ready. I already gave him my card number for it, okay? You just need to run in, snag it, and get back on over here. We've only got an hour or so left to get all this set up, then drive back out to the Point. Logan's already headed that way."

"Logan, who is not in his crazy tux jacket yet," she reminded her sister. "Unlike the rest of us. Why didn't he get your gravel?"

"Because he'd already headed out before I realized I was going to be short. And he can shrug on the jacket and cummerbund. It took me forty-five minutes to get that damn dress on you. And maybe I did it on purpose, okay? Making us wear these all day. It's only one day, but that's just it . . . it's only one day. Then boom, on to the next. We need to slow down a little, enjoy each of our 'only one days.' So this is sort of like a reminder for us not to take ourselves so damn seriously. We all do it, Hannah. You do. I do. Okay, maybe not Kerry. But we all worry, we stress, we go out of our way to please everyone else, and then worry we didn't do a good enough job at that, so then we bend over backward to do even more. We're uptight, overly conservative, ridiculously PC, because God for-freaking-bid we ever insult or offend anyone's delicate sensibilities, or make anyone feel uncomfortable, or step outside of our own boxed-up comfort zone. Oh my God, the world might come to an end." She stopped abruptly, and Hannah could hear her taking an audible deep breath. Then, with a shade of her more characteristic dry humor back and the overly shrill tone nowhere in evidence, she said, "And then where would we all be?"

"Fi—" Hannah began, now truly concerned about her younger sister.

"I just want us to have fun, Hannah," she interrupted. "You saw Logan and Alex together. She's good for him. When have we seen him like that? So relaxed, not looking like he has the weight of the world, our family, every one of our ancestors, and the entire town of Blueberry Cove on his big shoulders? He's happy. Truly, and utterly happy. And I don't know about you, but I don't want to wait for some-one to come along like Alex did for him, to help make me understand how important that balance is. You know? So the crazy clothes—and yes, maybe even being out in public in the crazy clothes—is like an in-your-face to everyone who really needs to get a life. Starting with me. And maybe, I think, a little bit, with you, too."

Hannah sat there in her car, in the parking lot of Fergus's pub, staring unseeingly out the window as she let Fiona's fervently delivered speech sink in. "So . . ." she said quietly a few moments later, love and concern tangled up in equal measures inside her head, and her heart, "when did you get to be the smart one? I thought that was my job."

"How about we take turns?" Fiona said, relief so evident in her tone, Hannah was glad she hadn't immediately jumped in with the cross-examination questions that Fiona always gave her a hard time about.

"Deal."

"So . . . you'll get the gravel for me, Scarlett?"

"Yes, dear." They both laughed, then Hannah added, "But if you think for one second there will be no consequences to your little 'Look at me having fun by publicly embarrassing myself' gambit, well—".

"I'm okay with that. Just think how much fun you'll have plotting your revenge," Fiona said with a laugh, already sounding a little better. Or a little less maxed out anyway. "See? My evil plan is already working."

"You've got the evil part right," Hannah said, putting the car back into gear and backing out of the parking space. "And I'm calling Owen and having him meet me at the curb. I think I've had all the streetwalker-Scarlett *fun* I can handle for one day."

Chapter Six

"I appreciate the mayoral insight into the new direction the town is taking," Calder told Owen Hartley. "And the history lesson." He leaned his hip on the hardware store counter, thinking he could have saved himself a lot of time and energy if he'd just talked to Hartley first. Brodie had mentioned him as a good source on all the goings-on and he'd been spot-on about that. With a good word from Brodie, Owen had already given Calder a general outline of what was happening in terms of town growth and who the main players were and how they all interconnected. For his part, Owen knew Calder was in town at Winstock's behest, to take on the construction of the yacht club, and that Calder was hoping to use the deal as a way to open dialogue between the two sides of his feuding family, but was curious as to why Winstock would bring him in, in the first place.

"I don't know if it will help you any," Owen said, brushing off the front of his shop apron. He was a slender man in his late forties with ginger hair and glasses, looking far more college history professor than shopkeeper or mayor.

But when he talked about the town of Blueberry Cove, or its residents, it was clear he had a deep, abiding love and respect for both, which likely made him very good at both of his jobs. "It's a complex matter. I will say, you did well, going directly to Jonah. He'd never let you know that, of course, far too proud, but I know the man. He's fair, cares very deeply for those he's responsible for, and he's smart enough to do what's right. He's stubborn, but not close-minded, and there is a difference."

Remembering Jonah's lecture the day before, Calder wasn't so sure he agreed with Owen, but he kept that opinion to himself. "You said you beat out Winstock's son-in-law, Ted Weathersby, for mayor. If you don't mind my asking, how has Winstock handled things since then? If Ted was formerly the head of the town council and had political aspirations above and beyond the mayor's office, Winstock can't have been happy with that result. Given what you've told me, it seems reasonable he hoped to use his son-in-law's influence to help him see his harbor plans through."

"Oh, no doubt about that," Owen said, his quiet manner managing to make him seem both honest and humble at the same time. "It's a good part of why some of the folks here asked me to consider running. Ted has become something of a polarizing figure, and when the former mayor sided with Brooks—Mr. Winstock—and awarded him the property the diner had been on, well, that didn't sit too well with a lot of folks, either. Brooks and Ted were both surprised when I ran and even more when I won the election—frankly, no more surprised than I was. But while I've felt the heat, so to speak, within the council because there are those who still support both men, neither Brooks nor Ted has come at me personally. I can say Brooks isn't one for dwelling on what's done—he's more the type who finds another way to move forward."

"Kind of odd that a man whose family tree stretches back—what did you say, five or six generations?—that he doesn't seem to have a strong sense of historic preservation. I could see if he was some recent transplant wanting to bring change, but this is unusual, isn't it? Speaking from my own experience, anyway, folks around here tend to cling to the past rather . . . stringently."

Owen nodded and understood Calder's reference to his own family feud. "Some do, maybe more than some, but I think in Brooks's case, his motives are more self-serving. He wants to build his own legacy here. I'm just not sure he's going about achieving it the right way."

"Do you think there's something going on with him that's making him push like this? His health? Family? Money issues?"

Owen shrugged. "Not that I've heard whispered about, and I think there would be that and more if there was even a hint of any of those things. I mean, I know he's been disappointed that his only daughter—Camille—hasn't given him any grandkids, but I can't see how that has anything to do with this."

Owen's offhand comment hit Calder close to home. Made him think about his own father's disappointment over his oldest son's divorce . . . as much because of the potential loss of an heir as anything else. Two of Calder's three brothers were married, with two kids apiece, all of them daughters, but his dad wanted a Blue to continue on with the family business. So, to him, though he doted on the girls, they didn't count as Blue heirs. Calder had pointed out that the girls were Blues, too, and might well want to take over the family contracting business one day. *And wouldn't that just solve all your problems.* But . . . yeah. Calder refocused his mind on the matter at hand.

"Maybe if Winstock doesn't have a living, breathing legacy to carry on the family name, he feels he has to put a permanent stamp on the Cove some other way."

Owen looked a little surprised by Calder's insight. "You know . . . you might actually be on to something there. I mean, I never gave any serious credence to Brooks's talk of wanting grandkids; it just sounded like what all people say when their kids marry and settle down."

"So, is it that his daughter and son-in-law don't want them or can't have them?"

"Not sure. They're both rather . . . self-focused. That doesn't sound particularly gracious of me, but I imagine the sentiment would be echoed pretty much everywhere you go here. My feeling is the only reason Ted and Cami would have kids was if they thought it would benefit Ted's political aspirations. They'd have a litter if they thought it would make a difference. And hire a few nannies to handle the rest."

Calder's brows lifted. "I see. So, maybe it is a legacy thing."

"May well be." Owen half smiled, but looked like he felt a little sorry for them, all at the same time. "Guess if I'd thought more about what split your people apart, it might have occurred to me sooner."

Surprised, Calder said, "Meaning . . . what? Jeremiah Blue wanted to fish the open seas and stay in the Cove, build on what he and his brother had begun. And his twin Jedediah was more of an explorer, liked to fish, but also liked to hunt and trap, so he set off into the wilds, ended up settling in what would eventually become Calais. Didn't start up anything as big or lasting as what the Blues have here, but he used his trapping and fishing skills to provide for his family. I think every man—and woman—should be able to follow his or her own path." He might have said that last part a bit more fervently than was absolutely necessary to the moment, but he sure as hell meant it.

Owen was studying him, listening, but clearly something else was going on inside his head.

"You think Jed should have stayed with the family business here?" Calder asked. "That it was a betrayal to leave? I know it put a strain on what the Blues had begun here and, depending on who is telling the story, could have destroyed it, but while I can see the two brothers having a falling-out, I never understood how it pitted family against family for generations."

Owen nodded, but didn't say anything straight off, until finally Calder said, "I'm guessing the Cove Blues have a different telling of that story? That's fine. I'd be surprised if they didn't. I'd long since figured each side had to have embellished the wrongdoings of the other to pacify themselves that they'd done the right thing, cutting themselves off so entirely. And for so long."

After another moment, Owen said, "I think it's safe to say that a number of the Blue family members here haven't ever taken the time to hear the story, no matter who's doing the telling, but have simply followed what they've been told to feel, and behaved accordingly. Here it's about loyalty, and family honor, no explanation required. Do as you're told, stick by the clan, and you have a place here always. Go against us, then good luck and Godspeed."

Calder smiled. "Yes, that does have a very familiar ring to it."

Owen seemed to relax a little, his mouth curving in a faint

smile of his own. "Is that how your family feels about you being here?"

"There are . . . varying opinions on that subject," Calder said, without elaborating. He didn't need or want to explain that the current generation of Croix River Blues was doing its damnedest to start its own divisive feud. He was pretty sure Owen could fill in the pertinent gaps. Speaking of which: "Care to fill in the gaps from my side? I'm sensing there's something I don't know that might help me understand."

"Oh, possibly." Owen's smile turned a shade rueful. "Probably." Concern filtered into his expression and voice then. "But it's not my place. Jonah should be the one—"

"Jonah has no desire to discuss family with me. He's made it clear I'm not welcome back on Blue property. I'd appreciate your take. I'm figuring it has to be more objective than Jonah's is likely to be anyway."

"Yes, no doubt true. It's just . . . it's going to color how you think about things. Knowledge is power, but it's not always a power that rests easily in the mind, or in the heart."

Now Calder frowned. "Okay. Now I think I'd really like to hear it." He lifted a hand when Owen seemed to waver. "I appreciate that whatever the story is, you're uncomfortable being the one to break it to me. I won't shoot the messenger. I love my family, and I take great pride in my ancestors, but I'm well aware we're all fallible. Myself most definitely included. So, I can't see how I would hold something—anything—that one of our ancestors did a hundred years ago, against any one living member of my family now. And that's all that matters to me."

Owen was nodding his head as Calder spoke. "I share that sentiment." He took a breath, let out a little sigh. "Well, as the story goes, and this comes not only from journals kept by Blue family members, but from the diaries of other townsfolk, some of which have become part of the public record. At least, if a person were so inclined to want to read them, anyway."

"Something the local historian might have done."

Owen smiled briefly, still looking somewhat troubled over having gotten himself into this particular conversation. "Indeed," he said. He paused and Calder was just about to ask him where he could gain access to those journals directly when he continued. So Calder fell silent, and simply listened.

"When Jedediah and Jeremiah had their disagreement, initially Jed wanted to keep the family empire united, but he didn't want to be tied down to the Cove. He thought of it as branching out, expanding on the empire rather than splitting it. Jeremiah wouldn't hear anything of the sort. They were fishermen. Period. They'd settled on Pelican Bay to chart their course, and to his mind, that meant building a fishing company. There would be no branches. It would take every bit of blood, sweat, and tears they and their kin had to make a go of what they'd already begun. Each brother felt betrayed, for not having the support of the other. Perhaps as twins, they felt this betrayal more keenly than most, but I'm just supposing there. It was well known they were very, very close and shared a unique bond, so the dissension between them was all the more troublesome and painful."

"Sounds like that's in keeping with what I know."

"Yes, well . . . so Jed ultimately decided to leave and chart his own course. When he did, he took his family with him."

"Yes, a wife, two sons, and a daughter, as I recall."

Owen nodded, then sighed a little, not quite meeting

Calder's eyes. "Thing is . . . they were Jeremiah's wife and kids. Not Jed's. Well, Jeremiah's wife, at any rate. There was speculation, of course, about the children's parentage after that."

Calder's eyes widened, then widened some more. He leaned more heavily against the counter. He had no idea where he'd thought this was going, but it hadn't been this. "So . . . what was their story?"

"Well, Jeremiah was intensely devoted to launching the family fishing business, so much so he dedicated every waking, breathing moment to it. Now he'd always made it quite clear he did what he did for his family, his kids, and their future. Building Blue's Fishing Company was his legacy." He looked at Calder. "Which is why your comment on Brooks struck me."

"So I'm guessing Jeremiah's wife was tired of being left home to fend for herself and the kids and somehow got tangled up with Jed?"

"Hard to say. Was a long time ago, and if Bettina—Jeremiah's wife—had a diary, she took it with her. Maybe your side of the family has something along those lines."

"So . . . okay." Calder had to take a moment to let that information filter in. "I know divorce wasn't looked upon lightly then, and if Jeremiah had strong religious beliefs, he could have had even stronger feelings than personal betrayal when his wife left him for his brother. But—"

"Well, as I said, there was some dispute then over whose kids they were. The oldest was only five at the time, the youngest barely six months, but with the brothers identical in appearance, there was no way to know from looks. It was all just speculation. For his part, Jeremiah publicly denounced Jed and his wife, and abdicated all responsibility for the children, claiming they were bastards. But this is where journals from the viewpoint of observers become interesting. Gossip was rampant. From the point of view of the observers whose journals I've read, Jeremiah might have denounced his brother, his wife, and his children, but he never stopped loving any of them. In fact, losing them essentially destroyed him. Historically, it's a fact that he never divorced her, and more than one journal passage noted that he wore his wedding ring until the day he died. But he poured his life and soul into the one thing he had left—the fishing company. Some said he was 'driven like the devil,' to quote a passage, to make it succeed as his own form of revenge or validation. He was never the same man. He'd been a hardworking man always, but that pain, the depth of that betrayal, caused him to more or less single-handedly work himself into an early grave. He gave everything he had to build his business and this town, so it's not hard to see how his efforts could have swayed not just the remaining Blue family kin, but the entire town to take up against Jed and Bettina, and what they'd done."

"Hard to believe no one in town knew about the affair between Bettina and Jed. Given the size of the town, it would seem impossible—"

"Except for the fact that the two men looked exactly alike."

Calder rubbed a hand across the back of his neck. "Yeah." He swore under his breath. "Sounds like a bad soap opera."

Owen smiled briefly. "Well, it gets more so."

Calder looked at him in surprise. "I'm afraid to ask. What's the rest of it?"

"The word that came back this way was that when Jed and Bettina took off and made their way up the St. Croix, they presented themselves as man and wife, and claimed the three kids as their own. The kids might well have been, but Jed and Bettina were most certainly not man and wife, at least not legally. No one there was ever the wiser as far as I know. No telling what they told their children, but they were young enough still that they likely believed Jed was their father. Their only father." Owen paused, then said, "It's highly possible that, all this time later, the kin on your side believe Jed and Bettina's story is the truth. They were a young married couple who struck out on their own with their kids and the Blues here never forgave them. Clearly they didn't want anyone who was part of their new lives to know the truth for legal reasons, if for no other. I'm surprised they let it be known they had kin back here in Blueberry Cove, but clearly you knew that much."

Then the real impact of the story struck him. "So, if those kids were really Jeremiah's, then our entire branch of the family tree would trace directly back—"

"Here. Yes. To Jeremiah. Not to Jed."

Calder was just shaking his head. Then he chuckled, still somewhat in shock. "All this time, so many years spent reviling the other side of the tree for being so selfish and hateful about not letting Jed and Bettina do their own thing . . . and we all might be direct descendants of the Cove Blues after all. Well . . . isn't that some shit." He looked back to Owen. "So . . . you said Jeremiah worked himself to death. He never remarried?"

Owen shook his head. "He was a devout man, and considered himself married until death. He didn't reach fifty."

"Wait, I thought—isn't Jonah in direct line from Jeremiah? How is that possible? None of the kids ever came back, did they? At least, we have no record of that happening."

Owen shook his head. "I doubt those kids ever knew the

truth, whatever that truth was. Like I said, they may well have been Jed's. That was, what now? Five generations back? Six? Your side has stayed loyal to your family. Is there much chatter about the Blueberry Cove Blues at this point?"

Calder shook his head. "Not really, other than at family reunions, that kind of thing, and it all comes off as so much folklore really. There isn't any actual animosity on our side, it's more just a kind of head-shaking bemusement over how narrow-minded and hateful this side was, way back then. No particular curiosity to find out where things might stand today, or change things, either. Blueberry Cove Blues were considered distant, long-forgotten relatives at best."

"And yet, here you are."

"Because Brooks Winstock reached out to me on the job bid. I knew the story, well, our version of it, in a 'how the Blues came to settle in Calais' kind of way. I knew I had a distant family history here, but I didn't even know if there were any Blues left in the Cove. I looked into it, though, trying to figure out what Winstock's angle was, poked around a bit, asked some questions of the oldest members of my family."

"And?"

Calder grinned. "Well, that stirred up a bit of a hornet's nest. They didn't often talk about this side, but go poking and prodding, and they were more than happy to give me their opinions on the matter. Which, collectively and quite succinctly, could be summed up as 'don't waste your time on those assholes.' Pardon the language."

Owen shook his head, looking more relieved than anything. "No offense taken. Guess it's not so hard to see why no one ever came looking."

Calder shrugged. "Not that I'm aware of anyway. It all

seemed kind of ridiculous to me, but now, hearing this . . . well, it definitely explains Jonah's open hostility and his unwillingness to communicate with me, both before my arrival and since. So who is Jonah descended from, if not Jeremiah?"

"They had a younger sister, Josephine. Her husband died young, shortly after they'd all settled here. She wasn't even twenty yet, had two babies already, both sons. Story goes that Jo's husband died soon after Jed had taken off, so Jeremiah took her under his roof and helped raise her kids. Not as his own, per se, but they were Blues, nonetheless. And—Cove history is wishy-washy on this, though I'm sure Jonah has records somewhere—but whatever his sister's married name had been, those kids used the surname Blue. Jonah descends from them."

Calder took a moment, letting all the information settle a bit.

"You have family?" Owen asked.

"No kids, if that's what you mean. I have three brothers. All younger." He smiled at Owen's wide eyes. "Two are married, two daughters apiece. The baby is still in college. Not a one of them cares a lick about what's going on out here." *They're too busy arguing with me.* "So . . . yeah, we weren't really raised to even think about this side."

"Well, Brooks will sure stir up a nest by getting you here, I can tell you that."

"I appreciate you telling me all this. I'm glad you did. I'd have rather heard it from you anyway. Factual and dispassionate. Though, while I understand Jonah's stance now, I still maintain it's ridiculous to hold the children responsible for the sins of their fathers. And mothers."

"Agreed. But if Jonah knows the whole story, then it's possible he isn't sure what you know, or—more to the point—what you don't know. He may think you're here to make some kind of claim on Jeremiah's descendants and their property, as a rightful descendant yourself."

Stunned, Calder opened his mouth, closed it again, then finally said, "Jesus. I never would have thought of that. But you're right." Then another thought struck him. "Do you think Winstock plans to use my potential gene pool connection as some kind of leverage to weasel Jonah's property out from under him? Although, off the top of my head, I can't imagine how that would play out."

"Hadn't occurred to me, but . . . sad to say, I wouldn't put it past him. I always thought him a fair man in his business dealings, but the way he's gone about securing this whole harbor renovation project of his has made me think otherwise of late. Now I don't know where he'd draw the line. Or if he even has one. He's . . . determined. And he has the wealth, power, and influence to push forward almost any agenda he wants. But to actually change the course of the Cove's future, its destiny . . . yes, he's resorted to some less than aboveboard methods. I'd be careful if I were you."

Just then, the shop phone rang, and Owen shot him an apologetic look, then picked up and immediately smiled more broadly than Calder would have thought possible. Possibly in relief, after their heavy conversation. Then Owen said, "Why hello, Hannah, so good to hear your voice. Home for the big event, I assume?"

At the mention of her name, Calder lost his train of thought, and found himself listening to Owen's end of the conversation.

Owen grinned further as he listened, and it was obvious how sincere his affection was for her. "Now, don't call me Mayor Hartley," he said, a pink hue staining his pale, freckled cheeks. "Owen will do fine, as it always has. And yes, your sister called." He placed his hand on top of the bag of white crushed gravel presently lying across the counter. "I have it right here." He listened, then said, "Sure thing, just toot the horn and I'll bring it on out." His face reddened further. "Well, I don't know about the shining armor part, but you know I'm always willing to pitch in and help. And please tell your sister if she needs help setting things up out on the Point for Sunday's ceremony, just give me a call. I can put together some folks to come set up chairs and tables and the like." His smile grew. "Good to have you back." Then he clicked off and looked at Calder. "Hannah McCrae. Hasn't been home in . . . well, more years than I can recall. Good to have her back, she's good people."

"Being sister of the police chief probably doesn't hurt, either."

Owen's brows lifted. "So you know her, then? The whole family is good people, always have been. Her brother has done an enormous service to this town. The girls all scattered early on, of course." His expression was one of honest and deeply held affection. "I'm sure they're enjoying the family reunion. I know we're happy to have them back in town again, all three together."

"Any reason they don't come back more regularly?"

"Well, Fiona pops in the most, usually making it up for a holiday or two, and at some point over the summer. Hannah used to, before her star started to rise on Capitol Hill."

"Politician?" That surprised him.

"Litigator. Good one, too."

That was more like it. "I'll bet," Calder said. "I've met

Fiona. Interior designer." *And cuckoo for Cocoa Puffs.* "What's the deal with the third sister?"

Owen's face creased in a grin so wide, his eyes twinkled.

"Wow," Calder said, chuckling. "I'm almost afraid to hear this."

"Kerry," the older man said, fondly. "She's the baby, the wild child of the bunch. Took off to see the world at barely eighteen and has only made a rare pit stop back here since. She's quite the handful, always was. She's the kind who makes a mark wherever she goes." He chuckled. "Some of her stories will curl your hair."

"Does sound like a handful." Calder tried to imagine all three women together at the same time, and decided that was better left unimagined. Being the oldest of four brothers himself, spanning twelve years from oldest to youngest, Calder could only think that as the eldest sister, poor Hannah likely had her hands even more full than he had.

The short blast of a car horn sounded from outside the front door. Owen went to heave the twenty-five-pound bag off the counter.

"I'll get it," Calder said, and easily hefted the unwieldy, thick plastic sack. "I appreciate the conversation. And the background. More than you know."

"Thank you," Owen said, nodding at the gravel. "And no problem. Any time. I don't know if it added any clarity to your situation, but, like I said, information is power. I hope it helps more than it hinders."

Calder hefted the bag to his shoulder. "Winstock has pushed our meeting back again. To dinnertime now. I'll be very interested to hear what he has to say."

Owen's brows lifted a bit at that. "You actually planning on building the yacht club?"

"I don't know. I'm not here for the job. Not really. I'm here to find out why Winstock wants me for the job."

Owen nodded. "Well, if you're looking for an in to help mend family feud fences, I don't think taking that particular job is the way to do it."

Calder nodded. "I'd already figured out that much. I'm not sure it will make a difference one way or the other, though, to be honest." He turned back at the door. "You've given me the various sides of the story, about how the town feels about the growth going on here, I mean. You haven't told me what you think. What's your personal opinion?"

"Well, as mayor, I think about what's best for everyone, and in that regard, I'm torn, as people's needs vary widely. As a shopkeeper, I think about what's best for me, and for my daughter, who is helping to run the place now and says she wants it to be hers someday." At Calder's pleased smile, a look of pride came into his eyes. "I'll admit that took me a while to really wrap my head around. I guess I had other dreams for her, something bigger and, well, beyond this place."

"Sounds like you've made this place a very good home for her. What's not to love about that? Seems to me like a wonderful future to hang one's hat on."

He nodded, beaming. "I've come to realize that, too. I'm very proud of her, don't get me wrong. And . . . to be honest, I love having her back here again, full-time. It's . . . well, you don't need to hear me get all sentimental."

"No, but it's nice that you are, all the same," Calder said, thinking how funny it was with families and patriarchs. His father wanted his sons to think of nothing other than the company he and his father had built, Jeremiah Blue had felt the same about his venture, and both were losing or had lost that battle, on some fronts, anyway, because of the sheer rigidity with which they pursued their goals. And here Owen was trying to cut his young one loose, only to have her stubbornly stick herself right back in the nest and claim it as her own. He thought about the McCraes, specifically Hannah, and wondered what their story was, one staying, the rest leaving.

"An increase in town revenue wouldn't be a bad thing for her as she takes this business forward another generation," Owen was saying. "And . . . who knows what that next generation's needs and responsibilities might be?"

"And as the town historian?" Calder asked.

Owen paused, then said, "The town historian knows that things that stay static tend to die, either from lack of forward energy, or from neglect, from being taken for granted. Change is inevitable. Change has come steadily to the Cove since its inception, or we wouldn't still be here. Now, what we do with, for, and about those changes, is what matters. And that can only be up to each one of us to decide."

Calder thought Hartley's wisdom applied to a whole lot more than town growth. "A cautionary tale?"

Owen smiled. "Or a celebration of the endless opportunities of life."

"Good point." Calder grinned. "We should grab a few beers sometime. I'll probably have more questions after meeting Winstock. If you don't think they'll run you out of town for being seen with me."

Owen seemed surprised by the offer, then nodded. "Oh, it would stir up some chatter, to be sure. But no harm in chatter. I'd enjoy a few beers." He smiled, and Calder noticed again the sharp intellect behind the somewhat mild-mannered outward appearance. "Of course, in return, I'd appreciate your insight into what you think Winstock is about, dragging you into this."

"Sold, Mr. Mayor," Calder said.

"Owen," he replied. "Thanks again." He motioned at the gravel.

Calder nodded and pushed through the door, thinking it was nice to discover at least one member of the town was sane.

Chapter Seven

As the door swung shut behind him, Calder squinted at the bright late-morning sunshine. *Interesting day.* Idling at the curb was the blue beast . . . and a pensive-looking Scarlett. *And it's not even noon yet.* He'd expected she'd be testy from being kept waiting. He really needed to stop assuming the worst about her.

"Your gravel, ma'am," he said and motioned toward the trunk.

She looked up, clearly startled from her thoughts, making him wonder what had brought that brooding expression to her face. Then her eyebrows climbed even higher. "You. Again."

"Small town," he replied, motioning again to the trunk.

She leaned down and reached around for the lever, then popped the lid for him. "Why are you here?"

"According to you? To destroy the Blue family and civilized life in the Cove as you know it."

She gave him an arched look. "I meant here at Hartley's, but never mind, it's none of—just never mind. If you could put that in the trunk, I really need to get back over to the pub. Careful, the steamer trunk is still in there."

She was flustered. Again. He hid his grin behind the

popped hood of the trunk and put the gravel in the back, then moved the steamer to keep it clear and closed the trunk. He walked around to the driver's-side door before she could pull away from the curb and leave him eating her dust. Again. "So, I feel as if I'm forced to ask now." He gestured to the outfit. "Some weird chick-flick-movie-themed bachelorette party?"

"And here I was thinking more Adam Sandler meets Tim Burton. Or *Hangover 6*."

He chuckled. "Point to Scarlett. Don't worry. I won't ask what the gravel is for. I don't have time to testify in court."

"Given our history, brief though it may be, I'm thinking you're the last person I should ask to be a witness. And I don't know about the gravel. I didn't ask." She might have smiled a little then. "Same reason."

He grinned. "Smart move, Counselor. On both counts."

She glanced up, surprised. "How did you know I was an attorney?"

"Owen. He mentioned it after taking your call. He can't sing your praises highly enough. So, you've only been home one day and already you're hot-rodding through intersections, taking out local signage, imitating Scarlett O'Hara in public, the questionable big bag of gravel . . . you're not afraid of being disbarred or anything?"

"I wasn't hot-rodding," she said, sounding impatient, meaning he hadn't been the only one to toss that in her direction. She glanced down at the dress, and her annoyance deflated a little. She sighed, and he wasn't sure if her resignation was aimed at him, or her sister. Probably both. "Fiona thinks we're not having enough fun, that we're all too uptight and conservative, hence the bad bridesmaid dresses for the wedding rehearsal."

"I take it the 'from hell' part at the end of that is a given."

She might have cracked an actual smile at that. "The

dresses are from hell, no doubt. But my family all gets along really well and just as likely Fi is right and it will be a hilarious blast. I'll probably love every minute. Just as soon as I get away from the Cove and everyone I've ever known since birth and back out to the Point." She gestured to the ensemble as a whole. "Not exactly the welcome-home impression I was hoping to make."

"Owen said it's been a few years."

She gave him that arched look again. "Owen sure had a lot to say."

Calder laughed. "You have no idea. But, where you're concerned anyway, you and your family, it was all glowing." He nodded toward the dress. "I figured the rehearsal was at the pub."

"Post-rehearsal party, dinner, whatever. We're decorating now."

"With gravel."

She lifted a shoulder. "I'm sure whatever it's for will be spectacular."

He lifted a hand, palm out. "I plead the fifth, Counselor."

She looked insulted on her sister's behalf. "She's very good, you know. Award-winning, actually."

"Considering the outfit you have on at the moment was her idea, and the one she had on yesterday, when it wasn't rehearsal day . . . you'll understand if I take that part on faith."

"How do you know this outfit isn't mine?"

He put his hand on the side of the door and leaned down a fraction, so she had to tip her chin up to look at his face. "It's not that I don't think you'd wear whatever a good friend—or sister—asked you to wear. But my sense is that any friends you have on Capitol Hill are very unlikely to have a wedding that tasteless."

She frowned. "How did you know I worked on Capitol—never mind."

"Owen," they both said at the same time.

She smiled at that, and honest affection warmed her dark eyes. Not for Calder, of course, but for Owen, he assumed. Even with the abundance of makeup, the crazy hat, the banged-up lip, and the bandaged nose . . . she was a beautiful woman. A fortunate gene pool had seen to that. But her wry sense of humor and that light in her eyes . . . yeah, those things made her attractive to him in an entirely different way. *Danger, danger, Blue. Walk away. Hell, run if you have to.*

"I asked him out for a few beers," he told her, referring to Owen. "He's an interesting man." His grin spread. "He didn't turn me down."

"Yes, well, he's not good at saying no when he should. How do you think he ended up as mayor? Too kind for his own good."

"I'd think he'd be a very good mayor."

"Oh, he is. Best we've ever had, to hear Logan and Barb tell it."

"Barb?"

"Sergeant Benson. You met her yesterday. At the station house."

"Right. Five feet of fearsome."

Hannah did smile at that. "Indeed."

"From what I've heard so far, sounds like maybe Hartley is just the thing this town needs right now. Neither too progressive nor too conservative. Give the folks some much-needed historic perspective."

"For a man who just got to town, you certainly seem to have nosed around a good bit."

"Not really." His grin deepened. "You all are a chatty bunch."

"Can be," she said, assessing him again, her expression making it clear she wouldn't have been one of the forthcoming ones. Not with him, anyway.

Maybe it was the impervious expression she was trying so hard to maintain, or the fact that he liked her better flustered, but he found himself crouching down beside the car door and folding his arms on the open window frame. "Offer to hijack you out of this mess is still open."

She smiled at that, even as he could tell she really didn't want to. "Don't you have your own business to attend to?"

"My meeting with Winstock was pushed back. Again. When do you have to be back for the rehearsal?"

"You're incorrigible." She didn't say it in a way that was remotely flirtatious.

Which, perversely, just made it that much hotter. "Look at it this way, in that getup, you're safer than you would be in a medieval chastity belt."

Her eyebrows lifted and he saw her mouth pinch a little in distress. He was close enough again now and with the angle of the sun, he could spy the dark shadows under the heavy makeup. So she was sporting a healthy pair of shiners under all that. Dammit. He liked making her smile, taking her mind—and his—off of their immediate agendas. But he wasn't trying to make her more uncomfortable. *Well, just what* are *you trying to do, then?*

Hell if he knew.

"I should get on my way," was all she said by way of reply. She put the car into gear.

Something about a woman dressed like a bad Vivien Leigh stunt double, but still looking as cool as Grace Kelly on her best day, driving a hot rod—and a stick shift, no less—turned him right around. And on. That was also a woman he had no business getting caught up with. Not even for an hour, a day . . . *a lifetime.*

"I'm sorry," he said.

That seemed to surprise her. "For?"

He lifted one hand and very gently pushed a wayward tendril of hair from her bruised and heavily made-up cheek, careful not to touch the tender skin. "The accident. Putting a painful damper on what sounds like an otherwise joyous family weekend."

"Wasn't your fault. And the weekend will be joyful. Is joyful."

He chuckled at the way she'd said that, like a closing statement meant to brook no further comment. "Yeah. You sound overcome with it."

She looked at him squarely then, which drew his fingertip along her cheek, down to her chin. "I'm very happy for my brother. I couldn't be happier for him."

"Then why do you look so miserable? I figured it was from getting smacked in the face with an air bag. You got some other sort of unrest going on back at the plantation, Miz Scarlett?"

She gave him a penetrating, no-bullshit stare, much the same way he imagined she'd look at someone she was about to cross-examine on the stand. It was impressive. But because he wasn't on trial, it didn't faze him in the least. He also noted she didn't shift away from his touch. Now *that* fazed him.

"No unrest. Everything will be fine," she said. "Is fine."

He smiled, which spread to a grin when she scowled. "Good thing you're not on the stand right now. You're perjuring yourself."

Despite herself, she smiled a little at that, then flinched when it pulled too much at her injured lip.

Despite his better judgment—because why start now?— he let his finger drift over her lower lip, stopping just short of the banged-up part. He felt her breath hitch a little, but he didn't think it was because he was causing her any distress. A quick look at her eyes and those rapidly expanding pupils confirmed that.

He traced his finger over the pad of her lip, down over her chin, then along the side of her neck . . . and slowly across her collarbone. She let her eyes close and he felt a light tremor race across her skin.

"What are you doing?" she said, her voice barely above a whisper.

"Relieving a little pressure," he said, and slid his fingers under the seat-belt strap, lifting it away from her injured shoulder.

She relaxed a little into the back of her seat, and he felt as much as heard the sigh of relief. "That's really . . . nice," she murmured.

"I am sorry," he said. "About the pain."

She kept her eyes closed, tipped her chin up slightly so the sun hit her face under the brim of her little hat. "Like I said. Not your fault."

"Still don't like you being in pain."

Her lips curved at that . . . and suddenly he needed to relieve a little bit of pressure, too. Inside his jeans.

"Why do you care if I'm in pain or not?"

He stroked his finger back and forth over her collarbone, keeping the strap lifted away from her tender shoulder, off of the lovely curve of her breast, which admittedly the dress did some justice to. "Maybe I'm just a humanitarian. I don't like seeing anyone in pain."

Her smile deepened. Even when she winced a little as it stretched her bottom lip, the smile remained.

"What?" he said. "I'm just another heartless contractor? Tearing down the old to build the new. A bit cliché, don't you think, Counselor?"

"Did I say anything?"

"Didn't have to. Your condescending grin said it all," he replied, but he was smiling too.

"Tell me about your farm," she said, surprising him. Her eyes were still closed, and a smile, though softer, smaller now, continued to curve her lips.

You're so damn beautiful, he thought, wanting her to open those stormy eyes of hers, to look at him. Into him. She could. Her natural beauty would not normally have been a plus in his book. In his very personal experience, looks like hers became all too centrally important to their owners. But her beauty went past the surface. *Hannah*. She was more like her name implied: no frills, essential, stripped of artifice. Which was ridiculous when you factored in how much fooffy lace she was sporting at the moment. And yet . . .

"What animals do you have?" Her voice was gentler now, more relaxed.

He continued to trace his fingertips over her bruised collarbone, then along her shoulder, back up along the side of her neck. Along the shell of her ear, prodding the netting of the hat aside as he did.

"Horses, mainly. A few pygmy goats."

Her wider smile returned. "There's a combination."

"Goats come in handy. They keep the pastures manageable. But you can't ride 'em. So . . ."

"What kind of horses?"

"Do you ride?"

She shook her head, just once to either side, as if she was too relaxed to do more than that. "Never had the opportunity. I like horses, though."

"I have four at the moment. Two quarter horses. A Morgan. And a Tennessee Walker."

"Just you?" she asked.

"I have barn help, but yes, all four are mine. Bought two at auction, got them off the block, saved the quarters when they were rescued from a neglected farm by the county."

Her smile deepened. This time she made a little noise when it tugged her lip, but that didn't hinder her smile. "You are a humanitarian."

"Well, I tried to tell you."

Still leaning back against the headrest, she turned her head, and opened her eyes, looking directly into his. "When is your dinner meeting?"

He felt . . . poleaxed. He was the one doing all the touching. So why was it he felt as if she'd just reached out and grabbed him? Hard. "Not until five," he said, finding his voice. "Why?"

"I was just thinking about something my sister said to me today."

"About what, not having enough fun?"

"About trying too hard to please other people. About not having balance. Not making fun part of the balance. She has a point. It shouldn't be a reward for good behavior. It should just . . . be."

He searched her eyes, but couldn't read her. Something was going on in there, likely something that had a lot to do with that uncertainty she'd spoken of when they'd run into each other earlier that morning. He wasn't sure that should matter. It was her issue. She was an adult, making her own choices.

"Good point. So . . . what do you want to do? For fun."

She held his gaze, then slowly straightened in her seat, trapping his fingertips under the seat belt as it was pulled taut once more. "I want to hijack you."

His eyes widened briefly. The exceedingly snug fit of his jeans, however, remained an abruptly increasing concern. "Don't you have a rehearsal to get to? A sister in dire need of white gravel?"

"We can drop the gravel off at Gus's. She'll understand the rest. It was her idea, after all."

"I'm thinking maybe I was too quick to judge your sister. We are talking about the same one?"

"Crazy chick in the wacked-out bridesmaid dress driving the Prius?" she said, settling in her seat now and putting her hands on the steering wheel. Looking like a woman on a mission. And her mission was him.

"You know, it wasn't that bad a bridesmaid dress," he said.

"It was horrid. Asylum horrid."

"Yeah. It was." He laughed, even as his body started to get rather indignant about getting itself upright and out of the potentially emasculating position it was currently in. "Still . . . I'm sure she had a good reason."

Hannah turned and pinned him again with that look. He'd have pled guilty to just about anything when she looked at him like that.

"Fun," she said. "That was her reason."

He slid his fingers free from the shoulder harness, then, when she shifted to look forward, he pressed them under her chin and turned her face to his. Very slowly, very deliberately, so she had time to back off if she didn't like where he was going, he lowered his mouth to hers.

"My lip," she whispered, at the last second, but her gaze was fixed firmly on his mouth by then.

"Shh," he said, and kissed the opposite corner of her mouth, then the soft, smooth edge of her bottom lip.

She let out a slow, soft, shaky breath.

So he kissed her chin, then the side of her jaw. Then ducked under the net of her hat and kissed, very, very gently, the soft, swollen skin at the edge of her cheekbone.

"Fun," he murmured, tugging briefly, gently, on her earlobe with his teeth. "I think your sister is on to something."

She sighed, and he liked—very much, maybe too damn much—the little shuddery sound that accompanied it. He wasn't sure he could even stand upright at the moment without doing serious damage to himself.

"Well," she asked, opening eyes that had drifted closed again at some point during his foray.

"Well what?"

"Get in."

"What?" He hadn't thought she meant it. Not really. It just didn't seem . . . her style. She'd just been toying, teasing. Playing with him, as he'd been doing with her.

She reached forward, turned on the engine, then gunned the gas pedal as she shifted it into gear and looked squarely at him. "Get in."

No frills, essential, stripped of artifice.

Yeah. This wasn't a woman who teased or toyed. This was a woman who attacked, pounced, and dismantled as part of her profession.

The same woman now trying to figure out how to be playful. With him.

She had an interesting way of going about it, to be sure,

but damned if he wasn't tempted. "I don't think so," he said, surprising himself more than he'd apparently surprised her.

She didn't look insulted, or even all that upset. It wasn't confidence or arrogance he saw, either . . . just respect for his choice. Apparently, for her, a no was just a no. Nothing personal.

Made him want to take her right there in the front seat of her little blue rocket in broad daylight. And wasn't that the damndest thing?

"Afraid I'll crash us into a moose or something?" she said.

No, he thought, *I'm afraid you're going to hurt something a lot less hard than my head.*

"I'd let you drive, but I borrowed this from a friend."

"It's not that."

"What then?"

He couldn't tell if she even cared what the answer was. She was still smiling, but her expression, her eyes, had shifted back to something less personal, less intimate. She was the cool, calm, collected litigator again. Never let 'em see you sweat.

For some reason, that irked him, though for the life of him he couldn't fathom why. He'd been the one to make the hijack offer in the first place, only to be turned down flat. Now they were even, though that wasn't why he'd said no. *Why did you say no? Afraid you might get tangled up? She clearly doesn't care one way or the other. Why do you?*

Irked with himself now, he straightened, swearing silently when his knees told him what they thought of being in a crouch for the past ten minutes, and swallowing a wince when another part of him complained about cramped quarters. He bent down, intending to brace his hands on the car door so as to block that particular body part from immediate view, only then she was tipping up her chin and it seemed the most natural thing in the world to slide his hand behind her neck and very carefully, very slowly, draw her mouth up to his as he lowered his head to hers.

She didn't pull away, didn't stop him. Didn't make that little shuddery sound, either. He kissed the corner of her mouth again, then again, then gently pressed his lips to the fullest part of her lower lip, before soothing it with his tongue. She shuddered then, just a little tremor, and he felt her shoulders relax as she turned her body toward his. As her eyes fluttered open, he slid his lips to her ear and whispered, "Because when we have fun together, Scarlett, we'll need more than the hour it will take me just to get you out of that dress."

Chapter Eight

Hannah slipped out the front door of the pub and let it swing quietly shut behind her. Not that anyone would have heard if she'd slammed the thing. Dear Lord, but her head was one giant throb. As were her face, her mouth, and her shoulder. She wanted nothing more than to crawl into her bed back at the Point and bury her head under a mound of pillows. Really soft, cool pillows. And maybe never crawl back out again.

At least she'd finally been able to get out of that awful dress and hat. She and Delia had pulled their co-maid-of-honor rank and defeated Fiona and Kerry on wearing those ridiculous getups a minute longer once the rehearsal was over. Privately—though Hannah would never admit it to Fi—it had been pretty hilarious as they'd rehearsed the actual walk down the aisle. All of them together looked like the cast of *One Flew Over the Cuckoo's Nest Gets Hitched*. In all honesty, the laughter and snide comments they'd shot back and forth had been the best sort of distraction, keeping her mind off of all those thoughts she'd worried she'd be having as she stood by and watched her brother and Alex go through their wedding motions.

She still had the actual wedding to get through, but right

now, it felt good to be wearing comfortable jeans, canvas boat shoes, and a thin, soft sweater. Better than good. Pulling them on had been like stepping into a familiar old shell. Hannah Before. Before the frantic need to climb the partnership ladder had consumed her every waking minute, before she'd begun to believe that was the only way to be a success, before she'd fallen for Tim, before . . . everything. She liked the feel of their softness, like a trusted caress against her skin. They were clothes she kept at the Point house, having no need for them otherwise. Back in D.C., even her comfortable clothes had been stuffy. She'd been stuffy.

When exactly had that happened to her? And why had she let it? Was she a stuffy person? Icy? Cold? Tim hadn't thought so, but then Tim was a lying, cheating bastard who'd say anything to get what he wanted. His opinion counted for less than nothing.

She took a sip from the bottle of ginger ale she'd been nursing for the past half hour, having decided early on that painkillers with a beer chaser, though tempting, probably weren't a good idea. She started to crouch down to sit on the pub steps, since she'd only come out seeking a much-needed break from the noise, but decided to go for a walk instead. It was a beautiful, late-spring night. Only a very light breeze was coming up off the water from the harbor below and the clear night sky was studded with grand, celestial sweeps of stars.

Once away from the pub lights, she paused and simply stared upward. She'd always been awed by the night sky here. As a child, she'd often wished she could soar up and out to them, through them, to the galaxies hinted at beyond. She smiled, thinking that didn't sound like such a bad idea now, either. "To infinity and beyond," she murmured, and lifted a ginger ale toast to the cosmos.

Smiling now, she continued on her walk, content with a lazy stroll. Back in D.C., she'd never strolled. At work it was run, run, run, too many things demanding her attention, never enough time. At home awaited another list of demands. Run to the market, run to the dry cleaners, run to this lunch appointment, that dinner meeting, the next social function. Hurry, hurry, don't be late! Someone else might beat you to the punch!

Now all she could think was . . . *what freaking punch?*

She crossed the road and started making her way down a steep side street that led to the waterfront in the pocket of the harbor and the Monaghan shipyard, and beyond that, Delia's Diner. Or where Delia's had been, she realized. She faltered a step, thinking maybe now was not the time to see yet another part of her life that had been filled with such love and fond memories gutted and leveled to the ground.

She took another sip, then tipped her head back and drew in a slow, restorative breath of cool evening air as the fizzy soda tickled its way down the back of her throat. The silence felt good. Even the chill in the air felt good. Her thoughts drifted to what else had felt good that day . . . namely Calder Blue. The way he'd touched her, stroked her skin. And that kiss . . .

She abruptly tipped her chin forward again and continued on her walk. However nice it might have been to have a little attention thrown her way from a good-looking man, she was smart enough to know she'd only let him because it had soothed her self-esteem, which Tim had left battered in his duplicitous wake. So, yes, a moment of weakness, an understandable one even. But not one she planned to repeat anytime soon.

Yes, it had felt good. Okay, better than good, if she was honest. It had been . . . *Jesus, it had been electric*. She took a steadying breath, another fortifying sip, put a more determined pace in her gait. Feeling . . . well, anything, right now, was probably unwise. She wasn't ready. She needed to be stronger, more distanced from what had happened, more settled on her new path, before including anything like that—or anyone like that—in her life. At the moment, what she needed was to stay comfortably numb a little longer.

She shoved thoughts of men, past and present, from her mind, and smiled as the music from the Rusty Puffin echoed after her down the hill. She always loved it when Fergus got out his fiddle, and tonight he'd rustled up a few local musicians to join in for a full-blown, traditional Irish *ceilidh*. She'd enjoyed watching everyone dance, had even taken a step or two herself. She smiled, picturing Kerry trying to teach them some Maori tribal dance, but in the manner of Irish step dancing, which . . . God, only Kerry. Hannah would have stayed longer, stayed forever in that cocoon of love and family, but her head had had enough. Logan and Alex would understand. Fiona had already asked her a half dozen times if she wanted to go on back home again to get some rest.

Home.

Hannah paused at the bottom of the hill to look out over the harbor. Yeah, what home meant to her now was . . . complicated. So she let her thoughts shift instead to how it felt to be back in the Cove. For good. To how it felt to not have any cases pending. At all. Of course, she worried about the ones she'd handed over when she'd tendered her resignation, worried they wouldn't be handled the way she would have handled them. She'd spent significant time with the new counsel for each case, made sure each had her contact information if clarification or assistance was needed. Her last day had been ten days ago now, and she'd been on the phone a dozen or more times, answered an avalanche of e-mails on various notes and proceedings, but it otherwise hadn't been as bad as she'd thought it would be.

When she'd walked out the door that last day, she'd had this feeling that she'd never be able to truly leave that part of her life behind, that it would dog her, as had all the rumor and innuendo, forever. She'd been so deep in it, her every waking moment so consumed by it, she honestly couldn't imagine it ever being truly over.

And yet . . . standing here, tasting the salt in the air, and feeling the utter calm that surrounded her . . . she realized that it just truly might. She laughed at herself as she began walking along the harbor road. And how pathetic was she? All she'd wanted was to escape, to put all the ugliness and hurt and pain behind her, and if that meant leaving her thriving career behind too, then so be it. The one had become inextricably linked to the other anyway, so she couldn't even lose herself in her work to drown out her personal pain. Not when her personal pain had marched its pregnant self right into her office and announced its presence to God and the world. Her world. Her former world.

And now she was feeling, what . . . miffed? A little insulted that the legal whirl on Capitol Hill hadn't come to a crashing halt because she'd decided to exit it, stage left? Okay, maybe she was. A little.

The caseload that had defined her life for more days, weeks, months, and years than she could remember was gone. Poof. No problem. Hand the files over and walk away. Don't let the office door hit ya on the way out. Easy come, easy go. See ya later, bye. *That's what you wanted, remember?*

So what if it seemed that both Tim and the profession she'd dedicated her life to could let her go. So easily, and so swiftly. Easily forgotten, easily replaced.

If only it could be that way for her.

Now her biggest problem was figuring out how to never be either of those things again.

She paused at the shipyard, looking up at the dark, shadowed spires that were the four tall ship masts, soaring so improbably high up into the night sky. Incredible. She made a note to ask Logan when the launch date would be. She wanted to see it being rolled out into the harbor, as the Cove's ancestors had done so many times in centuries past.

Her thoughts drifted to the other changes coming to Half Moon Harbor. The yacht club. For God's sake, who had let that plan get through? Without her wanting it to be, her gaze was pulled past the shipyard, to where Delia's Diner would have been standing, and she felt a gut-deep pang to see the spot was nothing more than a flat lot, graded over, parking lot, deck and all. The docks that went along with the property were still there of course, but otherwise it was just a gaping hole, waiting to be filled.

She understood how that felt.

She let the memories roll in, almost defiantly now, all the times she'd spent at Delia's, how much a part of her life it had been, and O'Reilly's—Delia's grandmother's restaurant—too. Birthdays, graduation dinners. Older kids going to prom. O'Reilly's had been gone before Hannah had reached prom age, but she remembered family dinners as a young girl, watching the teenagers coming in, boys all awkward in their tuxedos, girls in their fancy dresses, hair pinned up, corsages on wrists and boutonnieres pinned crookedly to lapels. It had all seemed so romantic to her.

Hannah forced her thoughts away from what she thought about romance these days, and thought instead of Delia as she'd been that afternoon, in the awesomely appalling bridesmaid dress she'd worn to the rehearsal. The gothic, almost funereal, punk-style getup—complete with studded collar and chainmail chastity belt—had made Hannah feel positively stunning by comparison. Delia was about ten years her senior, but they'd been like family for all of Hannah's life, which was probably how Delia felt about pretty much everyone in the Cove. They certainly felt that way about her. Delia and Alex had become good friends, hence the co-maid-of-honor designation. Alex's way of honoring both her ties to the Cove and Logan's family, which Hannah thought had been beyond kind and thoughtful, given they hadn't even met yet.

Her phone chirped, startling her. She juggled her bottle of ginger ale and dug the phone out of her jeans pocket, not bothering to look at the screen before answering it. It would be Fiona. "Hi, I'm okay. I just decided to get some—"

"Glad to hear it," came an unfamiliar male voice. "Do I have the right number? Is this Hannah McCrae?"

Her mind wiped clean of all thought by the sudden shift, she took a beat to switch gears. She glanced at the phone, but the number was unknown to her. Putting it back to her ear, she said, "I'm afraid you have me at a disadvantage. Who is this?"

"Mike Garrison. Over at Thompson, Craft and Banks. Got a minute? I have a proposition for you."

The knowing note he'd injected into that last part had her hackles rising. "I'm afraid I don't, Mr. Garrison. It's quite late, and I'm not—"

"From what I understand, late nights aren't a problem for you."

So. Apparently her past wasn't done with her quite yet. *Yippee*. She lowered the phone, too tired to be pissed off, too numb to care, her thumb on the END button, then stopped and put it next to her ear again. "I sincerely doubt you understand much of anything. You'll have to take your proposition elsewhere." *Preferably up your ass.* "I'm not with Holcombe and Daggett any longer."

"Don't be so quick to judge. I know you left them—that's why I'm calling."

"The only one guilty of snap judgments, Mr. Garrison, would be you. Whatever you thought to propose, I'm not interested. Good night."

"Wait! Listen, maybe that wasn't the right approach, okay?" He chuckled. "I should have known you'd want a little more foreplay. My bad. I just wanted to say that H and D is a stuffy firm and I don't blame you for walking. But not all firms are like that one. Some of us have a more . . . open-minded view of the workplace. I think there might be a place here for you. I'd love to meet you for drinks. Feel you out." He chuckled again, and it made her skin crawl.

"Thank you once more for the incredibly insulting and demeaning invitation, Mr. Garrison. You're right, I don't belong at Holcombe and Daggett. And given your description, I can say with equal certainty that I also don't belong at Thompson, Craft and Banks. It does sound, however, as if you've found exactly the right spot. Best of luck with that."

"Stone-cold, straight-up bitch," he said before she could click off, and worse, he made it sound surprisingly complimentary, then actually chuckled again. "Heard that about you, too. Like to make a man work for it, huh? Well, I like a challenge. Given your taste for the forbidden fruit, though, I hope it won't put you off when I tell you I'm single. But I can promise you—"

She found the END button then and clicked off, barely resisting the urge to turn and fling the phone as far out into the harbor as she could, as if by doing so, she could fling Mike Garrison, and everyone just like him, out to sea with it. She would have hung up sooner, should have, but once he'd started in, she'd just gone still, shut down. Now she stood there, trembling in disgust, in anger, and yes, in hurt and humiliation, and—*dammit*—feeling the chill of the harbor breeze suddenly straight through to the bone. Deeper, if that were possible.

"Hey."

She let out a short shriek and her phone did fly up in the air as she whirled around at the sound of the deep masculine voice coming from just behind her.

Calder Blue lifted a hand and snagged the phone from the air mid-descent as easily as an outfielder shagging a pop fly. He handed it back to her. "Sorry. I was trying not to startle you."

"Epic fail." Heart pounding now in addition to her head, Hannah tried to steady herself—again—but she was simply wrung out. In every possible way a person could be. She took the phone from his outstretched hand. "Thank you."

She had nothing left, and certainly wasn't up for yet another encounter with Mr. Tall, Dark, and Everywhere. Now more than ever, all she wanted to be was alone. She moved around him and started walking back toward the shipyard. Now she did want to go home, only she wondered if she'd feel safe anywhere. She felt . . . betrayed, that the ugliness of her past had reached out and so easily invaded—poisoned—her one haven. Her one safe place.

Maybe she wouldn't be able to leave the past behind after all. Maybe it would haunt her forever. But dammit, if she was going to be remembered for something, needed for something, what the hell did it say about her that propositions like Garrison's were going to be the legacy she'd be leaving behind?

"Scarlett—"

She stopped, whirled around to find him a few feet behind her. "Don't. Just . . . don't."

In response, he slid off the jacket he was wearing and handed it to her. When she didn't reach for it, he said, "You're shivering."

She realized then she was clutching her elbows, arms folded across her middle. She could have told him the shaking was caused by something much deeper, and far colder, than a simple harbor breeze, but she didn't have the energy. "I'm good. Just heading back to the pub. Good evening, Mr. Blue." She turned and continued walking.

"You're not, you know."

She dipped her chin, sighed, then swore under her breath. *Keep walking.* She did, but she also spoke. *Dammit. What was it about this guy?* "Not what, heading to the pub? I assure you I am. It was a mistake to leave. Or did you mean I'm not cold? Is that some kind of mind-over-matter suggestion?"

When he next spoke, he was once again just behind her, at her elbow. "No, I know you're cold. You're not a stone-cold bitch, though. Who was that asshole, anyway?"

It was surprising she didn't trip and stumble, that somehow, for once around this man, she remained upright. He walked casually enough, spoke even more casually, as if they strolled together often, chatted together often. She didn't look at him, kept her focus forward, but couldn't seem to keep her mouth shut around him. "How on earth would you know that?"

"That he's an asshole? It's a quiet night, you held the phone away from your ear. Voices carried. I wasn't trying to eavesdrop, but it was hard not to hear."

"What *were* you trying to do? I know Blueberry Cove is a small town, but even as small towns go, our paths have crossed an inordinate number of times in the past twenty-four hours."

She wasn't looking at him, but she could hear the smile in his voice when he said, "My meeting was postponed.

Again. So, since I was here, I was walking the harbor, trying to get a sense of what Winstock sees in his mind's eye, what his future plans are, how he might go about implementing them."

"It's close to midnight. Wouldn't it make more sense to do that in the daylight hours?"

"Lots of people out during the day, followed by lots more speculation if they spied me wandering about."

"Pretty self-important, assuming everyone knows who you are."

He chuckled, apparently not stung by her waspish tone. "I live in a small town, too. Given my surname, and who brought me here, it seems naïve to think folks don't know who I am. And I'm not naïve."

She thought about the smooth, easy—far too easy—way he'd slid in and round and past all her carefully constructed defenses earlier that day. She'd wasted thirty whole minutes after driving away from him the last time, convincing herself it was the combination of the accident, the exhaustion, the pain, and the wedding craziness, not the least of which was the getup she'd had on, that had caused her to lose her mind for five seconds and beg him to run off with her. To do what, exactly, she'd had no idea, then, or now. But he'd made it clear he had a few ideas of what they could have been doing. *No, he definitely isn't naïve.*

She shivered from the memory of his touch, his taste . . . his kiss. Even a half kiss from him had been enough to knock the sense right out of her. If a kiss to the corner of her mouth and a light stroke along her collarbone could turn her into a puddle of needy—

His coat landed on her shoulders, jerking her thoughts mercifully away from that dangerous path. She didn't bother shrugging it off and flinging it at him. Her little rant on the phone had zapped whatever defiant posturing she had left straight out of her. Instead, she pulled it closed in front of her, and tried not to breathe in the smell of him. Tried to make herself believe she hadn't thought about that very scent well past the time she'd convinced herself that the whole scene in front of Hartley's had just been an unfortunately timed chance meeting. Sort of like smashing into Beanie's sign. Only less painful. Maybe.

"So you graciously spared the town more needless gossip," she said, struggling to pick up the thread of the conversation . . . and ignore his scent, which was literally wrapped around her. "A Good Samaritan and a thoughtful humanitarian."

"But humble. Don't forget humble." The humor was still there in his deep voice. "I figured this town has had enough gossip where the St. Croix River Blues are concerned, so why contribute more where I don't have to?"

Hannah was surprised to hear the laugh—her laugh—as she said, "First of all, if you wanted to spare us that, you should have stayed back on your farm. Not that it would matter. This town thrives on speculation. It will never have enough. If not about you, then it would be about something else. And if you think for one second that no one knows you're skulking around down here after dark, well . . . you don't know small towns as well as you think you do."

"I don't skulk. And the only person I've seen is you."

"Doesn't mean I'm the only person who has seen you."

He dipped his chin for a moment, smiling. "Point to you, Counselor."

She shouldn't smile at that, either. In fact, she shouldn't be doing anything with him. And yet, she seemed to be doing something with him with alarming regularity. "Why do you care what Winstock's future plans are? You said this was just a job."

"It is a job. But the job is not the only reason I'm here.

Well, that's not entirely true. I wouldn't have come except for this job offer, but it wasn't the job itself, but the offer, that drew me here."

"That hard up for work in Calais?"

"That hard up to find a way to mend my family."

She did slow her steps then, and she did, finally, look at him. There were no streetlights on the harbor road, but there were lights dotting the larger piers that stretched out into the water, and they provided enough ambient glow for her to see his face. "Do you think it can be? After all this time?"

"Has anyone ever tried?"

She opened her mouth, then closed it again, thinking. Finally, she said, "I don't know. Not that I'm aware of. At least, no one from your side has actually shown up here. I'd know that. I can't say if anyone from here has tried to come to your neck of the woods."

"How would you know? You don't live here."

"Everyone would know that. Owen would have told you. He'd definitely have known. Besides, once a part of the Cove, always a part of the Cove."

"You're about as much a part of the Cove as one could be, from what I understand. Descendant of the founding family."

"One of them. But that wouldn't matter in this instance. Blueberry has a way of claiming you, of making you part of it, no matter how you got here or at what point in your life you show up. In return, the Cove has a way of holding on to its own, whether born here, or adopted. I think that's part of the larger concern, about the new development on the harbor."

"Meaning what, exactly?"

"This isn't a transient community. People don't just come and go from here. We're not a tourist destination. We're a village, a tightly knit one that has survived a lengthy and somewhat colorful history by sticking together, making us a self-supporting community, in every sense of the word. If you come here, it's not to visit or to see the sights, it's for a purpose, and if that purpose has merit and you respect those who are already established here, then our arms are open, and you won't find better allies to your cause."

"And if the purpose is deemed without merit? Or worse?"

She looked directly at him now. "Then we close ranks. And you don't stand a chance."

"Another point to the counselor," he said, a wry smile on his handsome face. "So . . . what do you do when the problem is within the ranks of the already established? Generations of established? Employs a good percentage of the other established folks of the town?"

She turned her attention back to the road. "All towns, all places, go through internal conflict. It would be a highly unusual place if it didn't." They walked on in silence a few moments, and then she said, "In this case, it's not a matter of whether the club is coming. Winstock has the property and from what I understand, all the proper paperwork in order to see it through."

"You checked on that, did you? I thought it wasn't any of your concern?"

"I live here. Of course it's my concern. And I didn't have to check on it. All I had to do was spend five minutes with my brother, and any one of my neighbors, to be brought pretty thoroughly up to speed."

"I see," he said, sounding thoughtful.

She shot him a sideways glance, but didn't ask him to clarify. "My point is, the tall ship is here, the lighthouse has been renovated. Those are done deals. Now the yacht club will happen, and, all combined, it will make us something of a destination for outsiders. Not just the new club members, either, but businesses who will want to cater to the needs of folks with that kind of money. Those being very different needs from most of the folks who live here. The question before us now isn't should we or shouldn't we. The question now is what we're going to do about what's definitely coming. The conflict is coming from different people having different ideas on how they want to handle that new reality."

"Owen said much the same thing. Change is always happening. If it isn't, then things wither and die, either from neglect or lack of energy pushing it forward. So, Hannah McCrae of the founding McCraes and defender of justice . . . how do you want to see this newest change handled?"

She lifted a shoulder, stifled a wince when she belatedly realized it was her bad one. The pain meds were wearing off. A moment later, his broad palm, warm and gentle, pressed to her lower back, then slid up to her neck. She started to shrug him off, but he stepped behind her, and gently slid his thumb under her hair, and up the back of her scalp.

"Just accept some help, okay?"

"I've been accepting your help all day. I can't seem to get away from accepting your help," she said, only the words didn't come out as sharply as she'd intended, because his hands were on her. Again. His breath was warm on the nape of her neck as he moved her hair aside. His body was big and broad, and blocked the breeze coming off the water, making her feel warmer, protected.

But who's going to protect me from him? She started to step to the side and move away, but he brought his other hand up and pressed both thumbs gently against spots on either side of her spinal column, right at the base of her skull. She groaned as the tension in her neck and shoulder released, and the pain abated. "Calder—"

"Shh. Just let me." He moved his fingers to another spot, this time lower on her neck, and pressed again.

She might have groaned again. Just a little. The relief made her want to weep. She was just so tired of hurting. Her head . . . her heart.

Then he moved his hands up under her hair, massaging fingertips against her scalp, letting her hair cascade over the backs of his hands and run through his fingers, creating that delicious tingling feeling you get when someone plays with your hair. She should move away. And she would have. But then he very gently massaged her temples, and it felt too good—so damn good—she decided she might be persuaded to let him work his magic. For another minute. Or two. He wasn't seducing her, after all. He was just . . . helping.

She might have possibly been leaning a little back against him when he lifted his hands. She all but had to swallow her tongue to stifle the moan of disappointment that rose in her throat. But then he was moving her hair aside again, and he leaned down so she could feel his warm breath on her neck.

He'd tasted sweet when he'd kissed her, a little spicy, and she shouldn't be remembering that, thinking about that. Only instead of pressing his fingers to those delicious, tension-relieving spots, he pressed his lips to the curve of her neck. *Now what's that if not seduction?*

Any other time, she'd have jerked away, made it clear that he couldn't just . . . invade her personal space. So casually, so confidently. She wasn't easy, she wasn't . . . what they said she was. Far from. *You're a stone-cold bitch.*

Only she wasn't that either. She was just a woman who'd fallen in love with the wrong man. A woman who'd had her heart shattered into a million pieces and handed back to her on a platter of public humiliation. She wasn't ready for kisses, confident, casual, or otherwise. Not even if they felt like . . . *oh, they felt so good*.

His lips were warm, firm, and tender all at the same time. He smelled good, he felt good. She wanted to sink in, to drown, to let everything fall away and simply float along on the lovely tingling sensations he was eliciting from her body. She was teetering, so close to that edge . . . then he pressed a kiss just below her ear, and her hair was swinging back into place, his jacket once again nudged up onto her shoulders. She didn't—couldn't—resume her casual stroll. She wasn't sure her legs would function properly. She felt . . . wobbly. And not just in the knees.

"Is, ah—" She had to pause, clear the hoarseness from her throat. "Is that what they teach you in humanitarian school?"

"Acupressure school, actually," he said. "I learned it to help the horses. They weren't in great shape."

She melted, there was no help for it. She turned to face him. "Seriously, stop it."

"You have something against using acupressure on livestock?"

No. I have something against you being wonderful, against the things you're making me feel. She turned away again, thinking she needed to simply walk back to the pub, snag the first set of keys she could find, drive out to the Point, and not leave again until Calder Blue had left Blueberry Cove and headed back home to his river and his farm. She had so much to figure out. She needed a clear head for that. Phone calls from jerks like Garrison made it hard enough, but Calder . . . he made clear thinking close to impossible. *Okay, all the way impossible.*

"No," she managed finally. "Of course not. It sounds

like those horses won the lottery jackpot." *Time to go home, Hannah. Wherever the hell that's going to be.* She slid his jacket off her shoulders and turned to hand it back to him. "Thank you. For . . . everything. Good luck with your meeting. I need to get back to my family."

To his credit, he seemed to know when it was time to stop pushing. He didn't follow her. In fact, she made it halfway up the steep road leading back to the Rusty Puffin before he called out, "Miz Scarlett?"

She shouldn't have smiled. She shouldn't have had even that brief moment of thinking, *Yes!* She shouldn't have. But she did. She turned. "Yes, Mr. Blue?" she replied, a bit of Southern accent sliding into the words to match his. *So unwise.*

"You ever have a hankering to ride a horse?"

"I try not to hanker, Mr. Blue." *Liar. You're hankering something fierce at the moment.* "I'm learning life is simpler that way." *Or will be. Just as soon as you cut that out.*

"I'm talking about the kind that come with four shoes and a saddle, not a gas pedal and a stick shift," he added, as if she hadn't said anything. "In case there was some confusion on that point." She could see his grin flash, even in the dim glow of the pier lights.

"I'm afraid I'm quite busy with a wedding at the moment. And don't you have a little yacht club or something you need to build?"

"Wedding will be over in a few days. Ground won't be broken on the club until Winstock and I haggle out the details."

"I wasn't aware there was haggling yet to be done."

"Until there are signatures on the dotted line, there's always haggling to be done."

"Hope you have a good attorney then."

He walked up the hill toward her, his long legs eating up

the distance more quickly than his casual stride made it seem possible. He stopped in front of her. "Don't think I need one." He smiled. "But in case I do . . . know any good ones?"

"Contract law isn't my forte."

"Right. You take down the bad guys."

"I make sure my clients get as fair a deal as possible."

His expression shifted to one of surprise. "You represent the bad guys?"

"I represent folks who pay my law firm to secure the best legal representation they can get. In my line of work, it's not about guilt or innocence. It's about achieving justice as defined by the letter of the law. You try and screw over one of my clients, I will do everything in my power to yank the screw free, and find a nice tender spot in which to return it."

He let out a low whistle, but otherwise said nothing.

She smiled, but felt the chill return. The internal one. "Rethinking your opinion on how cold my stones are?"

He let out a bark of laughter at that. "No. In the courtroom, I have no doubt you could strike fear into the slimiest of corporate snakes." He surprised her and stepped in, not aggressively, but as smoothly and easily, as if deep in her personal space was the most natural spot in the world for him. He didn't touch her, he just moved his body close enough that she had to tip up her chin to see his eyes. It was as intimate a position as two people could be in without actually touching. She couldn't help it; she liked how his superior height and breadth of frame—well, those shoulders anyway—made her feel sheltered. And not just from the harbor breeze. *Don't romanticize him. Or this. Any of this. He parried, and you thrusted. Now it's time to end this little flirtship. Go home, Hannah.*

"Outside the courtroom," he said, "I'm betting that's another story."

The comment wasn't delivered in the way sleazy Garrison had said it. Calder didn't even know about that, about what had happened. Still, her thoughts went there, and she stiffened, she couldn't help it. It was an ingrained response by now. She stepped back, but he took her elbow—gently, but with intent.

"Hey. I'm sorry. I—that sounded—" He stopped, swore under his breath. "I was going to say I'm not an asshole like that jerk on the phone. But that's exactly what it sounded like to you, I'm sure."

"I don't know how else I could have taken it." She didn't say it stiffly, but there was distance now. And a coolness in her tone. She couldn't help that either. Her self-defense mechanisms had taken some time to kick in back in D.C., but once they had, she shored them up as fast as she could. It didn't make it hurt any less, but it did help ensure nothing could hurt her anymore. Nothing. And no one.

"When I said that, I wasn't thinking about the way you tasted, or the look in your eyes when I kissed you," he said, and her gaze flew back to his, but there wasn't anything aggressive or even suggestive in his gaze. It was simply direct, open. Honest.

Like you'd know an honest man if you tripped over one.

"I was thinking about how you defended your sister, the honest love you have for her, even though she clearly drives you crazy. I was thinking about the clear affection in your eyes when I mentioned Owen Hartley's comments about you. And just now, the way you came to the defense of your hometown, your neighbors, their way of life. What used to be your way of life." He lifted a hand, caught a wayward strand of hair the breeze had kicked up, tucked it behind her ear, barely brushing his fingertips over the sensitive curve.

Her body wanted to get all wobbly again, wanted to lean toward him, but he'd already dropped his hand away.

"That's what I meant. You might be aggressive and all powerful when you're on the clock, fighting for your clients. But to do that, you have to have passion, and not just for the job, or justice. You have to care about . . . something. Deeply."

She looked at him, studied him, but she'd be damned if she could read him. "You don't know me."

"Am I wrong? About any of that?"

She paused, then said, "So what, did they also teach you people-whisperer skills in humanitarian school?"

He grinned at that. It was slow and wide, and made him even more attractive, but there was nothing overtly seductive about it, or even flirtatious. She knew that much; she'd seen that look from him, too. It was . . . potent. Turned out so was this one. It was . . . friendly. Honest. Like a man enjoying a good conversation with someone he liked. *Someone whose pants he wants to get into.*

She wanted to shove that thought aside, reject it out of hand. It seemed wrong. Unfair. *Don't blame all men for the sins of one*, she reminded herself. Only . . . that didn't mean that only one man was capable of committing that particular sin. In her work, she'd learned to listen to her gut, trust her instincts. Tim had taken that ability away from her, too, shattered it. It was, she'd realized, the cruelest twist of all. Losing faith in herself.

He tapped a fingertip to her temple, gently, then ran it softly along her cheekbone. "So much going on in there," he murmured. "Do you ever take a break?"

She felt wobbly again. She needed to go home. She needed to get away from him. Far, far away from him. Because this, him, all of it . . . felt good. Easy. Helpful. Nice. She couldn't afford to accept any of those things from him. *Stick with what you know, and who you know. That's the only way you'll relearn the ability to trust in yourself again.*

"That's why I'm here," she said, finally looking away, moving back a step.

He smiled. "And how's that working out for you so far?"

What was it about him that made it impossible for her to get a decent mad on and hang on to it for more than ten seconds? "Can I get back to you on that?"

He chuckled. "Sure."

She held his gaze a moment longer, then gave him a brief nod. "Good night, Mr. Blue."

"Night, Miz Scarlett."

She turned then, but he didn't let her get even five feet this time.

"Hannah."

He'd said it quietly, all teasing gone from his voice.

And because she apparently couldn't stop herself from responding to him, she turned. She'd intended to simply look at him, but, just as quietly, she said, "Calder."

His eyes did flare, just for a brief second, but it made something flare inside of her. He was the one to look away then, a brief glance down the hill, toward the harbor, out across the water. She didn't know what he was seeing in his mind's eye, but she doubted he was seeing anything in that harbor.

"How long are you here?" he asked quietly. "And— don't evade, just . . . how long?"

"What does it matter?" she replied, not defensively, simply asking.

"I—" He broke off, let out a self-deprecating laugh and looked skyward as he shook his head. "I have no idea." He shifted his gaze back to hers, his own eyes intent, searching hers. For what, she didn't know. "It just does."

Then she was searching his gaze, wishing she didn't understand, wishing his interest in her was the complete mystery it should be. But it wasn't, because she felt drawn to him in that exact same, nonsensical, why-can't-I-just-walk-away-I've-got-too-many-things-going-on-and-you're-a-complete-stranger kind of way.

"Calder, I—" But she never got the chance to finish the sentence, because at that exact moment, a small boathouse at the end of one of Blue's smaller piers exploded into a ball of flames.

Chapter Nine

Calder whipped his head around in the exact same instant he instinctively pulled Hannah into his arms and shielded her with his body. "What the—"

She squirmed in his arms. "Calder, let go. I need to—"

He set her away from him. "You okay? Call nine-one-one, or you probably know the entire fire crew by name. Get them here. Then stay here. I'll be back."

She'd already been trying to dig her phone out of her jeans pocket. "I'm on it, but—"

He leaned in, eyes right on hers, and kissed her, banged-up lip and all. "Stay here. Please." Then he turned and took off at a run toward the docks.

"Calder!" she shouted after him. "What are you—don't go down there! You don't know what else might—"

He looked over his shoulder just long enough to make sure she wasn't running after him, saw that she had the phone to her ear and was talking into it, presumably to the dispatcher, and let out a sigh of relief.

Then he turned back and focused on the burning boathouse, which looked like nothing more than a Norse effigy at this point, as parts of it sank into the still, dark waters of the harbor. *Please let everyone be safe.* It was past midnight now, so hopefully the boathouse had been empty. Things could be replaced. People could not. Family could not.

He heard the wail of sirens just as his work boots hit the main pier. It was a maze getting out to the smaller piers, but the blaze lighting up the night sky illuminated everything in a wash of flickering gold. "Jonah!" he shouted as he closed in on the main boathouse, the one Jonah had walked back to after their conversation. "Fire!" he shouted. "Jonah!" He banged a flat palm on the heavy wood panel door that closed off the end of the boathouse. He had no idea if the old man lived out here or if it was just the business part of the operation, but he couldn't take any chances. The explosion should have woken up anyone within a mile of the place, but—his thoughts broke off when a light came blazing on in the upper level of the boathouse. *Thank God.*

He turned back to look at the fire, which was still five or six short connecting pier lengths away, and as far out into the harbor as any of the piers went. He had no idea what might have set it off—could be any number of things, fuel tank, faulty wiring, anything. But his gut told him that it was no accident. He hoped like hell his gut was wrong.

There was a metal clanging sound on the other side of the wide panel door, then a loud groan and screech as the heavy wood door was dragged open along the metal tracks it was connected to overhead. "What in the name of God Almighty—" Jonah's gruff voice, made even more gravelly by sleep, broke off as he looked past Calder's shoulder. "No." He said it like a command. As if he could simply order the fire not to be happening. "Goddammit!"

That's more like it. "Emergency vehicles are already—"

"I can hear that," he barked. "I'm not deaf."

Calder didn't point out that he clearly hadn't heard the explosion, which had to have rocked the pier they were presently standing on. "Was there anyone down there?"

"What?" Jonah's gaze was fixed on the fire; then he spared a brief glance at Calder. "No. Tools and supplies." He looked back out to the burning boathouse and Calder saw a bleak expression enter his eyes.

Not a small amount of tools and supplies, he gathered.

Catching Calder's gaze, his expression went hard. He drew himself up to his full height, which, even in an old white T-shirt and frayed pajama bottoms, was impressively imposing. "Thought I told you to stay off this property."

"Fine," Calder barked right back at him. "Next time I'll let your ornery ass hide burn along with your precious property."

"Grandpa?"

Both men went momentarily still, then Calder looked down to find a tiny wisp of a thing clutching at Jonah's meaty paw. She couldn't be more than five, Calder guessed. Soft, dark curls tousled around the face of a pouty, sleepy angel.

"It's all right, Little Bit," Jonah told her, his voice as gruff as always, but with a thread of love running through it. "You go on back to bed now."

"Pawpaw, look," she said, her eyes growing wider as she came more awake. She pointed past him, at the glow of the fire.

The boathouse was a skeleton now, the roof gone and the vertical boards that had comprised the walls nothing more than a row of burning spears, like a black spiked fence, holding the fire within them. One by one, they were collapsing and falling in on themselves.

There was a thundering sound and all three of them turned as a team of five firemen came pounding down the pier in a regimented run, pulling hoses behind them. At the same instant, there came a horn blast from out in the harbor, and as the whine of the sirens died down, Calder heard the loud thrumming engine of what proved to be a Coast Guard vessel. They were spraying the surface of the water while the fire crews put out what was left of the blaze.

"Keeping the fire from picking up on any fuel in the water from the boat engines," Jonah said, apparently seeing the questioning look on Calder's face as he watched the Coast Guard crew.

"Holy sh—" He broke off, looked down at the little girl. He'd been thinking that the entire pier the boathouse had been connected to might have gone up and had envisioned the fire racing through the piers like a giant domino board set into motion. It hadn't occurred to him that it could literally light the harbor itself on fire.

He looked back at Jonah. "I'll go talk to them."

Jonah looked at him as if he'd lost his mind. "Like hell you will."

Calder dipped a chin toward his great-granddaughter. "Is there anyone else here to look after her?"

Jonah looked down at her and Calder saw his expression tighten. It wasn't anger directed at the little girl for being an imposition. He was pretty sure it was anger that she could have been hurt, or worse. Anger possibly directed at himself, since it had taken Calder to wake him up to the situation.

"I can watch her," Calder offered. "I have nieces her age," he added, thinking how it had affected him to see Jonah as more than the stubborn family figurehead, to see him as Pawpaw. Maybe if Jonah knew he came from a real, whole family, too, he'd see Calder in a new light. "I'm a stranger, though, so . . ." He looked back at the boathouse, now reduced mostly to embers. "Let me go let them know you're all right. I'll send whoever is in charge directly here to you."

Jonah looked lost again as he stared at the smoke and embers, then shook it off and glared at Calder. "I'll thank you to get off my property," he said shortly, and so coldly, Calder felt his hackles rise. Jonah might have just suffered a shock and what appeared to be no small setback to his business, but he seemed well in command of his thoughts now.

"Do we really need to—"

"Leave now, or I'll have you arrested for trespassing. I expect you'll be getting a visit from one of our boys in blue regardless. So don't leave town." He didn't wait for a response, but hiked his great-granddaughter up into his arms so she straddled his hip. "Come on inside now," he said to her, gentling his tone slightly. "We've got to make a few calls."

A moment later, the boathouse door was shoved closed again with a resounding clang, right in Calder's face.

"What the hell does that mean?" he asked, then propped one hand on his hip and scrubbed the back of his neck with the other. Not that it did any good. He had a sick feeling that while the fire had been put out, the repercussions of the blaze had just begun. And somehow he'd just landed himself square in the middle of it.

"Calder!"

He turned to find Hannah running down the pier toward him. "Hannah, you shouldn't—"

"Is everyone okay? Jonah? Bett?"

He reached out and caught her by the elbows as she all but skidded to a stop in front of him. "They're safe, they're fine."

"Oh, thank God. Did you talk to Jonah? What did he say? Was it some kind of fuel leak or something?"

Calder took a moment to look past her at the crews working on cleanup now that the fire was out. The Coast Guard boat had also ceased its operations and was chugging back to its pier, which was just around the harbor on the other side of Blue's, alongside the piers where the harbor tugboats were docked. He'd noticed them on his first drive through town and recalled thinking how smart it was to have them all in a central location together.

"I—uh, I don't know," he said, pulling his thoughts back to Hannah. "I haven't been over to talk to the firemen. I came straight to the main boathouse."

"I should go find Jonah. Logan is down here somewhere, too. I called Fi right after I dialed nine-one-one and she said he was being radioed about it as we were talking."

"Maybe you should go back up to the pub, with your family. Tell them no one was hurt. I'm sure your brother will have the full report as soon as they know what actually happened."

She finally turned her own distracted gaze away from the activity on the far pier, and looked back at him. "What aren't you telling me? Where's Jonah? Is he over there? Who's watching Bett?"

He cocked one eyebrow at that. "Why do you think I'm

not telling you everything? I don't know anything else. Jonah is inside." He nodded toward the boathouse behind him. "With his great-granddaughter. He said he had some calls to make. Possibly to get someone to watch her so he can go handle the fallout. I offered to—"

"You did?"

That same eyebrow went from cocked to arched. "Yes. I have two nieces about her age. Two more a few years younger. They happen to like me a lot. I'm great with kids."

"What aren't you great with?" she said under her breath, but he caught it just the same.

"What's wrong?" She started to pull out of his grasp, her attention once again on the far pier, but he tugged her back to face him. "What aren't you telling me?" he asked, flipping her question back at her.

She sighed impatiently. "Something else is going on here and if you're not going to tell me, I'll go find out myself. I know you think I'm fragile from the accident and—I don't know what else. But I'm not. I've handled cases that would make your blood run cold. I can handle a simple dock fire."

He held on again when she tried to shrug free, but before she could light into him with the full force of her litigator's awesome fury, he said, "That's just it. I don't think it was a simple dock fire. And neither does Jonah."

She stopped pulling at his hands. "What? Why?"

He started to explain, then thought better of it. "Not here."

"Why?" She didn't fall into step beside him, forcing him to stop or he'd be dragging her along.

"Let's get off Jonah's pier. I think you should hear what I have to say. So you can decide."

"Decide what?" she asked.

"If you'd be willing to represent me. I'm pretty sure Jonah's in there right now, talking to God knows who, claiming this was an act of arson—which I think is right. Only I'm pretty sure he's also painting me as the number-one suspect."

Chapter Ten

"Of course we're having a bachelorette party," Kerry assured Fiona. "Why else would we get here four days before the main event?"

"Because some of us are putting together the entire event, which we can't just whip out of our collective asses. It takes time, patience, and planning to create a memorable moment."

"Hang some streamers, bake a cake, and throw some rice," Kerry said. "The people make it memorable, not the color of the pebbles in the centerpiece. And what the hell are those anyway?"

"Terrariums. With little miniature tableaus set amongst the live plants and succulents. They're called fairy gardens and they're like little lasting wedding day memories. In this case, each one depicts a seaside scene, something meaningful to the bride and groom. Their centerpiece will feature our lighthouse."

"By the time they see them, they'll only be thinking about how fast they can ditch the after-party so they can hop a plane and go boink like bunnies."

"Oh, thanks." Fiona, who was lying flat on her back in the middle of her bed, moaned and put her hands over her eyes. "There's another visual I never needed about my big brother."

Kerry grinned. "I wonder if they like to do it in the shower."

Fiona threw a pillow at her. "Hannah, make her stop before I need therapy. Or more therapy," she muttered.

Hannah shot Kerry a quelling look, then hid her smile when Kerry very kindly stuck her tongue out at her oldest sister, adding a wink as she did. *Cheeky monkey*. Fergus had often called Kerry that, with exasperation, affection, and—far too often—admiration mixed in. Hannah identified with all of those feelings.

Hannah stared at her bare face in Fiona's vanity mirror while her sisters continued to haggle over the bachelorette party, with Fiona insisting she knew what Alex wanted and Kerry equally adamant that she knew what the bride-to-be needed. Hannah tuned them out and made a frank assessment of her post-accident-trauma appearance.

The accident had happened Wednesday afternoon. It was now Friday morning, and the color under her eyes was turning a lovely shade of seaweed green with a *soupcon* of eggplant purple. It gave her a certain Zombies of the Apocalypse *je ne sais quoi*. "How does she get that color to look so . . . *Night of the Living Dead*?" she mocked under her breath. "Maybe she's born with it." *Maybe it's Maybelline*. She smiled as the familiar jingle played in her mind. If only. There wasn't enough Maybelline in the world to fix her face.

"Earth to big sister," Fiona said. "Did Logan say what the verdict is on Blue's boathouse?"

Hannah turned to find them both sitting on the edge of the bed, shoulders pressed together, hands joined and resting on Kerry's lap. They'd always been like that, too. Fight like cats and dogs, then literally kiss and make up in the span of a breath. Then two seconds later, right back to Rock 'Em Sock 'Em Robots. Good thing neither one of them could hold a grudge for more than a blink. Hannah wished she had their forgive-and-forget gene.

"Word is it's arson," Hannah said. "Not particularly cleverly disguised to look like anything else, either."

"Why would anyone torch one of Blue's boathouses?" Fi asked.

"Not just any boathouse," Kerry added. "I heard it was basically his bait and tackle storage shed. Cost him large, losing that inventory."

"I mean, he wouldn't have done it himself for the insurance or anything, would he?" Fiona went on. "Blue's is doing okay, right?"

Kerry gave her sister a knuckle in the shoulder, earning her a scowl as Fiona rubbed the spot. "*What?*" Fiona demanded. "Who else would have a motive to do that?" She looked at Hannah. "Unless he pissed somebody off, which, you know, we're talking about Jonah. Has he fired anyone recently? Dropped a big-ticket vendor or something?"

"Why are you asking me?" Hannah wanted to know.

"Because you just absorb this kind of stuff," Kerry said, "you know, through legal osmosis or something. I mean, you were always getting to the bottom of things when we were growing up."

"What things?"

Kerry's eyes twinkled. "You really need a list?"

"Oh, you mean we're talking about me uncovering and deterring *your* shenanigans? Well, pardon me for wanting to keep my baby sister from getting a rap sheet longer than my arm. Before she was seven."

"Suspects?" Fiona asked, pulling Hannah's focus back

to the point of the conversation. "Did Logan say they had any?"

Hannah hedged, then figured what the hell, it was going to be common knowledge before the day was out. "He's going to talk to Jonah's great-nephew. Calder Blue."

"The guy who ran you off the road?" Fiona said, eyes bugging wide. "I *knew* he was bad news!"

"He didn't run me off the road. I ran the stop sign and almost hit him. And he's not bad news." *At least, I hope he's not.*

Fiona folded her arms. "Well, we'll see, won't we?"

"Why him?" Kerry wanted to know. "Because of that stupid ancient family feud? Does Jonah think he just suddenly came all the way down from Calais to firebomb one of Blue's boathouses because a century ago, his ancestor ran off with one of Jonah's ancestors? I mean, come on. And that doesn't even make any sense. Calder's ancestor was the villain in that little scenario, not ours. If anything, it would make more sense for it to be Jonah doing something to their side."

"See? You're just as bad as the rest," Hannah said, then sighed. "It's ancient water under a very old bridge and has nothing to do with this."

"Tell that to Jonah and his firebombed warehouse," Kerry said archly.

"Did Jonah accuse Calder of the crime?" Fiona asked.

"Jonah's just . . . well, he's a lot of things," Hannah said. *Stubborn, mule-headed, looking for a scapegoat.* "He's upset and not thinking clearly."

"So, who else are they looking at?" Kerry asked. "I mean, who else could it be? It's a little too much of a coincidence that someone from the Croix River Blues shows up after all this time, then *boom!* Up goes Jonah's boathouse."

"Which would make that coincidence seem a bit overly obvious, wouldn't you say?" Hannah replied, trying to keep her calm. Actually, it was good listening to Kerry play devil's advocate—her favorite role—because it was a useful preview of what she'd likely hear later today.

"So who else are they looking at?" This time it was Fiona asking.

"No one just yet," Hannah grudgingly admitted. She planned to change that, however. Just as soon as she covered up the *Night of the Living Dead* face that was staring back at her in the mirror.

"Logan will figure it all out," Fiona said confidently.

"Logan is getting married on Sunday," Kerry reminded her. "Then he and Alex are heading out to destinations unknown for a week."

Fiona's indignant posture wilted slightly. "Damn. You're right. Who'll be in charge of catching the culprit then?"

Both sisters looked expectantly at Hannah, who looked at them via the mirror with eyebrows raised. "Once again, why are you looking at me?"

"You're the closest thing we have to an investigator."

"I'm a lawyer."

"You worked on some fairly big criminal cases."

"Corporate crime. Huge difference. I deal with things like fraud, embezzlement, intellectual property rights, the occasional insider trading scandal."

"So this should be a piece of cake for you. Small-town arson. Your pool of suspects is limited."

Hannah swore under her breath. No point in trying to keep secrets. Okay, more secrets. She still hadn't told them she'd quit her job. Or about Tim. Or that she was moving home. "I'm not going to be doing any investigating.

We've got a wedding to pull off. And . . . well, I'm sort of representing Calder Blue."

Kerry hooted and Fiona's mouth dropped open in outrage. Which . . . was pretty much exactly the reaction she'd anticipated.

"I thought you just said he was innocent?" Fiona demanded. "Why does he need counsel if he's innocent?"

"I'm just helping to expedite the process, that's all, so they can focus on finding out what really happened."

"What do you think really happened?" This from Kerry, whose expression shifted from her initial delighted reaction to something more serious. It wasn't a side of her Hannah had seen too often. "Are you sure he's innocent, Han?"

Hannah felt a pinch in her heart, then she remembered that neither of her sisters knew about her colossal mistake in judgment where Tim was concerned. "Well, I can personally vouch for his whereabouts when the fire started. And given his reaction, I think it's safe to say—"

"Whoa, whoa, whoa. Hold up." Fiona raised her hand, palm out. "Last night was the rehearsal party. How could you have been—" She broke off, then looked accusingly at her big sister. "You said you went out for a 'walk.'" She made air quotes around the last word. "What's really going on?"

"I did go out for a 'walk.'" Hannah mimicked the air quotes. "I ran into Calder—"

"How con*ven*ient," Kerry murmured, the delighted look back in her glowing emerald eyes. "I'm liking this. Who's involved in some shenanigans now, huh?"

"At midnight," Fiona went on, shooting a glare at Kerry. "You just happened to bump into him. At midnight. By the harbor. *Where the fire started.*" She slapped her palms on her thighs. "And you think he's *innocent?*"

"Which is exactly why I'm representing him," Hannah

said calmly. *That, and because I apparently can't say no to the man.* Which was something she was going to have to get past and quick. "I do think he's innocent. And because he was down by the docks, it does look suspicious."

"*Look* suspicious?" Fiona barked. "It *is* suspicious. And hold on another minute. If you were down there with him, then how can you represent him? I mean, aren't you like, what do they call it, like an accessory? Or something? Aiding and abetting?"

"We were walking, Fi. And talking. No one was doing any aiding or abetting." *We were too busy trying to keep our hands off of each other. And failing.* Well, his hands had been on her. And sure, he'd just been doing some kind of acupressure voodoo, but there had been that kiss at the end. And holy . . . wow. There had been that kiss there at the end, all right. She cleared her throat. "Like I said, I was there. I saw his reaction. Which was the same as my reaction. And the first thing he did was to race down there and save Jonah and his great-granddaughter. Which no one seems to be mentioning."

"Well," Fiona said, stalling, wheels clearly turning. "What better way to make himself look innocent? I mean, you have to admit it's a rather extreme coincidence that he was down there when this happened."

"He was scoping out the harbor, trying to figure out Winstock's plan."

And then it all clicked in Hannah's brain, even as Fiona added a sarcastic, "At midnight? Really, Han? Did he try to sell you some swampland while he was at it? Or maybe a bridge for the harbor?"

"Winstock," Hannah breathed. Now her wheels were turning and she tuned her sisters out and focused on the trail that was forming in her mind. She turned to Fiona.

"How fast can you work your magic on this?" She made a circular motion around her face with her hand.

"What are you going to do?" Fiona wanted to know.

"We have a bachelorette party we're apparently hostessing this evening."

"I've got that covered," Kerry said with an airy wave of her palm.

"That's what worries me," Fiona said.

"Just get my face to look more professional and less zombie and then the two of you can carry on with the wedding and bachelorette party plans. I should only be gone a few hours. Three max. Or four. Adding in drive time," she said, since she was out at the Point. "Are you doing the bachelorette thing in town? Because then I could just meet you."

"It's nine in the morning," Fiona told her. "Whatever we do won't be until later this evening."

"Unless!" Kerry bounced on the bed. "What if instead of girl bonding over drinks and half-naked male strippers— or all naked, if we're lucky—maybe we could do a spa day? Mani, pedi, facials, massages, lunch, the works." She batted her eyelashes at Fiona. "Would that meet your oh-so-prim-and-proper standards of bachelorette party acceptability?"

Fiona opened her mouth for the usual retort, then stopped, looking momentarily stunned. "Uh, yes. Actually, it would. That's an awesome idea."

"Then why are you frowning at me?" Kerry wanted to know.

"Because you're the one who came up with it, so I'm going over the plan in my mind to see where the loopholes for inappropriateness are. Because we both know there are some."

"You mean other than a spa day would be done by dinner-time, so plenty of time for us to get our freshly mani-pedi'd selves all dolled up for the drinking and half-naked men part later? That kind of loophole?" Before Fiona could sputter her reply, Kerry threw an arm around her sister's shoulders and pulled her close for a shoulder-to-shoulder hug. "Oh, and make sure Delia can come with us today. She's free this evening, but not sure what she has going on today. Something, I'm sure, because when is she ever not working?" Kerry lifted her hands, palms out, leaving the previously leaning Fiona to sprawl heavily across her sister's lap. "So, I'm totally not kidding, but how about this? How about we take the spa day, and feel Alex out about the evening plans, and if she's into it, we go, and if not? We respect the bride's wishes." She grinned even more widely. "And go by ourselves!"

Kerry waggled her eyebrows, which was when Hannah noticed the tiny silver ring that was pierced through the outside corner of the left one. How had she missed that? *Oh, I don't know. You missed an entire pregnant wife, so an eyebrow piercing isn't all that surprising.*

"You feel Alex out," groused Fiona as she managed to get herself upright again. "But I'll play devil's advocate. And if she says no thank you, because, you know, she will be getting married less than forty-eight hours later, then you're on your own at the strip club. Which . . . where would there even be one?"

"Augusta," Kerry said, without hesitation. "Hey, you're not the only one who can do advance planning. Talk about making memorable moments." She nudged Fi with her hip. "Now make Hannah pretty. Or at least less living-dead-like, so she can go save the town, rescue her hero, and still meet us at the spa in time for facials and Brazilians."

"Who said anything about Brazilians?" Fi demanded at the same time Hannah said, "He's not my—oh, never mind."

She saved her breath and her argument, realizing the two

weren't even listening to her. They wouldn't have believed her anyway. She let them carry on as they pretty much had been since being born fourteen months apart, closed her eyes while Fi worked her magic . . . and started to plot out how she was going to work hers.

"Yes, I was in the harbor area," Calder told the police chief. "But I wasn't out on the docks and I didn't set the fire. I came here hoping to mend fences, not burn them down."

Chief Logan McCrae sat on the opposite side of the scarred heavy oak table in what passed, Calder supposed, as the interrogation room. It also appeared to be the break room, given the fridge in the corner, the counter with a sink, a microwave, and a few cupboards built in overhead.

Calder watched Hannah's brother make some additional notes, thinking brother and sister definitely had their fair share of family similarities. Both were tall and had dark hair, serious faces, and a very straightforward manner. He couldn't say if Chief McCrae shared his sister's smile, or her dry humor, as he'd yet to get either out of the man. Not that the situation was a laughing matter, far from. But a little gallows humor would go a long way at the moment toward helping him keep his annoyance and temper in check over being pulled in for questioning in the first place. He wasn't here as a witness, but as the prime suspect.

"Walk me through the events of the evening," Logan instructed.

"I gave one of your sergeants all of that last night after the fire had been put out. Voluntarily," he added.

"I'd like to go over it again. Once the adrenaline rush has passed, oftentimes other details emerge. Include as many as you can think of, even the most innocuous thing could be helpful."

Calder didn't bother to ask exactly what he'd be helping the chief to do. Clear him? Or nail him for a crime he didn't commit? "How far back in the day do you want me to go?" As the question was leaving his mouth, another thought struck his mind. If Logan wanted a detailed description of Calder's activities the night before, some of them were going to include Logan's own sister. *Oh, the day just keeps getting better and better.*

"Start with lunch and we'll backtrack if we need to."

Calder nodded, pressed his palms flat down on the table, then leaned back in his chair and propped one ankle on the opposite knee. He thought back over the previous day, and realized he'd spent more than just the last part of the day with Chief McCrae's sister. *Yeah, might as well lock me up right now.* He didn't have sisters, but he had nieces. And though the oldest was only eight, he could already well imagine his attitude, not to mention her father's, about any boy who came sniffing within a mile of her sweet little self.

Calder drew in a slow breath, let it out, and got his thoughts in order. "I was supposed to meet with Brooks Winstock the evening prior. Wednesday. To discuss the details of a job he's hiring me to do."

"Which is?"

Calder sighed. *So, it's going to be like that, is it?* McCrae knew damn well what he'd been hired to do, but was going to put him through his paces. Calder decided that was a good thing. Neat and tidy, all the facts lined up, i's dotted, t's crossed. "Building the yacht club. He acquired the property last August and originally had wanted the thing done by this July fourth, but the winter came in early, stayed late, and then he apparently had a falling-out with the architect, hired a new one, then the

original contractor walked due to the architect switch."
Calder lifted his shoulders. "When he—Winstock—accepted
my bid, he seemed pretty worked up about getting this
thing under way as quickly as possible. But he ended up
postponing our original Wednesday meeting to yesterday,
midafternoon. Then he pushed that to dinner last night,
then postponed it yet again. I went home to Calais Wednesday night, but opted to stay in town last night, to be available for this meeting the moment he could make it happen."

"When is it scheduled now?"

"He was supposed to contact me this morning, but I've
yet to hear from him. Your sergeant took my phone when I
came in, which I was happy to give her. Also voluntarily,"
he added. "Make sure you write that part down, too."

Logan looked up a little sharply at that, and Calder
worked again to tamp down his frustration. What annoyed
him wasn't so much that he was being dragged in, but that
it was giving whoever had really done the deed time to
cover his tracks.

"Go on," Logan prodded.

"I decided to spend the time trying to dig a little more
into what's really going on with Winstock."

Now he had McCrae's complete attention. "What do you
mean? Regarding what? The yacht club?"

"All of it," Calder said. "He's got this big new schooner
for tours, now this fancy yacht club. And he looked pretty
far afield for a new contractor. One who just happens to be
related to someone with a fairly large chunk of harbor real
estate."

"He came to you for the bid on the club project?"

Calder nodded. "I knew something was up from that
alone. I'm well aware—as is every member of the Blue
clan on both sides—of the centuries-old feud. We don't pay
it as much mind in our neck of the woods as the Cove side

apparently does, but I was curious to know more, I'll admit . . ." He let the sentence trail off, but in the face of McCrae's continued steady gaze, he said, "Family is important to me and I wanted to know what was really going on here."

"You think Winstock was somehow targeting your family back in Calais?"

"I have no idea what's on his mind, or what he's thinking or planning. In the end, I opted to throw out an outrageous bid. If he was just looking to trade on the Blue name to demonstrate he was respecting Cove history or some other such bullshit, he'd take one look at that number and walk. But if he wanted a St. Croix River Blue here for another reason . . ." He shrugged.

"And he took the bid. No negotiating the number?"

Calder shook his head. "Not yet, anyway. I expect that to happen when we finally meet. If we ever do."

"If you're looking to repair family ties, building a yacht club a hundred yards away from your great-uncle's fishing company won't be the way to get that done. You had to know that."

"I didn't know anything, honestly. There has been no other contact between the two clans for more than a century. I didn't know a damn thing about Jonah Blue until I looked into things after Winstock's bid request came through. When Winstock took the bid, I figured the only way to find out what was what, was to come on down and meet with the man who was trying to put this into motion. Find out why." He looked Logan in the eye. "I haven't signed anything, or committed to build anything as yet."

"So you just up and come to the Cove, with no agenda other than to find out what some deep-pockets guy here wants with you building his yacht club, because you think it might have something to do with family here that you've never met or had any contact with?"

Calder smiled. "That about sums it up." His smile faded just as quickly. "I don't like things that don't make sense, or that I don't understand, and when it potentially involves my family? I want to know what's going on. Information is power and so yes, I have technically been hired to build a yacht club here, but I've used my time since arriving to meet with Jonah and learn whatever I could. Jonah was aware I was coming, by the way. I contacted him when the bid was accepted to let him know what was going on, thinking he might be interested in that information and to let him know the deal didn't originate with me, but with Winstock."

"What was his reaction to that information?"

"I haven't a clue. Man's not exactly chatty. It was more like I left voice mails than had actual conversations. I figured I'd learn that when I got here, too."

Logan's expression hinted at that dry humor Calder had already come to expect from the man's sister. "And how did that work out for you?"

"It was about as productive a meeting as you might suspect. It didn't help matters any that I got a little hung up with the accident that happened as I was coming into town, which delayed my meeting with Jonah by quite a bit."

"Yes, about that. I do owe you a debt of thanks for helping to take care of Hannah after the accident."

"I'm just glad it wasn't any worse. Your sister is a very capable woman, but I wasn't comfortable leaving the scene until I knew for sure she could get help."

"Which I'm sure she didn't make easy," he said, more to himself than to Calder.

"Actually, it was your other sister, Fiona, who was more . . . shall we say challenging."

He thought he saw an actual hint of a smile, but McCrae quickly reined it in. "Yes, well, they're all pretty independent. Most Mainers are, which I suspect you understand." He cleared his throat. "Again," he said, more businesslike now, "thank you. So, what did Jonah say when you met with him?"

"Not much. That I wasn't welcome, by him or the town. Then he invited me to leave and warned me never to return. I respected that request."

"And yet, by your own admission, you were down at the docks last night."

"At them, yes. On them? No. Winstock cancelled our dinner plans late, very last minute. Or should I say his assistant did. I've yet to actually speak to the man himself since arriving in the Cove. I opted to stay here rather than make the round trip to Calais and back, got a room at the B and B on the edge of town—the Hurleys, nice couple—and then took a walk down along the waterfront trying to get a mental picture in my mind of what Winstock's plans might be."

"What makes you think he wants anything more than a yacht club?"

"Common sense. In the span of, what, eighteen months? He's tried to take a chunk of the shipyard, but failing that, hired the guy who owns the property to build him a replica of a historic four-masted schooner; then he literally pulls the land for the yacht club out from under someone I understand is some kind of local icon. As you said, he has deep pockets, but he's not using his money to win friends and influence anyone here, or he'd have bought out the shipyard owner up front and paid off that town icon. Instead, his maneuvers seemed to have cost his son-in-law his shot at being the mayor, and riled up the town against him. I'm just trying to figure out why a man smart enough to have amassed a fortune is going about all of this so ham-handedly. I don't know him, but it doesn't seem to make any sense. Bringing me in would seem to add more fuel to that fire, not dampen it. I spoke with the current mayor—"

Logan lifted a surprised brow. "You spoke to Owen? When was that?"

"Earlier in the day yesterday, when my first meeting was postponed. I learned a great deal of new information about my family history, but, other than some theories, Owen didn't offer anything that directly explained Winstock's thought processes about what he's doing to the Cove, other than to say his actions aren't really in keeping with how he's done business in the past. Although he owns a fair amount of real estate in the Cove, both private and commercial, he's never tried to make over the place in the way he is now."

"What were his theories?"

Calder lifted his hands, then let them fall back on his propped-up calf. "I wondered if maybe the man was ill or in some other compromised situation that would make him act so rashly about the things he's doing, but Owen felt he'd have heard whispers to that effect. We did wonder if perhaps, with no grandchildren, he's hit an age when he's decided to create a legacy of his own design, in order to leave something lasting if he does end up the last Winstock in the line. Well, his daughter would be, but you know what I mean."

Logan nodded, but didn't say anything.

"So, with that theory in mind, I was walking the harbor road, scoping it out from a contractor's viewpoint, trying to see it as Winstock might envision it. With the shipyard out of his reach, the only real place he could have a presence on the waterfront would be in Blue's spot. After that, it's government-owned property with the Coast Guard, and then you're out of the pocket of the harbor itself into less showy property units."

"What makes you think his vision includes more waterfront property?"

Calder shrugged. "That's all he's gone after so far. If he wants to make his mark, and especially if he envisions tourists being any part of his scheme, the waterfront is really the only place to do it."

Logan made more notes, but said nothing.

"Bottom line, I can't help but think Winstock is using me, somehow, some way, to get to Jonah. I told Jonah as much the day we met, and that was before my talk with Owen. It's the only reason I can see for Winstock to reach out to me. I just can't figure out what he's trying to achieve." He let his foot drop to the floor, and leaned forward again, forearms on the old table now, gaze directly on Logan's face. "And then the boathouse goes up in flames. And I'm right there. And Jonah sure as hell thinks I have something to do with it, despite the fact that my first instinct was to race toward the fire to save his sorry hide. Which I did. He slept right through the explosion. And his little great-granddaughter was there with him." He shook his head. "I'm not the villain here. I didn't burn anything," Calder reiterated, in case it needed saying again. "But someone sure as hell did."

Logan was quiet for another moment, then said, "You're the first Blue from your side of the family to set foot in Blueberry Cove for a century. Thirty-six hours later, a rather valuable piece of property belonging to the patriarch of the other side of the same family goes up in flames." Logan leaned his elbows on the table, and Calder had to admit, for all that Hannah's brother had been calm and cool up to now, he didn't doubt the man could pull off the bad-cop role with equal effectiveness. "And now you're telling me that one of the wealthiest men in this town, one whose family has been here for five generations, is somehow at the bottom of all of it. Help me understand how that could possibly be true."

"Why would I burn Jonah's boathouse? What could I have to gain from that?" Calder asked, his patience fraying again. "The Cove side still holds a grudge against my family, and I understand more clearly now why that is, but they're the angry ones. Not me, not anyone from my side. We look at it more like something they should get over. Ask any Blue in Calais and they'll tell you we wrote off this side of the family a very long time ago. Now someone— this very same wealthy man—is pulling the hated side of our family back into this town to build something the Blues here surely don't want to see built. It seems to be a very deliberate thing on his part, otherwise why come to me seeking a bid? And why accept one that's clearly beyond anything I should be asking for? What other purpose is he trying to achieve?"

"Why haven't you asked him that very thing?"

"I plan to," Calder said, quieting his voice, trying to corral what was left of his patience, rather than shouting the words as he wanted to. "If we ever sit down. It's not a phone-call kind of question. I want to see his face, read him, when I broach that topic. He doesn't even know what my motives are for being here, hasn't asked. I can only assume he thinks I'm here for the big payday, too stupid, foolish, or greedy to consider that anything else might be going on. Figuring out the real story is the only thing I'm interested in getting from him, or this town. I just want answers. And if that helps me to mend this ridiculous tear in our family, great. But my father and brothers could give a good goddamn about that, and in fact, think I'm wasting valuable time being here." He shot Logan an arched look. "I'm beginning to think they have a point."

"What did Jonah say about all that, during your face-to-face? Did you tell him your suspicions? About Winstock?"

"I did, and that I was here to figure out why I was hired in the first place. I told him it made sense that Winstock would target his property, since he first targeted Monaghan's place and will still be using his docks as a base to operate the schooner trips, and then he took Delia O'Reilly's diner property. Blue's is the next property on the harbor, and a big, lucrative one at that."

"And Jonah's response?"

"He was even more pissed off at me. He assumed I was saying he could be bought, when I was actually warning him that Winstock wouldn't likely offer him a dime, either because he knew Jonah wouldn't budge, or because—who the hell knows why? He hasn't been buying his way into this legacy he's building, he's been taking it. Or trying to. I spoke to Monaghan—I know what happened with the shipyard property, and how he came to build Winstock that boat, and how Winstock tried, and to some degree succeeded, to co-opt the future of the shipyard. Monaghan was only able to thwart the bigger plan because of an equally deep-pocketed ally. But Jonah ordered me off his property, made it clear I was never to set foot on it again."

"Yet you did."

Calder felt his temper climb as his pulse rate sped up. "It was a warning I heeded immediately and had no intention of disobeying, until I saw his boathouse blow up. I figured he wouldn't mind me being on his property if it meant saving his life." Calder paused, then looked down and shook his head. "Apparently I should have left him and his great-granddaughter there to possibly—" He couldn't even finish that thought. He looked directly at Logan. "Why does he think I would do such a thing?"

"What? Rush in to save him? Or torch the boathouse?"

"Either. Both." Calder lifted his hands, then let them both fall to rest on the calf of his propped leg. "I think the person we should be talking about is Brooks Winstock. He's the only one, as far as I can tell, with any kind of motive to burn the place."

"What motive would that be?" Logan lifted a hand. "I know what you've already said, but spell it out for me, from your viewpoint, what exactly you think he stands to gain by blowing up that boathouse?"

"I understand the boathouse that burned stored a large part of Jonah's inventory. I saw his face that night, when he looked at the fire. It was a bleak, defeated look. Maybe Winstock plans to ruin him, or put him in such dire financial straits that he'll have to sell. I don't know. Again, I'm not the one you should be talking to about that." He shoved his chair back, his patience at an end. There wasn't anything else to say and he was done repeating himself. "But clearly meaningful dialogue is not something this town is interested in. Except perhaps for your mayor. Good man, decent guy. Ask him about our conversation, get his insight on this, on me. Because I have nothing else to offer you and you don't seem interested in what I have to say. Now, unless you plan on charging me with something, I'm done with this particular meaningful dialogue." He stood.

"Sit down, Mr. Blue," Logan said, his tone as even and infuriatingly calm as ever.

"Are you bringing charges?" Calder asked, just as evenly. Okay, his teeth might have been on the edge of being bared, but if the police chief just wanted a scapegoat, then apparently it was going to be up to Calder to find out who'd actually destroyed property and put two lives at risk. He couldn't do that standing in the police station.

"I have a few more questions. If you don't mind."

"He does mind."

Logan looked up. Surprise etched his rugged, stony features for the first time, but Calder barely noticed as he turned to face Hannah, who'd just come directly into the room, without any preliminaries.

"Hannah—" both men said at the same time, then broke off and glared at one another. It was the first inkling Calder had that Logan was a damn sight more pissed off about this whole thing than he'd let on. If Calder weren't so annoyed and frustrated, he'd have given the man a nod of respect for being pretty damn good at his job. But since McCrae's intent was apparently to railroad Calder into some kind of guilty plea, he wasn't feeling particularly generous at the moment.

"Why are you here?" Logan asked, before Hannah or Calder could say anything further.

Hannah stepped in, cool as a cucumber and looking every inch the expensive Capitol Hill litigator she was. In slim black pants, black jacket, white blouse, all exquisitely tailored to fit her wandlike frame, she looked so crisp he was surprised he didn't feel a chill rolling off the high-thread-count fabric. Her hair was pulled back in the same sleek manner it had been when he'd first met her, in yet another tasteful and pricey-looking clasp. Small, understated gold earrings and a single thin gold necklace completed her litigator look. Someone had done a hell of a job with makeup again, because other than the thin bandage on the bridge of her nose, covering the stitches, and the slight puffiness of her lip where the cut had also been expertly concealed underneath barely there lipstick, there was no visible trace of the trauma she'd suffered just two days earlier.

"Hannah," Calder said, as Logan also stood, but she merely nodded at him before turning back to her brother. It was only then that he noted she was carrying her leather day planner, and—a briefcase? Who brought a briefcase with them while on vacation for a family wedding?

Hannah McCrae did. He found himself fighting a smile as he pulled out the chair next to his. "I won't need that," she said to him, "but thank you." She looked at Logan. "Calder didn't torch Jonah's boathouse," she told him. "And you're wasting valuable time you could be spending on finding out who actually did."

"Excuse me, Counselor," Logan interrupted, appearing surprised, but otherwise not at all perturbed by her sudden intrusion. "I'm not done questioning Mr. Blue. I'll be happy to talk to you separately. In fact, you're next on my list."

"There's a list?" she asked. "Good. That's very good. But I'm not leaving." Calder shifted behind the chair, and pushed it in for her as she apparently changed her mind and took a seat.

He sat back down in his chair, and a now more annoyed-looking Chief McCrae did the same. Funny how quickly things could change, Calder thought, his frustration taking a backseat to amusement. At least for now.

"You were there," Logan said, directing the comment to Calder. "Which makes you an eyewitness, at the very least. Given the hour, the area was otherwise empty. Blue's was long closed. Delia's Diner is gone, Brodie's boat-building operation would have been closed by then, too. The other new shipyard businesses aren't open yet. Leaving you—"

"And me," Hannah put in. "Along with the person who

actually set the fire, as at least three people who were down by the docks that night. And it doesn't take a crowd, Logan. Only one. The fewer witnesses around, the better. I was only there because I needed a break from the noise at the rehearsal party. My head was pounding." She looked at Calder. "I assume you explained your presence."

Calder nodded, but didn't add anything. She seemed to be doing a fine job all by herself, and more importantly, her brother actually seemed to be listening to her. Frankly, when she got that look in her eye, he doubted there was a person alive who wouldn't hang on her every word. Whether in fear, in admiration, or . . . in whatever the hell she was making him feel. He shifted a little in his seat, acknowledging how she was making him feel, and tamped down a smile.

She'd already turned back to her brother. "Then you have our statements. I believe the person you need to be interrogating is Brooks Winstock. Unless Jonah has an angry ex-employee or vendor he's fired, Brooks is the only other person I can see with a stake in Jonah's livelihood."

"Other than the Blue family member presently seated beside you," Logan replied, still with infuriating calm.

Though, now that Calder could view the scene more objectively, he noticed there was tension in the man's face, at the corners of his eyes, his mouth. And in the grip he had on the pen in his hand. He wasn't calm at all. He just hid his agitation very well. Once again, Calder hid the urge to smile. "He has no reason to destroy Jonah's property. He holds no ill will toward the Cove Blues. Quite in reverse actually. And being thrown off Jonah's property hardly set him off so badly he decided to torch the place. He has no record, no history of anything like that."

Logan must have seen Calder's raised eyebrow, because

he looked at him now. "You have something you'd like to add? You look surprised."

"That she knows my criminal history or lack thereof? Yes, I am. But, it's true, I've got nothing to hide. A fact she just confirmed, I believe. Feel free to check, all the same."

Logan looked between the two of them; then he might have sworn under his breath. "You are the only two eye-witnesses we have." He looked at his sister, and something of his real feelings on the matter edged his words as he said, "I realize we're not in a fancy Capitol Hill deposition room, but I would like to talk to each of you separately."

"Oh please," Hannah said, and laid her briefcase on the table and flipped it open. She drew out a small recorder, which she set on the table between the two men, and a yellow legal pad, and a small iPad, which she also set up, and plugged her phone into.

"Hannah—" Logan started, sounding more exasperated by the moment, much to Calder's enjoyment, but she lifted a hand, effectively shushing him.

She closed her briefcase and set it aside, checked her tablet to make sure her phone had provided her with the hot spot she needed to be connected to the Internet. Then she very deliberately leaned forward and pressed down the RECORD button on the small cassette player. "Old school," she said, "but I like it." She said the date and the time. "Blueberry Cove Chief of Police Logan McCrae questioning Mr. Calder Blue in reference to the fire and subsequent loss of Jonah Blue's bait and tackle boathouse in Half Moon Harbor." She straightened. "Please, start from the beginning."

"This isn't necessary," Logan said.

"On the contrary, if you're talking about separating us to take statements, then my client deserves—"

"Your *client?* You can't represent him," Logan stated and Calder delighted in the vein that started to rise up just above the man's left temple. "You're an eyewitness."

"I will give you my statement separately when we've finished. You already have my separate eyewitness account on record from last night." She recited into the recorder the name of the officer she'd given her statement to, along with the date and the approximate time. "As you well know, but for the record, I am licensed to practice law in the state of Maine, something I believe you suggested I do soon after passing the D.C. bar, to help protect our family interests here, if ever needed. So, I am well within my rights to offer Mr. Blue my services as counsel."

"That's not what I mean, and you know it."

For his part, Calder just leaned back and propped his booted foot on his knee again. He didn't need Hannah's help, but the entertainment value alone made it well worth any potential future complications. Professional or personal. He liked seeing Hannah in litigator mode. Anyone who thought her cold must not have been paying attention. She was fiery, passionate, anything but icy. He felt other parts respond to that train of thought and deliberately looked back at Logan. *Yeah, that took care of that. For now.*

Calder spoke. "I've already explained to your brother, the chief here, that I was looking out over the docks and the harbor after my meeting was canceled, trying to figure out what Brooks Winstock's bigger plan might be, when I ran into you lecturing some poor jerk in D.C. who was trying to hire you—"

"That's not pertinent to this investigation," she inserted calmly enough, but he'd been watching her and hadn't missed the brief flash of surprise and—had that been panic?—that crossed her eyes. Seemed so uncharacteristic for her, he questioned whether he'd seen it at all, but he was fairly certain he had it right.

Was Logan such a protective older brother? They were both in their thirties, for God's sake. She hardly needed looking after. Not to mention she'd handed the asshole's balls back to him on a silver platter. So, was it possibly something else? And if so . . . what?

As Hannah explained to Logan that they'd run into each other and talked about inconsequential things, like the wedding plans—though he noted she didn't mention their little acupressure session, or the kiss—Calder thought back over the phone call he'd overheard. From what he'd pieced together, both from her side of the conversation and from what he could hear of the guy on the other end of the line, Limp Dick had been trying to hire her for his law firm, using rather suggestive innuendo to lure her in.

Calder didn't know how things were in a big metropolitan city like D.C., but he'd be surprised to learn that that method was a popular recruitment technique for someone of Hannah's obvious caliber. He'd only known the woman a few short days, but he could state with fair certainty that even if it was, sexual innuendo was about as wrong an approach as someone could take with her. Not because she was a cold fish—far from—but because she oozed class, and, if anything, carried her polished professional demeanor too far into her personal interactions. Why on earth that guy would think she'd be swayed by—wait. That part of the conversation clicked off as something she'd said clicked in. *It's true, I no longer work for Holcombe and Daggett.*

Calder chewed on that tidbit for a moment, then glanced casually between brother and sister. It was purely a guess on his part, but could she be worried about her brother finding out that she was no longer employed by her legal firm? Didn't mean she hadn't taken a position elsewhere, but piece that together with her comments about having too many other things going on to add him into the mix, and—

"Calder?"

He snapped his attention back to the room and its occupants, glancing toward Hannah. "I'm sorry, I was . . . going back over every step of last night."

She held his gaze a moment longer than was absolutely necessary, and her expression didn't falter or change by so much as a single flicker. But somehow he knew what she was trying to telegraph to him. There was no way to reassure her that he wasn't going to out her recent job shift, or mention their more personal interaction, since neither thing pertained to figuring out who'd gotten busy with some matches and gasoline. All he could do was show her.

"Have you spoken to Jonah at all since he went back inside his boathouse last night?" Hannah asked Calder.

He shook his head. "I offered to talk to the firemen, direct them to where he was—he had his great-granddaughter to oversee—and I even offered to help with her so he could go talk to them himself. Instead, he ordered me off the docks and went back inside. You arrived right after that, and you and I both exited the property together. Then you went directly to the pub, and I went back to my room at the Hurleys' place." He looked to Logan. "I'm sure some of the crowd that was gathering by that point could verify that we exited the docks together and left the immediate area, and what time it was when we did so."

Logan looked at Hannah. "Why were you on the docks at all? Why not go directly back to the pub after the explosion?"

"I called nine-one-one, then called Fiona. She said you

were being radioed about it as we spoke, and Calder had already raced down the hill to go rouse Jonah if he was there. The firemen were already on the pier leading to the burning boathouse by then, so I went down to where Calder was to see if I could offer any assistance. But, as Calder said, Jonah had already come out and gone back inside. He knew they were okay, and he told me Jonah had told him to leave the property. So we did."

She leaned forward and her voice gentled a bit, more sister to brother now, instead of defense counsel to police chief. "Logan, I saw Calder's face when that place went up. His immediate gut instinct was to protect me. Then it was to race directly down there and try to help. I've looked into the eyes of a lot of guilty men. He's not one of them."

"I know," Logan said, quietly.

Calder shouldn't have been as massively relieved to hear that as he was . . . but it was a load off, there was no denying.

"Well, then why all the—"

This time, Calder cut Hannah off. "He's just doing his job." He looked at Logan, his concern shifting to how they were going to find the true culprit. "Have you talked to Winstock? I can't imagine he went down there and did this himself, but if you have no other leads, he's got to be the connection."

Logan tapped his pen on the table. Then he leaned over and flipped off the recorder before turning his steady gaze back to Calder. "Are you staying in town?"

"Are you asking me to?"

"No, not as long as I have contact information from you for any follow-ups I might have." He closed his notebook, tossed his pen down.

"Would you like me to stay in town? I still have a meeting to attend with Winstock."

Logan flicked a gaze at him, held it for a beat, then let the hint of a smile curve his mouth. "I'd like to think I'd have your support if I need it."

"Logan—" Hannah began, but neither man was paying attention to legal counsel at the moment.

"I'd be more than happy to do whatever I could," Calder said. "Jonah might be family in name only—to his way of thinking anyway—but my name has been dragged into this now, too. Getting to the bottom of it matters to me for several reasons. I want to know what's going on, same as I did when I got here. Whether it's related to the fire or not. If my getting the answers I came here for can help sort that mess out, too?" He lifted a shoulder. "Two birds. One stone."

Both men held each other in silent regard for a moment longer. Then Calder's lips twitched when he heard Hannah sigh and mutter, "Am I the only one who hears the score from *The Good, the Bad and the Ugly?* You're too old to play cowboys, you two, but don't let that stop you."

Logan stood and stuck his hand out. Calder shook it. Both men grinned. "There," Logan said to his sister. "We played nice. Happy?"

"Men," Hannah muttered, but Calder didn't miss the relief on her face.

"Leave your contact info with Barb on your way out when you get your phone back," Logan said. "I'll be in touch."

Chapter Eleven

"No strippers?" Kerry shook her head at the other three women. "If Delia were here, she'd side with me."

"She finally got the inspector out at her new place—no way was she missing that for a mani-pedi. And it would still be two against three," Fiona said, beaming smugly.

"My disappointment, it is deep," Kerry replied gravely. "It's like you all have lost your will to live."

"Maybe we've just lost our will to drive several hours to see men disrobe in front of a room full of women," Fi shot back, smiling even more sweetly.

"You all can go if you want to," Alex said hastily. "I just—" She shrugged. "I'm good with the hot, naked guy I already have."

"Nobody likes a spoiled winner," Kerry said, but she was giving Alex a high-five as she did so.

Fiona groaned and clapped her hands over her eyes. "Bad images, bad images. I'm happy for you, but seriously, consider the audience."

Kerry rolled her eyes and slung an arm around Fi's shoulders and pulled her in for a side hug. "That reaction is precisely why you need a night at a strip club. I think you've forgotten what a naked man looks like. You know, one who's not your brother." Still grinning, she winced at Fi's carefully placed sharp elbow to the ribs, but held on. "We can replace those bad images with some good ones. Some really, really good ones, if we're lucky." She waggled her newly shaped eyebrows. "A shame to waste our freshly mani-pedi'd selves on this lovely Friday night."

"Some of us are okay without having a naked man in our life," Fi groused, ducking out from her sister's arm. "But you go right ahead."

"Hannah?" Kerry said, not even remotely put off by Fiona's comment.

"She already has a hot guy," Fiona said. "Tim, the Titan of Finance."

"You've been talking to Barb, haven't you," Hannah said, giving her younger sister a dark look.

"There's a Tim? I don't see a Tim," Kerry said, looking around. "Do you see a Tim?"

"I thought you were with Calder Blue," Alex said, looking confused. "Who's Tim?"

At Alex's comment, Fiona's mouth dropped open and Kerry's eyes lit up with glee. Hannah glared at them both to no avail, then looked at Alex. "Who said I was with Calder? I'm merely his—"

"Logan might have mentioned something about the two of you at the station house earlier," Alex said, looking instantly guilty. "Don't worry, he said nothing about your statements. Those are obviously part of the arson investigation. He just thought—you know, never mind. Boys can be dumb."

"They can be," Kerry agreed, her gaze still fixed on Hannah's face. "But our big brother is usually pretty sharp. So, big sis, what's the story? What have I missed? You just got here and already there's something steamy going on. Does he have brothers? And you've got another man tucked away back in D.C.?" She pretended to wipe away a tear and mock sniffled. "And here I thought you were hopelessly uptight and prudish. I'm so proud." She put her fist out for a bump.

Hannah just looked at her with a flat stare.

"I am sorry, Hannah," Alex said. "I didn't realize you were with someone already. I mean, trust me. It's all fine. No one is gossiping or anything. It was only because the two of you . . . you know what? I'm shutting up now."

"She and Tim have been together for almost—what, has it really been two years?" Fiona asked, raising a questioning brow in Hannah's direction. "Wow. Time does fly. Now I'm even more bummed he's not coming. We need to meet this guy. It must be pretty serious. You haven't been with anyone that long since you graduated law school. I mean, I know you've been fast-tracking the career, so there hasn't been time, but—wow. Two years." She smiled and lifted Hannah's hand, tapping her ring finger. "Maybe I'll get to plan another Cove wedding shortly? Hmm?"

"Wedding?" Kerry said. "How can you be talking wedding and I don't even know about this guy?" She looked at her sister. "How do I not know about this guy?"

"Seriously, Ker?" Fiona rolled her eyes. "We're lucky to hear from you once every few months. And then it's usually your illegible scribble on some mangled postcard that looks like a wildebeest slept on it."

"There aren't any wildebeests in Australia. That was the Serengeti. Which is in Africa. You're thinking wild boar." Kerry looked back at Hannah. "And that still doesn't answer the question. Two years and I've never even heard his name?"

Hannah's mind was spinning like an out-of-control hamster wheel as she tried to decide how to handle this latest conversation bomb. Between her brother thinking she was an item with Calder—her brother, who didn't know she'd broken up with Tim, so God only knew what he thought of her now—and Kerry sinking her teeth into the Tim issue—Kerry, who was like a mongoose with a . . . well, Hannah didn't know what mongooses hunted, but whatever it was, that's what she felt like. She was going to have to tell them, dammit.

"When we get the chance to chat," she told Kerry, stalling as she searched for the right words, "you're usually more concerned about my securing a bail bond or fast-talking you out of some tribal conflagration than asking about my social life."

Fiona spun on her younger sister. "Bail? *Bail!*" She spun back to Hannah. "Oh my God. Why didn't you tell me?"

"Oh, I don't know," Kerry said dryly. "Because I worried you might overreact?" She looked at Hannah. "See what you've done now? I suppose you're going to out me to Logan now, too."

"You know," Alex interjected in an overly bright voice, "I've changed my mind. I think we should go watch the strippers. Lots of dollar bills tucked in many a sweaty G-string, and frosty glasses of nice, cold alcohol." She looked at the three sisters, none of whom was paying any attention to her. "Really big, frosty glasses."

Kerry stepped over and looped Hannah's arm through hers, her green eyes already twinkling again. "Of course, all is forgiven if you tell me every delicious detail. Have you talked weddings? When is he going to pop the question? He'd better be planning something majorly amazing and romantic. You should give me his contact info. Fi and I will make sure he does it right." She tossed a brilliant smile at Fiona. "Won't we?"

Fiona tried not to smile, but ended up sticking her tongue out at her younger sister, then moving over so she could loop her arm through Hannah's free one. "We'll take care of it for you." She tipped up on her toes and whispered in Hannah's ear. "But to be safe, just give the contact info to me."

"I heard that," Kerry said.

Hannah stood between them feeling miserable. Not, for once, because of what Tim had done, but because she was going to put a damper on things by telling them the truth. She had to, she knew that. It was one thing to simply avoid mentioning why Tim hadn't accompanied her to the wedding. Quite another to tell a bald-faced lie about the state of their relationship.

"So, what's his deal?" Kerry asked. "Spill. We want details. Is he really a titan of finance? Is he amazing in the sack?"

"Kerry!"

"He's—" Hannah started, then stopped. She had to tell them, but she didn't have to tell them everything. "It doesn't matter what he is, because we're no longer together."

Fiona looked immediately stricken and Kerry just looked pissed. "Who ditched whom?" she demanded. "Never mind. Clearly he's a loser and an ass if he let you get away, no matter the circumstances."

Tears sprang instantly to Hannah's eyes at that, which was dangerous because she really wasn't going to say any more on the subject. In fact, she realized now, they never had to know the details. She could bury them, just as she'd buried the rest of her past.

"You're making her cry," Fiona accused, then pulled Hannah into a hug. "I'm so sorry. You should have told us."

Hannah sent an apologetic look toward Alex over Fi's

shoulder. "I'm sorry. I was trying to avoid this. It's your weekend."

"Life doesn't wait until it's convenient," Alex said. "And I have a lifetime with Logan. This weekend is for us to celebrate with family and I'm just thrilled to get to be part of yours." She stepped forward. "I'm really sorry, because being at a wedding probably sucks right now. But, if it helps, I'm really, really happy you're here."

"Oh, now I'm crying," Fiona said. "Group hug!" And she and Kerry pulled Alex into the sister circle and they all held on. "I'm so glad you picked our brother to marry," Fi said, snuffling.

Hannah simply closed her eyes and soaked in the love that was her family—all of her family, Alex included. *You're a lucky, lucky woman. No more tears. Not for Tim, not for yourself.*

"Did someone die?"

Hannah turned to find her brother in his big, police-issue SUV, idling at the curb. "No," Hannah said, sniffling and smiling as she wiped her eyes. "Just . . . sister stuff." She reached down for Alex's hand, and squeezed it, felt better when Alex held on just as tightly.

"I'm getting calls," he said, mildly. "If you guys are going to keep this up, could you at least do it somewhere less . . . public?"

Hannah looked back at the other three, then glanced past them to the gold letters painted on the shop window. They were all still standing outside Linda's Nail Emporium on High Street. "Oh," she said, looking back at Logan. "Right." She gave Alex's hand a final squeeze, then let go and walked over to the curb.

"Actually," Kerry called out, "we were just talking about The Lumber Yard. You know, that male strip club in Augusta."

Logan's eyebrows did a slow climb as he looked from Kerry to his lovely bride-to-be.

To Kerry's delight and Hannah's surprise, Alex simply smiled at him and waved.

"I thought you were having some kind of bachelor thing tonight," Hannah said, yanking his attention back to her.

"Owen, Dan, Fergus, and a few others are going to shoot pool after I get off work. It's not that big a deal."

"No strippers then," Hannah deadpanned.

"Really?" he asked her. "Even you?" He shook his head as she laughed. "I count on you to be the one to rein the other two in."

"Who's going to rein in Alex?"

"She doesn't need—" He broke off and her grin spread as she saw his jaw work.

"I only kid because you're making it too easy not to," Hannah said.

"I just want Sunday to get here so we can get on with it." He lowered his voice and nodded toward Kerry, who was once again talking animatedly to Fiona and Alex. Hannah was certain the strip club issue was being revisited.

"The longer this stretches out, the more I worry about keeping that one"—he nodded toward Kerry—"from getting into some kind of trouble. And now you're talking strip clubs? Really?"

"I'm not talking strip clubs. She's thirty now, by the way," Hannah reminded him. "Not thirteen."

He merely lifted a skeptical brow and gave her the *And, your point would be?* look.

"I had them talked out of it until you came riding in here all Gary Cooper in *High Noon*."

"I thought I was Clint Eastwood."

Hannah grinned. "That's not *High Noon*. That's *The*

Good, the Bad, and the Ugly. I'll let you pick which one
you get to be."

"Your fiancée said she was happy with the hot, naked
guy she already had," Kerry called over, making sure her
voice was louder than it had to be. "I'm not thirteen or
deaf," she added.

Hannah shot a look at Alex, who'd turned about three
shades of red, but was giggling and sending a sheepish
wave to her husband-to-be, while Fiona tried to physically
corral her younger, taller, and far stronger sister closer to
the building, away from the street. Hannah turned back to
her brother, took one look at his smug smile, and rolled her
eyes. "Oh, so we can't stand here and hug it out and cry
happy tears, but if it's announced to God and everyone that
your soon-to-be-wife is happy in the sack with you, that's
perfectly okay."

Logan shrugged, completely unrepentant. "I'm a guy."

"How convenient for you," she shot back, but a smile
hovered on her lips, too. "Did you need to give me any
further instructions for the evening? Do you want me to
have her hold a sign at the strip club saying 'happy with my
hot fiancé, leave me alone'? Or am I free to go, Officer?"

"You're really going?" he asked, and she relished the
look of uncertainty that filled his handsome face for a full
three seconds before he spied the twinkle in her eyes.
"Okay, that was fair," he said, smiling sheepishly himself
now, but then that faded and his expression turned more
serious. "Actually, I was going to come looking for you
anyway; the calls just made finding you easier."

"I have my cell phone. You could have just—wait,
calls?" Hannah said. "Plural. Really? Must be a slow
grapevine day in the Cove."

"On the contrary. Do you have time to take a little ride
with me before the evening's debauchery commences?"

"I do, sure. Where?"

"Nowhere, actually. I just want to talk to you about Jonah and the case and I wanted some privacy." He sent a meaningful glance at their siblings. "This seemed the safest bet."

Hannah hadn't forgotten the revelation she'd just made to the others before Logan had rolled up. For no other reason than to avoid further questions about Tim, or any follow-ups to Alex's comment about her and Calder being an item—which led her to remembering why Alex had made that comment in the first place—she turned back to her brother.

"Actually, I have a few things I'd like to discuss with you, too."

It was clear from his expression that he understood he was in the doghouse somehow, though he was unsure why. "Um, sure," he said cautiously. "But me first."

"Deal." She explained to the girls that she needed to do some follow-up on the arson case with Logan, but would meet up with them later. "Not in Augusta," she clarified, then looked at Fiona. "I'm counting on you to be the level head in my absence."

"Party pooper," Kerry called after her as Hannah climbed into the passenger seat of Logan's SUV. "And don't think we're not going to grill you later on this whole Calder Blue thing," she added. "Because I saw him earlier today and *rowr*! Are you representing more than just his legal interests?" She wiggled her eyebrows again. "Inquiring minds want to know!"

Hannah simply rolled her window up, letting that be her response. Undeterred as always, Kerry grinned and threw kisses at her, and Hannah knew she was in for it later. Kerry. Mongoose. If the moniker fit . . .

Logan pulled away from the curb as Hannah settled into her seat, thankful the seat belt went over her good shoulder. "Okay, Chief, shoot," she said, when they were a few blocks further down High Street.

"Actually," he said, "I want to follow up a little on what Kerry was just saying, first."

"Seriously? Since when do any of us want to go voluntarily down Kerry's path?"

"When that path leads to our number-one arson suspect?"

Hannah didn't so much as blink. She folded her arms and shifted toward her brother. "Really? Okay, I'll go first then. You mean the very same suspect whom you mentioned to Alex as someone you thought I was having a thing with? Which is why Kerry is on that track, thankyouverymuch."

"Are you?" he asked, also not missing a beat, and quite serious.

"Why does it matter?" Hannah asked, rather than quantify whatever it was she was having with Calder. Although it was nothing. Sort of.

"Arson suspect?" he repeated.

"You said you knew he wasn't guilty. I know he's not guilty. He's no longer a suspect. So the subject is moot."

"I believe he didn't do it, but so far, we can't turn up any other credible leads. And I have no actual proof exonerating him. Unless . . ."

"Unless, what? Unless I told you I was standing about a hundred yards away from the boat pier, talking with Calder, when the boathouse blew up, and he didn't do anything or say anything, or act suspicious in any way prior to the explosion. And that, after it happened, his reaction was the same as mine. Utter shock. Oh, wait, I already did tell you that." Her eyes darkened. "Or did you want me to tell you we were off somewhere doing hot and sweaty things when—"

"Okay, okay, uncle," Logan said, waving one hand. "I'm not questioning where you were when it happened. I wanted to know if your statement could in any way be called into question because of whatever is going on between the two of you."

"Wow. I can't even believe you'd have to—"

"Before you get all high and mighty, last I heard you were in a long-term relationship with Tim Underwood. Then you sit across my interrogation table and—"

"Oh please, it was the break room and I was nothing less than one hundred percent professional, nor is there anything unethical—"

"You sit across from me," he reiterated, talking over her, "and it's quite clear to me and anyone else with eyes in his head that there are enough sparks striking off the two of you to have started that fire from halfway up Hill Street." He flicked a gaze at her, then back to the road. "So, what's going on? No details, just—" He broke off, blew out a breath, and his shoulders relaxed a little, as did his two-fisted grip on the steering wheel. "I'm sorry. I just . . . I've known for a while something is wrong, with you, or in your life, or . . . something. I wanted to say something, but I didn't know what to say, so I figured you'd come to me when you were ready. I had a few things going on in my world, but that's no excuse."

"Tim and I are no longer together," she said, just putting it out there, boom, done. He'd hear about it from Alex or their sisters anyway.

He glanced at her, then reached over and put his hand on her arm, squeezed gently, before returning it to the steering wheel. "I should have called, or pushed, or gotten Barb to push. I'm—you know I'm not good at this stuff."

"Logan," Hannah said quietly, abashed now, her irritation fleeing as quickly as he'd stirred it up. "I—I guess I owe you an apology. The whole family. Barb, too. I should have said something. Maybe not when it happened, but at some point since then. I just . . . I had to deal with it on my own. I didn't say anything at the time, because we broke up over Christmas. I knew it was a special holiday for you and Alex, you'd been together a whole year." She smiled over at him. "Fiona spilled to me in an e-mail that you were going to pop the question over the holidays." She punched his shoulder, and he mock winced. "Who knew you were such a romantic, you big softie."

She looked away, ducked her chin briefly, then looked out the windshield. "So, when everything happened, I—I couldn't—wouldn't—intrude. It was a good thing, and I wasn't going to spoil a good thing with my bad thing. It's okay, I handled it." She didn't say more, and wasn't sure she ever would. Logan had always been protective of his sisters, maybe a little overly so in their younger years, but while it had made her feel good, and loved, and safe, she also knew it was part of the burden he carried, whether his siblings wanted him to or not. She wasn't going to add to it.

"I'm sorry," he said. "About Tim. About . . . everything there. I want you to be happy."

"Seeing you and Alex together makes me happy," she told him, never more sincere. "Being here, being home, makes me happy." It was on the tip of her tongue to tell him the rest, that she'd quit her job, was in the Cove to stay, but without going into greater detail on why she was moving back, she wasn't really sure how to explain. She should have prepared something.

Then he said, "So, about Calder Blue. How well do you feel you know this guy?"

She frowned. "What is that supposed to mean? And once again I ask, why does it matter? He's not a suspect."

They'd left the town proper at this point and were heading south, in the opposite direction from their home on Pelican Point. Logan turned onto a narrow, paved road that wound its way down to one of the many tiny inlets off of Half Moon Harbor. He drove only a short way, then pulled over, leaving the engine running. Now he shifted to look at his sister. "It means I want to hear your take on the guy. Beyond the facts. How well do you know him?"

"I just met him a few days ago. We've crossed paths a number of times since. We've had a few conversations. Casual conversations. I don't know him that well."

Logan sighed, then looked out the windshield, his expression somewhat conflicted.

"Oh, for heaven's sake, spit it out."

"I have an eyewitness who saw you getting a little cozy with Blue in front of Hartley's."

"Did Owen say that?"

"You know I can't tell you. Calder did mention to me he'd spoken to Owen. Is the eyewitness account true? Because then I need to understand *casual* as you mean it."

"Are you asking as the chief of police, or as my big brother?"

He looked at her, eyebrow raised. "Should I be asking as your big brother?"

She swore under her breath. "I wasn't doing anything illegal, Officer."

"Stop it."

"No, you stop it," she said, then relented, her shoulders drooping. "Logan, I don't know what's going on."

"Just give me your gut opinion on the guy. Good guy? Possibly not a good guy? What do your instincts tell you?"

Hannah didn't know whether to laugh or swear. *My instincts about men. Good question.* "All I can tell you is that in my conversations with him and my interactions with him, he's been polite and well mannered, and has gone out of his way to be helpful." She recalled something else. "He has known from the first moment, or close to it, that you were my brother. I mean, that my brother is the police chief. Fiona told him at the accident site. So why would he be getting chummy with me if he was planning this supposed arson?"

"Because who better to get close to, to cover his ass?"

She rolled her eyes, but she hated to admit that Logan was planting seeds of doubt in her. Her rational mind said no way, but . . . given how blind and stupid she'd been about the last man she'd allowed into her life, what if she was wrong? "Did you run that check on him?" she asked. "Of course you did. So you know he's got a clean record." *Please don't let me be wrong.* She'd bluffed about having run her own check. She'd considered it, but hadn't wanted to make use of any of her old contacts. More than that, she couldn't determine whether she wanted to know as his lawyer, or as a woman, and was annoyed enough with her uncharacteristic uncertainty that she hadn't acted. "He's too responsible a person," she said. "Works for a generations-old family firm. Has three younger brothers, a handful of nieces. Runs a farm. Rescues horses. Even learned acupressure to help relieve their pain."

Logan's mouth twitched in a smile. "And yet you hardly know the guy."

"Stuff comes up in conversation," she said pointedly, "even casual ones. Why are you still pursuing him, or my take on him, if you know he's not guilty?"

"Because without finding anyone else, I need to prove he's not guilty. You know how this town works. Just because I think he's clean—"

"Don't underestimate your opinion. The people of this town adore you and respect you. Instead of looking for proof of who didn't do it, find who really did do it. Did you talk to Winstock?"

He nodded. "He has a solid alibi. He was down at his yacht club in Bar Harbor."

"He was supposed to be having a dinner meeting here in the Cove with Calder. Why would he be hours away in Bar Harbor? He canceled at the last minute, so if he was all the way down there, he knew he wouldn't be able to make it long before he actually cancelled. Did you check?"

"Of course. And he was there. I don't know what the deal is with his delaying his meetings with Blue."

"You questioned him, though, I presume, so what did he say was the reason?"

"He didn't. Once we established he wasn't in the Cove during the fire, he politely excused himself and invited us to contact his lawyers if we had any further inquiries."

"And you don't think that reaction was a little over-the-top?"

"I think it was classic Brooks Winstock, but it doesn't matter. I've got nothing to go on there, and without anything connecting him to Calder Blue other than this supposed contract they have—"

"Supposed? Did Brooks deny there's a deal between them?"

"I didn't say that. My point is without probable cause

to suspect Winstock, I can't get clearance to dig into his personal information."

"Like to see if he paid someone to bomb Jonah's boathouse, you mean? Because who else would have a direct stake in causing Jonah Blue trouble so he'd either sell the place or have to close his business?"

"We don't know for certain that it's that complicated. Could be he just pissed off a supplier, or one of his guys, and they torched the place."

"First, I'm sorry to say this, but I don't think any of Blue's guys would be smart enough to set a boathouse fire that is clearly arson, but manage to do it in a way that leaves absolutely no trace and no trail behind."

Logan nodded. "Agreed. Doesn't rule out a vendor."

"No, it doesn't, though it's still an extreme reaction. Did you talk to Jonah about who might be mad enough at him to wish him or his property harm?"

"You know we did. And no, he doesn't have any names."

"Because he wants to believe it's Calder."

Logan didn't deny that, which was the same as saying she was on the right track. "What I need is a credible lead—any lead—that will take me in a different direction," he said. "And the sooner, the better."

"Are you getting some kind of pressure about this?"

"You mean other than from Jonah? No. But I'm getting married in less than forty-eight hours, and then I'll be gone for ten days."

"Right." She shook her head. "Crap. Of all the times for something like this to happen." She looked at him. "You don't think whoever did this chose the timing of it to coincide with your being gone, do you?" She leaned more heavily into her seat and let her mind go down that trail.

"I can't rule it out, but it doesn't seem likely. Not based on what I know at the moment, anyway."

"Except you don't know anything."

They both fell silent for a moment and she ran through the previous night again in her mind, then started to list everyone connected with the docks, with Jonah, with the proposed club . . . but nothing stood out, nothing niggled, nothing seemed off. Except Winstock. Who had a lock-tight alibi.

Then Logan suddenly swore under his breath.

"What?" Hannah demanded. "What just occurred to you?"

"There is one other thing after all," Logan said quietly.

Something in his tone made her feel a thread of alarm. "Just tell me already."

"A possible motive for Calder Blue."

"What reason could he possibly have—"

"You know the family feud story, that the children Jed took might have been his, or might have been Jeremiah's."

"That was over a century ago. What on earth could tie that to—"

"If they were Jeremiah's kids, or even one of them was . . . it's possible then that Calder is a direct descendant of Jeremiah. Not Jedediah. And that property of Jonah's is an inheritance that has been handed father to son in the hundred-plus years since."

"You think Calder is here to put some kind of claim in on Jonah's property as his rightful inheritance?"

"I don't know. I will say I talked to Owen, and he said it appeared Calder knew nothing of that side of the story."

"Well, there you go then. If you can't trust Owen's judgment—"

"I do. That's not the point. It helps explain Jonah's

reasoning for suspecting him with such certainty. And the inheritance could be used against Calder, as an argument that he did it."

"Even if he'd known about that particular family secret, it still wouldn't explain burning the boathouse. Why burn up the inheritance you're hoping to claim?"

"I didn't say it was a perfect motive, just that we need to keep in mind every possible slant to this. Cover our asses, his ass, figure this thing out. Not just to nail who did it, but to keep them from nailing an innocent man and getting away with it."

"So, just to be clear, you still think Calder is innocent?"

Logan nodded, but it was obvious his mind was still spinning on this latest potential connection.

"I'm sorry, but I keep circling back to Brooks," Hannah said. "From his hiring Calder in the first place, to the fact that he keeps ducking their meetings." She looked at Logan. "Do you think it's a ploy to keep Calder in town, maybe get him a little frustrated, then boom, up goes the boathouse, so it looks as questionable as possible?"

"But how could the person—whoever it is—know how things were going to go down after Calder's arrival?"

"It doesn't take a rocket scientist to figure out Jonah was not going to welcome him with open arms," Hannah said. "And it has to be Brooks, because he's the one who got Calder here, then stalled him. Maybe he waited to see how things went with Jonah. Maybe he had some other idea in mind on how to use Calder's connection to Jonah to get what he wanted—namely, Jonah's property." She snapped her fingers. "Maybe he planned to find a way to exploit Calder's possible genetic tie to the property! It would be exactly up his alley, just like the end runs he tried around both Brodie Monaghan's property and Delia's claim to the diner property."

"How?" Logan asked.

"Who knows?" Hannah said. "But it's something to give some thought to. Because, beyond Brooks's contract offer, Calder is only connected to one thing here—Jonah Blue. So, maybe Brooks waits, watching how things play out. Jonah acts true to form, so Brooks either puts an already-decided-upon plan of action into play, or he comes up with one, making it up as he goes. Either way, he's set it up pretty brilliantly to not only put Jonah in a possibly precarious financial situation—have you found out just what the damage is there, by the way? But he also sets it up that although he masterminded the deed, someone else takes the fall. Someone the town considers an enemy, in a general sense. A wrong-side-of-the-tracks Blue, for lack of a better term. So he might even feel justified. I mean, I don't know what he's thinking, but maybe that's all there ever was to this." She looked at Logan. "And it's working."

"I follow you, and I might tend to agree with you, except for one thing. How could Winstock possibly know that Calder would wander down along the docks last night, just because he canceled dinner? The night before, Calder drove all the way back to Calais after their meeting time was shifted."

"Maybe that's why he waited until the last possible second, and left the new time dangling, to keep him here. Maybe it didn't matter where Calder was when the boathouse blew up, just that he was in town at all. For all I know, he talked to Jonah and planted some other seed of doubt there, but I'm guessing Jonah jumped on the Calder blame train all by himself." Another thought came to her and she sat up straighter, alarmed.

"What?" Logan asked. "What is it?"

She turned to him. "If we're right about this, so far, things are working out exactly how Brooks wants them to."

"You just said as much. What's on your mind now?"

"Did you find out the monetary damage to Jonah?"

Logan nodded. "It was pretty substantial. Not enough to ruin him, and he's got the whole summer season ahead to recoup, but the loss will definitely set him back, and, for some period of time, anyway, reduce his ability to operate at full capacity to recoup that loss. Not only because he lost the inventory, but because he has nowhere to put new inventory."

"So, what if Brooks wasn't planning to just blow up one boathouse? I mean, this puts the hurt on Jonah, but it doesn't finish him off. Maybe Winstock didn't plan or want anyone in the vicinity of that boathouse blowing up. He just needed Calder to be in town for Jonah to point the finger at. He most definitely didn't want anyone else there, like me. Because now there is a witness saying Calder didn't do it."

"So you're saying he has something more planned?"

"It's all gone according to plan so far, but that wasn't the final nail in Jonah's financial coffin, just the first." She shuddered a little on that last part, not wanting to believe Winstock would actually risk hurting anyone physically, but Jonah and his great-granddaughter hadn't been that far away. What if she and Calder hadn't been down there so she could call 9-1-1 and Calder could wake him up?

"But with all this attention already focused on Calder," Logan said, "wouldn't it be a stretch to believe he'd do something else to Jonah?"

Hannah sat back again. "Good point. But the more I think about it, the more this doesn't feel like the whole shebang. It feels like step one. Jonah's down, but he's not out. Yet." She looked at Logan again. "Maybe he only needed Calder for the first step."

"But if something else happens to Jonah now, and it's clearly not tied to Calder, that would only serve to lift suspicion from him. So that defeats the purpose of making him the scapegoat in the first place."

Hannah nodded, but her mind was in full litigator mode. When she was working a challenging criminal case, she had to look at everything the opposition had on her client, and try to find anything that wasn't right, that didn't jibe, that she could use to point the finger of guilt away from her client and, if she was even luckier, on to something or someone else. "I hear what you're saying, but without there being a more obvious culprit here—fired employee, angry vendor, etcetera—it's got to be Brooks. And you know, the irony is, if Brooks hadn't brought Calder here, we wouldn't have any real tangible connection between Brooks and Jonah at all. So the tool he's using to get what he wants is the same tool that is leading us right to him."

"Won't matter if it works," Logan said.

Hannah nodded. "I know. We just have to figure out how to find whoever Brooks hired to set the fire. That would be the weak link. If only you could get a look at the Winstock financials, see if he'd paid anyone a sum lately that seems sketchy."

"A man with an empire as big as his, something like that would be too easy to bury, too impossible to find on a cursory scan of his personal banking information."

"True." She fell silent, and let the wheels spin. It felt good to get her brain back in that groove; it was the one place she felt confident, certain. She just wished this were about some impersonal corporate client and not Calder Blue. *A man you want to get very personal with*. She frowned and pointedly ignored the little voice as she circled back to the other key point they'd stumbled across. "Who gets the case when you leave on your honeymoon? Dan doesn't have the experience and Barb—"

"We haven't worked that out yet. It may be that it sits and waits for me to get back. It's only ten days."

She boggled at him. "Ten days to let someone with Brooks's resources cover his ass? And what if I'm right and this was just the first volley?"

Logan rubbed a hand over the back of his neck and swore under his breath. "Then we'll cross that road when we come to it." He kept talking when she would have jumped right back in. "I'm not canceling my honeymoon. It took too long to figure out the logistics in the first place. I won't do that to Alex, and if you say anything, she'd be the first one to do it herself to help me."

"No, no, I wouldn't want you to and I'm not going to say anything, I promise. I just—can't someone you trust in a nearby precinct step in to handle things? Machias maybe? Or Lubec? It's a hike, but they have more resources than we do."

"If something happens, then yes, at least temporarily until I can get back." He looked at her. "If something happens, I will come back immediately, Hannah. But without any proof other than a string of hunches on your part—and mine," he added when she gave him a steady look, "that's all I can do. That and work it as best I can right up until the minute I walk down the aisle."

Now she swore under her breath. "I'm sorry," she said. "That all this is happening at a time when you should just be happy and looking forward to marrying Alex. Nothing ever happens here, and then this, and now of all times. I still have to think that's not a coincidence. But I'm sorry it's happening, all the same." She fell silent, and so did Logan.

After a moment, he said, quietly, "And I'm sorry about Tim. I thought it was a good thing. I mean, I worried about you and your work, and that you were getting so busy you weren't having a life, but I thought maybe he would balance that." He leaned across the seat and kissed her on the temple. "I have no problem driving down to D.C. and beating him up for you, you know," he murmured against her hair.

She sniffled a laugh through a sudden, fresh threat of tears. "Thank you. Not necessary, but thank you."

"Because you already kicked his ass?" Logan asked, leaning back and shifting forward again, putting the truck in gear.

"Something like that," she said, smiling, blinking the tears back more easily this time.

"So . . . about Blue. Calder," Logan qualified, then sent a sideways look at her as he turned the truck around and headed back to the main road. "Do I need to beat him up?"

She laughed again. "No." Her smile spread. "I can kick his ass on my own, too," she said. "If it comes to that."

They started the drive back toward town; then, sounding truly uncomfortable for the first time, Logan said, "Did you know he's divorced?"

Her thoughts had gone right back to figuring out how she was going to catch a break in this case before Logan walked down the aisle. "What? Who?"

"Calder."

She frowned at him. "He said something about it. Why are you mentioning it? Divorce isn't like a scarlet letter, you know."

"I do know that. I just—divorce is hard and so who knows—"

"Seriously, are you saying to me that I need to be careful because I might be his rebound fling? I'm not sixteen. And we're not having a fling."

He glanced at her, his expression filled with compassion and concern at the same time. "No . . . but you're also just out of a relationship."

She tried not to stiffen at the implication. "Thank you, Dr. Phil. If anything was happening, which it's not, I believe I can make my own choices without advice from the peanut gallery. Also, how do you know he's divorced? Because of his background check?"

"No, that was just a criminal records check. I had a contact. Or more like a contact through a contact, in the Calais department. So I used it."

She swung on him so fast he actually pulled the steering wheel just a hair to the left before self-correcting. "You called someone in Calais and asked questions about Calder? Regarding an arson incident? Does he know that?"

"I didn't inform him, nor am I required to. Why are you so bunched up over it? I mean, given there's nothing going on between you and all."

"Don't turn this back on me. He's here trying to find a way to mend a stupid family feud and causing a fair amount of strain on his immediate family by doing so. I have the feeling there's more going on there as well, but, like I said, I don't know him that well, so I don't know the particulars. Telling someone—anyone—in his town, which might be bigger than ours, but not by much, that he's being looked at in some kind of arson case in Blueberry Cove? Are you kidding me?"

"I have to go where the case leads. I can't help it if— what are you doing?"

She lifted a *one moment* finger, having just pressed in a number on her cell phone and now holding said phone to her ear. Probably she should have thought this through a bit more, but what the hell. If she was going to learn to go with her gut again, she had to start somewhere. "Calder?" she said a moment later. "It's Hannah. Are you still in the Cove?" She paused, then sighed in relief. "Good. We need to talk."

Chapter Twelve

"Please tell Mr. Winstock that my patience is near an end here. He either wishes to go forward on this project with me as his contractor, or he does not. Given the considerable delays he's faced already, I'd think he'd want to get moving on this sooner rather than later. I'll be staying in Blueberry Cove till Sunday evening and hope Mr. Winstock can adjust his schedule accordingly. After that, I will be returning to Calais and my other business concerns and he'll have to find someone else to build his club." Calder barely stayed on the phone long enough to listen to Winstock's assistant make additional mealymouthed assurances before ending the call and tossing the phone on the passenger seat of his truck.

He scrubbed a hand over his face and considered his options for dinner now that he knew he wouldn't be meeting with Winstock that day. He had no intention of signing that contract, but he wanted—needed—to sit across from the man and at least try to get a sense of what was really going on while looking him straight in the eye. He snatched his phone back up and called Hannah. "It's Calder," he said, when she answered. "Sorry I couldn't talk longer before. I was on hold with Winstock's office. How about an early dinner?" He grinned, listening to her reply. She was in crisp, lawyer mode. Why that made him happy, he didn't know. It probably boded trouble. But he was discovering that trouble where Hannah McCrae was concerned was the kind he didn't mind getting into. "Sooner is good," he said. "I can do sooner. Just tell me where and I'm on my way."

Twenty minutes later, he was pulling into the lot of a small diner about fifteen miles south of the Cove, on the outskirts of Machias. No blue beast was parked in the small gravel lot, but he was sure he was in the right place. There was no other establishment in sight. Other than a boat repair shop and an old, run-down gas station, long since closed, he hadn't passed a single other place of business since leaving Blueberry. Surprisingly, or maybe not if it was the only game in town, there were a few other cars in the lot.

He started to get out of his truck, thinking he'd grab a table and maybe order himself a nice, cold beer, when his phone rang. Assuming it was Hannah, he smiled as he slid it out of his pocket, then was surprised to see his father's name pop up on the screen instead. He sat back in the truck, took a breath, then answered. "Hey, Pop. I got your e-mail this morning. I faxed the adjustments on that warehouse bid to Eli about an hour ago, along with some suggested changes to the specs. I made pencil marks on the blueprint to show him what I had in mind. It's a better fit in those corners and saves us a hassle in getting those custom collar ties and ceiling joists made. Not to mention the cost. Tell him to check the floor in the office, sometimes those long sheets slide right off the fax tray."

"I'm not calling about the goddamn warehouse project!" Thaddeus Blue's gravel voice was even rougher than usual, and twice as tight.

Calder tried not to tense, even as he swore under his

breath and prepared himself for whatever this latest storm was going to be about. His father had been quite vocal in his lack of support for his oldest son's latest endeavor, and was even less of a fan of Calder's continued stay in the Cove. The lack of a signed contract with Winstock was definitely not helping.

In the few conversations they'd had since Calder's initial arrival in Blueberry, his father hadn't asked a single question about Jonah or the Cove Blues, and Calder hadn't offered. He didn't now, either. "What's going on, then?" Calder asked, hoping maybe it was another one of their job sites giving them grief, but bracing himself for yet another lecture on how he was wasting his time and company money, complete with barked orders to get his ass back to Calais.

"What in the living goddamn hell is going on down there?"

So, okay, not just angry. Try livid. "You know why I'm here," Calder replied, both resignedly and doggedly. He hadn't backed down when his father and Eli—the next to oldest and most company-dedicated of Thad's four sons—had flipped their collective shit when he'd announced the bid and resulting job offer that would put half their resources on a job ninety-plus minutes away, not to mention the whole family feud aspect. He sure as hell wasn't backing out now. As he'd reminded his father in heated situations before, Thaddeus wasn't the only Blue mentioned in the name of their company.

"I left word with Carrie with my schedule for the remainder of the weekend," he continued. "I'll be back in Calais Sunday night, and I'll know what's next then." Carrie was the secretary and all around wrangler for Blue and Sons Contracting. "Is there something specific I can help with? Is Kendall giving you a hard time over that increase we had to make on the gravel? Because he's just going to have to suck that up. It's his own damn fault for not telling us about the drainage issue he'd already been having—"

"It's not about the fucking gravel," his father shouted. He was actually screaming. "What is this about a burned-out boathouse and some ridiculous shit about them looking at you for arson? And I have to hear this from goddamn Malcolm at the sheriff's office?"

Well, shit. "Dad, Dad, calm down. I don't know what Sheriff Lonergan heard, or told you, but I'm not in any trouble here. I'm a witness, nothing more. There was a fire. Someone torched Jonah Blue's—"

"I don't give a living, breathing fuck about some goddamn fire and I sure as hell don't want to hear you so much as whisper that man's name ever again. The Cove Blues have been nothing but trouble for us, and clearly a hundred years hasn't changed that." Thaddeus was so angry, his voice trembled with rage. "Now get in your goddamn truck and drive your ass home. And in case you forgot where the hell that is, it's not in fucking Blueberry Cove! And it's not on that godforsaken, run-down, piece-of-shit property you're calling a farm. You're not a goddamn farmer. And you're not a fucking missionary. You belong here. With me, with your brothers—who are a damn sight more grateful for what I've built and the life it has provided than you've ever been. They're having to pick up your slack, doing the good and fine work that they and you were put on God's green earth to do. So, get on it!"

The line went abruptly dead as his father disconnected. Which was just as well since an aneurysm or heart attack had sounded imminent. Calder wished he could say that that kind of behavior was an aberrant thing, or that he felt guilty for being responsible for pushing his father into such a state. The truth was, for too many years, Calder had shouldered that burden and more. However, as an adult, working with his father, seeing all the ins and outs of his father's day—and not just the parts he dragged home and shared, often at top decibel, with his family—Calder had come to realize that his father was just made like that. Belligerent, bullheaded, with a hair-trigger temper that ran as wide as it did deep. Fortunately, he wasn't given to physical violence of any sort, and Calder, as well as his brothers, knew that his anger blew out as fast as it blew up. They'd still been kids when they'd learned to simply take the blast, wisely refrain from responding in any manner, and then continue on about their business. Until the next time.

"So . . . sooner wasn't soon enough, I guess."

Calder shifted around to find Hannah standing at the edge of his open truck door. He swallowed a string of swear words and not a little embarrassment. "I guess you heard. You and everyone within a five-mile radius."

"I'd hoped to warn you. Logan talked to the local law in Calais as follow-up. I should have just told you that over the phone, but I was with Logan at the time, and—well, anyway. Water under bridge now, I guess. I'm sorry."

"I'd apologize for my father," Calder said, "but I've learned it's not my responsibility to do so. I will apologize that you had to listen to that. He's actually a well-educated man, though you'd never guess it by that language."

"Calder—" she said, sounding abashed for him, but thankfully not pitying. "Consider us even, for the call you overheard," she said at length.

He held her dark blue gaze, and noticed there wasn't quite as much of a makeup mask in play this afternoon. And she'd changed since their meeting that morning at the station house, into a soft floral, sleeveless sundress with a scoop neck, the hem of which dropped all the way to her shins, though it wasn't any less sexy for its loosely shaped silhouette. Her hair was brushed back from her face, but worn down and loose, and he thought he'd never seen her look so soft and feminine, then realized that wasn't true. She'd never been anything but in his eyes, no matter the wrapping. "How're the injuries? You look better."

She made a face, but smiled briefly. "I feel better, thanks." She flashed her hands at him, showing off short nails painted a pale pink. "We had a girls' spa day and that helped, too." She touched her cheekbones lightly. "Swelling is mostly gone, just puffiness when I first get up, and late in the evening. Still aches a bit, and the stitches are starting to itch like mad, but I guess that's a good sign."

His gaze dropped to her mouth. "And the lip?"

He saw her throat work and had to swallow the urge to grin. Because looking at that mouth worked him up a little, too.

"Looks like I'll get to keep it after all," she said wryly. "My ability to whistle is saved."

He grinned, and it was all he could do to keep from pulling her into his arms, sliding his hands beneath that silky waterfall of dark hair, and sinking into a deep, slow kiss. Only, he knew if he put his hands on her now, he wasn't sure either of them would stop at a kiss. Between the situation he'd found himself in with Jonah's boathouse, Hannah now acting as his lawyer, and his father having apoplexy over the whole thing, it would probably be wise to keep his hands off her. Period.

"Well," he said, trying to clear the sudden roughness from his voice. "Since we're here, we might as well go in and grab a bite." No reason they couldn't eat a meal together, he told himself. She was his lawyer, after all. Then he paused. "Unless you'd rather get back to the Cove. I appreciate your trying to warn me about the call to Sheriff Lonergan, and keeping that as private as possible, I truly do, but I'm sure there's probably some wedding-related function you should be attending. Wedding-day prep? Bachelorette party?"

Her expression shifted slightly at that last one.

"Ah, girls' night out it is, then. And a Friday, to boot. Wait—you didn't let your flakey sister plan that too, did you? Because—"

"Fiona's not flakey," Hannah said, somewhat coolly, instantly closing family ranks. "She's smart and sharp and a creative genius." She relented slightly when he merely continued to stare at her. "Okay, maybe a bit eccentric, but the best creative minds are."

"And she's lucky to have a sister who loves her like you do," he said with a smile.

"She'd step up for me, too."

"I have no doubt of that." Even though he and his brothers spent a fair amount of time at odds with each other, he'd have done the same. And their conflicts were largely due to the fact that three of them worked together full-time, along with their cantankerous father—which was putting it kindly—and the youngest only thought he knew everything because he was still in college and didn't know any real damn thing yet.

Calder hopped down from the cab of his truck and put his hand on the small of Hannah's back, shifting her away from the door so he could push it shut behind him. Just pressing his palm, even that briefly, to the slender curve of her back, feeling the softness of her cotton dress, being close enough to get a whiff of the faint lavender scent she wore, sent a jolt of awareness through his body so sharp and keen, there was no mistaking the clear warning it was. No matter how many silent, rational lectures he gave himself, his control around her was shaky at best, and about one touch away from crumbling completely.

"This place any good?" he asked, sliding his hands in his back pockets, just to be safe. He glanced at the small building. It was a square box of a place, with old shake siding, painted white, or once painted white, and a tin roof mostly still painted dark green. A neon sign in the window proclaimed it was J.T.'S, though half the T and the apostrophe no longer lit up.

"I don't know," Hannah said. "Never been."

Calder lifted a brow. "This place looks like it's been here since the dawn of time and you grew up not fifteen miles from here."

"I know, and you're right, it's been here longer than I've been alive. But we had Delia's, so I never needed to come here."

"Why today?"

"Because I wanted to warn you about Logan talking to your sheriff, and I also wanted to talk to you about the arson case a little more and what Logan and I discussed today. We did a little brainstorming on what we think is going on with Winstock and I wanted to get your feedback, see if you could add anything. So, I wanted some privacy."

"Assuming small towns here operate like small towns up in my neck of the woods, I don't think fifteen miles is going to be much of a challenge for the Cove grapevine to conquer."

"I don't care if the town talks about us, but at least the conversation itself will be private and that's all that matters."

"Fair enough," he said, but his mind was stuck on the town talking about them. The way she said it was like folks were already whispering. He added that to the list of things they were going to discuss over their meal. Halfway across the gravel lot, he stopped in his tracks, and said, "I have a better idea."

She paused beside him and simply gave him a questioning look. And he still wanted to taste her so bad, his teeth ached. His hands went right back into his pockets. And not where they wanted to go, which was cupping those small breasts, thumbing her nipples through that soft cotton dress, running his palms down the slender curve of her back, cupping her, pulling her into the cradle of his hips and—

"A talk," he said, rather more abruptly than he'd intended. "And a meal. But not in there." What was left of the rational side of his brain was all but yelling at him to turn himself right back around and march the two of them into that very public diner.

Yeah, he decided he was going to ignore that voice completely. Or at least for the next few hours. Life was short. And he was tired of being the dutiful one.

He motioned back toward his truck. "Lock up the blue beast and climb in the cab. Just shove whatever is on the seat into the back."

She said nothing to that, but stood still and watched him as he continued to walk toward the diner. "Where are you going?"

He turned around, continuing to walk backward a few steps. "You like steak and cheese? Lobster roll? Or do you eat sissy girl food?"

"I'm more of a haddock sandwich kind of girl."

He grinned. "Perfect. Give me ten minutes."

Took him a little longer than ten minutes, but to his relief and absolute pleasure, Hannah was still waiting for him, leaning against the passenger door of his truck when he stepped out carrying two brown paper bags and two bottles of root beer. He had a water bottle under his arm, just in case she wasn't a fan of soda. When he'd kissed her the night before, down by the docks, she'd tasted like something sweet, not like alcohol as he'd expected since she'd come from the party at the pub, so he thought soda might be the thing. "Why didn't you climb in? Need a hand up? Shoulder still bugging you?"

"A little, but mostly I didn't because you locked it."

"No, I—" He stopped, shook his head, laughed. "Sorry. Force of habit."

"Crime a big problem in Calais?"

"Only of construction materials and tools. In my occupation, you learn to lock things as you go." He juggled the two bags into her hands and popped the locks with his key fob. "Here—"

"I got it," she said, then left him half gaping when she gripped the folded bag tops between her teeth, pulled the door open and swung up into the seat like she was some kind of long-haul trucker. She set the bags on the seat next to her and reached toward him, wiggling her fingers. "Drinks?"

"Well, okay then," he said, handing the bottles to her, but keeping the water. He couldn't stop staring, and only partly because she kept surprising him.

She rolled her eyes. "What, did you think hotshot D.C. lawyers only ride around in little red sports cars?"

"So now you're a hotshot, are you?"

She merely leaned out, and pulled the door closed in his face, then smiled at him through the raised window.

Grinning, he shook his head and circled the truck, realizing the scene with his father had already been shoved to the back of his mind and hopefully hers as well. Whatever else happened that afternoon, he could kiss her just for providing him relief from spending the next few hours chewing on that phone call. Which would have been the least of it. He settled in the driver's seat and found her exploring the contents of the two brown bags.

"Both haddock?" she asked, glancing up at him from the

bag holding two thick sandwiches wrapped in white wax paper.

He nodded. "Should be a thing of tartar in there. Wasn't sure if you liked it."

"What's in the other bag then?" But she was already opening it, and immediately groaned.

"You hate hush puppies?"

"The exact opposite of hate," she said, her voice taking on a somewhat reverent tone. "It's bad enough I'm eating a fried fish sandwich a little over a day out from having to wear a fitted and tailored bridesmaid dress, but hush puppies? And root beer? Which is my guilty pleasure, by the way, how did you know? It's all just—" She stopped, shook her head, her dark eyes all but glowing, as if she were looking at forbidden fruit.

He shifted in his seat, feeling his own forbidden fruit stir, and held out the bottle of water. "Does this help?"

She clutched one bottle of root beer close to her chest. "Don't even think about reaching for this bottle."

It might have been that specific moment, he thought, with her hair swinging against her shoulders, the pretty sundress softening her curves as she held on to her root beer for dear life, her beautiful dark eyes sparkling, all but daring him to make a grab for it. Or maybe it was the culmination of all the moments leading up to it, from the way she'd ordered him to be on his way while still strapped into her wrecked sports car, to how she'd felt stumbling into his arms with a restored vintage trunk and that Scarlett O'Hara dress pushing her breasts up for his viewing pleasure, to the smooth, professional litigator who had stormed the precinct in his defense just that morning. All he knew was that he wanted her. Right now in this truck . . . and in his every-day life. He'd known her for only a few days, and yet the thought of her not being in his orbit was simply something he didn't want to contemplate.

He wanted Hannah McCrae. He wanted her in the seat next to him, he wanted her defending him in a court of law, he wanted her riding down the highway next to him, and galloping across a field. . . . He wanted her warm in his bed at night, and every single morning. He wanted her wherever he happened to be. He could picture her anywhere, and everywhere in his world, and he knew, looking at her now, she'd fit right in.

And he had absolutely no idea what to do about it.

"Your root beer is safe with me," he said. Then, chuckling as she kept hold of it anyway, he stuck his key in the ignition. "Buckle up, Scarlett," he told her, then shot her a wink and a grin. "Guess I'm hijacking you after all."

Chapter Thirteen

Hannah had been trying to decide how she felt about this latest turn of events, and what she should do about it. The only thing she knew was what she wasn't doing about it, and that was stopping him.

He didn't continue down the highway to Machias, or turn back toward Blueberry Cove. Instead, he took the side road from the parking lot and headed toward the ocean. The Maine coastline was made up of thousands of little inlets and coves, and though she'd never been down this particular side road, it would eventually wind its way down to the water.

He didn't say anything, so she let the silence settle over them, enjoying the comfort of it. She used a napkin to unscrew the metal caps from the bottles of root beer and tucked them in the drink holders on the dash. Then she opened the bag of hush puppies, inhaled the sweet and crispy scent before rolling the edges of the bag down and tipping it toward him.

"Thanks," he said, fishing one out.

She did the same, then groaned as she sunk her teeth into the warm, breaded cornmeal bite. So what if she had to borrow one of Fiona's Spanx camisoles for the wedding?

These were just too good to pass up. And, frankly, indulging in something that felt good, even if it was just a heavenly bite of hush puppy, took the edge off the other sensory pleasures she'd been missing for some time now, and was suddenly craving once again. She purposely kept her gaze off her copilot . . . and his hush puppies. "You want your sandwich now or when we get to the water? Assuming that's where we're heading."

"I'll wait," he said, then continued winding his way slowly down the point.

It wasn't long before she could see stretches of bright blue water backing the occasional beach cottage property on one side of the road or the other, as the land narrowed toward the point. Piers extended out into peaceful coves, boats with brightly patterned sails bobbed at anchor, awaiting their next adventure. Colorful clusters of old pot buoys hung from garage doors and mailboxes. Boats and lobster traps dotted various yards in almost equal quantities.

Hannah let the familiarity and comfort of it wash over her and seep deeply inside, wallowing in the pure pleasure of being home again, of feeling that fortifying sense of belonging to something. Something good, something strong, something that welcomed her happily and readily, with open arms instead of sly, knowing glances. For the first time since coming back to the Cove, she didn't feel like this was merely a safe haven to hide away in while licking her wounds. Rather, this was the place she felt strong, and good, and happy. The last thing she wanted to do here was hide.

All along the stretches that ran between the freshly cut lawns were clustered spears of pink, white, and purple lupines, adding more warmth and charm. Hannah smiled, thinking maybe it was just as well she wasn't driving. She'd been looking at the lupines right before she almost sideswiped Calder's truck. She didn't share that thought with the man himself, but when she sent a sideways glance in his direction, he quickly let his gaze slide from her back to the road, an amused smile playing at the corners of his mouth, as if he'd guessed her thoughts anyway.

She dug out another hush puppy and handed him the bag again. Given the events of the last twenty-four hours, and the tension that usually sang between them, the ride was surprisingly peaceful, soothing. Gulls soared and cried overhead as they neared the shore and Hannah let the natural ebb and flow of her surroundings relax her and smooth out the last of the rough edges she seemed to carry with her all the time now, no matter how much she tried to simply let things go.

The road ended at an old boat ramp, fronted by a small dirt and sand lot barely big enough to turn the truck around. There were no houses down here, at least none right on the rocky shoreline of the little harbor. There were no roads that wandered around the shoreline either, though with the tide out, a swath of seaweed-strewn sea floor between the receding waters and the rocks had been exposed, creating a temporary beach of sorts.

Calder angled the truck so that they faced the open waters of the small harbor, with a view of the ocean beyond it, at the edge of the horizon. He pushed a button on the console and lowered both of their windows, then cut the engine. Other than the cries of the gulls and the water lapping the shore, the peace was complete.

He picked up the other bag containing their sandwiches and handed Hannah hers and a few napkins. He set the containers of tartar sauce on the dash between them. She didn't unwrap hers right away, instead letting her head loll back on the headrest as she took in a nice, long breath of the briny air, then let it out slowly. "I feel like I'm a world away and home, all at the same time." It was only when he answered that she realized she'd spoken out loud.

"Well, in a way, you are both of those things, right?"

She nodded, then started unwrapping her sandwich. "It's funny, though. Part of me feels that way, and yet another part of me feels like I've never left."

"You said it's been a few years?"

"Yes. Work. Relationship. More work. I've visited, but I've never been back for long. Always too busy, too focused on my new world. The one I thought I wanted so badly."

"But . . . no work now. Or, not the work you were doing." When she looked at him curiously, he said, "On the phone, the night of the fire. You told Limp—uh, that guy that you weren't working for your firm any longer."

Her lips tilted as she mentally filled in the rest of the moniker Calder had tagged the jerk with. Probably right, too. "Yes, I did. And no, I'm not with my old firm any longer." She wondered how she'd answer if he asked her where she was working now, whether she'd tell him the truth. Probably. Why not? It wasn't as if he was going to tell Logan or her sisters. And she only had a few more days to get through before they would know anyway. Only that wasn't the direction he went.

"And the relationship?" he asked, seemingly just as casually, but she noticed he'd stopped eating while he waited for her answer.

"No," she said, the single word a bit rougher than she'd have liked. "Not any longer. Not for some time now. If there had been, I wouldn't have let you—" She broke off, took another bite of her sandwich as she looked out over the water.

"Good to know," was all he said. Then he went back to his sandwich as well.

She took a few more bites, debating whether to ask what

she wanted to know, then decided what the hell, fair was fair. "How long has it been?" she asked. "Since you . . . became single again. You mentioned you were divorced, the first day we met," she clarified. "Assuming you still are, that is," she added, realizing she hadn't established that, really, either. Not that it mattered, she told herself. She wasn't getting involved with him, anyway.

"A little over two years ago now. Longer if you add in the separation. And no, there isn't anyone else."

She could feel his gaze on her like a physical caress when he added, "I wouldn't have kissed you, or even touched you, if there had been."

She swallowed, hard, and was thankful there was no food involved, or she might have choked. His voice did things to her, had, since the first moment he'd spoken to her when she'd had a face full of air bag. Only she couldn't blame shock or trauma for the effect it was having on her now. "Good to know," she managed, echoing his earlier reply. "Mutual decision?" she heard herself ask, then quickly added, "Never mind. None of my business."

He answered anyway. "Mutual in the sense that she delivered an ultimatum and I didn't pick the option that included us staying married."

"Oh," Hannah said, wishing she hadn't asked. "I'm sorry. Regardless of why, it can't have been easy. I shouldn't have pried."

"I don't mind," he said, sounding a little surprised by that. "We were married five years. I wanted family, and a different life from the one that had been carved out for me. My father got to know her father through business dealings and we were introduced at a company function. Both sides were very happy we hit it off." He leaned back in his seat a little. "A business merger and a family merger."

She glanced at him. "That sounds . . . less than romantic."

"It was . . . and it wasn't. We did hit it off, and I did love her, but I don't know how much of that was because everybody else was just so damned happy we were together, so we were reveling in the joy and glow of it all and sort of overlooking the differences between us—I mean, how could so many people who loved us be wrong?"

"You're the oldest, right? Was she?"

He nodded. "I am, yes. And she's an only."

Hannah made an *ooh* face. "That can be even trickier."

"Indeed." His grin resurfaced then, and she couldn't seem to look away.

"Since you asked, I can do the same. How long ago? And who ended it?"

"We were together a year and a half, though I'd known him a little longer. Business connections. It ended six months ago," she said, and for the first time, it felt like it had been a lot, lot longer ago than that. *Thank God.* "And I guess it was mutual, though neither one of us did the deciding. His pregnant wife took care of that."

She couldn't quite believe she'd said that. Out loud. To a stranger. Almost stranger. Okay, he didn't feel at all like a stranger to her now, but that didn't bear examining too closely.

"Wow," he said, but calmly. He took another bite of his sandwich, as if nonplussed, or musing over her response. "I'm guessing you didn't know."

"About the wife? Or the pregnancy?"

He looked at her, looking amused even as he finished chewing and swallowing his last bite. "Either," he said, then wiped his mouth with a napkin and crumpled that and the sandwich wrapper up, shoving them both back in the paper sack.

"What makes you think I wouldn't sleep with a married man?"

"You mean other than the fact that you just said you wouldn't have let me kiss you if you were in a relationship?"

He surprised her by reaching over and taking her sandwich wrapper and the half-empty bag of hush puppies, scooping it all up and depositing it in the backseat. Then he flicked off her seat belt, but when she tensed, thinking he meant to reach for her, he surprised her again by opening his door and sliding out of the truck.

He was at her door before she'd gathered her now scattered thoughts. He opened it and lifted his hands as she turned and swung her legs out. He took her hips in his broad palms as easily and smoothly as if he helped her from the truck all the time, as part of the normal course of things. He had helped her down, once before. But he'd taken her hand then, not her hips. And when she'd stepped to the ground, he'd stepped back a respectful foot or two. Unlike now, when she slid out and directly into his personal space, and he stayed right where he was.

His hands stayed on her hips, too, and she tipped her face to his, thinking she should probably do something, anything, to keep this from going where it was most assuredly going. But then he said, "I know because you've been hurt. Badly. And not just by Beanie's Fat Quarters sign."

She tensed a little, not liking the idea that she was so obviously wounded. It made her feel pathetic, and she was just starting to feel whole and strong again. "Like I said, breakups aren't easy on anyone—"

"Shh," he said gently. "That's not why I know you were hurt." He searched her eyes, then let his gaze roam her face as he lifted a hand and traced a calloused but gentle fingertip along her temple, over the still-tender skin at her cheekbone, then along her jaw, until his gaze came back to rest on hers. "It was the way you looked when you said it. Your voice was calm, smooth . . . but those eyes of yours were anything but. Someone capable of inflicting that kind of hurt wouldn't have been that hurt."

Hannah's thoughts shifted instantly to Tim, who had absolutely been someone capable of that. She remembered their confrontation after his wife's surprise appearance at her office. He'd been contrite and apologetic, then angry and accusatory when she wouldn't forgive him. One thing he hadn't been, she realized now . . . was hurt. Hurt that he'd done something so callous and cruel, hurt that he'd betrayed his wife and unborn child, or even hurt that he was going to lose her because of it. Mostly, he'd just been pissed off at having been revealed for the man he truly was.

It was like a weight lifted from her. She'd been plenty mad at Tim, once the shock and hurt had settled into something more rational and manageable. But the feeling that came over her now wasn't so much renewed anger at him, it was . . . well, it was a sense of pity, of all things. Because Calder was right. Someone who could willingly and knowingly do what he'd done, to people he claimed to love, could never truly feel what she'd felt for him, never understand how glorious it was to love and feel loved in return. Tim's love had turned out to be empty and hollow, but hers for him had been real and true. And rather than make her feel stupid and foolish, the knowledge made her feel proud, and strong, for having the ability to feel that way at all. She'd chosen wrong, yes, but she'd go on to love again. Tim would never love, not truly.

She looked at Calder, and blinked back . . . not tears really, but tamped-down emotions that were suddenly swirling inside her. "Thank you. For saying that. Not about me, but—"

"It took me a long time to get that," he told her, stroking her finger along her chin, "to truly be able to see what I thought we had, what I knew I had, versus what she was capable of having. With anyone."

"Then you've saved me untold months of emotional wrangling," she said, surprised to hear the laugh come from her. "I feel like the grip on my heart just loosened a little, if that makes sense."

"Perfect sense," he said, and she believed him.

"What happened?" she asked. "To finally bring about the end, what with the family support and all. It couldn't have been easy."

"No, disappointing them was a big part of the problem," he said. "What about your family? I'm sure it's been good to have their support. I know it was important to me, from my brothers. Invaluable, really."

"Actually," she said, "I just told them earlier today. And I didn't tell them why, just that it ended." She hurried to explain before he could say anything, just wanting to get the rest out and change the subject. "I didn't tell them when it happened, because it was Christmas—"

"Six months. Yeah, I guess it would have been. Well, isn't that some—awful," he said. She was sure he'd been about to use the kind of language she would have. "I'm sorry."

"I was, too. But I knew Logan was going to propose to Alex over the holidays, so the last thing I was going to do was dampen their happiness with my crap, and then the crap sort of hit my professional fan, too, so I was in scramble mode. Only no amount of scrambling was going to fix that particular storm."

"Why would your personal life affect your job? How

did your firm even know about it? Unless—did you work together? He's a lawyer, too?"

She shook her head. "No, his wife marched into my office—recall, his very pregnant wife—and told me and everyone within shouting distance, to leave him alone."

"Jesus," he said; then he did swear, though under his breath. "I'm so sorry." He paused for a moment. "So, that's why that asshole on the phone thought you would be interested in—?" He broke off, swore a little more under his breath. "That's just not right. Surely, they knew you weren't—?"

She laughed. "Oh trust, me, they thought they knew. I had something of a reputation. 'Cool under fire' would be a nice way of putting it. So something that salacious and tawdry? Oh, I was a marked woman instantly. It got real ugly, real fast." She waved her hand, then got the rest of it out. "Anyway, I didn't say anything to my family because of the impending proposal, then the fallout kept me pretty occupied and I really didn't want to discuss that with my family, and now I'm here for Logan's wedding, so I'm not going to put a damper on that. But as soon as the wedding is over, I will come clean—or would have, but I sort of got outed today instead." She thought again about the rest of that particular conversation and decided she'd said enough. She didn't need Calder knowing folks in town were gossiping about them, and that included the police chief and her sisters. "I didn't tell them why, but eventually I'll have to explain why I quit and came home for good, so, I guess—"

"You're back in the Cove to stay?"

She realized too late what she'd let slip. "I am. Or at least, that's the current plan. I haven't done anything about it yet, because—"

"You haven't told them that part yet."

She nodded. "I will, but not until the wedding is over. I really wanted Alex and Logan to have their moment and just be here to support them. Logan deserves all the happiness in the world and—"

"And then boathouses are blowing up and family feuds are reigniting," Calder said. "So much for a peaceful wedding."

Hannah sighed and slumped a little, and now he was the one squeezing her hand. "And now they know about me and Tim—my ex—so they'll all be tiptoeing around me at the ceremony, which I will hate and was also why I didn't mention the real reason he wasn't here with me."

"Doesn't make the wedding part any easier," he said.

"No, but—" She broke off and looked up at him, peering closely at him until he laughed a little self-consciously.

"What, do I have hush puppy in my teeth?"

"No," she said, "your teeth are as perfect as the rest of you."

Now he laughed outright. "What is that supposed to mean? Because you do not make it sound like a good thing, and, for the record, I am far, far from perfect. Ask any member of my family, and they'll happily regale you with my shortcomings for days." He made a face. "On second thought, only ask my brothers. You don't need to hear what my father has to say."

Hannah smiled dryly. "I'm pretty sure I already did."

"So, back to fair being fair, you didn't tell me what brought your marriage to an end. I've revealed enough now that I'm not even going to apologize for asking. I deserve equal ammo," she added with a cheeky grin. Kerry would be so proud of her.

"Well, it's no secret to anyone why my marriage ended."

"You said you had differences all along," she said, steering herself back on track. "So did something else happen? You said you wanted a family—was that one of the differences? I know that would be a hard one to get past."

"Tenley was sharp, pretty and very smart. I liked her for her intellect as much as I did her . . . everything else," he finished with a grin that was somehow both endearing and wolfish.

"Such a guy."

"Guilty, but in the beginning, it was true."

"So, what were the tarnished spots you missed?"

"Nothing on her. She was always exactly who she was, from the beginning. I just chose to think the differences wouldn't matter, that the good would outweigh the problems.

"But when I figured out the kind of life I really wanted, the one I knew would make me happy . . . it wasn't what she wanted."

"She liked the family merger thing," she guessed. "Being married to the oldest son of a successful company owner, groomed to take his place, from a good family herself, maybe used to that lifestyle and assuming her life would be more of the same. Am I on the right track?"

"Yes, Counselor," he said, both a rueful smile and teasing glint on his face, each lethal to her senses in their own way.

"So, did she? Try it your way? You gave her dream life a chance. Did she give yours one, too?"

"No," he said, quietly. "That was where the ultimatum came in. She already knew what she wanted. She had what she wanted. I was the one who wanted—needed—something different."

"Your farm?" Hannah thought back again to his father's harsh criticism of Calder's horse farm.

He nodded. He opened his mouth to add something, then apparently thought better of it, and closed it again.

"What?" she asked, wanting to reach up and smooth the

creases that had formed at the corners of his mouth, his eyes. She didn't trust herself to do that, though. She wasn't even strong enough to step away from his touch. "Just say it."

"You're right. She married the guy who was being bred to take over his father's contracting business."

"In the end, you had to save yourself if there was going to be anything left to give to anyone else."

His gaze narrowed speculatively and he looked deeply into her eyes, searching them, again. "Is that what you did? When you left your firm? Rescue yourself?"

She nodded, but she looked away then, and didn't add anything to that.

"So you know the guilt that comes with that. The sense of failure for not being what your partner wants you to be, who they want you to be," he said, but he didn't make it a question. "In your case, I'm guessing it was feeling like you were failing family, but still. It's never an easy decision."

"Did you get past it?" she asked, after a moment of shared silence.

"I don't think you get past it as much as you come to terms with it. I don't regret the choice I made." He cupped her cheek in his palm and tipped her face up to his. "Not with my farm, the marriage, or the one I'm going to have to make with my father and the company, once I can make the farm self-sustaining. Doesn't mean it won't hurt, or that I won't feel guilty, or sad, but I did come to understand that we only have one life, and it's up to us to live it as honestly and forthrightly as we know how. For ourselves and the ones we're here to take care of. My father will never understand that or see it that way. His mission statement is very different from mine and leaves no room for reinterpretation."

"You inherit what I provided for you and you're grateful for it, or you're a total loss," she murmured and saw the answer in his eyes. "I'm so sorry," she whispered. "What is your vision for the farm?"

"I have a couple hundred acres. I don't want to do vegetable farming, but some cows, more goats. Mostly I want to expand the stables, build a few more paddocks, a show ring eventually. Become a boarding facility, as there aren't many out where I am, hire a trainer or two to give riding lessons. Personally, I'd like to get involved in providing a place for horse rescue and rehabilitation. Maybe combine that with some groups who work with kids who have certain genetic issues, and have found horse therapy to be very rewarding. It would be a great way to put those two things together. But that's all a ways off yet, and I wouldn't just up and leave the company high and dry. My youngest brother graduates college next spring and, as of now, anyway, plans to come on board. So that's sort of the target date for me, too. My father will just have to accept that that is how it will be."

"Your plan for the farm is . . . well, it's practical and smart, but it's also beautiful. You'd be very good at that. Wonderful, even." He was, she already understood, a rescuer by nature. And not just for broken-down horses. She suspected her heart was in her eyes a little, but he made it damn hard not to feel that way. "Maybe in time your father will come to see the good you'll be doing."

Calder grinned again. "You know, Counselor, I might just have to invite you to a Blue family dinner sometime. Maybe you could sway the judge and jury on my poor, sorry behalf."

She smiled, and didn't think he'd be offended by saying, "I'm good, but I don't know if I'm that good."

He barked a laugh at that and pulled her fully into his arms as smoothly as if that were where she spent most of her time anyway. She went into them, just as smoothly, and decided, for the moment, simply not to question the whys or wherefores.

"Hannah McCrae," he said, tipping her mouth up to his. "I'm going to kiss you. Really kiss you."

"Why, is that a warning, Mr. Blue?" she asked, a faint bit of the South coloring the words. "Should I be concerned for my virtue? After all, you're a suspected felon, are you not? What if being kissed by you besmirches my good name?"

The slow slide of his grin matched the slow slide of hers. His lips were just a breath from hers. "Frankly, my dear, I suddenly don't think I give a damn."

Chapter Fourteen

He tasted like hush puppies and root beer, Hannah thought, and decided that might just be the best thing ever. But whereas the food had been a comfort, Calder's kiss was anything but. This was no gentle, exploratory kiss meant to incite desire, or something fast and hard, delivered in the heat of the moment. This was slow, deliberate, and very, very thorough. He kissed, he nibbled, he nipped. He slid his tongue slowly, languorously between her lips, then seduced hers back between his. He didn't coax her to lower her walls, he merely set about systematically destroying them, until she wanted to shove him aside and tear them down for him, if it meant having more of him faster, deeper, harder. More of his kisses, more of his hands on her, just . . . more.

He allowed her no time to think, to decide, to be objective, much less rational. He was too busy making her feel, and what she was feeling was simply too damn good to stop just so she could overthink things.

"Your lip," he murmured when she made a soft sound of protest as he left her mouth and continued his campaign along the curve of her jaw, then the tender skin along the side of her neck, before working his way over her collarbone, this time with his tongue.

"Calder," she breathed, having no idea what she thought she was going to say.

"Shh," he whispered, then turned her in his arms so her back was cradled against his body, nudged the fall of her hair aside with his cheek so he could kiss the nape of her neck.

A low, needy moan slipped out as desire raced like a live wire straight down her spine, where it sparked, hot and ready, between her legs. He slid his palms down her arms, then cupped her hips. She braced herself, knowing when he pulled her back against him, she'd feel him, hard and aroused, pressing into the soft curve of her backside. She didn't know if her knees would hold her up. She felt drugged, intoxicated, like the worst sort of addict, trembling in need of a fix. If she were capable of rational thought at all, she'd tell herself her response was just a knee-jerk reaction to feeling desirable again.

Only that would require linear thought, of which she was entirely incapable at the moment. Her thoughts were like seeds in the wind, scattering about, drifting away on whichever current was the strongest. Which, at the moment, was the current making every muscle between her legs clench so tightly they ached, her nipples so hard they felt like little knots of pure need.

So she braced herself, wanting nothing more in that moment than for him to tug her back into him, press against her, then slide his hands around her body, stroke his fingers over those most sensitive parts, and release the almost excruciatingly sweet tension he was building as he cradled her with his wide palms and pressed hot kisses to the nape of her neck.

She held her breath, feeling his, so warm, on her sensitive

damp skin, feeling his fingertips press more firmly into her hips as the trembling need shaking her legs took hold in earnest. She gasped when he nipped her shoulder, moaned as his fingers dug more deeply still in an instant response to the sound, and was a split second away from reaching down and gripping his thighs for support.

"Hannah," he breathed, the word a rough rasp that was almost as devastating to her senses as his touch, his kiss. "This . . . us—"

"Don't," she said, forcing out the word, not wanting to chance that something—anything—he might say, would bring her back to sanity and end this perfect, erotic interlude. She felt him go still behind her, and realized he'd misunderstood her. It was his instant response to her request, his very ability to not push her, even though she knew he wanted it every bit as much as she did, that shoved her past any hope of reclaiming rational judgment. "Don't stop, Calder," she gasped. She reached down, back, grabbed the sides of his thighs, sank her fingers in, and was rewarded with a low, guttural groan that exactly expressed the ripping need she felt for him. "That's what I meant. Don't stop."

She felt him press his forehead against the back of her head, and thought for a split second he was going to pull away anyway. And she would have let him. She would, but she might have sobbed immediately afterward. Only this time it would have absolutely nothing to do with any aspect of her life that had existed outside these blazing-hot moments with Calder Blue. There was nothing else in her thoughts except the pooling heat, the feel of his hands on her, and his warm breath on the bare skin of her neck.

She slid her hands around to the backs of his thighs just as his mouth came down on the curve of skin between her neck and her shoulder. She moaned, a long, almost keening sound of want and need, as he growled when her hands grabbed the bottom corners of those perfectly snug back pockets of his jeans and tugged him mercifully, blessedly, *finally* forward, so their bodies met . . . and fit, in perfect, exquisite torture.

Instead of assuaging her needs, the feel of him, so rigid, so hard, pressing into the soft curve of her backside, only served to ramp them up to a fever pitch she hadn't been aware existed until that moment. He was kissing, biting, then soothing with his tongue, along her neck and shoulder, shoving aside the collar of her sleeveless sundress to get at more bare skin. For her part, she was, God help her, pushing back against him, moving her hips into the cradle of his, groaning fiercely when he relented and thrust back.

"Calder," she panted. "Please."

"Please what?" he asked, though it came out as more of a demand. "Tell me what you want."

"Your hands," she said, then gasped when his grip on her hips tightened and his fingers slid a dangerous inch or two forward, the tips of them curling over her hip bones. "On me. Touch me." She was begging now, only she felt absolutely no shame in it. If his uneven breath, the urgency in the way he was nipping at her earlobe, all but devouring the side of her neck with hot, damp, kisses, wasn't enough of a confirmation that he was in this every bit as deeply as she was, she could feel him jerk and throb against her every time she moved against him.

"Stop," he told her, his voice tight. He gripped her hips fully now, keeping her from moving them, even while holding her body in full contact with every ramrod hard inch of his. "You're driving me crazy. I won't last. And I want to make this last. I want—"

He broke off and tugged her back fully into his arms, cradling her, then slowly slid his fingers around the front of her, until she thought she might go mad and jump straight out of her skin as he drew closer to the apex of her thighs. They were both fully clothed and that mattered not one shred of anything, because she knew the moment he moved those big, strong fingers of his over her—

"I want to feel you fall apart for me," he growled against the shell of her ear and her body shook with the promise that he would make her do exactly that. He slid the fingertips of one hand very deliberately, with the most perfect, delicious precision, over and between her legs, as the other traveled, flat palm, over her belly, then higher, until he found first one nipple, and rolled it, then the other, just as he pressed the tips of his other fingers right on the exact—

She cried out and shook hard as she came instantly, even with layers of cotton and silk between her throbbing body parts and his wicked, wicked fingertips. Wave after wave of intense, blazing pleasure rocked through her core and radiated outward as he continued to play with her nipples, continued to claim the nape of her neck. She shouldn't be able to even tolerate his touch, she was so hypersensitive. Instead . . . she climbed straight back up again.

"Oh," she gasped, shocked and more turned on than she'd ever been in her life. "Calder." She gripped his thighs hard as she shuddered and gasped through another climax. She was surprised the force of it didn't topple them both straight to the ground.

He'd planted his legs apart and held steady, like the wall of solid muscle that he was, taking her weight completely against him, wrapping her up in him, and taking her straight to the stars . . . and keeping her there. How did he keep her there? She held on to his thighs still, dug her fingers into his backside, and—she couldn't help it, had no say in it—ground her hips back against him, and came again as he continued to play with her body and growl against her skin, his own body bucking, but not giving in, not yet.

She might have been whimpering—okay she was absolutely whimpering. She only knew she wanted the part of him she could feel pressing against her, thrusting deep inside of her. Now, immediately, do not pass go, no more delaying the inevitable. Because that's what it felt like, had felt like, she admitted, since he'd first spoken to her in the seconds after the crash. She'd wanted him just like this, to be taken just like this. She simply hadn't understood that, the power of it, the very existence of that kind of need, until now.

"Calder, please—"

To her shock, he chuckled against her ear, and it was the sexiest, earthiest thing she'd ever heard.

"Greedy," he said, sounding pleased, his voice a deep, ragged whisper. "More please," he said, in a mock British accent, and she was gasping, laughing, and almost crying with need, all at the same time. Only Calder could quote *Oliver Twist* at a time like this, and make it sound carnal and wicked.

"You," she managed. "I want more—of you."

She felt the shudder that ran through him, right out to his fingertips, and then he was turning her in his arms, pulling her against him, into him as he buried his hand under the waterfall of her hair, and cupped the back of her neck so he could bring her mouth fully up to his . . . and sink himself into it.

They both groaned and she tried to move even closer, wanting, needing, for the hypersensitized parts he'd brought so screamingly to life to come into contact with any part of him. Then he was growling, running his hands down her sides, her back, cupping the curve of her backside, until she growled too as he tucked her against the rigid, oh-so-beautifully hard length of him. It still wasn't enough and he must have thought so too, because he gripped her hips and said, "Hold on." He lifted her up. "Wrap your legs around me, Hannah."

Just hearing the need in his voice, so thick, so deep, vibrating over her as delectably as his fingertips had, made her go a little wild. He slid her sundress up past her knees as she wrapped her legs around his waist, his hands sliding underneath, up her thighs, until he cupped her cheeks through the silk of her panties, her soaked panties, his fingers so close, so close again.

"Calder," she whispered raggedly, then buried her face against the side of his neck, reveling in the heat of his skin, the thump of his pulse, the smell of him, crying out as he touched her, stroked her. "Oh!" she cried, "yes!" Whatever she had thought passion could be before was shattered to smithereens now, because this? Was unlike anything she'd ever experienced.

He turned them toward the truck, until her back met the door, and with that support, she could pull him in more tightly between her legs. She let out a soft cry of disappointment when his hands slid down her thighs again, only to cry out again when he hitched her legs higher, so he could move even more snugly against her.

"This isn't—we're—too many clothes," was all she could get out as he started those devastating nibbles and kisses along the side of her neck again. She was panting and could hear his labored breathing as well. It was primal, and raw, and—and still not enough. "Calder, I want . . . more."

He shifted and she shivered in anticipation as she felt him all but rip open the button of his jeans, wrenching the zipper down.

Then he froze. "Dammit, Hannah. I don't have—I've

got nothing, no protection." His voice was a rough, sexy growl that made her shudder with need. "I wasn't planning this." He lifted his head and looked at her, his eyes having gone from rich honey to deep whiskey gold. "I wasn't planning on you."

She felt ensnared there, in his gaze, and realized that while they'd been all but clawing at each other, this was the first moment their eyes had met. She felt a split second of panic that looking at each other would make it somehow too real, and she didn't want to think, didn't want to be rational or safe or smart. She just wanted this, wanted him, and every other last thing in her entire world could simply wait until she'd gotten it.

"I'm protected," she said, her voice a rasp, her breathing still hard and thick. "I—IUD," she stammered. "I still have—I never had it taken—I'm—"

He cupped her face, and even in the blazing, animal heat, with the hardest part of him pressing so intimately against the softest part of her, his fingers were gentle on the still-tender bruised skin of her face. "Are you sure, Hannah? I'm—you don't have to worry about me, I'm safe, but—"

"Me, either. After I found out—after—I got tested. I didn't know who, or what he'd—I'm okay." She was stumbling and stammering, but her tongue was as tied up in the need for him as every other part of her.

The way he looked at her had robbed her of her voice. Her throat was thick with an unnamed emotion as the truth of what she'd thought she'd had with Tim was shattered into a million tiny, shallow, superficial little shards. Calder didn't look at her as if she were some precious object he'd delightedly discovered he could possess, or something perfect and porcelain to be stroked and worshipped and made love to as if it were some kind of beautiful reward, some kind of special prize—which she now realized was exactly how Tim had always taken her. At the time, it had made her feel loved, cherished, but she knew now he'd just wanted what he thought he couldn't have, delighting in getting to have her, in making her want him in return.

Calder looked at her like a man who wanted her for who she truly was, just as she was, busted nose, skinny body, shattered life, and all. A woman who had maybe made him laugh, made him think, made him want again. It was heady stuff, but in a completely different way. This felt real. It felt honest and normal and earthy. And the truth was, he was all of those things to her. Honest, open, flawed. Real.

There was no worshipping here, no claiming of a prize. It was equal want to equal want, partner to partner, man to woman, basic, honest.

"You need to be sure," he said. "It's been two years for me, longer. Not since my divorce. I—"

She silenced him with a kiss. Something about the combustion of how their intimate parts felt—all but fused together below—contrasted with the softness of her kiss—the way she took his mouth, claimed his mouth, slid her tongue between his lips, and this time seduced him back between hers. It made her heart swell to almost bursting.

He broke the kiss, panting hard. "Jesus, I want you. I've wanted you since I laid eyes on you, I—"

"Then take what you want," Hannah told him, turning his mouth back to hers, until their gazes clashed and caught again. "Because I want you, too." She leaned in and kissed him again, keeping her gaze on his until the last possible second, then letting her eyes drift shut as his hands slid down and gripped her. His fingers dug into the soft flesh of her bottom as he jerked her against him, pushed against her. "I'm sure," she whispered against his mouth. "So very, very sure."

And though some part of her was well aware she might be anything but sure later on, in that moment, it was the God's honest truth. And what happened later mattered not at all.

He groaned in acceptance, and took her mouth, growling, "Hold on tight." Then he was wrenching at his jeans and reaching under her dress to tear the lace straight across the front of her delicate panties, so the silky panel between her thighs dropped away.

That act alone drove her straight back to the edge, and she knew he'd find her wet—no, drenched—as she finally felt the heat of him, velvety smooth and deliciously hot, against her finally bared skin. "Yes," she cried as he teased her. "Please."

"I swear to God, you're going to kill me," he ground out, then took her mouth as he gripped her hips. He pulled them down and surged inside of her in one, deep thrust.

She cried out, and when he instinctively began to pull out, she dug her heels into his buttocks and locked him in. "No," she said, raggedly, then pressed her cheek against his neck before biting his ear and growling, "More please," in guttural, Brit-inflected English.

"Why yes, Miz Scarlett," he said, laughing and groaning at the same time. "I believe I shall."

And how it was that they could be almost insane with lust and desire for each other, and laughing at the same time, she had absolutely no idea, but it felt . . . gloriously freeing. And good. And strong. And . . . real. She'd never laughed in moments like this. Actually . . . she'd never laughed with Tim even in moments not like this. Not that she and Tim had ever had moments anything like this. And then Calder thrust into her again, and that was the last time she'd allow Tim Underwood into her thoughts, no matter the moment, ever again.

Calder kissed the side of her mouth. "You feel . . . like—"

"Home," she finished, not knowing where the word even came from, only knowing it was right. She shifted so he could sink even more deeply inside of her, and they both moaned.

He took her again, and again, and she rode him every slick, sliding thrust of the way, moaning, gasping, alternately crying out and grinning like a loon at the insanity of the pleasure they were able to give each other. "Yes!" she cried, her hands fisted in his hair as he drove her up to the edge yet again. She pulled his mouth back to hers as he picked up speed. "Yes, yes, yes," she murmured between kisses. Then she took his tongue and sucked on it in matching rhythm to his strokes until he shuddered against her, his growl deep in his chest as his climax ripped through him. It made her feel exultant and all powerful and more intensely female and desirable than she'd ever felt in her life . . . and that took her over the edge right after him.

Chapter Fifteen

Calder held on to Hannah with one arm and braced the other against the side of his truck. His breath was labored to the point of wheezing, and his legs were shaking. He'd never had—that was, he didn't know it could be—because it never had been . . . *damn*.

"I'd stay inside you for the rest of my—but I don't think I can—" He slid out of her and she unwrapped her legs from around his waist and let her feet and the hem of her dress drop down as he rolled to his back against the truck. He kept her tight against him, wrapped up in his arms, holding them both up as they panted and laughed through their gasping breaths.

"I don't know what that was," Hannah said, sounding as stunned as he felt. "But I know I'll never make myself believe it was real. And I was there."

He slid his hand up her spine and sank his fingers into her hair, which wasn't a sleek, shiny waterfall now. It was wild and tousled, and he loved that he'd mussed her up a little. "Scarlett, that was about as real as it gets. I don't know how we're still upright."

She giggled at that, and he thought it was the very best sound he'd ever heard. "I think saying we're standing is more a technicality due to the position of your truck than an accurate assessment of our current abilities."

He let his head loll back against the door frame and let out a wheezing snort. "Indeed, Counselor, I do believe you have a point."

She rocked against him and snickered. "Well, one good point deserves another."

He thought he might choke on the laugh that swelled up in his chest. "You never cease to surprise me," he managed.

She lifted her head and said, "I'm not sure how to take that," but the affront in her voice was cancelled out entirely by the wicked gleam in her beautiful, storm-blue eyes.

"Oh, in a good way. In a very good way." He thought about how he'd initially assessed her, and though he'd discovered within minutes of that assessment just how flawed it was, she continued to be nothing like he'd assumed she'd be, or maybe, more accurately, how he'd been afraid she'd be.

She'd struck a spark in him from the moment he'd opened the door to her ruined little sports car, and denying that, or worrying that it was a mistake to give in to it, had clearly gotten him nowhere. *Except right here. Where you wanted to be all along.*

He closed his eyes and kept her bundled against his chest as he let that truth sink in. And now that he was there? Now what?

He didn't know. Had no idea. The only thing he knew was that holding on to her, laughing with her, talking with her, even arguing with her, were the parts of his days, of his life, the ones he held on to, the ones he thought about, the ones that made him smile.

"You need oil for those gears," she murmured against his chest.

"What?" he said. He emerged slowly from his thoughts, and realized they were no longer clinging to each other for support. Their breathing had steadied, evened out. They were wrapped up in each other now because . . . because that's where they still wanted to be.

She slid her fingers up his neck and through his hair, making him groan with pleasure, as his body considered a miraculous twitching return to life. Then she knocked gently on the side of his head and laughed into his shirt. "I can hear the gears turning in here," she said.

"You're a mind reader now?" he murmured, holding on to the moment, holding on to her.

"You've either returned to the real world," she said, and he could hear the smile in her voice, "or you're desperately afraid that the seagulls are going to come down and pluck me away." She wiggled slightly, just enough to make him realize he was holding on to her rather tightly.

He relaxed his arms, but didn't let her go, and was surprised by the relief he felt when she didn't make any move to disengage herself. "Sorry," he said, then leaned down and kissed her temple. "And if I'm under oath here, Counselor, the answer is . . . a little bit of both."

She lifted her head then and leaned back so she could look up into his eyes, which he'd opened enough to look right back into hers. Her eyes were still a dark and drowsy blue, the look of a woman well pleased, and his body twitched again. Her knowing smile added a little zip to that burgeoning need. But he hadn't missed the way she was probing his eyes, his face. Even supremely relaxed, she was still focused, still intent. His smile grew at that, because he realized that rather than put him off, or make him think her too stiff or stuffy—something he knew quite intimately not to be true—he found her always-ready sharpness, her intellect, to be a big part of his attraction to her.

And it wasn't until that moment that he realized some part of him had always had a bit of an issue with Tenley's sublime lack of interest in what was going on around her. Well, he'd known it had bothered him, he just hadn't fully understood why. Tenley hadn't had a full-time occupation, but she had filled her time both with making a home for the two of them and with her family's charitable work. He'd been proud of her, hadn't resented her lack of drive or ambition. She might have been a bit overly emotional about things he couldn't understand, and she wasn't particularly self-sufficient when it came to entertaining herself, always needing to be doing something, talking to someone, running off to somewhere, but for all of that, she wasn't stupid or flakey. She just hadn't been . . . aware. Tuned in. Paying attention.

"I can assure you that the seagulls won't be interested in carting me off. You won't have to use your mad Samaritan skills to rescue me again."

He slid one hand up her back, then pushed back the wild tangle of hair next to her face. "You don't always have to rescue yourself, you know."

Rather than be annoyed by that, or defensive, she laughed and the tone was decidedly self-deprecating. "That's not the problem. The problem is needing to be rescued at all."

He leaned down and caught her face to his, kissing her slowly, but thoroughly, until they were both a little needy again. Her eyes drifted open as he lifted his head. "What was that for?" she asked, and the soft heat in her voice did amazingly restorative things to his very recently depleted manhood.

"Everyone needs to be rescued from time to time," he said. *Sort of like what you're doing for me, right now.* He straightened up until they were both steady on their feet. "Tide's out," he said. "Take a walk with me." He nodded to the exposed floor of the inlet.

"Okay," she said, sounding both surprised and pleased, making him glad he'd gone with the impulse.

He just wasn't ready to let go quite yet.

He zipped up while she reached under her dress and slipped off her ruined panties, and the idea that she was commando under that pretty floral sundress shouldn't have made him so hungry, given what they'd just been doing, but the truth was, as wild as it had been, he hadn't actually seen any part of her naked. Yet.

He went around to the back of the truck and pulled out two pairs of old Wellies, setting them both on the ground. The tide might be out, but what was exposed wasn't beach so much as ocean floor. Not for bare feet.

"So attractive," she said, but rather than nix the stroll, she simply lifted her skirt, bundled it to the side and tied it into a sort of giant knot the way some women did with long T-shirts at the beach. She looked at him and laughed. "What? I've already forfeited any style points I had by putting on those things"—she nodded at the mud-spattered green rubber boots—"so going into negative numbers isn't exactly going to hurt me."

He picked up the smaller pair, which belonged to one of the young guys he'd hired on as summer barn help and set them down in front of her, then provided his shoulder while she slipped her slender feet out of her sandals and into the boots.

"There's like, straw in these. Or something." She looked up at him, her hand still on his shoulder. "I probably shouldn't ask." Her blue eyes were sparkling and he wanted her even more than he had an hour ago.

"Safer bet," he told her, then kicked out of his work boots and tugged on the other pair, over the legs of his jeans. He held out his hand. "Shall we, Miz Scarlett?"

"Why, I do believe I've left my bonnet in the cab of your surrey, Mister Blue."

He laughed and gave her a questioning look. She hadn't been wearing a hat.

Seeing his expression, she said, "I saw a baseball cap on your backseat. Could I borrow? I'm not supposed to have my face in direct sun what with the stitches, black eyes—"

"You're beautiful," he told her, knowing she wasn't fishing for compliments, which made it that much more fun to give them. "I can't vouch for what condition the ball cap is in, but . . ."

"I'm sure it will be fine. Thanks," she said, as he opened the door and dug around under the lunch leftovers.

It was a Blue and Sons company hat, thankfully not in bad shape. He kept it, along with a hard hat, in the truck for walking job sites, so it didn't see too much wear and tear. Still, he dusted it off on his thigh before handing it to her.

"Thanks." She scooped her hair up in a high ponytail, popped the hat on her head, slid the ponytail through the strap opening in the back, then pulled the strap snug, all in a matter of seconds.

"I'd almost believe you'd done that a time or two before," he said.

She tilted her head and he thought there wasn't anything she couldn't make look good. "What makes you think I haven't?"

"Well, neither the sundress you have on now, nor the lawyer suit you had on earlier, looks like it goes well with a ball cap."

She laughed easily, and it was that self-deprecation thing that always caught him off guard. Tenley had been very worried about her appearance, always wanting to present herself in the best light, and there was no teasing her on the subject. And Lord help him or anyone who made her mess up her hair. Calder was not interested in making anyone feel bad about herself, but even he had to admit the minefield of his ex-wife's insecurities had been exhausting at times.

"I will admit that my current wardrobe—or the one I had when I left D.C.—was not conducive to ball cap wearing. I didn't even own a pair of jeans." At his raised brow, she said, "I was never doing anything that informal."

"I'm sorry," he said, and meant it.

She laughed again. "I know, right?"

He nodded toward the waterfront and they made their way down to the washout and started picking their way between the kelp beds and other flotsam and jetsam. She occasionally stooped and sorted through the tidal detritus with a stick, leaving him to marvel over how she could go from cool, sleek, and elegant lawyer—which she'd been, even in her soft cotton sundress—to baseball hat-, knotted-up dress-, and muddy boot-wearing beachcomber. Both suited her like a second skin.

She crouched down and was picking up shells, discarding some, rooting some more, when she let out a particularly content-sounding sigh. "I used to do this all the time growing up. I never got tired of it. Like a treasure hunt." She glanced up at him. "Which is where the mad baseball-cap-wearing skills come from. Apparently some things you never forget." She laughed rather delightedly, and went back to digging.

The sun was shining on the thick fall of her ponytail, which was wild and messy from their earlier adventures; her knees, which were exposed as her knotted dress had ridden up her thighs, were somewhat knobby, he noticed. Which made him smile, because somehow that was the last thing he'd expected on her sleek frame, and yet, in that moment, he thought, of course they were knobby. And suddenly he wasn't having as hard a time picturing her on his farm. Not having a hard time at all.

"Aha!" she shrieked, and straightened, then wobbled when her boots sank in the muck.

He reached out a quick hand for her elbow, steadying her, and she turned into his arms. *I could get used to this, Hannah*, he thought, feeling both protective and possessive, certain she wouldn't be grateful for either emotion. *I could get used to you.*

"Look! Sea glass." She turned the small, blue, pitted piece of saltwater-worn glass in her fingers. "For Kerry, it was fossils, and for Fiona, it was rocks and shells." She looked into his eyes, hers a brighter blue, sparkling like the water beyond. "For me? It's always been sea glass. I had jars of these at home, all shades of blue and white and green. I wonder where those jars are now?" She looked down at her dress. "No pockets. Figures."

She went to toss it back, but he caught it before the speck of blue left her fingertips.

"It's okay," she said, looking sheepish. "It's no big deal."

If she'd seen her own face, the delight in her eyes, she'd know it was definitely a big deal. He took the smooth pebble of sea-washed glass and slipped it in his shirt pocket. "Fortunately, I have pockets."

Instead of rolling her eyes, and turning back to her hunt, she rose up on her tiptoes, her boots making a sucking, popping sound as the heels came out of the muck, making them both grin, and she kissed him on the mouth. "Thank you. You're always rescuing me," she said. Their kiss tipped up the brim of her cap and she put a muddy hand on the top of it to keep it from falling off, her mouth curving in a dry smile. "I don't know why I'm surprised any longer."

He grinned, turned the brim of her cap sideways, then pulled her into his arms and kissed her. Deeply, slowly, thoroughly. She moaned into his mouth as he parted her lips; then he groaned when she readily welcomed him. "Hannah," he said, raggedly, when he finally lifted his mouth from hers.

"Mmm," was her only response; then she slid her arms around his waist and nestled more deeply, more perfectly, in his arms, and pressed her cheek to his chest.

Something inside of him seemed to settle, almost like a part of him physically clicking into place, when he had her in his arms this way. He couldn't question it or wonder about it; he could only accept it, and how it made him feel. *Like I'm home. She's home.* He wrapped her up close and held her there, looking out toward the receding harbor waters, but not seeing any of it. *I don't want to let you go. I don't want to let this go.* Of course, he'd have to do both. He let out a slow, quiet sigh and pressed his cheek to the top of her ball cap, wishing life weren't so complicated, for either of them.

After a few moments, she shifted in his arms, slid her hand down, and took his as he let her go, then silently continued on their walk, not releasing his hand, even when she crouched down to continue her hunt. It wasn't clingy, or needy. In fact, there was something both sweet and very intimate about it, a connectedness that was somehow more powerful than when he'd been buried deep inside of her.

By the time they got to the end of the small cove, he had a breast pocket full of sea glass and a few more chunks in the front pocket of his jeans. He'd just opened his mouth to ask her if she had some time the following day—Saturday—to drive out to his farm with him. He wanted—needed—to see her there now. Even though he knew it might be the stupidest thing he could do. She'd just come home to her family, a place she clearly loved, and seeing her here on the water, he felt pretty positive that she'd made the right choice. Would she want to go back to D.C.? Only time would tell. But was she in any real shape to make some other big leap? Say, in the direction of Calais? *You're an idiot. And since when are you in an all-fired hurry to take any big leaps yourself?*

He still had one to take with his father, and his brothers, about his future with the company. And that would have to wait until after he'd gotten out from under the arson situation here in Blueberry Cove. So the very last thing he should be thinking about was tangling her life up with his any further, much less imprinting the memory of her in any part of his life on the farm. That was his new life. *His* life. No regrets. No . . . *foolish ideas of happy ever after*, his little voice supplied.

It was probably divine intervention when his phone rang before he could issue an invitation. He hadn't realized he'd shoved his phone into his back pocket until the ringer went off. He couldn't help going tense, but he'd be damned if he'd let his father intrude on any of the remaining time he had with Hannah. "Sorry," he muttered, and slid the phone out. Then he paused in his steps, bringing her to a halt alongside him, as he looked at the name on the screen. He looked to Hannah. "It's Winstock. Or his office, anyway."

She nodded, her face instantly going into sharp, legal-eagle mode, and damn if that didn't make him grin, too.

He answered the phone. "Calder Blue." Then his eyes widened when none other than Brooks Winstock himself came on the line.

"I'm back in the Cove," he said. "Dinner meeting, seven o'clock?"

So much for preliminaries. "I can make that work," Calder said.

"Come on up to the house. I'm buried under a mountain of stuff here and I can have the cook rustle us something

up. More relaxed that way. Sounds like we could both use
a little of that."

Calder wasn't entirely certain what Winstock was allud-
ing to. Their protracted attempts at meeting? That both of
them had been questioned regarding the arson fire? He
didn't sound amused or pissed off, just . . . direct. So Calder
didn't probe for clarification. "Sounds good."

"I'd give you the address, but anyone can direct you.
Why don't you ask your lawyer?" he said, and for the first
time, there was the barest hint of an edge to his voice. "She
knows exactly where I live." Then the line went dead.

Calder slowly pocketed the phone again and looked at
Hannah, who, standing as close as she was, had clearly
heard both sides of the conversation. "So," he said. "That
was fun." He smiled, though it was rueful. "I wonder if he
knows my father?"

Her smile matched his. "Do you want me to go along?
As counsel? Arbitrate the contract?"

"There won't be any contract," Calder said.

She grinned. "He doesn't need to know that."

He laughed outright, and pulled her into his arms for
another fast kiss. "I believe you have bridesmaid debauchery to attend." She made a face, which made his grin
deepen. "I'll handle this one on my own." He leaned in,
kissed her again, but softly, then deeply, until she moaned
again. He ran slow kisses along her jaw to her ear, his
body leaping in response when he felt the shudder of pleasure race through her. "But I reserve the right to request
counsel later."

Chapter Sixteen

Hannah stood on the stretch of lawn that separated the old keeper's cottage from the lighthouse, marveling over the stunning transformation of her childhood protector. At least that's how she'd always thought of the Point light, though she'd never told anyone that. She cradled an oversized mug of her brother's famously delicious coffee between her hands, and thought about how, while listening to her grandfather's many stories about the McCrae lightkeepers and the lighthouse itself, her seven-year-old self had considered that if roadways had the same sort of beacon lighting as Pelican Bay, maybe her parents wouldn't have crashed their car during that ice storm when she was five. Maybe they'd all have remained one big, happy family.

She'd loved listening to her grandfather's stories of when the lighthouse had been operational, of her ancestors and their families who had been both lightkeepers and cottage caretakers. After the accident, those stories had become a great comfort to her, as had the tower. She'd somehow come to believe that as long as she had the lighthouse in sight, or in her heart, nothing bad could happen to her. "And we see how well that worked out for me," she murmured as she brought the mug to her lips again and sipped.

Although, if she were honest with herself, she hadn't really kept the Point light in her heart, not in any meaningful way. She loved her home and her family, but she'd let her life in D.C., her goals, her dreams, her relationship all hold sway over her, until they consumed her every waking thought, pushing her home, and even her family, to a distant second place, especially the past few years. Standing there now, she wondered how she could have possibly gone a full three years without seeing her brother, or either of her sisters, without her beacon.

"What a lovely setting for the wedding."

Hannah didn't start; she'd heard the approaching footsteps. She turned at the sound of Owen Hartley's voice, a sincere smile of affection creasing her face. "Isn't it? They're calling for sunny and clear tomorrow, just like today. It's going to be beautiful." She turned her head so her hair would catch in the wind off the water and blow away from her face as she laughed. "Though they might have a tough time trying to say their vows in the ever-present sea breeze."

Owen smiled as he leaned in for a quick one-arm hug, careful not to jostle her coffee mug. "Somehow, when your brother looks up and sees Alexandra at the end of the aisle, I doubt anything else will register in his mind." He smiled as he stepped back and shifted to stand beside her, both of them looking over the preparations that were under way for the following day's festivities. "From talking to Alex, my sense is she'll have the same feeling, looking at her groom."

Hannah smiled, and then relaxed shoulders she realized she'd tensed as Owen had started talking about the wedding. She'd been subconsciously waiting for that ping of hurt and betrayal to nip at her, followed by the guilt of letting her own ugly past mar her joy for her brother's well-deserved happiness. But that ping didn't come. In fact, rather shockingly, when Owen had mentioned Alex looking at her groom, the person Hannah had pictured hadn't been Tim. It had been Calder.

She closed her eyes briefly, hid behind her coffee mug as she took another long sip, and tried to block out exactly why Calder Blue dominated her every thought. And it wasn't because she knew he was, at that very second—hopefully—finally sitting across a table from Brooks Winstock. She'd gotten a short text from Calder the night before, letting her know he'd arrived at the Winstock estate only to be greeted with the unbelievable news that Brooks had been called away at the last second. Calder had been put up in the Winstock manse for the night with a promise of a breakfast meeting right there in the family dining room the following morning. Hannah supposed she shouldn't be so surprised, but the gall of the man was incredible. Calder had promised her that he wasn't leaving the house until he'd seen Winstock. She smiled into her coffee as she recalled the other thing he'd texted her after she'd asked again if he wanted representation during the meeting. He'd responded by telling her exactly how he'd like counsel to be representing him in the king-sized bed he'd been assigned for the night.

"It's good to have you back in the Cove," Owen was saying.

Hannah tuned smoothly into the conversation again, lowering her mug, and simultaneously thinking she needed to find a way to raise her rapidly dwindling defenses where Calder Blue was concerned. It was one thing to have a hijacked afternoon of crazy behavior. Quite another to be thinking about the man while watching town volunteers help to set up chairs for her brother's impending nuptials. "It's really good to be back," she told him sincerely, and renewed her determination to keep her thoughts exclusively on her family, her sisters, the wedding, the town—anything but the man who had taken her body up against his truck, then claimed far more fragile pieces of her by taking her hand for a stroll down a tide-gutted cove.

"How is life treating you down there in our beautiful nation's capital?"

She was surprised to hear herself laugh so easily, and stunned to realize she wasn't forcing it. "The city is lovely, but life? Mmm, it's been better."

His pale brow knitted in concern. "Your brother has mentioned that you put in a lot of hours." He rested a hand on her arm. "Make sure you take some time, find some balance." He smiled a bit sheepishly. "Something I'm learning the importance of more and more lately."

Her face brightened. "That's right! I haven't officially congratulated you on your mayorship, Mr. Mayor."

"You said as much on the phone, no need to fuss over it," he said, and charmed her with the blush that rose to his pale cheeks.

She leaned in and kissed one of those cheeks. "Now it's official," she said, smiling gaily as his blush deepened. Owen wasn't old enough to be a father figure, maybe more like a much older brother, or beloved uncle. She'd known him her whole life and he'd always been kind, always offered a willing shoulder, always been a safe port. *Safe ports. Beacons. Funny how you're framing everything in terms of safety this morning.*

"So, I had the chance to meet Jonah's great-nephew," Owen said, inadvertently turning the subject directly to the one person she was trying not to think about.

"I heard," she said, looking once again at the white folding chairs being set up in neat little rows. "Calder was very grateful for the Blue family background you shared with him."

"I was surprised he didn't know," Owen said, after a brief moment of apparent surprise that she knew of their conversation. "On further reflection, I suppose it's not so shocking given the history. Do you know how things are progressing with him and Brooks? When we spoke, his meeting had been cancelled—more than once, I believe. Then there was that awful fire . . ." He let the words trail off, shaking his head.

"I hope you know he had nothing to do with that fire," Hannah said, telling herself she was rushing to Calder's defense as his attorney speaking to the town mayor, nothing more. "You met him, you're a very good judge of character. Surely you—"

"I don't think he did it," Owen said, "and I've been vocal about that with the council, if that helps."

She took his arm, squeezed. "Thank you," she said, knowing her reaction had nothing to do with being Calder's counsel of record.

"I know the investigation is proceeding," Owen said. "I feel awful that it's happening now of all times." He nodded toward the wedding preparations. "The council wants me to press the chief for answers."

"He's doing everything he can," Hannah assured him.

Owen nodded. "Oh, I know. I do. To be honest, I suspect the pressure from the council members was coming from Jonah, looking to get his pound of St. Croix River Blue flesh." He glanced at her, a rueful look in his soft eyes. "Sorry. But you know how he can be when he's on a tear."

"Don't apologize for him," she said, hearing the edge in her voice. Just because she'd known Jonah Blue her entire life, and his great-nephew less than a week, did not mean Jonah automatically earned her support. And, in this instance, she was fairly certain she'd feel that way whether or not she'd ever laid eyes on Calder Blue. "I do know. But you're saying the pressure isn't coming from him?" At Owen's quick shake of the head, she sighed. "Let me guess. Brooks is pressuring them. Not surprising. And I probably shouldn't say this to you, but I have to think the reason Brooks is pushing this to a rushed conclusion—while the finger is pointing in a different direction, namely at Calder— is to keep suspicion from shifting to him. He's the one with something to gain by Jonah's business taking a bad turn. Assuming he wants to continue with his one-man harbor revitalization kick."

"What does your brother—I mean Chief McCrae— think about that?"

"He agrees that there is logic to the assumption, but that's all it is. An assumption."

Owen nodded thoughtfully, looking a bit absent for a moment.

"I'm sorry," Hannah said. "I have put you in an awkward place."

"No," he said, still sounding caught up in his personal thoughts. "I mean, yes, you're right. I just—" He broke off and made a humming sound in his throat.

Hannah's gaze narrowed slightly. "What aren't you telling me, Owen?" She asked calmly enough, gently even. "Logan doesn't think Calder did it, either, but there's no evidence proving anyone else did. And if the council is pressuring him—and you know something that might lend credence to my theory, or some other person—"

"Nothing tangible," Owen said, blinking, looking back at her. "No proof of any kind. Obviously I'd have given anything like that to the chief." His gaze cleared completely as he looked at her more directly. "I share your concerns. About Brooks. About his possible future plans for the harbor. In fact, Calder and I spoke about that very thing, about what his motivation might be. Especially since he's been uncharacteristically ruthless."

"I thought the same thing. He's richer than Croesus, and yet he seems more interested in swindling folks out of their harbor property than approaching them head-on. I know he's very aggressive in his business and that's a large part of why he's been so successful, but I've never heard of him going to such lengths to get what he wants." She paused. "Of course, how well do we really know anyone?"

"We did theorize a bit on that score," Owen admitted.

"Yes, Calder mentioned something about thinking Winstock might want to leave a bigger legacy given he has no direct heir to his throne. But he already owns, what? A quarter of the town's property at least, maybe more. How much legacy does he need?"

"I think he wanted to do something that would change the course, the future, of the town, something that would be more . . . I guess for lack of a better word, historic. Owning property, even as much as he has, isn't the kind of thing that gets more than a footnote in the history books, even if those books"—Owen made air quotes of the word—"are the local lore handed down from generation to generation."

"Hasn't he ever heard of charitable works? I mean, if he wants to leave a more lasting impression that will change the course of the town, why not build a park, a senior home, whatever. Slap his name on it for all eternity."

Owen lifted a shoulder. "I don't know. I do know that it's not Brooks directly pushing at the board. It's coming more indirectly, from his son-in-law. I'm assuming, however, that it's being encouraged by Brooks. And knowing Ted, he's happy to comply, to demonstrate that even after losing both his head council seat and his bid for mayor last year, he can still throw his weight around, and prove the same to his father-in-law."

Hannah's head swung around as the words struck her, and struck hard. "Is Brooks still upset with Ted for losing his seat? I mean, has it been a publicly divisive thing between the two of them?"

Owen looked momentarily surprised by the intensity of the question, but took it seriously. "I . . . I suppose you could say that. I mean, I've felt a certain amount of animosity from Ted. No more, I think, than he'd have directed at anyone who dared to challenge him. And Brooks was definitely not happy that he lost his direct link to the council, but, in all honesty, he seemed to move on. I think he doesn't waste much time wallowing in his defeats. He usually moves directly forward to the next conquest. I told Calder as much."

"His next conquest being to continue his makeover of Half Moon Harbor to reflect his own ideal of what this town should be."

"Yes," Owen said, looking confused now. "That's why he's a suspect in Jonah's boathouse burning down, right?"

"Right," Hannah said, only more to herself than to Owen. Her mind was spinning. Brooks had been around a long time, and while his methods had been less than compassionate—the way he'd tried both to take part of Brodie's shipyard, and to get ownership of Delia's property—all those maneuvers had been legal. Why resort to arson, then? It just didn't jibe. "Think about what has changed from the time he took the diner property to the time of the arson," she said, thinking out loud. "Only one thing stands out."

"Ted lost the election," Owen said, scrambling to follow her line of thought.

"Exactly. Brooks's son-in-law no longer holds any political power in this town. I mean, he still has some political clout, no doubt, through whatever allies he still has on the council, but any actual, immediate power? Gone. And to get it back, he'll have to start over again."

"All true. But I'm not sure I see how that connects—"

She looked directly at Owen now. "It's never been a secret that Cami married Ted for his political aspirations, and that both Winstocks, father and daughter, have been grooming Ted to ascend the mayoral throne here, mostly as a launchpad to state politics, and perhaps further. Given the shenanigans both of them get into outside their marriage, clearly there is nothing else between them. No children, nothing. And, as you said, no grandchildren for Brooks, no heir to the family throne; the family legacy ends with Brooks."

"No political career for Ted, no family legacy there either," Owen said, slowly catching on.

Hannah's eyes lit up as the rest of the pieces fell into place.

"You're amazing!" She grabbed Owen's face and kissed him square on the mouth, then grinned. "You figured it all out!" She pressed her coffee mug into his hands, then took off in a sprint toward the house.

Leaving a crimson-faced Owen standing there, clutching her mug, saying, "I did?" He smiled, looking a little dazed. "Happy I could be of some help," he called out.

Chapter Seventeen

"Mr. Winstock will be with you shortly. He asked that you please enjoy your breakfast. What can I bring you to start?"

Calder wasn't used to having a crew of people attending him inside someone's private home. *Must be nice,* he thought, then decided, nah, he'd hate having people hovering around him all the time. Sort of creepy, really. "Thank you," he said. "Just coffee is fine. Black."

The young man, dressed in a crisp white linen button-down shirt and tailored black slacks, looked somewhat concerned at that. "Are you certain, sir? We have a world-class chef. Perhaps an omelet to start? Or maybe you'd prefer the quiche? Fresh lobster this morning. It's top-notch."

We spared no expense, Calder thought, and the line from *Jurassic Park* did nothing to dispel the heebie-jeebies this whole charade was giving him. "Fine," he told the obviously relieved young man. "That sounds good." He only hoped the guy didn't stand behind him and watch him eat.

A cup of steaming black coffee was placed in front of him with alarming speed. Did they have eyes in the wall? He straightened his shoulder against the prickle of awareness that lifted the hairs on the back of his neck. He felt ridiculous for letting his surroundings get to him, but he still couldn't shake the feeling that he was the hapless extra in a bad horror movie.

A different door opened, one of the double doors leading to the main hallway. He looked up, pasting a polite, businesslike smile on his face, expecting to greet his host, but a woman walked in instead.

She was average height, maybe a little shorter. It was hard to tell in the tottering spike heels she was wearing. She was a blonde, with a figure that could only be described as bombshell, wearing a tight-fitting, perfectly tailored suit the color of the bright blue waters of the bay that sparkled in the huge picture window just behind her. That she not only could compete with such a spectacular view, but quite easily trump it, seemed to be something she took as her due.

Calder had the rather uncharitable thought that if Tenley had had access to the kind of fortune Winstock wielded, she would have aspired to be someone almost exactly like the woman he was looking at. Unkind, perhaps, but no less true.

"My, my, I wasn't aware I'd have such handsome company at breakfast this morning," she said, her perfectly modulated voice only a fraction above a purr. "You must be Calder Blue. Daddy said something about your dropping by. Quite early," she added. "You must be eager." Her dark eyes sparkled. "I like eager."

Calder had stood when she'd entered the room, partly out of ingrained politeness, and partly because she had a rather regal way about her that seemed to demand that sort of thing. But before he could step around the table to assist her, the young man who'd been attending Calder earlier rushed in from the side door and whisked her chair out for her instead.

They do have eyes in the wall, he thought, amused. *Good to know.* He absently wondered if they could monitor something as small as his text message screen, because he'd said some rather naughty things to Hannah the night before. He smiled, thinking about it.

"Bring me some hot tea, Thomas," she instructed the young man as he pushed her chair in once she was seated. "Not that abominable brew from yesterday morning. In fact, have Chef make a tray for me please, and bring an assortment." Her gaze lifted to Calder. "A woman likes to have choices."

"Yes, ma'am," Thomas said. "Right away." He scurried off as if the hounds of hell were at his heels.

Calder took his seat again, thinking despite her perfectly put-together outfit, artfully tousled hairstyle, and ruthlessly applied makeup, he probably wasn't far wrong in his assessment this time. "I'm afraid you have me at a disadvantage," he said. "You seem to know my name, but—"

She laughed, and it was as perfectly modulated as the rest of her, a delightful little waterfall of sound that made every hair on his arms stand straight up. The theme from *Jaws* echoed through his mind. "My apologies." She was sitting catty-corner to him, at the end of the long table nearest the picture window. She lifted a hand to him. "Camille Winstock Weathersby. My close acquaintances know me as Cami."

He wasn't sure if he was supposed to shake her hand, or kiss the ring on it, but he took her fingertips in his, and bowed his head slightly, in some awkward combination of the two. "Brooks's daughter," he said, rather than address the issue of what he would be calling her. "A pleasure to meet you. You're married to Ted Weathersby, is that right?" His smile grew as hers dimmed. "Just trying to keep all the names and connections straight," he said, sounding perhaps a bit more aw shucks than necessary.

"Indeed," she said, her smile turning to something a shade harder, the gleam in her eyes a bit more brittle. "Keeping connections lined up, especially when you're new in town, is rather important."

Calder wasn't sure if that was another come-on, or a thinly veiled warning of some kind. If so, he wasn't particularly interested in obeying either one.

"I'm so sorry to hear of Ted's recent loss in the mayoral race." He paused to sip his coffee, and watched the remnants of her polite smile fade altogether. "I'm sure he's had many offers, though. Man with his background." Of course, Calder knew absolutely nothing about Ted Weathersby's background other than the part he'd just stated, but she was clearly annoyed at the turn of the conversation, which made it an obvious line to pursue. "Or is he working for your father now?" Calder smiled. "I work in a family business myself, though I don't think my brothers would want their spouses working alongside them. Perhaps it's different with your family."

"You're not married then?" she asked, a spark of interest flashing back to life in the dark chocolate depths of her eyes. "Seems rather a shame," she said, making it sound like she personally thought it was anything but. She ran her gaze over him, casually, carelessly, then let it drift back to his face. "I don't think the women in this town would let an eligible man such as yourself go to waste."

"I'm not married, no," he said, then surprised himself when he added, "though I'm not exactly eligible, either." His thoughts went to Hannah, and he smiled to himself, thinking she probably wouldn't appreciate him slotting her in the spoken-for category alongside himself.

Cami's gaze narrowed as she took in his smile. "Fortunate woman," she murmured, then glanced up as her tea service tray was delivered. "Don't dither, set it down," she instructed the young man with snappish impatience.

Calder felt he should apologize to the young steward, given her animosity was likely directed at him and not the hired help, but he was too busy trying to interpret why Winstock's married daughter was hitting on him in the first place. Right under her father's roof.

"Do you often have breakfast with your father?" he asked, as his quiche was quickly set in front of him, along with the assorted appropriate flatware. "I'm sure he must enjoy that. You're the only child, right?" He flashed her a grin. "I can't tell you how many times I wished I was an only."

"How many brothers did you say you have?" she asked, steeping her tea strainer in a dainty china cup with a pattern matching that of the single-serving-size teapot that had been delivered with it.

"I have three. All younger."

Her perfectly penciled eyebrows lifted. "And all of them married? However did you escape the noose?"

"Two of them. The youngest is still in college. And I didn't," he said. "Escape the noose, I mean."

Interest sparked right back to life in those soulless depths, but was quickly hidden behind a moue of sympathy. She had quite a mouth on her, he'd already noted, the kind of full, bowed lips a man would go to great lengths to get pressed to various parts of his anatomy. A man other than himself. He thought of the banged-up and bruised set of lips that had consumed his every waking thought for the past four days. Well, the woman they belonged to had, anyway.

"Divorced then," she said. "That can be such a difficult thing."

Some shred of another emotion in her voice had him looking up from his quiche. "It was," he said, curious now. Then added, "Very," to see if that encouraged her to open up.

"How long ago?"

"Two years," he said. "Longer, I guess, if you add in the separation."

She nodded, still looking at him, though her thoughts seemed to be elsewhere. She mindlessly added sugar to her tea, and though he didn't know her, he thought it wasn't in character for her to not be paying attention to every tiny detail, even how much sugar she added to her tea.

So he pressed on. "She was close to my father. My ex," he clarified. "He very much approved of our relationship, so that didn't help matters any."

She looked at him now. "So I take it you were the one to end it? Does your father blame you?"

"It was more a . . . mutual decision," he said, intentionally making it sound anything but. "But yes, my father absolutely holds it against me. He's always expected a lot from me, not the least of which was a long successful marriage and at least a few grandkids." He smiled ruefully. "Seems my brothers are going to be far more adept at that than I am."

"No children then?" she queried. "And your father disapproved?" She didn't wait for him to answer, but sighed as she took the strainer from her teacup and let it clatter to the silver service tray. "I know a little something about that myself," she said, sounding frustrated and annoyed. She took a sip of her tea, and regarded him over the rim of the fragile cup as she lowered it again. "What is it about men and their legacies? Their inherent, obsessive need to create offspring—male offspring, mind you—as if it's the be all and end all of achieving success?"

He smiled. "I'm probably not the one to ask."

"And yet you decided not to follow that path." Her gaze narrowed and he thought he'd really hate to be on the receiving end of her temper. "Or is that why the marriage ended? She couldn't pop out a litter of pups for you?"

His eyes widened at the sudden impolite turn of conversation. He wondered what she'd say if he told her that Owen Hartley had used that exact same expression—litter—only regarding her own motivations, not his. He thought it best for Owen's longevity not to go there. "No, our marriage ended for other reasons, but we did have a difference of opinion on having a family of our own."

Her annoyance shifted to interest once more, and again, the hairs on his arms lifted. "You don't want children? How . . . refreshing."

As it happened, it was the reverse of that, but his feelings about children had nothing to do with creating heirs or leaving legacies. Telling her would also end any chance he had of uncovering more of the situation between her and her husband. With Winstock in the crosshairs of the arson investigation, the more he learned about the inner workings of the man's family, the better. "I'm more concerned with living my life as I want to live it rather than worrying about what I'll be leaving behind when I'm gone, or that there will be someone to leave it to."

Her eyes sparkled as a smile curved her perfectly plumped lips. "Exactly! Why is it that people have such a hard time understanding that? I wasn't put here to be a broodmare; I was put here to have a life, same as any man. I have my own goals, and it just so happens, marshaling a herd of rug rats isn't one of them. Is that so wrong of me?"

He shook his head. He honestly felt no one should be forced by family or society to marry, procreate, or, for that matter, take over a family business, if it wasn't what they wanted to do. "Not at all. Seems to me that only brings suffering to more folks." He laid his fork down, his lobster quiche still untouched. "Do you have an interest in taking over your father's business concerns? Is he not . . . receptive to that idea? Because you're not a son?"

"Daddy has somewhat antiquated ideas about such things, it's true. But I'm nothing if not resourceful."

He lifted an eyebrow, and let a grin lift the corners of his mouth, making it seem as though his interest—which was sincere—was perhaps inspired by something less than polite. "I'm beginning to see that," he said.

She glowed at the praise. "I married a man with political aspirations, who had much the same mind-set as myself." She leaned forward, tapping her uniformly tapered and painted nails on the pale yellow linen tablecloth. "Teddy and I have always had an understanding."

He let his suggestively raised eyebrows ask the question for him.

The speculative gleam that entered her eyes made him shift slightly in his seat, but not because the fit of his pants had suddenly grown uncomfortable. If anything, his pants had just become distinctly looser-fitting. But she didn't have to know that.

"Teddy's family is well off enough, but they aren't otherwise connected. He had a good enough pedigree though, and good schools, but he needs my background, my connections here in the Cove, to reach his own goals."

"And you needed him for . . . ?"

"For his Y chromosome. Not to have children, though

my father was quite hopeful about that. But he could help me groom Teddy for political greatness, and that would allow me to add to Daddy's legacy and be seen as an asset to him."

Wow, Calder thought. Her father would only see her as an asset if she either produced more Winstocks, or added to the family legacy with a mayoral spouse, perhaps a senator, or greater? How sad. And yet, wasn't he in much the same place with his own family? "Did you ever consider running for office yourself? I mean, you're bright, sharp, attractive. You could have achieved that without—"

"Kind of you to say," she said, all but preening at his words of praise and not the least bit humble about accepting them. "But, as I said, my father has rather antiquated ideas about a woman's role in society. We are the icing, the cake topper, the arm candy. We throw perfect parties, keep an immaculate, well-appointed home, have the perfect progeny, connect with the masses via our charitable work." She looked him dead in the eye, and the fury he saw behind the bright gleam actually alarmed him. "We do not become our own successes, or further our own causes. Certainly not at the expense of our spouse, or our father. Just ask my mother."

"I—" He wasn't sure how to respond to that.

"She left when I was a little girl, with a man who apparently thought she had more to offer than whether or not pleated chiffon drapes looked good as a backdrop when paired with Meissen china."

So there's a minefield you wandered into. Nice. He stalled with a sip of coffee, then said, "I'm sorry to hear that. I take it you and your mother aren't close, then?"

"I haven't seen or heard from her since the day she left."

He was sure he looked as shocked as he felt. "That's—

harsh. I'm sorry, it's not my place to say," he added. "I don't know the circumstances, but if you were young—"

"I was three. I don't remember her. And don't hold it against my mother. I thought for years she simply didn't want us, me or my father. I found out later that she'd been paid rather handsomely in the divorce to leave me with my father." Her smile could best be described as acid. "Part of the property settlement, no doubt." She set her teacup down, very carefully, and just as carefully schooled her features back to something softer . . . or as soft as she was capable of. She even added that little hair-lifting laugh. "I shouldn't speak so ill of the man. After all, he was just trying to do right by me. Any woman who would run off like that—how was he to trust her with his only child?"

Calder suspected she was reciting Brooks's exact explanation, word for word. "That was some time ago. Your father never remarried?"

She shook her head. "He doesn't handle failure well." She waved a hand. "Not in business, of course, because one can always turn failure there into a success elsewhere, not that he has many failures. But when it comes to life outside of business, it's not so easily controlled, or manipulated."

I don't know about that, Calder thought. Brooks Winstock seemed to be pretty damn good at doing just that. Both with men like Calder, whom he'd been jerking around like a puppet on a string, and with his own daughter, whose life he'd seemingly gone out of his way to control and neatly map out as well.

"He doesn't like it when life doesn't go according to plan," Cami went on.

I bet he doesn't, Calder thought, and wondered what that might mean in regard to the boathouse burning. Winstock's life had taken an unexpected turn when Ted hadn't won the mayoral race, and had lost his council seat as well. Was that why he'd made the desperate attempt to harm Jonah in the only way that could benefit Winstock's future plans? Was he tired of waiting, afraid of something else unraveling his carefully made plans, and taking illegal shortcuts now?

"Ted's loss must have hit him hard then," he said, trying not to show his own avid interest in her response.

"You could say that," she said, mildly. "In fact, that's one of the reasons I'm here this morning. To discuss . . . options."

"I'm sure it's very frustrating. What will Ted do now? What does he want to do?"

"I don't know," she said, then took another sip as a contemplative look crossed her face. But that look was quickly usurped by a slow smile. A smile that was completely at odds with the hard glint in her eyes as she looked at him and said, "It's not my problem. I've informed him I'll be seeking a divorce."

Calder's eyes widened at that. "I'm—sorry to hear that. As you said, it's never an easy thing."

"No," she said, quite matter-of-factly. "No, it's not. But, as I've long known, life isn't fair. Sometimes you're dealt a raw hand, and tough choices need to be made." She blotted the corners of her perfectly painted lips with the linen napkin that had been spread in her lap, and dropped it unceremoniously on the tea service tray. Calder couldn't help but think it appeared she was discarding her husband with the same careless indifference.

"True, I suppose," he said. "I am sorry, though." Then another thought struck him, and suddenly, things began to make a lot more sense. "How long has he known?"

Her gaze narrowed very briefly at the question. He thought he might have overplayed his hand, but she seemed to shrug off her suspicion and lifted a casual shoulder.

"Several days ago. He's experienced a number of losses of late, so I knew he wouldn't take it well."

Calder wondered if that was the reason, or one of them, that Winstock had continually postponed their meeting. Ted apparently didn't work for Brooks, and Cami didn't seem overly emotional about the situation, or at all emotional, actually, but a divorce still had to be something that father and daughter would have to discuss at length. If for no other reason than it would be big news once the word got out. Naturally they'd want to control the timing and manner the news was disseminated.

"I haven't been in town long," Calder said, "but I'm from a town only a little bigger than this one, and I know how challenging it is to keep that kind of news quiet."

"Actually, other than Ted you're the only person I've told." She smiled then, and a bit of that predatory spark came back into her eyes. "I'm not sure why." She leaned forward slightly, lips curving again, reminding him of a jungle cat circling its prey. "You're very easy to talk to. And, of course, we share this painful life event."

She tried to imbue the word "painful" with something he supposed was intended to look like discomfort, but it didn't play exactly true, with the gleam still there in her eyes. She reached out a hand and curled those talons of hers around his wrist. "Perhaps you and I can share a drink, or dinner, before you head back to your river. Although, I suppose if you're building Daddy's little club, you'll be spending a fair amount of time here." She let his wrist go and leaned back in her chair, taking care to slowly cross her legs in a manner that wasn't even trying not to be suggestive. He was only surprised she didn't run a pointed toe up the side of his calf.

"I appreciate the invite," he said, but that's as far as he got.

The hallway doors opened and in strode a tall man with a well-groomed mane of silver hair, wearing a golf shirt and slacks that on anyone else might have been casual attire, but managed to make Brooks Winstock look as if he'd just stepped out of his personal tailor's shop. In Milan.

"Daddy," Cami said, instantly all smiles. She unfolded her legs and rose gracefully, in one sweeping motion that, given the snug fit of her skirt, Calder thought almost defied physics. She leaned in for a hug as her father paused at her end of the table.

He kissed the top of her hair, careful not to muss it, Calder noted, then stepped back. "Look at you," he said, his lips curving, but his gaze more considering and observant than filled with fatherly affection. "Lovely as always. Fresh as a garden flower."

"Thanks, Daddy. You look good too. Hope the game went well this morning?"

Game. So Brooks had put Calder off . . . for a golf game? Calder had stood at the same time as Cami, tossing his linen napkin over the uneaten quiche. He silently hoped the steward and the chef didn't come under some kind of reprimand for his lack of appetite.

"Mr. Winstock," he said, extending his hand across the table as the older gentleman came to stand behind the chair opposite his, a polite smile on his face. "A pleasure to finally meet."

Winstock took his hand in a quick, firm handshake, but there was no corresponding smile on his face now. Once he'd looked away from his daughter, he'd become the consummate businessman once again, golf attire or no. "My apologies for dragging this out so long." He noticed the linen on Calder's plate with a quick flick of his gaze. "If you're done, why don't we head to my office. Here," he qualified, "in the house. Just across the hallway."

"I'll leave you two gentlemen to your business," Cami said, then looked at her father. "I'll be up in my rooms. We'll talk when you're through?"

"Absolutely. I'll send up for you. I'm glad you've taken my advice and plan to stay here. It's really for the best." He stepped around the table and leaned in for another hug. "It's good to have you home again, kitten."

Her smile didn't falter so much as a whisper, but Calder hadn't missed the oh-so-slight mist that had sheened her eyes as she propped her chin on his shoulder during the brief hug. It was gone by the time Winstock straightened, but Calder knew what he'd seen. Maybe she wasn't completely cold and calculating after all. At least where her father was concerned.

She turned to Calder and held out her hand again. "A pleasure to meet you, Mr. Blue." Her lips curved more deeply. "I enjoyed our conversation."

She'd extended her hand, fingertips curled downward, and once again he was left to consider just what she intended. He took her fingertips in a gentle grip, but didn't nod this time. "The pleasure was mine. Good luck with . . . your future plans."

She smiled then and it was at odds with the poor little girl look that had been on her face when her father had hugged her a moment ago, not to mention completely inappropriate given said father was standing just behind him, in clear view of what could only be described as a . . . hungry expression.

"Perhaps we can discuss exactly that," she said, then curled her hand to run the side of her thumb up the center of his palm. "Dinner and drinks, then. I look forward to it."

Then she was gone, leaving Calder to tamp down his

body's instant response to her unexpected little caress. Even if his body was one step ahead of his brain, her touch shouldn't have had that effect on him. He turned to find Winstock looking at him with a decidedly calculating expression on his face.

The man missed nothing, and Calder was left grappling for the appropriate thing to say, knowing such a thing really didn't exist.

"You'll have to forgive Camille," Winstock said, taking pity on him, if the half smile now curving the corner of his mouth was any indication.

Incredibly, that was even more unnerving than the look his daughter had just given him. *What the hell was with this family, anyway?*

"She's always been rather . . . assertive. I'm afraid she gets that trait from her dear old father. Unfortunately, she also has her mother's impulsiveness." He let out a short half laugh and lifted a shoulder in a casual shrug. "What's a father to do? She's my only and I find I can never bring myself to deny her anything. It's my one failing, I'm afraid."

Calder knew he must have looked alarmed, at least momentarily, because Winstock let out a sharp, almost delighted laugh.

"Don't worry, my boy. I won't feed you to that particular lion. Or should I say, lioness. I'll need you to stay sharp and focused for our little project. Although she might have something to say about that, so be forewarned." He stepped past a gaping Calder and walked through the double doors Cami had left open upon her exit. "Just this way."

Calder stayed right where he was a moment longer, trying to process what had just happened, and what in the hell he planned to do about it. *Good damn thing I have no intention of working "our little project,"* he thought. *Jesus.*

And here he'd thought there wasn't anyone who could make fatherhood look less palatable than his own father. How wrong he'd been about that.

He shook his head, straightened his shoulders, and followed Winstock into the hallway, which was more like a grand foyer, complete with twin arching staircases that led to a second-floor balcony, and two separate wings of the house. He knew this, as his room the night before had been located in the one that angled off to the left. He had another thought that if Cami had indeed been under this same roof the night before, he was damn lucky she hadn't known he was also in residence. A shiver of what could only be described as revulsion rippled through him as he thought once again about there being eyes in the wall. Cami . . . and her Daddy dearest. *Dear God, don't even go there.*

Winstock crossed the beautifully restored and polished cypress plank foyer and the blue stonework that had been inlaid in the shape of a star in the center of it, the soles of his leather golf shoes making not a single sound. *Lion raised by a panther,* Calder thought.

Winstock had just opened the matching double doors leading into a room that looked as if it might rival the Library of Congress for the sheer volume of leather-bound books from the floor to rotunda-like ceiling of the room, when a commotion at the massive front door caught his attention instead. Both he and Winstock turned as Hannah pushed her way past, well, Calder didn't know what to call him. The butler? Majordomo? Whatever his job description, he hadn't been able to stop the determined woman presently striding toward them.

Calder grinned. She was in uber-attorney mode, at least her expression was. What she was wearing was anything but classic D.C. lawyer garb. She had on wrinkled tan khaki capri pants, thin, no-heeled flats, and a peach-colored pullover. Her hair was down and reminded him of their walk on the shoreline the day before. His body responded instantly, to all of it.

"Brooks Winstock. Just the man I need to see." She spared a glance at Calder. "I'm glad you're still here. You haven't signed anything, have you?"

"Hannah?" Brooks asked, stepping forward, looking mildly concerned. "What is the emergency, Ms. McCrae? I'm assuming, given your brazen entrance into my home, there must be one."

She looked at Calder a moment longer and he gave a quick shake of his head, which she seemed to understand was in response to her question. So she turned to Winstock and drew herself up to her full, defense counselor magnitude, which was striking no matter what she wore. "I know you've been questioned in regard to the arson that took place Thursday night on Jonah Blue's pier."

Winstock's agitated expression remained, but his stance relaxed somewhat. "Ms. McCrae, I'm well aware of your brother's—or, I should say, Chief McCrae's interest in Calder. No need to come barging in here in some misguided attempt to save me from myself. I can assure you, I've been in business longer than you've been alive, and am quite capable—"

"Don't be disingenuous. I didn't come here to warn you about Calder. I'm his attorney, for God's sake. But you knew that."

Winstock's expression smoothed even as his gaze sharpened, and Calder thought, *Maybe more shark than panther.*

"Indeed," Brooks said. "Well, if you're here to wrangle some kind of confession out of me, or to warn your client—"

"I'm not here—" She broke off, and Calder was pretty sure he heard her swear under her breath.

His smile grew to a grin. His prim and proper little

lawyer was turning out to be anything but. Proving you could take the lawyer out of D.C., but you couldn't take the hometown girl out of the lawyer. He liked it. He liked it a lot.

"I'm here to warn you both," she said, and his grin instantly fled.

"What's wrong?" Calder stepped forward, all amusement gone. "What happened?"

"Nothing," she told him. "Yet." She looked at Brooks. "Mr. Winstock, do you know where your son-in-law is?"

For once, Brooks's expression went completely blank. "What?"

Calder had no time to enjoy the older man's uncustomary lack of words, because there was a gasp from the stairs behind them and they all turned to see Cami, stopped about halfway down, clutching the bannister.

"Oh God," she said, looking truly stricken. In fact, she was sheet white.

"What is it?" Brooks went immediately to the stairs.

"I just got a call from Chief McCrae." She sucked in a gulp of air, and still looked as if someone had just gut punched her. "Teddy is at the docks." She turned her stark gaze toward Hannah. "He's holding Jonah and his great-granddaughter hostage in the big boathouse."

Chapter Eighteen

Hannah drove so she could fill Calder in on the way to
the docks. "I put it together when Owen was talking about
Winstock's disappointment with Ted, and I realized we'd
been looking at it all wrong. Brooks is wily and borderline
underhanded—or maybe not so borderline—but he's never
done anything illegal, and for all he seems hell-bent on re-
creating Blueberry Cove in his own image, I couldn't see
him risking the rest of the empire he's built on an arson
charge that, by itself, didn't even get him what he wanted."

The sprawling Winstock property was on the outskirts
of town, on a high promontory overlooking the town and
the bay beyond. Calder gripped the dash as she took the
turn heading toward the town proper and the docks
below. She glanced over at him. "Don't worry, I'm not
thinking about lupines." At his *very funny* look, she
turned her attention back to the road with a partial smile,
even though her heart was pounding in her chest at the
thought of what could be happening on those docks right
that very second. "All those years driving in D.C., not a
single accident. You're safe." She smiled as she braked a
little harder than necessary at the same stop sign she'd

run the day she met him. "Ish," she added, glancing at him again before continuing.

She purposefully didn't look at the remains of Beanie's sign, however, knowing that would distract her. It was enough she had Calder sitting mere inches away from her. She'd already spoken to Beanie personally and worked out the details of getting the sign replaced, and any other restitution Beanie felt she was owed, given that in some ways, the sign was irreplaceable. The older woman had been remarkably understanding about the whole thing, but Hannah would feel better when the reparations had actually been made.

She put all that out of her mind as she sped past. "I started to think about who would be desperate enough to burn down that building," she went on, refocusing her thoughts. "Brooks might want what he wants, but he's got enough on his hands trying to get the damn yacht club started. Why would he be rushing ahead to the next thing? Then Owen mentioned Ted and I realized that of all the people in this town, Ted is the one who has faced the biggest setbacks. He lost his bid at mayor, and his seat as head of the council was gone because he got cocky and gave it up when he put his bid in for mayor. I did some checking before heading to Winstock's place, called a few people who would know what was what, and as far as anyone I talked to knows, since then, he hasn't been employed anywhere doing anything. Not by Brooks, not by anyone else, at least not in the Cove. Not even consulting, nothing. So I thought, there's a guy desperate enough to do something, to prove to his rich father-in-law, maybe his demanding wife, that he is still valuable, still worth something. And Teddy is a big enough weasel that he'd consider arson. Well, honestly, I didn't think he was that stupid, but desperate men taking desperate measures, and all that. Even so, I didn't see him doing something like this." She swore under her breath, finding it hard to even picture Ted waving a gun around in some kind of hostage situation. "He must be in far worse shape than anyone has guessed. Like, off-the-deep-end bad. I heard he hadn't been seen much the past few weeks, but what would motivate him to do something like this?"

"Yeah, well, I think I can shed a little light on that. Seems you would be right about his demanding wife." He broke off and rubbed a hand across the back of his neck. This had gotten so far out of control so very fast.

Hannah flicked a look at him as she slowed, coming into the town proper, then looked at him again. "She made a move on you, didn't she?" She laughed and reached over to pat his thigh. "Did the big bad she-monster come prowling around your room last night?"

"No, she prowled me directly at the breakfast table, in front of her father. And if I hadn't already known I wasn't building anything for Brooks Winstock, the little interplay between the two of them would have killed any deal completely dead." He visibly shuddered and rubbed a hand over his face. "I don't want to speak ill of folks you grew up with, but there is something decidedly off in that relationship. And I don't want to know what it is, either."

"It's pretty well known that Cami and Ted aren't exactly a love match. And whereas Ted is more the cliché of a sleazy used car salesman in his handsy approach to his extracurricular activities, Cami is quite the effective prowler. I can't say I ever understood how anyone would fall for Ted's line of bull, but no one doubts Cami's ability to take what she wants. As to her father—"

"Do I really have to know?" Calder asked, sounding pained and more than a little disgusted.

"Let's just say he can't say no to his daughter, so if she

wants something, he either doesn't stand in her way, or he does what he can to see that his baby girl gets her wish."

"That's just . . . I don't even want to find the word for what that is." He glanced at her now. "So, it didn't bother you to think that Cami might come prowling around my door last night?"

She slid him a look, one eyebrow raised. "Should I be bothered?"

He lifted a shoulder and actually had the confidence to look a little put out, which made her already dangerously wobbling heart tilt a bit further in his direction.

"I wouldn't expect a full-on catfight or anything, but a modest display of jealousy would have fed my manly ego at least a little bit."

She smiled as she looked back at the road. "Well, since we're being all honest and vulnerable here, I will reveal that when I saw her on the staircase behind you in the Winstock foyer, I might have felt my claws extend, just a wee bit." She glanced at him. "Better?"

"A little," he said, pretending he had to consider it.

She sighed, relenting, and said, "And, okay, when you did that little disgusted thing just now, rubbing your hand over your face at the very thought of her anywhere near you?" She slowed to make the turn down toward the docks, rolling to a stop long enough to look at him and hold his gaze directly. "I might have wanted to do a little victory dance." She held her hand up and put her finger and thumb close together. "Little bit."

He grinned then, and she thought it was a damn good thing they had a half-crazed man in a boathouse to deal with, because otherwise she'd have turned that car around and headed for the nearest desolate inlet and let him have his way with her, all over again.

Their smiles faded as they made the turn toward the

docks, and spied the flashing lights of the law enforcement and fire department response to the situation on the pier. She swore. "I grew up here and I didn't know we had that many vehicles with lights on top. Wow. This really is not good."

"What did Logan say when you called in?" She'd called the station as they'd raced out to her car.

"I didn't talk to him directly. He was already on his way down here. I talked to Barb." She slowed as she got closer, trying to figure out the best place to park. Ironically, she ended up pulling into the plowed-over lot that used to be Delia's Diner. "I called Logan before I left the house, to tell him what I thought about Ted. He agreed with me and said he'd go track him down and have a talk with him. But I don't know if that happened before—" She nodded at the cluster of police cruisers and fire trucks that completely blocked off street access to any of Blue's docks.

"Did Barb—Sergeant Benson—say what exactly happened down here?"

"All she knew was that Jonah had called and told them to . . ." She glanced at Calder, well aware that Jonah was his great-uncle. "Uh, come down and pick up Ted."

Calder smiled, though it was more of a grimace. "I imagine he used somewhat more colorful language than that. But you said Bit was in there with him."

Hannah took off her seat belt, and wrapped her arms around her waist for a moment as her heart clutched. She'd been trying to stay all prosecutor about this, as she'd long since trained herself to do. Even on the most heart-wrenching cases—though it was rare that things like corporate fraud and insider trading tugged at the heartstrings—she kept her cool. But these were people she knew, people she loved, and maintaining that professional, objective distance was proving impossible. "Yeah," she said, roughly. "And even Teddy at his most disgusting should know better than to do something like that. Jonah's a hard-ass old coot—" She looked at him. "Sorry, no offense, intended."

"None taken. I'd have to agree with you. I like it when you get mad enough to swear out loud."

She flashed him a confused half frown, then said, "I imagine he's holding his own in there, and given the size difference, my money would be on Jonah snatching the gun away and beating Teddy senseless with it."

"Maybe that's why he took Bit. Leverage."

She nodded, her throat closing over. "I still can't believe he's doing it, no matter how desperate he may be to prove himself to Brooks."

"I didn't get to finish earlier. Cami told him she's filing for divorce."

Hannah's head swung around so fast, she winced at the residual ache in her shoulder and face. "When?"

"Earlier this week."

"So he was about to lose everything."

Calder nodded.

She opened the door and he put a hand on her arm. "Don't rush in there. I'm sure your brother has it all under control."

"My brother," she said. Then, "Shit!" And she was out of the car like a shot. What the hell had she been doing, sitting there in the car, mulling over the ins and outs of the situation, when it was very likely, knowing Logan, that he'd gone in there guns blazing, at least metaphorically speaking. Or maybe not so metaphorically. He was getting married tomorrow, dammit. He couldn't go putting himself between crazy Ted Weathersby and—she broke off that mental train. There was a tiny girl at risk, likely scared out of her mind. Of course he was going to put himself between her and a bullet. "Dammit, I'm going to kill that sleazy weasel with my own bare hands."

She ducked under the yellow tape. A few local firemen and the men on Logan's force turned instinctively to block her, but all they had to do was take one look at her face, and they stood back and let her through. They closed ranks, however, on Calder.

"I'm with her," he said, nodding at Hannah's quickly retreating back. "And if you don't want her rushing in there and putting herself in danger, you'll let me through. I'm Jonah's—"

"We know who you are," said one of the police officers. "I'm sorry, but—"

Hannah had doubled back and grabbed his arm. "It's okay, Joe. He's with me. We might need him to talk to Jonah, keep him from doing anything stupid." She all but dragged him away.

Calder leaned his head closer as they bobbed and weaved their way through the crowd. "I'd be happy to, but I'm pretty sure the only thing I'd do is piss Jonah off enough to distract him and give Ted an opening."

They stopped behind two squad cars, parallel parked bumper to bumper at the end of the main pier leading to the boathouse. Officer Dan had a marksman rifle resting on the roof of the squad car, trained at the boathouse. And that's when it very abruptly became real for Hannah.

"Dan, do you really need to do that?"

She didn't even know he knew how to do that.

He didn't so much as blink, much less look her way. "Logan's behind the emergency truck," he said, looking and sounding far older and more mature than she'd have thought possible. Yet another reason to want to kill Ted with her bare hands.

"Thanks," she said. "Don't—uh—don't do anything rash."

"Ten-four to that," was all he said, keeping his eye on the target. "I'm having to pass up my mother's meat loaf for this."

That sounded more like the Dan she knew. "Come on," Hannah said to Calder, feeling a little better. She was still clutching his arm. "He's down here."

"So I heard," Calder said, mildly, but he didn't slow her down or try to stop her. Instead, he moved up next to her, removed his arm from her grip, and placed a steadying hand on her back as they wove their way through another throng of uniformed people. Some of whom she didn't recognize at all, which was when she realized that it wasn't just Blueberry Cove's finest clogging the waterfront with emergency vehicles. Logan had brought in reinforcements. Her heart rate jumped up another tick, until that was all she could hear, pounding in her ears. She all but skidded around the back of the emergency truck, and clapped her hand over her racing heart the moment she spied her brother, looking very severe, but mercifully very alive and not inside the boathouse with a crazy man. He was speaking to two other officers, both of whom were carrying the same kind of scoped rifle that Dan had been handling.

"Logan," she said, more breathlessly than she'd expected to sound. She tried to rein in her relief and find her prosecutor's calm once again. It didn't come as naturally as she'd have liked. "What's going on in there?"

"Hannah," he said—barked, actually—before giving the two officers a dismissive nod. They went to the two squad cars positioned at an angle to the pier and boathouse, and took up the same stance as Dan with even more lethal-looking weapons.

"Is that really necessary?" she asked, nodding at them. "I mean, it's Ted. He's an ass, but he's not—"

"He's not himself, is what he's not," Logan told her. "Why are you out here?" He looked beyond her and she knew he was an instant away from having one of the uniforms drag her and Calder back to the other side of the yellow-taped line.

"Calder has some additional information that might help." She all but shoved him in front of her. "About Ted and Cami."

"What?" Logan demanded. "Why didn't you—"

"I just found out."

Calder looked at Hannah as he stumbled to stand a foot away from Logan, then turned to her brother. "I was at Winstock's, for our meeting this morning, only his daughter showed up for breakfast first. And confided that she'd told Ted she was filing for divorce."

Logan's eyes widened. "When?"

"Earlier this week. Before the fire."

"Shit."

"Yeah," Calder said. "My reaction exactly. Have you been able to talk to Jonah? How is Bit?"

"She must be terrified," Hannah said. "I swear when you get him out of there, I'll strangle him myself."

"One thing at a time," Logan said to her, then looked back at Calder. "Did she say how he took the news? Anything specific?"

Calder shook his head. "No, but I think the who and the why are pretty obvious now."

"Yeah," Logan said, then swore again as he rubbed his palm across the back of his neck. "We should have seen this."

"How? I mean, Ted? Really? What does he want?" Hannah asked. "What does he want from Jonah? Or from you? Why the hostage deal?"

"He wants Jonah to agree to sign over his property to Brooks."

"Holy—" Calder finished that epithet under his breath. "Like we said before, Jonah would never agree to that, even over his actual dead body."

"That's what I'm afraid of," Logan said.

"Bit!" Hannah gasped. "That's why he has her—oh, Logan, what are you going to do? You can't let anything happen to—"

"I'm not planning on letting anything happen to her. That's why we got the SWAT guys here from Bangor. Lucky for us, they were doing some kind of training deal up in Lubec."

"Has anyone talked to Jonah?" Hannah asked. "Can't we just get him to say he's going to sign the land over, to end this thing, then Ted gets locked up and he goes on with his life? Life being the key word there?"

"That's what we'd like to see happen, but no, there has been no communication with Jonah as yet. Apparently Ted went to talk to him today about working out a deal to buy up the property, and, well, you can imagine Jonah's response to that. One thing apparently led to another, and now Ted's got the two of them in there at gunpoint."

"He had a gun the whole time? So it was premeditated?" Hannah was already running through the process of where this would go once they brought it to a conclusion. A peaceful and safe conclusion, she prayed silently.

"I can't be sure about that," Logan said. "I've tried to establish communication with him." He gestured to the bullhorn sitting on the hood of the nearest cruiser. "He just keeps saying it's between him and Jonah, that it's all up to Jonah."

"Do you think bringing Brooks or Cami out here would—"

Logan swung his gaze from the boathouse to her. "I don't want them anywhere near here."

Hannah could have told him that she was pretty sure both Winstocks were being barely restrained on the other side of the yellow tape, but figured he didn't need the added distraction. "I'm so sorry," she said, putting one arm around him for a quick hug. "This is not how you should be getting ready for your big day."

"Tell me about it," he muttered, relenting for a brief moment and giving her a quick one-arm squeeze in return, before straightening and turning back to the matter at hand. "What the—?"

Hannah spun around . . . and saw Calder with the bull-horn in his hand, walking down the pier. "Holy—Calder!" she half shouted, half hissed. "What do you think you're doing?"

He just waved her silent with a hand behind his back, keeping his gaze focused on the boathouse at the end of the pier.

"Blue, get your ass off that pier before I have one of my guys shoot you off," Logan barked. This was followed by the sound of guns being cocked and a murmur going up in the crowd being held at bay behind the rear cluster of squad cars and emergency vehicles.

Calder paused long enough to look over his shoulder. "Nothing else is getting through," he said, raising his voice just enough to be heard. "Let me try this. I might be the only one who can talk to him."

"Why on earth would he think that?" Hannah said. "He just told me he'd only piss Jonah off." She thought her heart would leap straight through her chest as she watched Calder inch closer to the boathouse. "He doesn't even know Ted."

"I hope Ted doesn't kill him," Logan growled. "Because that would rob me of the pleasure." He stalked off to bark orders at the SWAT guys and his own guys, leaving Hannah to stare, gripped by a fear she'd never felt before, at the pier.

She told herself she'd be freaking out no matter who it was putting his life stupidly in jeopardy, but she knew this went a lot deeper than that. Sometime over the past few days, somehow, he'd finagled his way a lot farther past her defenses than she'd allowed herself to truly admit. It was stupid and foolish and she was in absolutely no shape emotionally to even begin to think about having a relationship with anyone. And none of that, not one single bit of it, had kept her from falling for Calder Blue.

"Stupid Good Samaritan," she muttered. "Stupid good guy, stupid hero, always having to do the right thing." She paced back and forth, watching him move slowly closer, feeling her heart drop inside her chest with every step he took. "You know you don't have to rescue everyone all of the time," she called out to him, unable to help herself. She was about two breaths away from a full-on panic attack, and if Ted didn't kill him, and Logan didn't strangle him, well, she was third in line.

He stopped about thirty yards from the boathouse, then glanced over his shoulder, looking directly at her. Infuriatingly, he grinned, and winked, before turning back and lifting the bullhorn.

Chapter Nineteen

Calder's palms were so sweaty, it was a miracle he didn't drop the damn bullhorn as he fumbled with the ON switch. There was a loud, high-pitched squeal that made him and probably half residents of the Cove flinch. Then it faded and he lifted the speaker to his mouth.

"Ted? Hey, it's Calder Blue out here. I hear you want to talk a deal on this piece of property. Well, if that's so, then you've got the wrong man in there."

Even with the speaker, he could barely hear himself over his own heartbeat. What the hell had he been thinking, pulling this stunt?

Nothing from inside the boathouse. *Jesus*.

He lifted the bullhorn again. "You don't know me, but I came here a few days ago to see Jonah. I had the very same talk with him that you're having. He's a stubborn son of a bitch, I know."

He ignored the collective gasp behind him, and the resulting swell of murmuring voices. *Just focus on the boathouse*.

"You see," he said, then paused to take a breath, forcing the tremor out of the words. *Calm, casual, like you deal with deranged former council leaders every day.* "Jonah thought I was from the other side of the Blue clan, up in Calais. And that is true, I was raised on the St. Croix River. But the fact is, those kids that Jedediah took when he left? Yeah, turns out, they weren't his at all. They were Jeremiah's." *Keep going. You've got this.* "So that means I'm not Jonah's great-nephew. I'm the direct heir, straight from Jeremiah himself. Jonah is descended from his sister."

The gasp this time was bigger, as was the resulting fury of whispering and murmurs, followed by the barked order from Logan for absolute quiet.

"So, Ted, you see, I'm the rightful owner here. I have proof. Proof even Jonah had to listen to. The thing is . . . we're a lot alike, Ted. We both want the same thing. We're tired of the old men in our families calling all the shots. Tired of being made to feel like we don't know shit, like we can't call our own shots, build our own dreams." His voice took on more conviction as he spoke, only Ted didn't have to know it was his own father he was thinking about, his own life. "They were us once, you know, and they just can't let that go, can't understand that their time is over." He paused, wiped his free hand on his jeans leg, and swapped hands on the bullhorn. "It's our time now, Ted. Our time. Jonah knows that. And now so does Brooks Winstock. So . . . what do you say, Ted? Can we talk? Because I can't do this alone. And I think you're just the man to help me. The Winstocks of this town have had it their way long enough. Time for us to make our own mark."

He stopped talking then, not sure what else he could say. He waited one long beat, then another, feeling as if his heart were going to simply plow its way right through his chest wall. The seconds ticked on. Nothing. No response.

Defeat started to seep in, and he scrambled in his mind for what else he could say, how he could convince Ted that the only one with the power to give him what he wanted was Calder. He wondered if he should mention the man's wife, but figured that was far too volatile a subject, and he didn't know enough to go there. It had been a risk even bringing up Winstock's name. But assuming Ted was in there trying to prove his worth to both the man and his daughter, he'd felt it was a risk he had to take. Make Ted think he really knew what was going on, knew all the players.

He wiped a hand over his face, and was just about to bring the bullhorn back up, to say God knew what, when the boathouse door groaned and rolled slowly open on its tracks. There was a flurry of sound and movement behind him, and he waved his arm as authoritatively as he could, praying no one did anything stupid.

The door opened about three feet, then stopped. A moment later, Jonah appeared in the opening, his feet and wrists bound, forcing him to shuffle slowly into the open doorway. Then Ted appeared behind him. He was holding a wide-eyed, tear-streaked Bit. And a gun.

Okay, he thought, *so things just got more real.* At least he didn't have to worry about being able to hear over his pounding heartbeat, because that particular organ had just stopped dead in his chest.

He had to force his gaze from the terrified little girl to look at Ted instead. He was a tall man with the look of an aging athlete, and classically handsome, in that prep-school manner some men never outgrew. Of course, he'd probably looked better than he did at the moment. His hair was a bit wild, as if he'd raked his hand through it repeatedly. He was sporting a few days' worth of beard and the dark circles under his eyes either meant he wasn't sleeping, or he was on something, or both.

"Ted," he said. "Good to meet you. Calder."

"What—?" Ted started, then stopped, coughed a few

times, and wiped his forehead with his gun hand, dangerously bobbling the weapon, before steadying himself—
mostly anyway—and looking out at Calder, and the sea of
insanity behind him.

Calder prayed that the crowd didn't spook him.

"What's your offer?" Ted asked, finally, his voice sounding like rough gravel. "What are your plans?"

"That's just it. I'm not a developer. I'm a contractor. I
have the contract—my company does—on the yacht club.
My plan was to talk to Brooks about going in on a development deal with me on the rest, but to be honest, all he's
done is dick me around on this contract and I'm starting
to think he's not the man for this. He's too old-school,
thinks his money is better than mine because he's—well, I
don't rightly know why. Money's money, isn't it, Ted? And
my family has been here just as long as his. He thinks he's
better because he made his money sitting his bony ass
behind a desk, while my family made their fortune break-
ing their backs. Well, that's a bunch of shit now, isn't it,
Ted? But you know that. You were the one running this
town. You were the one getting things done. That's the kind
of guy I need on my team."

Ted just stared at him, looking half glazed, half vacant.
As if the enormity of what he'd done was starting to sink
in, starting to take its toll. And though Calder knew jack
about hostage negotiating, he'd stood across the table from
his father. When Thaddeus got on a tear, which was pretty
much every week, he acted almost as insane as Ted right
now. And what Calder had learned was that it was impera-
tive to strike with logic and clear thinking while his father
still had the capacity to listen. Because once he went
around the bend fully, there was no talking to him. In fact,
Calder had suggested to his brothers, more than once, that
they should have their father's mental health evaluated,

but they'd looked at him like, *Sure, you and what army?* Which . . . true.

"Hey, Ted, I tell you what," he pushed on, shoving away thoughts of his father and what awaited him back home when word got back about this latest stunt. If he made it back home, that is. "This is between you and me. Jonah and I already have an agreement, but he can stay, too, if you want. Though I don't see what good that will do. However, the last thing we need in there is some crying little kid. This isn't day care, Ted. That's all Jonah is good for, you know? Watching over the grandkids. We're the ones making plans, making things happen. No time for that bullshit. Let her down so we can focus on what's important here."

"I can't," Ted said, frowning, as if he was trying to sort through the logic of what Calder was saying. "I need her— she's leverage."

"But that's just it. We don't need leverage." He patted his breast pocket, like there was magically something in there, when quite clearly there was not. "I have it all right here. Jonah's signature on the dotted line. We don't need the kid, Ted. We've got all the power. Or we will, once you and I strike a deal. Brooks already let me down. I'm counting on you to be smarter than he was. I've already proven my worth to Jonah."

He glanced at Jonah for the first time then, and the fury in the old man's eyes was so ferocious, so intense, it was a miracle Calder didn't burn to a pile of soot on the spot. He noticed the gash on Jonah's temple then, and the blood that had run down over his cheek to his neck. He'd wondered how Ted had gotten the bigger man trussed up like he was. He supposed that answered that question. He also supposed the fury in the old man's face wasn't about the shit Calder was talking, but about the fact that he was putting his great-granddaughter front and center in this little tableau. *I'm trying to save her, old man.*

"How about it, Ted?"

Ted wiped his brow again, gun wobbling, and Calder switched his focus back to the younger man, blocking out the murderous look on Jonah's face. He couldn't die twice, so the guy with the gun had to be top priority.

"You're juggling enough," Calder said to Ted.

"I wanted kids, you know," Ted said abruptly. "I wanted them. I wanted to give Brooks grandkids. Wanted that, just like he did. It was Cami who didn't." His voice broke on his wife's name, and Calder thought that was a sign that bringing her up was not a good idea.

"Well, with this new deal we're going to make, the hell with Brooks and the hell with her, too. You're a young man, Ted. Young and virile, just starting to make your name. No doubt you'll be able to stake your claim wherever you want. Plenty of time to start a family, build your own dynasty, one with your name attached. Weathersby. Not Winstock. She'll regret not believing in you. Trust me, I know all about that."

He saw Ted truly begin to waver, saw him stand a little straighter. He also held the gun a little steadier.

"But I'm not talking to you as long as that kid is here. Let her go, then let's go inside, discuss this like men."

"Dumb bitch," Ted shouted suddenly. "Doesn't she understand? Doesn't she realize what it feels like?"

"I know what you mean. Put the kid down, and we can swap some stories. I know Jonah has a bottle or three stashed in there somewhere."

Ted laughed then, and it wasn't a pleasant sound. "Yeah. If I didn't blow that up along with his damn boathouse. He should have known then. Who was in charge."

"Like I said. He's too old-school. Too stuck in his ways to realize he's already on the way out. Well, he knows it now." Calder patted his breast pocket. "We have the power now, Ted. Put the kid down. Let's talk."

"Yeah, old man," Ted said, grinning as he popped Jonah on the side of the head with the pistol grip. "Who's got the power now?"

It took great effort not to look at Jonah, who reeled slightly from the blow, but kept his stance, though he briefly rested his shoulder on the door frame for balance. Calder kept his gaze on Ted. "The kid, Ted. Come on. You're smart enough to deal with me. Those are my terms. Jonah can go or stay, but I don't babysit. I make deals."

And just like that, Ted let Bit go, all but dropping her to the pier as she half slid, half dropped from his arms. Calder didn't look at her; he kept his gaze on Ted, who immediately stepped behind Jonah, and put the gun to the old man's temple.

"Everyone else can go now," Ted screamed. "It's over, okay? Just a business deal now." He cackled and tapped the gun barrel to Jonah's temple. "Just a business deal."

Yeah, so that's not exactly how I hoped that would go, Calder thought. Bit was still standing on the pier, looking up at her great-grandfather, tears welling again.

"You go on now," Jonah said, speaking for the first time, his voice gruff but otherwise surprisingly gentle. "See that lady? You go talk to her. I need to talk to Ted here. Then we'll get some ice cream."

Bit looked from Jonah to Ted, her bottom lip quivering.

"Go on," Jonah said, and Calder could see what the gentle tone was costing the man. He was visibly shaking. "See the nice lady? Go to her. I'll be done here in a minute."

Calder risked a quick glance over his shoulder, and what was left of his heart rose right up into his throat. Hannah was just behind him, about ten yards back, crouching down with outstretched arms, beckoning to Bit. "Hannah," he hissed, but she didn't look at him.

"I've got coloring books, Bit," she called out. "Let's go play until your Pawpaw is done, okay?" She wiggled her fingers.

Bit looked uncertain and Calder knew the window was closing.

"Go on now," Jonah said, a bit of impatience creeping into his voice. "You know better than not to listen to your elders."

She nodded, bottom lip still wobbling, but then she took off down the pier toward Hannah. Calder let out a breath so loud he thought he'd be light-headed. He didn't watch Bit, he watched Jonah. The man's gaze was locked on the little girl, so Calder knew the moment she and Hannah had made it off the pier, because that was the same moment a little of the tension went out of Jonah's frame.

Calder looked at Ted, and lowered the bullhorn, taking a few steps closer. "Do we really need him?" he said, talking conversationally now, as if the worst was over. When it was anything but. "Let him go with the kid." He looked at Jonah. "You go babysit while we do some real business, old man."

Even though Jonah knew, quite clearly, that this whole thing was a bunch of bullshit, the fury in his eyes when he looked at Calder was quite real. *I just saved your great-granddaughter,* he wanted to shout at the old coot. *So back the hell off.*

"I don't know," Ted said, looking stronger now, less uncertain, which Calder belatedly realized was not necessarily a good thing, since he was still holding a gun to Jonah's temple. "Maybe it's time he was really done. Show this town we mean business."

Calder tried not to show any of his real reaction to that; instead, he looked disgusted. "Seriously, Ted? We don't have time for this bullshit. And I don't have time to walk you through the legal minefield you're going to be in if you shoot the guy. He's a pain in the ass, no doubt. God knows I've wanted to shoot him pretty much every minute since I met him. But there's no time for that."

"Fuck this," Jonah said; then in a move faster than Calder would have thought possible, he brought his bound hands up, snatched the gun, turned, and cracked Ted in the skull with the butt. The younger man dropped straight to the dock in a limp, lifeless heap. Then Jonah shuffled inside the warehouse, pulled a gutting knife off the wall, bent over, and snapped the cords on his ankles with hardly more than a flick, then stalked down the pier, all while Calder stood there, gaping at the hulk of a man. "What?" he said, as he passed by. "You expected me to stand there with a gun to my head while you talked him to death?"

He kept on walking, popping his hands free a moment later, then sending the gutting knife, point first, into the pier as he crouched down while Bit ran into his arms. He held her tight as a team of EMTs, SWAT guys, Logan, and Hannah, all raced down the pier. Most heading toward a now-groaning Ted. Hannah, however, stopped in front of Calder.

She stared at him wordlessly for what felt like a day and a half; then she leaped into his arms, wrapping him tightly in her own, and buried her face in his neck. "That was the most selfless, brave, stupid, idiotic, foolish thing I've ever seen anyone do." She beat on his back with closed fists, then clutched them in his hair and leaned back to look in his eyes. "Don't ever do that again. Promise me."

He wrapped his arms more tightly around her, grinning as he held her so she stayed up face-to-face with him. "Promise," he said, hearing the shakiness in his voice. Which spread rapidly to his arms, then his legs. "Now, I think I need to go sit down. And maybe throw up a little."

Chapter Twenty

Hannah pulled into the Winstock compound and parked beside Calder's truck. They hadn't talked much on their way back. He seemed to need a little time to come down from the adrenaline rush and process what he'd just done, and she needed some time to figure out how she was going to keep from throwing herself at him.

"I didn't think to find out where Brooks and Cami got off to," she said, stealing a glance at him.

He looked . . . well, he looked wonderful was how he looked. But he also looked tired and a bit freaked out by what he'd done, which somehow made him all the more endearing to her. Human, imperfect. *Mine.* "Logan mentioned they'd gone off to the hospital where they took Ted for evaluation before booking him for assault, arson—" She waved her hand. "The list is endless."

"I guess he is still Cami's husband, so Brooks will want to do damage control."

"I'm not sure even his money and power can smooth over this kind of thing." She shook her head, then looked at him. "So, what are you going to do now?" she asked, not sure whether she was ready to hear the answer. But finding out she'd never see him again would at least thwart that whole throwing-herself-at-him part.

He leaned his head back on the headrest, but didn't reach for the door. "I tried to talk to Jonah, while you were talking to Logan and your sisters."

Fiona and Kerry had come down to the docks. Well, pretty much the entire town of Blueberry had been at the docks. It wasn't often—as in never—that they had that kind of hysteria in town.

"And?" she asked.

Calder shook his head. "Stubborn old coot. Wouldn't let me anywhere near him."

"You'd think, if nothing else, he'd want to thank you for what you did for Bit." She shook her head. "I've half a mind to go have a chat with him myself."

That earned her a brief grin from Calder. "I've half a mind to let you." Then he reached over and cupped her cheek with his palm. It was the first time he'd touched her, in any intentional sort of way, since they'd walked off the pier and been separated by Logan and the EMT crew, who wanted to look over Calder, check his vital signs, hydrate him.

She leaned into his palm, unable to help herself. He could have been hurt or killed. So many things could have gone so horribly wrong. And suddenly the crap that had happened to her back in D.C., the stuff Tim had done, all of it ceased to matter. Life was what mattered, living it was what mattered, enjoying every moment was what mattered. Not worrying over what had happened, or over what might happen next.

"It would be my pleasure," she told him, smiling, seeing the real weariness in his eyes, and suspecting it had a lot more to do with his own stuff than with what had happened on the pier.

"You know what would be my pleasure," he said, his head still pressed against the seat. "Making love to you again. Preferably on something flat. And soft. I'm not sure my legs are up to another round of against-the-truck at the moment."

She laughed, even as her body reacted with an instantaneous and resounding *yes* to that idea. She tried not to let herself wonder what he meant, if it was just about the sex, or if he wanted more than—*Stop it*, she scolded herself. What happened to living in the moment?

Yeah. She was pretty much going to have to work at that.

And Calder Blue was going to head back to Calais, and to his farm on the St. Croix River. Could she handle being with him one more time, knowing it would be the last? Because the first time had been mind-blowing and they hadn't even gotten naked. Of course, Calais was just an hour and a half away. She looked away from him, back through the windshield. *Is that what you want? Someone you occasionally go have sex with?*

Maybe that would be easier. At least no one would get hurt. No one would be betraying anyone or lying, because there wouldn't be the promise of anything in the first place.

"You want to borrow my oil can?" he asked, his voice deep and a little rough, still weary, but amused at the same time.

She wanted to push her hands through his hair, to kiss him slowly, deeply, then take his mind off of what he'd done, before sliding into a long, blissful nap, wrapped against his heated, spent body. "What?" she said, belatedly processing what he'd said.

"For all those gears spinning in your mind." He shifted in his seat, sat up straighter as the hand that had been cupping her cheek fell back to his lap. From the corner of her eye, she could see he was making a visibly conscious effort to shove the aftereffects of his hostage negotiating aside. "I know what I want, Hannah. And you're probably not ready to hear it. But I don't think I'm going to have the luxury of waiting until you are." He waited until she looked directly at him. "I do want to make love to you. Truly make love to you. I want to do a lot of things with you. In and out of bed. I don't know how it would all work out, given where you are and where I am, and what we're trying to figure out for ourselves. But if there was any way those things we're figuring could align—" He broke off when his phone chirped. He pulled it out of his pocket. "I'm sorry. Eli has called like four times, and I'm really not up for a family conversation. Let me turn this off."

"There were media trucks there," Hannah said. "At the end. Maybe they saw the news. You might want to see if—"

But Calder looked at the screen of his cell phone and what color had come back into his face washed straight back out again.

Now Hannah sat up straighter. "Calder, what is it?"

"Text. From Eli." He scrubbed a hand over his face. "I've been ignoring his calls because I wasn't up for another round with him or Dad. I knew I'd be back soon enough and whatever the crisis, it could just damn well wait."

"Calder—"

He looked at her, and she saw something she hadn't seen the entire time he'd been standing there on Jonah's pier, putting his life at risk for family members who didn't know him and—speaking for one of them anyway—didn't want to get to know him. She saw fear.

"My father collapsed at one of our job sites. Not a heart attack. Could be a stroke. They don't know—" And then he sort of blinked and reacted, shoving the phone in his pocket and all but kicking the door to the Mustang open as he fished his keys from his pocket. "I'm sorry," he said, almost absently, his attention clearly and understandably no longer on her. "I have to . . ." He didn't finish the sentence, he just climbed out of the car.

For her part, Hannah jumped out of her side and skirted the back of the car just as he unlocked and yanked open the door to his truck. "Calder. Don't race over there. I mean, don't—just be careful," she said, feeling beyond lame and useless, because if she'd gotten that news about any one of her family members, nothing would keep her from getting to him or her as fast as possible, and reckless driving would only be the beginning of the risks she'd be willing to take. She got to the driver's-side door just as he closed it. "Is he—?"

He lowered the window as he jammed his key in the ignition and gunned the engine. "He's at the hospital, in ICU. That's all I know. I'll call Eli on my way there."

"Okay," she said, and though she wanted to step up on the running board, kiss him, cling to him, imbue him with some kind of willpower and strength, she stepped back instead, doing the one thing she could do, giving him a clear path with those wide rearview mirrors of his, to back out next to her and get on his way. "Just be safe. And—let me know." She had no right to ask, but she couldn't not ask. She didn't know his father, but she knew Calder, and what happened to his dad affected him. And that mattered to her, if nothing else.

"I will," he said, but he wasn't even paying attention to her, not really. He threw the truck into reverse, then just as quickly slammed it back into park and looked at her. "Come here," he said, commanded actually, or maybe begged.

She all but leapt up on the running board, clinging to the

open window frame of the big dually. "It's okay," she said. "I understand. Go. Please."

"Nothing is okay," he said roughly, then reached out and gripped the back of her head, and kissed her as if his life depended on it. And maybe it did.

"You've been through a lot today," she said, breathless when he let her go. "Just be careful, please." She cupped his face now, and looked into his beautiful, honey-colored eyes, her own heart clutching at the fear and pain, the guilt and regret she saw in them. "I need you to be careful. Okay?"

He looked at her, truly looked at her. "I will," he said, so intently, he sounded almost ferocious. "I promise, Hannah." And then he yanked the truck into reverse and she jumped off the running board so he could back out. He looked at her through the passenger window as he shifted the truck to a forward gear, and held her gaze for what felt like an eternal, heart-stopping moment, then drove off without saying another word.

Chapter Twenty-One

Hannah stood in a bridesmaid dress she actually loved, tears swimming in her eyes, grinning madly as she watched Alex walk down the aisle, beaming at Hannah's incredibly dashing and handsome brother. Fergus was the bride's escort, and he looked about as thrilled as any good Irishman could be. And quite dashing in his kilt and full plaid regalia as well.

She watched Fergus lift Alex's veil, a tear in his eye as he leaned in and bussed her cheek. Hannah grinned, sniffling herself, as she saw the love glowing on Alex's face when she turned and looked at Logan, their gazes meeting as he took her hand, and they turned to face the minister. Hannah had been so worried about this moment, about how it would make her feel. And the only emotion brimming in her . . . was joy. Unmitigated, soul-filling, life-affirming joy. Seeing the looks on their faces, the love they had for one another, watching them smile, laugh as they shared a private whisper when Logan fumbled the ring he'd stowed in his tux pocket, all she could feel was joy, and all she could think was how happy they'd make each other, and how lucky they were to have found love, fortunate to be smart enough to recognize it, reach for it, hold on to it.

She felt Fiona's hand gripping her elbow, and let go of her bouquet with one hand, to reach down and cup her sister's fingers, pressing them tightly, as she glanced quickly past her to Kerry, who was gripping Fiona's other hand and letting the tears slide down her cheeks unabated. The three shared a watery little laugh, then Delia turned, saw the sisters grinning madly, and juggled the bouquets to reach for Hannah's other hand, her own eyes brimming now, too, even as she laughed at herself.

In the end, all four of them stood there watching Logan marry Alex, abandoning completely the traditional bouquet-holding pose, their hands linked, one to the next, bouquets clutched between them, tears tracking down their perfectly made-up faces, sniffling and grinning as vows were traded, rings slid on fingers, and the minister finally pronounced, "You may now kiss the bride."

A cheer went up from the gathered guests, and from the bridesmaids, who lifted their joined hands in a victory celebration as Logan bent his bride back over his arm, laid one on her, then scooped her up against him, leaving her dainty slippered feet dangling a good foot off the ground as he kissed her again. Then she was in his arms, scooped up against his chest, as he carried her down the aisle, Alex waving her bouquet at the clapping, cheering, laughing guests as everyone filed in behind them, and the celebration began in earnest.

Hannah lost track of how many hours had passed before she finally sat on the edge of Fiona's bed back inside the house. She wiggled her toes, her heels mercifully no longer on her very tired feet, and flopped straight onto her back, deciding the bridesmaid dress could wait a few more minutes. "Oh my God, I had way too much champagne. I can still feel bubbles tickling my nose."

Fiona flopped back beside her. "I had too much cake.

But it was Boston cream. So, really, I can't be blamed. I mean . . . seriously, who has a Boston cream wedding cake?"

"Alex does. Bless her renegade-wedding-cake-loving heart," Hannah said, with a deep, appreciative sigh. "Where's Kerry?"

"I'm not her keeper. Not today. Last I saw she was dancing with—I don't even know his name. Right now my sugar high is in dangerous risk of crashing. Which I'm pretty sure means I need more sugar. You know, to balance it back up again. Only the thought of one more bite of cake is making me feel a bit queasy."

"Just lie here for a minute. The feeling will pass."

"The urge to eat more cake, you mean?"

Hannah giggled. "No, silly. The feeling queasy part. Because you're right, that was ridiculously amazing cake."

"It would be, like, a crime, to waste it."

"I saw Delia stow a wedge of it in the fridge along with the top of the cake."

"We can't eat that. It's for their first anniversary. You freeze it, then take it out when you celebrate your first wedding anniversary. Tradition."

"I'm not talking about the topper. I'm talking about the wedge."

"Oh." Fiona grinned. "Well, yeah. We're kind of obligated to eat that."

"My thought exactly." Hannah let her eyes close, only the room seemed to move a little when she did that. "Maybe it's just as well Delia didn't stash any champagne in there with it."

Fiona giggled. "She didn't have to. I might have smuggled some up here earlier when I came to change shoes."

Hannah knew she'd be sorry. So very sorry, but she grinned, too. "It's going to be a good night."

Fiona reached over and twined her fingers with Hannah's. "It already is."

Hannah would have sworn she was cried out, and not from the heartbroken tears she'd been so susceptible to since . . . Lord, it felt like a lifetime ago now. But the happy-happy, joy-joy wedding tears had been pretty prodigious as well. She squeezed her sister's fingers. "Hasn't it, though? It was so beautiful. Every part of it. And who knew our brother could dance like that?"

"Fergus taught him." When Hannah lifted her head to send an amazed look, Fi laughed. "He did. It was a secret. Well, I knew, but Alex didn't." They lay there in silence for a few minutes, then Fiona said, "Have you heard from Calder? How is his dad?"

"I got a text last night saying he was still undergoing tests and they were waiting for results. They feel pretty certain it was a stroke, but the damage it caused isn't known yet."

"It's just awful," Fi said in hushed tones. "I mean, Calder goes and does something so massively heroic, and then that happens. Seems really wrong. I mean, on top of it being wrong anyway."

"I know," Hannah said. It had occurred to her, more than once that day, that beautiful, lovely day, just how much her life had changed in such a short time. It felt like a lifetime ago, another life completely, even, when she'd driven away from her newly sublet, fully furnished condo in Alexandria, a key to a newly leased storage unit in her pocket, heading to Maine with nothing more than a suitcase of clothes she hated and a bag of pity pretzels in her lap.

"So . . . what are you going to do about him?" Fiona asked.

"About Calder's father?"

Fi took their joined hands and popped Hannah in the

stomach. "No, doofus. About Calder. I mean, something *is* going on there, right? And you're going back to Virginia soon. So, are you just going to walk away?" She leaned up on one elbow, and added, "And don't say you can't go there because you just broke up with Tim. Fate is fate and timing is everything. Life doesn't always hand you chances when it's convenient or when it's best for you." She flopped back again. "I'm just saying, you should think about it."

"I am," Hannah said, after a moment.

Fi popped right back up on her elbow. "You are?" She leaned down and kissed Hannah on the forehead. "Good for you! I really didn't think you would."

Fi flopped back again and Hannah groaned, thinking she was going to be the queasy one if her sister kept doing that. "Actually," Hannah said, "I'm not going back to Virginia." *Best to just rip off the Band-Aid.* But she closed her eyes and squinched up her face, which made no sense since it did nothing to keep Fiona's squeal from pinging against her eardrums, and everything to make the still-tender skin on her nose sting as well. She covered her nose with her hand, and made an *ow* face under her palm. Maybe she shouldn't have been so quick to talk Bonnie into taking her stitches out before the wedding. But she'd refused to wear a bandage on her nose for the wedding photos.

Fiona let her hand go and flipped to her stomach, propping herself up on her elbows. "Tell me everything. I'm assuming you decided this before you came home, so just be aware, it's only because you're still in crash recovery that I'm not popping you one right now."

"Actually, if you don't stop bouncing this bed, I'm going to throw up on you, and you'll have much bigger things to worry about than why I waited until after the wedding to share that tidbit of news." She lowered her hand, happy to see there was at least no blood on it. "I thought you were queasy," she groused.

"You have zero room to bitch right now. Tell me."

Hannah sighed, then took a breath. "The breakup was not good." She spent a half second deciding if she should go there, and decided she was done giving Tim any stage time in her life. "But the truth is, I've been unhappy longer than that. The breakup was just the thing that made me review my life." She rolled her head to the left, looked up into her sister's compassionate gaze. "I thought I wanted to be a big city litigator. And, the truth is, I'm good at it. Really good."

"But being really good at something isn't the same as being really happy about doing it."

"No," Hannah said. "No, it's not. I just . . . I don't know. I feel guilty. Like I quit. Like I'm running back home again. And that's not it. At least, I hope that's not it."

"You know, when you went off to Georgetown, we were all so proud of you, so happy for you. I mean, if anyone could make the transition from a small coastal town in Maine to the most important city in this country, maybe the world, it would be you. You were the elegant one, the sophisticated one, the smart one."

Hannah rolled her eyes, despite being deeply touched by her sister's heartfelt words. "The last thing I was when I left Maine was elegant and sophisticated, and as for smart, we all have smarts." She laughed at Fiona's pointed look, knowing she meant their younger sister. "Just because Kerry makes rash, impulsive decisions, doesn't mean she's not smart enough to know better."

"Actually, you're right," Fiona said. "Not about Kerry. She doesn't have the smarts God gave a donkey. Wily and the nine lives of a cat, maybe. What you're right about is that it's true. You weren't elegant and sophisticated."

"Gee, thanks," Hannah said, wryly. "I think."

"I mean, when you were here, you were like we all were. Small-town girl, because, duh, what else could we be? But you saw yourself as what you could be. And because you saw that future so clearly for yourself, we saw it for you, too. Because we wanted for you what you wanted for you."

"So, are you saying I've just been faking it this whole time?"

"No, you were—are—definitely those things, and more. You're everything you always wanted to be." She took her sister's hands. "What I'm saying is, clearly you're unhappy. Or unfulfilled, or . . . something. Maybe it is just the breakup aftermath, leaving you feeling wobbly. Trust me, I know what that feels like." She eyed her sister with an affectionate smile. "In fact, we both know just how much experience I have with what that feels like." She laid her hand over Hannah's, which she'd folded over her middle, and squeezed them both. "But now I see you here, and see how you've so easily, so swiftly, so . . . naturally, slipped back into being the old Hannah." She laughed. "Okay, maybe the old Hannah with a bit of D.C. polish and prestigious law school smarts, but what I mean is, it's occurred to me that maybe you weren't so much faking it, as forcing it."

The words hit Hannah with such unmistakable truth, she couldn't even formulate a good dodge in her rapidly spinning mind.

"I mean, the minute you get here, you shuck all of your sophistication, right down to the clothes, the way you wear your hair. It's like you can't wait to be free of your other self." Fiona stopped, looked down. "I'm talking out of my ass. I don't know what's going on in your world. I guess maybe we all unwind when we're away, like you do on vacation. I'm sorry—"

Hannah covered Fiona's hands to keep her from pulling them away, and okay, maybe a little to keep her from flopping again. "Don't say you're sorry."

"I am. I wasn't trying to hurt you. I wasn't trying to—"

"You're trying to help me. To love me. And you are, and you do. You're also right. I think. Or maybe I know. Maybe some part of me has always known. I kept thinking if I finally felt like I'd made it, I could relax and maybe actually start to enjoy it." She looked at Fi. "But that feeling never came. So I climbed harder, faster. And the relationship, I guess I pushed that, too, made it out to be more in my mind than it really was, because that was even more proof that things were going as I'd planned. I actually thought he was going to propose to me. Can you believe that?" She shifted her head back to stare at the ceiling, then just closed her eyes. Her thankfully dry eyes.

"Oh, Hannah—"

"No," she said. "It's done, and it never should have been in the first place." She opened her eyes. "It's my past now. Along with the rest of my life in D.C."

"I'm so proud of you," she said, true excitement in her eyes. "What are you going to do? I mean, are you going to give up being a lawyer?"

"No," Hannah said. "I do like what I do. I just didn't like where I was doing it. Or the kind of work I was doing. If that makes sense."

Now Fiona did flop. "Oh, it makes perfect sense."

Hannah turned her head and frowned. "Sounds like you need to spill it. Is this what you said you wanted to talk to me about? The first day I got here?"

"Yes. Only now that I know you're coming back, I think I know the answer. I think I answered it myself. Just now." She turned her head to face Hannah's and their gazes locked. "Is it more scary or exciting? Ditching your old life? Coming back to everything you know, where you feel like you fit in, but have no clue how to take what it is you do and earn a living from it where there might not be an actual demand for it."

"Oh my God," Hannah said, almost on a whisper. "You want to leave New York! But I thought your business was booming."

"It is. In fact, I need to hire someone, maybe several someones. There's a magazine spread coming out soon, and I know that's going to hammer my already crammed calendar." She squeezed her eyes shut. "Which sucks."

"Because you don't think you can find good enough help? Or because you don't want to delegate?"

She looked at Hannah again. "Because I hate, with every fiber of my being, the kind of work I have to do in New York, for the most stuck-up, god-awful, ungrateful, bitchy, entitled pains in the asses I've ever had the gross misfortune of thinking I wanted to design for." She sighed. "There. I said it. God help me. I'm now officially the most ungrateful bitch on the planet."

Hannah lay there, dumbstruck for a moment, then burst out in a howl of laughter.

"I'm not sure how to take that," Fiona said, frowning.

Hannah pushed herself upright to a sitting position, groaning when it made her champagne-loaded brain spin just a little. She tugged on Fiona's hand until she sat up, too, and she groaned and pressed a hand to her stomach.

"So, I'm an idiot, right?" Fi demanded. "I worked so hard to live my dream, and unlike ninety-nine-point-nine percent of those who try to do that exact same thing, I actually, somehow, pulled it off. And now I don't want it. I want to come back to Blueberry Cove, and be broke and starving, and figure out how to make things that make me happy and also make other people happy, except I don't have a freaking clue how to do it." She looked at her sister. "Did I mention there's this big magazine spread? About my design firm? That I want to close?"

"Shit," Hannah said.

"At the very least."

"So, what are you going to do?" Hannah asked her.

She shrugged. "I don't know. What are you going to do?"

Hannah shrugged. "Well, I've already sublet my place. All the rest of my stuff is in storage. All I have, literally, is what's in my suitcase. And I even hate most of that."

"So, you're here then."

Hannah nodded, then looked down at her bridesmaid dress, then at Fi's. "For better or for worse."

Fi snickered, then Hannah snickered. Then they both laughed, and kept laughing until they fell back on the bed, gasping for air.

"I know one thing you should do," Fiona said.

"Good. Guide me, oh Obi-Wan."

"Oh no, that's still your job." She rolled to her side. "You're staying here. In Blueberry. Which is what, like an hour from Calais? Ninety minutes tops?"

"Fiona—"

"Hannah," she mimicked. "You might not know what kind of lawyer you're going to be here, but you do know a guy you'd like to have hanging around while you figure it out. I saw how he hugged you out there on that pier. Just . . . figure that out. Then the rest will fall into place."

"Says the woman who hasn't been in a relationship longer than what, six months?"

"I've been busy. And I'm not talking about me. I'm talking about you." She squeezed Hannah's hand. "Go to Calais. Figure that out. Then decide on the rest."

Hannah stared at the ceiling, and thought about what Fiona was saying. It seemed so simple. Obvious, even.

But the very concept of reaching for Calder, of reaching for something . . . *more*, when it came down to actually doing it, was terrifying. What if she failed? Now that his life was even more upside down, what if he didn't want her in it? She wanted to be happy. She was so very ready to be happy, and she was pretty damned sure she could be very happy with Calder. But only if he thought he could be happy with her.

Could she handle heartbreak again? What Tim had done had leveled her. But having Calder look at her and tell her he didn't want her in his life after all . . . she didn't know how she'd come back from that.

Chapter Twenty-Two

"You're doing great," Calder murmured, leaning forward so he could run his hand along the side of Vixen's neck. The mare's ears flicked back, then forward again, but she didn't break stride. They were ambling more than striding, making slow circles around the ring. Nothing major, as she still wasn't up to that. "You're going to live up to your name yet," he said, smiling as he steered her toward the fence, then stopped and dismounted. "Come on, let's go in and get you gussied up."

He was actually looking forward to the next hour, to the grooming, raking the stalls, bringing the other horses in for the night. The chores provided a routine that he found soothing, calming. Which was something he'd needed more and more over the past two weeks. They'd helped to take his mind off his father, the family situation. *Who are you kidding? It's Hannah you can't get out of your head. Family you're dealing with. One day at a time. Hannah, on the other hand . . .* "Yeah," he muttered. "Hard to take care of something that isn't there."

The thing was, he understood. He truly did. His life was upside down at the moment, and that wasn't going to change anytime soon. All he had to offer her was chaos and uncertainty, and that was the last thing she needed. She was trying to figure out her life, so no big surprise that figuring it out, for her, meant not getting involved in the crazy that was his world at the moment. Hell, if he had a choice, *he* wouldn't get involved in his own life. Not as it was, anyway. She'd come back to Maine because she wanted peace, she wanted a quieter life. Thinking back on the scene in the hospital just that morning, between him and Eli, coming almost to blows over what they thought was the best course of action for their father's care . . . yeah, that had been anything but peaceful.

But understanding didn't make it any easier. He told himself it was crazy to miss someone he'd only known such a short time. Sure, they'd experienced a lot in that short time, but it had been twelve days since he'd left the Cove for good. He'd known her what, five? "Yeah, you're a damn fool to think she'd want you with the baggage you have, after such a short time."

A damn fool who missed her sharp mind. The way she gave as good as she got. That she could roll her eyes at him one moment, then blush the next. That she had the best laugh, and an even better giggle. That she made this noise, like a half gasp, half moan, and said his name like it was both prayer and plea when she came. *Jesus, you really need to stop this.*

He had spoken to her. Sort of. He'd texted her that first night to let her know that his dad had indeed had a stroke, that the extent of his recovery was still being determined. She'd replied and had been exactly who she was, comforting, compassionate. She'd offered to come to the hospital, but he'd declined. That was the last place he'd want her right now. He'd texted her the following day when the scans Thaddeus had undergone had revealed that the cause of the stroke was a brain tumor. A fairly sizable one he'd apparently been carrying around for quite some time. So long, in fact, it had finally tried to kill him. The surgeon had confirmed that, given its location, it could have been a factor in his mood swings and over-the-top behavior. It had been the first time he'd been thankful that his father was one stubborn son of a bitch. Too stubborn to let a tumor kill him. So far, anyway. Now they had to figure out how to get the damn thing out of him without killing him in the process.

Calder had debated even telling Hannah. Technically, he was out of her life. But, frankly, the news had terrified him, and with his family leaning on him, he'd needed someone to confide in. Even then, he'd texted rather than called, only giving her the bare bones of it. She didn't need to know all the details, though she was smart enough to realize there was more going on than he was saying. But she was sensitive enough, compassionate enough, not to press. And she probably felt it wasn't her place. He so wished that were not the case; he wished it were exactly her place. And yet, how selfish was that?

He led Vixen into the barn and put her into the cross ties, patting and stroking the side of her neck. "Pampering time," he told her, then took his time taking off the saddle, the saddle pad. She hadn't worked enough to sweat, but he took the currycomb, smoothed her out where the saddle had been on her back, then used a hoof pick to clean her feet.

He hefted the saddle and the pad and strode down the short, dirt-packed aisle to the tack room to stow it. He stepped inside and lifted the saddle onto the rack and laid the pad on the stack on the floor, glancing out the single, small octagonal window on the far wall to gauge how much daylight he had left. He turned to head back to Vixen, then stopped, frozen.

He straightened, turned, and looked back through the

window again. For a split second, he wondered if tumors were genetic, or if he was the one having some kind of a stroke. Because he hadn't imagined it. He could swear that was the big blue beast parked outside his rambling, falling-apart farmhouse, about a hundred yards away from where he currently stood.

Only one person he knew drove a car like that. "Mustang Scarlett."

His heart was beating a rapid tattoo as he went back to Vixen, murmuring his apologies for not spoiling her a little longer. He led her to her stall, hung a feed bucket of oats inside, then tried really hard not to head to the house in a dead run.

A million questions ran through his mind as he crossed the packed-dirt path that led from the stables to the house. Why was she here? Had something else happened back in the Cove that involved him somehow? Wouldn't she have just called him if that was the case? And if that wasn't the case, then what had brought her all the way out here without advance word?

She wasn't in the car, or on the front porch, which was a good thing, since there were parts of it he was fairly certain wouldn't support even her weight. He went in the back way, through the mudroom, and shucked his boots since he hadn't bothered to brush them off before leaving the stables.

"Hannah?" Maybe his mind was playing some kind of weird trick on him. Maybe he was more stressed out than he thought, seeing things that he only wished were there.

He found her in the kitchen, which was big, and ran across most of the back of the house. It was one of the reasons he'd bought the place. Not that he cooked, per se, but it just seemed . . . homey. Friendly. Warm. Like a family should live in it, cooking meals, kids doing homework at the table, stuff tacked up on the old pull-handle fridge. Someday.

"Hannah?"

She jumped, then turned and looked at him guiltily. "Calder." Her smile was slow, and tentative, and he realized he must be looking at her like she had two heads. "Sorry. I didn't see you out around the paddocks, so I knocked, then stuck my head inside, and then I was kind of already in, so I figured I'd just sit here and wait. I—probably shouldn't have done that." She started to stand.

"No," he said, almost swallowing his tongue in his haste to keep her from getting up, from going anywhere. Praying she hadn't come on business. "Stay," he managed.

"You're mad. I should have called. I'm really sorry. You have so much going on, I don't know what I was—" She did stand then, and he finally snapped out of the almost out-of-body experience he was having, because she sounded almost exactly like he felt.

Nervous. Uncertain. Hopeful. But, hoping for what?

"Stay," he said again, less urgently. "Please." He couldn't stop drinking her in. Right there. In his kitchen. He could smell the lavender scent she used on her hair; he noticed the scar was healing really well on the bridge of her nose, hardly noticeable, and any other remaining traces of the accident were gone completely. And not hidden under layers of makeup. Because if he wasn't mistaken, and he wasn't missing a single speck of her, she wasn't wearing any makeup. "You look so . . ." *Beautiful. Delicious. God, I'm so hungry for you.* ". . . good,*"* he finally got out.

Then his gaze fell on the legal folder she was clutching in her hands. And his heart sank so hard, so fast, he leaned against the frame. *See? Told ya.* So, she was here on business. Though he couldn't fathom what on earth it would be.

Surely Winstock wasn't holding the club contract over his head.

He cleared his throat, and finally managed to get his act together. Though he kept his weight on the door frame, because he was pretty sure if he took a single step toward her, he'd have her hauled up against him half a second later. "What brings you all the way out here?" When she just continued to stare at him, seemingly as hamstrung by the moment as he was, he nodded toward the folder. "Business, I take it?"

She looked dumbly down at the folder in her hand, then back up at him. "Oh! Right. Yes." Then her gaze got tangled up in his again and he started to think maybe they'd both lost their minds, because she was just as tongue-tied as he apparently was.

Only, in her case, it was probably because he was staring at her like a feral animal left in the wild too long without food. She was probably worried he was going to pounce on her and fill himself right back up again. And he wished he could reassure her she was wrong. "Is it something with the yacht club?"

"What?" She dragged her gaze away from his, and looked back at the folder. "Right. Yes." She took a visible breath and he saw her try to regain her professional demeanor.

He wanted to tell her that if she wanted to go back to being the cool, elegant woman who had almost T-boned him in the intersection a few weeks ago, leaving her hair down and all wild like that, and wearing soft floral sundresses he wanted to peel off of her . . . with his teeth . . . was not the way to go about it.

"Yes, it is. Well, sort of, it is. I was going to call you about it, but then I thought maybe it would be better if I showed you."

There were a lot of things, a very long list of things, he wanted her to show him. And not one of them would be located in that folder. "Okay." He gestured to the table. "Here you are, then. And here I am. We should sit down."

"Yes. Of course." She pulled the chair back out and tried to sit, all while still looking at him as he walked into the room.

He pulled out a chair across from her and had to dig his fingers deeply into his palms to keep from reaching for her and finding her a far better seat. In his lap. "What's going on with the club? Do I need to sign off on something so Winstock can get another builder? Because I never signed anything to begin with—"

"There's not going to be a yacht club," she said, her gaze dropping from his face, to his hands, and then almost desperately back to the folder, which she all but slapped open. "A lot has happened in the past few weeks."

That was an understatement, and at the same time, it felt as if his whole world had been standing still since the day he'd driven away from her as she stood beside that damn blue muscle car, looking like a stiff wind would tilt her right over. And he wasn't going to be there to catch her. She'd hate it if he thought she needed catching. But she did. Everybody did. Sometimes. Right now he damn well did. *And here you thought she'd be the high-maintenance, needy one.*

He ignored his little voice. "Such as?" he prodded.

"Well, the whole thing with Ted, and then the divorce news, and Brooks coming off like he was somehow bullying Ted into taking desperate measures to stay in the family fold—though I have to tell you, I've spoken to Brooks personally and he was leveled by this whole thing. He did not see any of it coming. He didn't know about the divorce, either."

She'd gone from being tongue-tied to talking almost too fast.

"I'm surprised," Calder said. "Because it seemed as if Cami had moved back home the morning I was there, and Brooks made a comment that she'd made the right decision."

"Well, I don't know what that was all about. Maybe he thought they were having a spat, or that they were both moving in, with Ted not working. But I can guarantee you he didn't know Cami had asked Ted for a divorce. I think she planned to tell him that day, but then everything happened." She shook her head, seemed to take another breath, but her nerves were still apparent.

And he couldn't stand it another second. He reached across the table and trapped her hand under his. "Hannah, stop." When she laughed self-consciously and tried to slip her hand free, he held it more firmly. "What's going on? You're like the proverbial cat on a hot tin roof. I'm not upset you're here. It's—is something else wrong?" He groaned, and felt like an idiot for assuming her nervousness had to do with him. Without thinking, he slid his fingers through hers and something in him instantly relaxed at the connection. He didn't know how to take care of himself these days, but taking care of her, that felt like something he could do blindfolded. Every day. For the rest of his life. "What happened?"

She went still, her gaze dropping to their joined hands, then lifting slowly back to his. "Nothing," she whispered. "I mean, nothing bad. Winstock isn't going to build the yacht club." She fished around for the folder with her free hand, but gave up and just looked at him, as if she were drinking her fill of him, too, as if she might not get the chance, ever again. "He couldn't get the investors he needed."

"Investors?" Calder frowned. "Why did he need investors? He could build ten yacht clubs with his pocket change."

"I think the whole point of the club was to show off to his friends, make them see what a vital business opportunity his little private mecca would become. Only they apparently weren't buying it. That was why he was putting you off. He was trying to convince them it was a good deal, but frankly, they knew what we all knew. Blueberry Cove is too far north to be practical for most people, even wealthy people. Boat tours and a restored, historic lighthouse weren't enough to attract their interest, and a working harbor wasn't exactly the elite spot they were hoping for. He'd apparently let his anger about that slip to Cami, and she'd told Ted, which was why he made the desperate grab for Jonah's property. He thought the harbor would be more attractive to investors without Blue's in business."

"So, why did he bring me in then? What was the angle?"

"I think he was hoping you'd contest the rights to the property, then he'd work through you to buy it out, knowing Jonah would never sell. But he couldn't even get the concept of the yacht club to take root. Rumor is that the members of his club down in Bar Harbor were laughing behind his back about his little 'fishing town club.'" She made air quotes around that last part.

"I bet that went over not well at all. So . . . what is he going to do?"

"I don't know. He donated the land for the club back to the city, and walked away from it. Actually, he's more or less been a recluse since the incident with Ted. Ted has been recommended for outpatient psychiatric help, and he's also been arrested on a very long laundry list of things. He's been transferred to a larger jail facility near Bangor, where they can keep him from doing anything stupid to himself. I have no idea what will happen with the marriage. Cami hasn't been seen or heard from either. I think this really brought both father and daughter down so many pegs . . ." She trailed off, then shook her head. "It has to have changed them in some way, some permanent way. But it remains to be seen how."

"Might not be a bad thing," Calder said, "though not worth the danger folks were put in to get there."

"That's the thing, I think, that really got them. Brooks and Cami, I mean. Seeing Bit like that, in Ted's arms, with that gun." She shivered then, and he rubbed his thumb over her fingers.

"So, will your friend Delia get the land back now, build a new diner? Seems like the least the town can do, give her first dibs."

Hannah shook her head. "She's started in on a new place, so she's good." She looked from their hands, to his face, her gaze on his. "Actually, the town wants to build a community center there. The boat tours will happen, and Grace—Brodie's significant other—will open her inn there on the waterfront very shortly. Delia's place should be up and running by then, too. Brodie's boatbuilding shops are going well—the publicity of the schooner he built has brought him a lot of attention. He's got contracts from all over, even international interest. The schooner launches in a few weeks, with the town's tercentennial celebration, so that will officially get things rolling. But it's all . . . I don't know. Now it all seems to fit. Everything will stay slower, quieter, and the new businesses will still celebrate the harbor as it's meant to be, what with the historic Monaghan shipyard operating again, albeit on a much, much smaller scale." She smiled. "Though apparently Brodie will be building a yacht or two with the international contracts, so that's kind of ironic."

Her smile shifted from wry to hopeful. "There's talk of

turning one of his boathouses into a maritime museum, celebrating his family's contribution to founding the town, along with the other main enterprises that built the Cove and the harbor, like Blue's. Jonah is digging in, doing everything he can to rebound from the fire and the town is really rallying around him. It's all new, but it's all very promising. It feels . . . back to normal. Only better." She broke off, and looked down again. "I'm rambling. I shouldn't be so nervous. I don't know why I am. It's ridiculous."

He tugged at her hand until she looked up at him again. The tension in the room had lessened as she'd talked, giving them both a chance to take a collective breath. At least the nervous tension had decreased. Now when she looked at him, an entirely different sort of tension stirred.

"Why are you here?" he asked.

She opened her mouth, then closed it again. She shoved the folder at him with her free hand. "It's a contract. For your company. To build the community center. We felt it was the least we could do, seeing as you risked your life to save one of our own." She held his gaze. "You are one of our own. You made things right, that day. Forevermore, you're a part of our town."

"Tell Jonah that."

"Actually, Jonah has come around. A little," she added at his skeptical look. "But he's conceded that he might have been a little hard on you."

"A little." Calder shook his head, but he'd ceased to be annoyed with Jonah. His father's stroke had taught him that life was far too short, and too precious, to hold grudges. Especially when that's what had gotten the Blues into trouble in the first place.

"I wouldn't be surprised if you get a call from him. Jonah, I mean."

"Your doing?"

She shook her head. "Not me. But I know Owen had a long talk with him."

Calder smiled, thinking if anyone could get to Jonah, it would be the unassuming-looking Owen. "He's like the stealth mayor."

Hannah laughed. "Exactly!" Her smile lingered as she went on, though she sounded a bit tentative again. "I was thinking that you'd said your nieces were the same age as Bit. And, if you take the contract offer, you and your brothers will be coming in to do the work on the community center. Maybe your brothers' wives would come with them on occasion, bring the girls. There aren't that many young kids in the Cove and I know Bit would love having play friends."

A smile twitched at the corners of his mouth.

"What?" she asked, looking honestly perplexed.

"I'm surprised any of your cases went to trial, Counselor. You are quite adept at negotiating a settlement."

She smiled then, too. Lifted a shoulder. "Go with your strength."

It was all he could do not to pull her into his arms right then. "Why did you come all the way out here?" he asked her, his voice quiet now, but the smile still teasing his mouth.

"The contract. To get you to sign it."

"I know this house may not look like much, but our offices are actually very nice. Our offices, with the fax machines and everything."

"I wasn't sure you'd even look at the contract if I just sent it over. I didn't know how you felt. Or if you ever wanted to even think about the Cove again, considering all you have going on."

He rubbed the side of her hand with this thumb again;

then he turned her hand over, and rubbed it over her palm. She gasped, and he felt the shudder of response to his touch run through her. And his pulse went from steady to hot and thrumming, like a temperature spike. "Just the contract then."

She nodded.

"I'd think you'd have a better poker face," he said idly. "All that time in front of juries, and everything."

"I—"

"Would it help if I told you that I want you so badly I can barely breathe? That I think about you when I open my eyes in the morning, see your face when I close them at night, and that a good number more seconds than is possible, given all that is going on in my world right now, are spent doing that exact same thing, all damn day long? Every single day? Would that help? Because you need to tell me if it doesn't. And I'll find some other words."

"Calder—"

"I'll sign the contract," he told her. "There. Now your business here is done."

She just looked at him.

"Hannah," he said, the word rough. "Put me out of my misery. One way or the other."

He wasn't sure if she stood first or if he just dragged her across the kitchen table. But the folder went flying one way, the contract pages another, and he didn't give a good goddamn about any of it because she was finally back where she belonged again. In his arms.

Chapter Twenty-Three

Hannah framed his beautiful, handsome face with shaky hands. "I—didn't know if—I didn't know."

He was running his hands over her arms, tunneling his fingers through her hair, touching her face, as if making himself believe she was really there, reuniting himself with every part of her. And she rejoiced in every step of his rediscovery.

"Then you should have asked," he said. "What didn't you know?"

"Like you said, you have so much going on, and your life is upside down."

"Yours, too."

"Mine is my own, yours is anything but."

"I want you, Hannah. I never stopped wanting you. But . . . I don't have the right to ask you to tangle yourself up in my family madness. That's not why you came back to Maine."

"Shouldn't that be my decision?"

He looked startled. "Is that—why would you even consider it? Hannah, there is no part of my life that makes any sense right now."

"I'm good at making sense of things."

"I have no doubt. But that doesn't mean you should—"

She put her finger over his lips. "Will you be here? Does this madness of a life come with you in it?"

His gaze burned into hers and he nipped her finger, which she pulled away as desire flared in his beautiful golden eyes. "I'd say for better or for worse, only, sweetheart," he said, doing a really, *really* bad Bogart impression, "I'm afraid it's pretty much all for worse right now."

Hannah could only grin at him in response. And it felt glorious. "Why don't you let me worry my pretty little head over that," she replied, in full-on Scarlett. She realized it made no sense with his Bogey, but hearing him laugh, seeing the smile light up those eyes of his, she thought she'd do a lot, go to a great deal of trouble, in fact, to make sure he did that far more often.

"Hannah," he said, only it sounded more like a benediction this time. He traced his fingers over her cheek, slid his fingers down the length of her hair.

"Tell you what," she said, thinking that as nervous as she'd been while finally getting out why she'd come here, she was surprisingly calm now. "Why don't you kiss me, and we'll see how that goes. Then take it from there." She leaned in until her lips were just a breath away from his. "You remember how to kiss me, don't you? You just put your lips together and—" The rest of that was lost in a squeal as he took her mouth in a fierce, hard kiss. Then the sound changed to a long, keening moan, as the kiss changed into something slower, deeper, but no less devastating.

He shoved his chair back so she could straddle his lap, but he was half shoving her dress up her thighs and she was tugging at his shirt when he said, "No, not this time." He wrapped his arms around her. "Hold on."

She didn't question him, because she had no intent of

letting him go anytime soon anyway. She crossed her ankles around his back as he stood, and nibbled the side of his neck as he half stumbled, half walked them through the house, stopping every few seconds to pin her to a handy wall and plunge right back into another soul-searing kiss.

She was panting heavily by the time they reached the bedroom. "I was pretty sure I'd blown that whole day by your truck into something unrealistic in my mind."

He laid her on a bed the size of a small ocean and climbed right down on top of her. "And now?"

She smiled up into his face, wondering why in the hell she'd waited so long. "Now I think I didn't do it justice."

He grinned, his eyes going all caramel hot, and she squirmed under him. She started tugging at his shirt as he undid the small row of buttons that ran down the bodice of her sundress. He finally leaned up enough to pull his T-shirt off over his head and toss it aside, but when he came back down, intent on nibbling his way along her neck, she stopped him, her hands going to the small blue talisman drilled and knotted on a piece of twined rope, tied around his tanned neck so it dangled in the hollow of his throat.

She fingered the pitted, rounded surface, then looked up at him. "Sea glass," she said. "Is it from—you didn't have this on before."

"I found it in my jeans pocket. It was what I had. Of you. Of that perfect day."

She smiled, her throat growing tight. "I don't know how perfect it was. I looked like an extra from *Dawn of the Dead*, and you were—"

"I fell in love with you that day, Hannah," he said, and her throat closed right over. "I was halfway there, maybe all the way there, even before then. But the way you gave yourself to me, completely and utterly, then watching you walking the tidal pool, your delight in just . . . in just being there. You're life, and breath, and sunshine. And hope. I—"

She lifted her head and kissed him, not knowing what else to say, awed to silence by his declaration. When he lifted his head, the look in his eyes leveled her. The honesty there, the truth of what he'd just told her, was laid bare for her to see. She felt humbled and not a little awed that this man, this good, honest, kind, decent, sexy as hell, hard-working, family-loving man, felt that way about her. "You, uh—" She had to clear her throat, because she wanted to say the words back to him, but she didn't want him to think she was just parroting his. She needed him to know she truly believed every word. "You don't strike me as the jewelry type."

His gaze didn't waver from hers. "There's an ancient belief that if you wear a piece of something you gathered in a meaningful place, carry it with you, you'll go back there someday."

"You want to go back to the Cove?"

"I wanted to go back to you."

"Oh, Calder," she said on a hushed whisper. If she thought she'd been loved before, cherished before . . . she knew now she'd had no idea of the real meaning of the word. And if she thought she'd known love, known what it felt to feel love, to give love . . . it paled in the face of what she felt when she looked at him. "You never left me. Not for one second. You've been inside me, in my heart, my head, every part of me. I never wanted you to leave."

"I—"

"No, I don't mean leave to come back home. I know why you're here, what you have to do. I meant . . ."

He leaned down and caught her lips in a slow, tugging kiss, then seduced his way between them, much as he had that very first time, when she'd been in the car dressed in that ridiculous, awful getup. She ran her hands up his arms, framed his face and kissed him back, taking him, seducing him, showing him, telling him, in all the ways she could, all the ways she knew she'd never stop showing him, what he meant to her.

The kisses changed from slow to deep, from deep to hot, and from hot to breathless. Her dress was tugged off and sent to some far corner of the room where she hoped it would stay for hours. Days. Weeks. His jeans followed, along with every other stitch of clothing they were wearing. She pulled him down on top of her, but he resisted, leaning up on one elbow to look down at her.

"I didn't get the pleasure of this last time," he said, tracing a finger over her collarbone, and down to the tip of her breast. "I want to explore every inch of you. Of this lovely, very naked you."

She gasped, arched, and said, "I think you might have to wait until next time. After which, I'd really—really—like to return that favor."

He laughed, then groaned as she slid her legs up the sides of his thighs and angled her hips so he could—"Oh," she said as he slid deep inside of her, all the way, until she was full with every hard, perfect inch of him.

She groaned. Then she squealed when he slid out, and cried out when he thrust back in. "Maybe the time after next," she panted, as he kept up the pace, and she matched him, thrust for thrust and they both drove each other up, up . . . and over.

She was still trying to catch her breath when he finally slid out of her, and started working his way down her body, lingering over her most sensitive parts. "Calder, I can't—"

"It's next time—"

"I know, but I need time to—"

"You'll be fine."

"No, I know what I—" Then she gasped, then she moaned.

He chuckled against the inside of her thigh. "You're so much more than fine."

"I—I believe I am," she said, arching and crying out as he found her and took her directly to the edge, and shoved her flying off of it.

It was another few times later, when they finally lay spent, sprawled over each other in a tangle of arms and legs, all hot and damp and sweaty . . . and delicious. She laughed.

"What's funny?" he said, his face half smushed into the mattress.

"This can't be right."

"If this ain't right, then I pray to God we keep getting it wrong."

She laughed again, and he managed a chuckle, which came out like more of a wheeze.

"Are you okay?" she asked, pushing his hair back from his face.

"I might have been doing a little more actual work than you," he said. "Just give me five minutes."

She ran her hand down his back, and over his very, very fine backside, which, it turned out, far exceeded even her initial expectations that day she'd first admired it, sitting inside her wrecked Audi.

He groaned. "Okay, maybe ten."

She laughed again, then squealed when he reached out and tugged her so she was pinned half under him. "No more wandering fingers," he told her, his voice getting drowsier.

She ran her tongue over his shoulder. "How about a wandering this?"

He slid a finger over her lips. "Shh."

"What if I wanted to say I love you?" she said against his big, wide finger.

He rolled his head and opened one eye. "That you can do. But you'll have to tell me again later. Maybe more than once."

"Because you think you'll forget?"

He moved more quickly than she would have thought possible, given his half-drugged stupor. She was suddenly flat on her back and a very revived Calder was pinning her to the bed. "No," he said gruffly, "because it's the best thing anyone has ever said to me." He leaned in and kissed her. "And I'm greedy like that."

She wiggled under him. "I like greedy."

Now he barked a laugh. "I think perhaps I've awakened the real beast. It's no wonder you like that car."

"I bought it," she said proudly. "Well, I traded it. For the Audi. Sal got permission from his nephew. I think it suits the new me."

"The new you."

She nodded, then slipped her hands free of his grasp and tugged his face down to hers. "The me who loves you and drives a blue hot rod and tries really hot court cases about who stole whose lobster traps and pot buoys, and maybe figures out how to help you turn this farm into the place you're dreaming it will be even faster, so as soon as your family is put back together, you can be here full-time. Where we can do a lot more of this."

"Oh," he said, a devastatingly sexy smile starting to curve his lips. "That new you."

"I love you, Calder Blue."

He leaned down and nuzzled the side of her neck, and slipped between her thighs again. "How'd you like a last name to match that hot rod of yours?"

She gasped, then shoved his face back to where she

could see it. "Is that what I—did you just—really? Here? Is it because you're hormone addled—?"

"Come here, Scarlett, and let me love you some more. We'll talk cars and last names later."

"But—"

"I love you, Hannah McCrae. From Blueberry Cove. Hmm. Blueberry. I'm seeing a pattern here. I don't know how I missed it."

She grinned and it felt as if her entire body had just expanded to include the entirety of the universe, because that was the only way she could describe how full of joy she was in that moment. "Me, either."

"We should think about that."

"Okay." Then she flipped him to his back and straddled him. "But frankly, right now, Mr. Blue?" She wriggled back onto him and sighed. "I really don't give a damn."

Epilogue

"I've got five dollars that says she'll chicken out as soon as that thing goes faster than a slow limp."

"That thing is a Tennessee Walker. Who will be quite beautiful again one day. Calder's doing a good job with her," Alex said.

Kerry climbed up and sat on the paddock fence next to Alex, and looked at where Fiona stood next to them, elbows resting on the top of the fence, her feet propped up on the bottom rail. "I'll take that five and see you twenty."

Fiona eyed Kerry, then looked at their eldest sister, who was presently taking a very slow stroll around the edge of the paddock on said Tennessee Walker. "Really? Why? She looks okay now," she said, well aware she'd just been the one doubting that very thing. "Maybe she'll be awesome."

Kerry snorted. "Do you see the way she's holding those reins? And she cannot sit a saddle. Her tight ass will not ever let that happen. She is just not made for this. Poor Calder."

"I don't know," Alex MacFarland McCrae said. "A month ago she was scared to even walk through the barn when the horses were safely in their stalls. And look at her now." She grinned at Kerry. "I give her even money."

Kerry hooted and looked triumphantly at Fiona. "Ha!"

Fiona scowled and kept her attention on Hannah, feeling a rush of pride that their sister was out there, conquering one of her fears. Fiona needed to find a better way to tap into that conquering spirit. "Shouldn't you be on a plane, train, or slow mule to China or something by now?" she groused to Kerry. How was it that Kerry was still in the Cove and it was almost August? It was a mystery to everyone except Kerry, who, for the time being, was helping Fergus run the Rusty Puffin and seemingly not in any big hurry to depart on her next worldly adventure.

Privately, Fiona thought that was a good thing. Lord knew Uncle Gus was loving it, and even she had to admit it was nice having her sister back where they at least knew she wasn't in danger of being eaten by cannibals or anything.

The news that Hannah was staying in the Cove for good had been met with happy cheers by everyone, although, technically, she was really staying in Calais. But she was back in Maine, and that's what mattered. Fiona felt like her family was coming full circle, back to where they were meant to be.

That said, the news that Fiona was going to shut down her business in Manhattan and return to the nest as well? Yeah, well, only Hannah knew about that. For now. In fact, she'd only come back home this weekend to scope out a place to launch the new business idea she'd been working on since returning to New York after the wedding.

Her gaze went back to Hannah, and a smile curved her lips as her eyes dropped to the sun glinting off the rock her oldest sister was sporting on her engagement ring finger. There was going to be another McCrae wedding.

So you have a deadline now. Back in the Cove for good by Hannah's wedding.

"Yeah," she murmured under her breath, trying not to let herself feel overwhelmed by everything that was going to have to happen between now and then to make that a reality. "Good luck with that."

Kerry's gasp made Fiona look back into the ring. Under the close tutelage of Calder, who was riding behind her on his own mare, Vixen, Hannah had increased her speed to a slow trot.

Alex put her fingers in her mouth and whistled, then frowned when Kerry ripped her fingers out of her mouth. "What?"

"You'll spook the horse."

"Oh!" She looked immediately worried. "Sorry!" she called out. "What do I know?" she said to Kerry. "I fix lighthouses."

"So I guess that means you're next," Kerry said, nodding to the ring.

When Alex, who routinely hung off the side of said lighthouses, blanched at the idea of being on horseback, Kerry hooted.

"You're so doomed right now," Fiona said, then sighed happily and rested her chin on her folded arms. "Have I mentioned how glad I am to have another sister?"

It was all going to be okay. Coming home for good was the best decision she'd ever made.

Here goes nothing! She smiled. *And here comes everything.*

Recipes

Alex & Logan's
Boston Cream Pie
Wedding Cake

I'm a big fan of the untraditional wedding cake (mine was red velvet, which was scandalous back in the day!) and in this story, Logan and Alex celebrate their nuptials with a Boston cream pie cake. I might have been projecting my own wedding-cake rebelliousness when I decided on Alex's cake, but I know I would love to find a stunning stacked and glazed Boston cream pie sitting on the table at a wedding reception, wouldn't you? Mmm, I want a slice right now!

Boston cream pie first showed up at the Parker House Hotel in 1856, the creation of Armenian-French chef M. Sanzian. It has since been declared the state cake of Massachusetts, and has long been a New England favorite. It's called a pie because pie pans were used in its original creation—those were more plentiful in those days than single-layer cake pans—but it's actually a luscious, rich layered cake, sliced in the manner of a traditional pie.

Below is my version of Boston cream pie—the measurements listed make a regular-sized cake—which is a recipe cobbled together from my grandmother's yellow cake recipe, a family-favorite custard cream filling recipe, and my own chocolate ganache glaze recipe. Yes, it's a triple-threat cake and that means three times the yum! (See final notes on wedding cake tips!)

Warning! A little advance planning is in order, as the cake has to cool completely before it's sliced and filled with custard, and topped with that warm, rich ganache glaze. But the real warning should be to keep a fork handy! Rich, delicious, sinful . . . enjoy!

NOTE: Boston cream pie is often made by slicing a single nine-inch round cake in half horizontally to make two, thinner cake layers, with the custard then spread in between. The easier version is to bake two full nine-inch cakes and layer them as you would a regular layer cake, with the custard filling in between the cake layers. This is the recipe you will find below. Mostly I love it because, more cake!

Yellow Cake

½ cup sweet, unsalted butter, softened
2½ cups sifted cake flour
3 teaspoons baking powder
½ teaspoon salt
1½ cups granulated sugar
¾ cup plus 2 Tablespoons milk
1 teaspoon pure vanilla extract
2 eggs

Directions

Preheat oven to 375 degrees F.
Prepare two nine-inch round cake pans with butter
    and dust with flour.
Stir or blend butter until fully softened but do not
    overprocess.
Combine flour, baking powder, salt, and sugar and
    add to butter.

Add ¾ cup milk and the vanilla.
Beat for 2 minutes at low speed.
Add eggs and remaining 2 Tablespoons of milk.
Beat for 1 minute at low speed or just until fully
    assimilated.
Pour the batter into the prepared cake pans
Bake for 20 to 25 minutes or until a
    tester/toothpick comes out clean.
Turn the cakes out onto cake racks and cool
    completely.

Pastry Cream Custard Filling

½ cup sugar
3 Tablespoons flour or 1 Tablespoon cornstarch
    (I prefer cornstarch for a thicker custard.)
Pinch of salt
1 cup whole milk
2 egg yolks, slightly beaten

Directions

Put the sugar, cornstarch and salt into a small,
    heavy saucepan.
Stir in the milk.
Cook over low heat until the mixture thickens,
    approximately 5 minutes.
Stir in the 2 egg yolks.
Cook and stir for 3 minutes more until the custard
    is smooth and creamy.
Allow to cool completely before spreading over
    one room-temperature nine-inch layer cake.
    (For faster cooling: pour into bowl, cover with
    plastic wrap, and set in the fridge. Can be
    stored up to forty-eight hours.)

Carefully stack the other completely cooled layer
   cake on top.
Press down slightly if you like your custard to fill
   out past the edge of the cake.

Chocolate Ganache Glaze

⅓ cup heavy or whipping cream
7 ounces semi-sweet or bittersweet chocolate, chopped
   (I like to use Ghirardelli bittersweet baking chips
   for faster, smoother blending and rich dark
   chocolate taste.)

Directions

In a small, heavy saucepan, add the cream and
   bring just to a boil, immediately removing it
   from the heat.
Add the chopped chocolate, stirring with a whisk
   until the chocolate is melted and the mixture is
   completely smooth.
While still warm, spread or pour the chocolate
   ganache over the top cake layer and allow to
   drizzle down the sides of the cake, coating as
   much or as little of the sides as you like.
Allow to cool, then slice the cake as you would a
   pie, and serve in wedges.

Wedding Cake Tips!

If you're interested in making this a wedding cake, you have several alternatives, depending on the number of guests who will be indulging. For a small wedding, if you want something a little more impressive, you can make four nine-inch cakes and stack the cake taller, creating a four layer, with cream between three layers, then serve chilled, so the cake can be sliced into thinner sliver portions. For a larger gathering, you can tier the cake using plastic bases and posts/columns available at most craft stores to stack the cake recipe above into multiple sections (with columns in between). Or you can go the fun route and make individual-serving-sized Boston cream cupcakes and create your own tiered cupcake wedding cake display. (I've done this for a variety of occasions and it's always a big hit!) You can also bring this recipe to your wedding planner/baker, who would have industrial-size round pans for an even wider range of possibilities!

Happy baking! Enjoy!

Don't miss the next heartwarming story
in Donna Kauffman's
Brides of Blueberry Cove series,

Snowflake Bay,

coming this October!

*There's no place like seaside Blueberry Cove, Maine,
at Christmas—and there's nothing like a wedding,
the warmth of the holidays, and an old crush,
to create the perfect new start . . .*

Interior designer Fiona McCrae has left fast-paced
Manhattan to move back home to peaceful Blueberry
Cove. But she's barely arrived before she's hooked into
planning her big sister Hannah's Christmas wedding—
in *less than seven weeks*. The last thing she needs is for
her first love, Ben Campbell, to return to neighboring
Snowflake Bay . . .

As kids, Fiona was the bratty little sister Ben mercilessly
teased—while pining after Hannah. But Fi never once
thought of Ben like a brother. And that hasn't changed.
Except Fi is all grown up. Will Ben notice her now?
More importantly, with her life in a jumble, should he? Or
might the romance of the occasion, the spirit of the season,
and the gifts of time ignite a long-held flame for many
Christmases to come . . .

Something old might just become something new . . .

There should be a rulebook, she decided. Or at the very least, a tastefully done pamphlet. *The Bridesmaid Rules*. Fiona McCrae zipped along the Cove road, too distracted to even glance across Pelican Bay at the lighthouse perched majestically out on the tip of Pelican Point. *Too much to do. Too much to plan.* What on earth had she been thinking, taking this on?

"A list of basic, common-sense rules," she said, warming to the subject as she made the turn toward the Point. She'd have been quite happy to draw up a list, if anyone asked. She could think of a half dozen without even trying.

Bridesmaid Rule No. 1: No one should have to be a bridesmaid twice in one year. "Especially if said bridesmaid has yet to become a bride herself." She smiled wryly. "And the single ladies crowd goes wild." She made the universal hordes-cheering sound, and held on to her amused smile as she wove her way ever closer to home base. *Hmm. Bridesmaid Rule No. 2* . . . "No bridesmaid should ever be expected, asked, or guilted into also filling the role of wedding planner." Actually, that should probably be Rule No. 1.

If there were such a rulebook, being a bridesmaid twice

in six months *and* the planner for both weddings would be in serious breach of the bridesmaid code. On top of that, this time she was also the maid of honor. And she *had* been honored when her older sister had asked her to play that most special role in her big day. She'd done the big, sloppy cry, in fact. They both had. And there hadn't even been adult beverages involved.

At the time, Fiona had blamed still being joy-buzzed from watching her big brother tie the knot barely three months earlier. And now, suddenly—too suddenly to her mind—it was Hannah's turn to walk down the aisle.

Weddings were a happy thing. A thing she should be thrilled about. Downright joyful. So what if her family was falling in love all around her while her own life was falling apart?

Okay, so maybe *falling apart* was being a bit melodramatic. Except selling off her award-winning interior design business in Manhattan to move, lock, stock, and fabric sample binders, back to her hometown of Blueberry Cove, Maine—all without exactly firming up her new business model—pretty much felt exactly like that. She still couldn't believe she'd really made the leap, taken the plunge. "Jumped off the cliff," she added as she pulled in between her sister-in-law Alex's ancient truck and the shiny red pickup parked in the small lot outside her childhood home.

Fiona gasped as she cracked the car door open and the icy coastal breeze snatched her breath away. She wedged her booted foot out first to keep the door propped open, trying not to bang it into the truck as she climbed out, lugging the heavy satchel behind her. It was filled with an assortment of samples, swatches, wedding books, and magazines she'd carefully selected, along with a stack of planners she'd already begun assembling, the combined weight of which felt as if she'd packed up the proverbial kitchen sink.

She edged her way out between the vehicles, but didn't give the truck much notice otherwise, assuming it belonged to yet another of Alex's long list of subcontractors. The renovation work on the old lightkeeper's cottage was the last piece of the Pelican Point restoration project that Alex had been working on for close to two years now. Fiona did glance out at the Point then and took a moment to admire the beautifully restored stack of two-hundred-year-old stone and steel that was the McCrae family lighthouse. But only a moment.

No time for dawdling! There's a wedding to plan! "In seven freaking weeks," she muttered under her breath. *Seriously. There should be rules*. Fiona hauled the oversized canvas tote up higher onto her shoulder and dipped her chin down, tucking it into the scarf she'd wrapped repeatedly around her neck. It was a vain attempt to keep the wind that clipped relentlessly over the rocky promontory from whipping her cheeks to an even more chapped pink than they already were. In all of her daydreaming about moving back home to the Cove, how was it she'd managed to so utterly forget what the cold weather did to her fair skin?

She needed to get a tube of rehydrating cream to keep in her purse. And one for her car. And every other bag she carried. If she applied it a dozen times a day, she might have a slim chance of not resembling a cherry-cheeked elf at her sister's December wedding. And that was another thing. *Who gets married at Christmas? Who wants to have their wedding anniversary compete with Santa?*

"More to the point, who makes the big decision to get married at Christmas, when it's already only two freaking weeks to Thanksgiving?" She'd tucked her chin so far down behind the heavily wrapped scarf that speaking out loud caused the wool fibers to laminate themselves to her heavily balmed lips. *Lovely. Just lovely. Bridesmaid Rule No. 3: It has to be at least above freezing to have a wedding.* And while she was at it, *No. 4: There should be at least a six-month minimum wedding planning window. Better yet, nine. Hell, make it a year.* "But seven weeks from saying yes to saying I do? Insanity." She spluttered at the wool fibers now sticking to her teeth and tongue, too, as she clambered up the wide, stone steps.

It wasn't sour grapes, either. These were salient, perfectly rational points, all of which Fiona planned to put forth to her sister. And she would. Just as soon as she divested herself of the luggage-sized satchel she was grappling with, and scraped the scarf off her face. She'd be completely nonconfrontational, of course. She'd merely explain, in a calm, rational, don't-piss-off-the-starry-eyed-bride manner, that it would make so much more sense to have a lovely spring wedding. Coastal Maine was beautiful in spring. Well, if you overlooked the mud that resulted from all the snow melting. Followed by all the heavy seasonal rains. Not to mention the occasional crippling late snowstorm. Okay, so maybe she'd go with the nine-month minimum wedding planning rule after all. All the better, really. A summer wedding would be perfect. Just as it had been for Logan and Alex.

Plotting how she'd open the delicate-but-has-to-happen conversation, she banged her way to the side door off the wraparound porch hugging the gabled, shake-shingled house that had been home to generations of McCraes. Surely she could make Hannah see reason. "Knock, knock!" she called out as she let herself in. She shoved her body and the tote into the small mudroom, then heard a loud *thump* overhead, mixed with muffled voices, followed by laughter.

"Alex?" she shouted through the scarf, which was still half draped over the lower part of her face as she tried to maneuver herself around to reach for the door that led to the kitchen. There was another *thump* overhead and more laughter. Good. She'd recruit Alex into change-the-date mission. Strength in numbers.

"You better not be upstairs having crazy, naked newly-wed sex with my brother," she called out as she finally managed to nudge the kitchen door open. Grunting, she pushed harder when she and her bag got wedged in the narrower kitchen doorway. "Because that is an image I do not need to have burned into my corneas today."

She should have put her satchel down and taken off her scarf and coat in the mudroom before trying to jam herself inside. *Me? Plan ahead? Why start now?* She made one last determined push, sucking in air, as if it would some-how make even the satchel thinner, and finally popped through the door like a parka-clad spitball. She made a loud *oof* sound as the center work island broke her staggering trajectory. "Hannah?" she half shouted, half wheezed, as she slumped over the canvas tote she'd slung onto the new marble countertop before it slung her back onto her ass.

She needed to start working out again. All right, ever. And she would. That was part of why she'd come home after all. Okay, so perhaps not specifically to get into shape, but at the slower pace of life that was Blueberry Cove, surely she would have time for things like jogging and yoga.

Things she also had sworn she'd do when she'd moved to the big city, she reminded herself, recalling her gilded visions of getting all lithe and lean on her daily runs through

Central Park, topped only by the fabulous friendships she'd surely make with her newfound fellow artist gal pals in her thrice-weekly yoga classes in the Village. Yeah, somehow those items had never made their way onto her daily agenda.

Of course, she was older now, wiser, with her priorities clearly straight, which was proven by her recent exit from a stressed-out city piled high with even more toxic clientele, returning to her healthy, serene, simple-life roots. She tried to feel cheery at the thought of shopping for a yoga mat and cute running shoes.

Then again, she thought, it was winter. And in Maine that meant it was dark. A lot. And pretty damn cold. Jogging in the cold and dark seemed unwise. In fact, it seemed wrong, really, to have to work out like that at all in the winter. Ask any Mainer and they'd tell you that surviving a New England winter was pretty much the equivalent of participating in a full-contact sport in and of itself. *Yeah.* So, technically, she was already working out. She would be like a—a boxer, punching her way through a tough coastal winter, while simultaneously focusing her creative mind and spirit on plotting out the best way to apply her well-honed design skills to suit the needs of the sure-to-be sweeter, kinder, gentler clientele she'd find in the Cove.

Come spring, she'd be all bulletproof from winterizing herself, her new business model would be successfully created and implemented, and she would happily jog herself skinny, all while feeding her inner creative soul in a local yoga class. When you looked at it that way, it was all simply part of a bigger training regimen, really.

Feeling somewhat better about herself now, if not technically athletic, she disentangled herself from the satchel strap, then began mentally rehearsing a summer-weddings-are-so-beautiful speech while she looked around for something to scrape the wool scarf out of her mouth. Deciding to get herself unwrapped first, she fished out the end of the scarf. She could already feel her fair skin chapping even as she stood there with the warmth of the kitchen creating something of a sting in her thawing cheeks. The struggle with the scarf started almost immediately. It was as if her curls had begun actively weaving themselves into the knitting, becoming one with every loop and knot.

So, she was more wrestling with the scarf than unwrapping it, really, swearing somewhat creatively, possibly a wee bit passionately even, by the time a deep male voice that was quite decidedly not her big brother's baritone spoke from far too close behind her.

"I've got bolt cutters in my truck. We could just cut you out."

Fiona froze. Stock still. And not because of anything having to do with the coastal winter weather or being out of shape. She wasn't breathing hard. In fact, she might never draw breath again. It had been, what, ten years? Longer. She'd lost track. *Or, more truthfully, you've blocked it from your memory banks.* Blocked it back when the owner of that voice left Blueberry Cove for college in Boston, excited to get started on fulfilling his dreams—none of which included coming back to his hometown. At the time, that had seemed the only way she'd ever survive not having him in her daily orbit.

She felt his big, broad palms cup her shoulders, turning her slowly around to face him, and stupidly squeezed her eyes shut, as if that would change this sudden new reality. All it did was delay the inevitable.

"Fireplug?" he said, as the top half of her face became visible when he pushed the curls from her forehead and the scarf from where it was now haphazardly draped diagonally across her face. There was sincere surprise in his voice. "Is that you inside all that sheep's clothing?"

Fireplug. All of the air came back into her lungs in one big, sucking gasp. Emphasis on the sucking. Her cheeks burned again, only the sting of remembered humiliation, coupled with the memories of her pathetic, unrequited crush on her older sister's first serious boyfriend, far, far outstripped anything a Maine winter could do to her fair skin.

They were both many years older now, she reminded herself, and that meant wiser as well. Although she didn't feel wiser at the moment. At the moment, she felt instantly thirteen again, pining after a guy who'd barely noticed her, and when he did, saw her as nothing more than the nuisance kid sister of the girl he was trying to impress.

Of course, that girl was now engaged to another man, and for all Fiona knew, her childhood crush was married himself, with a bundle of kids stashed somewhere. Hell, for all *he* knew, so was she. Which meant, yeah . . . the distant past was just that. Distant. And past.

She prided herself on taking an extra moment to steady herself, let her breath ease out, then slowly back in again, before opening her eyes. Okay, so she was still half tangled in a woolen neck scarf and she wasn't exactly making eye contact with him, but it was a start. A mature, grown-up start. Between two, mature, grown-up people.

So why is your heart racing like it's the first time a man has ever touched you? More to the point, why are all your other more mature body parts clamoring for him to touch a whole lot more than your shoulders? You're both potentially married with kids, remember?

Only she wasn't married. Didn't have kids. Not even the

dimmest of prospects of either on the horizon. A horizon that, at the moment, was completely consumed with a big, tall, rugged reminder of all that she didn't have. Had never had. A reminder, it should be noted, who still had his hands on her . . .

GREAT BOOKS, GREAT SAVINGS!

When You Visit Our Website:
www.kensingtonbooks.com

You Can Save Money Off The Retail Price
Of Any Book You Purchase!

Visit Us Today To Start Saving!
www.kensingtonbooks.com